20,000 KILOS
UNDER THE SEA

A Modern Retelling of the Jules Verne Classic Adventure

20,000 Kilos Under the Sea: A Modern Retelling of the Jules Verne Classic Adventure by Richard Wickliffe

Copyright © 2022 Richard Wickliffe

Interior design by Jacqueline Cook

ISBN: 978-1-61179-398-7 (Paperback)
ISBN: 978-1-61179-399-4 (e-book)

10 9 8 7 6 5 4 3 2 1

BISAC Subject Headings:
FIC002000 FICTION / Action & Adventure
FIC028010 FICTION / Science Fiction / Action & Adventure
FIC047000 FICTION / Sea Stories

Address all correspondence to:
Fireship Press, LLC
P.O. Box 68412
Tucson, AZ 85737
fireshipinfo@gmail.com

Or visit our website at:
www.fireshippress.com

Dedicated to my wife Anthea, my travel partner for over thirty years, with many more voyages to come

Preface

• In 2021, the Colombian navy intercepted thirty-one submersible vessels known as "narco-subs" funded by cartels, a leap from twenty-three in 2019.

• A Miami taskforce, "Operation Odessa," identified men planning to buy a Soviet submarine for the Cali cartel. The men met with officers at a Russian naval base to prove to the cartel the deal was possible, but one of the suspects ran off with $10 million before any deal could be finalized.

• If the sale had taken place, over eighty percent of our oceans are "unmapped, unobserved and unexplored," according to the National Oceanic and Atmospheric Administration.

20,000 KILOS
UNDER THE SEA

A Modern Retelling of the Jules Verne Classic Adventure

RICHARD WICKLIFFE

Cortero
An Imprint of FIRESHIP PRESS

PART I
TERRA FIRMA

Prologue
The Shark, a Minnow, and a Hawk

Despite nightfall, the predator watched its prey with ease from beneath the surface. It was even darker twenty meters below, yet it could see its victim as clear as spying a duck paddling on a lake. But this was no duck, and the immense Gulf was no lake.

Like a graceful beast, the predator halted, silent. As with any hunt, it was imperative to preserve the element of surprise. The predator focused on its feeble prey. As with any hunter-hunted relationship, it wasn't personal. And only a complete slaughter would be acceptable. No survivable wounds, where it might escape, crying back to its guardians. The target would be completely devoured, with its innards used to nourish, consumed from the bottom of the sea.

The hunter began to ascend, careful to not have its dorsal fin or tail breach the surface, yet. And there it waited. Patient.

Unknown to the predator, another set of eyes watched from the skies. The hawk's view filled an infrared monitor with static, struggling to produce a surveillance image.

"Lookout for a vessel," a garbled voice called out. "It departed Mariel, north-northeast. Zero-one hundred hours. Over."

The static cleared to depict an infrared aerial view of the coast. A field of black, then a blip of color. It was a small boat.

"Copy, JIATF Key West," a voice responded. "Confirmed target: a single vessel, triple engines, and low profile. Over."

"Hold. Is that something following its tail?" the first voice asked. "What is that?"

Chapter One
El Monstruo

The silhouette of a thirty-three-foot boat appeared on the horizon. A crescent moon projected a silver thread on the vista, with just the tranquil lapping of waves. The serenity was pierced by a boat's engines, and then the sound of a crying infant.

"Silence that child or it goes below!" the smuggler barked in Spanish to the scrawny eighteen-year-old mother.

The eyes of a dozen Cuban migrants turned to the girl. They were clustered on the boat's deck in a virtual heap. They sat gaunt and terrified, only wearing rags.

The hands of the young mother, Mariela, trembled as she struggled to comfort her bawling three-month-old son. The child inhaled and howled, inconsolable.

The swarthy smuggler stood at the console of the Renegade powerboat. He was barefoot and fat and wore a squid-stained Cristal beer t-shirt. Beside him hunched the captain, who'd made the run a thousand times. The leathery man had pointed shoulders and knees that quivered with energy.

"Our cargo below is worth more than a kid," the captain shouted in Spanish. "The baby goes overboard if Rao is not here soon!"

Mariela gasped. She cowered over her child, creating a shield. The refugees around her huddled closer. The smuggler laughed. The captain flicked a cigarette at them.

All heads snapped towards the drone of a vessel. The captain rummaged through his cluttered console to find binoculars. He aimed them to their rear.

"It is a Scarab," he adjusted his lenses. "Thirty feet long." He turned to the smuggler, "It is Rao. Finally!"

Everyone onboard squinted to watch. Two hundred yards away, the approaching boat's lights twinkled through the gloom.

The captain lifted his radio. "Rao! Hurry or we'll all be dead!"

The Scarab accelerated towards them.

Mariela blinked at the comment, *all be dead?* What if their lights are seen by authorities? Was there a chance they could be saved? Mariela involuntarily smiled at the fantasy racing through her mind. *Saved. Brought to America. Proper care for Ernesto.* She turned to the men at the controls. One fat, one skinny and both repulsive. They would certainly rather flee, endangering all their lives to save their own.

Mariela looked to her right and left. Jumping overboard with a baby would be futile. They were miles from any shore. Her son would certainly drown. Perhaps they had a better chance of survival remaining on the boat. Mariela held her son closer to her throbbing heart.

She glanced at the others. They'd been picked up at a port in Mariel, forty kilometers west of Havana. Cobbled together by a local gang after they'd each paid their *tarifa de boleto,* passage fee. Mariela knew none of them. They remained in tight cliques, only murmuring to each other. No one spoke to her, and everyone glowered when her son cried. Mariela inhaled, suppressing another surge of tears.

Everyone watched the Scarab accelerate towards them. The deep growl of its engines became more prominent. The migrants looked at each other, unsure what this meant. The smugglers had said something about a delivery.

Within the lull of waiting, the refugees traded silent glances. They'd been scolded to not open their mouths. All eyes conveyed the same emotions: fear, despair, curiosity. The three-foot seas sloshed their boat, and the incessant diesel fumes were nauseating.

After a pause, everyone jolted at a deafening crash. It was the Scarab, a hundred yards away. The air filled with an abrupt crunching of steel.

In a flash of confusion, they saw the Scarab's lights launch as if striking rocks. Before anyone could grasp what they were witnessing, the Scarab exploded into a fireball.

"*Dios Mio!*" the smuggler shouted. "Was it a missile?" He looked skyward.

The captain tensed. He then revved the boat's triple Yamahas.

"*Mira! Allí!*" Elderly migrants pointed behind the boat. *Look! There!* They motioned to a sudden wake following in their trail. Fifty yards away, a wedge-shaped spew of water was approaching fast in the darkness. Froth sprayed off its edges as if it were an immense fin.

The smuggler looked back at whatever they were screaming about. The fin appeared over four meters tall. As the spray grew closer, they could see two glowing orbs, one on each side of the wake.

"*Son esos ojos?*" A woman shouted, horrified. *Are those eyes?*

The captain pushed the throttle forward, summoning every ounce of speed.

"*Monstruo marino!*" another woman screamed, creating a frenzy.

The men and women pointed. The wake was advancing at a greater speed.

The captain glanced at his sonar. A shadow was following them; it was cigar-shaped and advancing like a torpedo.

"That is no whale!" the smuggler shouted. He crouched on the pounding deck.

The refugees huddled in a tighter mass, crying in confusion. An old woman clutched her rosary beads.

The Renegade raced across the surface. But the impending wake was faster, a hundred feet behind them. Then fifty. Then twenty.

The boat crunched from the rear like a giant accordion. The hull splintered and the engines sparked. When the smugglers looked back, it was like stepping into a buzz saw, instantly slaughtering them into a pinwheel of crimson.

The refugees' faces were stung with flying debris. The bow launched up, plunging them into the sea. The vessel shattered down its center, flinging humans to both sides like ragdolls.

In the ink-black chop, the migrants grasped debris. They cried and splashed, shouting to locate loved ones in the darkness. Whatever had raced through them was gone, leaving a roiling churn in its wake.

Mariela's wet clothes weighed her down. With salt burning her eyes, she struggled to hold her son above the waves.

Bobbing heads coughed and cried, unsure what to do. Only seconds had passed. Their eyes adjusted to the flicker of light from burning pieces of the hull floating around them. Flames licked over the waves from splattered fuel. Several men helped the older women. One lady cried that she couldn't swim. Desperate hands clutched each other through a choir of prayers.

"*Esta regresando!*" a woman screamed. *It's coming back!* She pointed into the blackness.

With her son bawling above her shoulders, Mariela squinted to see the two eyes in the darkness, the glowing orbs. Fifty yards away, the creature was turning back.

The men and women shouted in despair. There was nowhere to swim or hide.

The enormous beast stopped turning. It appeared to face them, head-on like a bull. It then lunged forward, waves trailing off its giant dorsal fin.

Mariela embraced her son and closed her eyes. Tempted to peek, she cracked an eye to see the beast racing closer. *Those eyes.* She struggled to pray within the cacophony of screams.

Simultaneous gasps, then silence.

Mariela opened her eyes. The creature had submerged. It was gone.

A blinding light irradiated from the skies as if a switch had been turned on. All heads looked up, squinting at a thunderous gust.

Chapter Two

Intercepted

The hawk swooped down from the heavens. A Coast Guard MH-60 Jayhawk.

The survivors narrowed their eyes at the turbulent drone from the helicopter. Its spotlights revealed the men and women clutching debris among flaming wreckage.

"Heat signatures from…nine survivors," the pilot's voice announced to the team. "Holding position for search and rescue."

From seemingly nowhere, blue, and red strobes ignited the scene. A forty-three-foot interceptor powerboat came to a splashing halt beside the survivors. Everyone turned to the vessel, crying in panicked confusion.

The Jayhawk had been equipped with a SeaFLIR Multi-Spectral Surveillance System, an imaging system designed to track smugglers, terrorists, or any other threat, night or day, on the roughest seas.

However—despite its advanced technology—it hadn't been able to see everything. Even with the pattern of recent occurrences, the exploding vessels hadn't been anticipated. And refugees weren't supposed to be there.

The intel had been accurate about the boats. But nothing about their imminent destruction. Was it some sort of new weapon? A turf war among cartels? If so, where had the weapons been deployed? The Jayhawk hadn't seen any unauthorized air traffic within fifty miles.

"You heard the man," Agent Kurtz's voice crackled from the interceptor. "Nine survivors, get movin'!"

Standing on the bow of the DEA interceptor, Agent Kurtz aimed a Maglite to see the shattered boat, with flames unfurling from a fuel slick.

"Grab these folks before the tanks ignite!" Kurtz shouted. He was mid-fifties with a silver buzz cut. "Ruiz, throw ropes!"

Agent Ruiz, his boyish junior partner, tossed several ropes with life rings attached. A female agent threw life jackets toward the thrashing survivors. A fourth agent automatically aimed his nine-millimeter. When he realized the wretched condition of the men and women, he holstered his firearm.

A trail of flames began to spread on the waves like tentacles. The interceptor's flashing lights added a beat to the scene; a countdown that time was running out.

Like a well-rehearsed exercise, the agents heaved ropes to grapple the refugees and pull them aboard. The younger helped the elderly.

"There's a baby!" Kurtz shouted and pointed, "That young lady!"

The female agent leaned broadly over the side and stretched her arm. She finally touched the hand of the young mother. Mariela offered her infant to the agent, and both were pulled aboard.

"That's it! *No mas!*" Ruiz shouted. "Let's go!"

Flames on the water climbed higher as shards of plastic and Styrofoam fueled the blaze. Thick smoke drifted towards the interceptor. The weary refugees coughed, turning away from the radiant heat.

Kurtz roared, "Randy: full speed!"

The DEA interceptor had been a confiscated drug powerboat, enhanced with triple MerCruiser engines. It spun and launched forward like a rocket. In their wake, the smugglers' gas tanks exploded with scorching light.

The refugees cringed at the blasts. Seated together in the stern, they calmed to watch the ironic beauty of the fire reflecting on the Gulf. An unexpected peace from knowing they'd been saved. They comforted each other; tears replaced with smiles of gratitude.

"Pass these out," Kurtz opened a large ice chest filled with bottled water. "As much as they can drink." Agent Ruiz and the others handed them out to the men and women. Plastic bottles crackled and they gulped the water as the vessel raced north at fifty knots.

Kurtz then distributed Mylar blankets. "Make everyone use these whether they want to or not." Though the air was seventy-eight degrees, it was protocol for hypothermic exposures. Considering the condition of the survivors—some of them elderly—they were also wet. The high winds could suck any remaining heat from their bodies.

Ruiz helped the group, explaining everything in Spanish. The survivors obliged, covering themselves in the foil blankets. He asked if anyone was injured. A few described how the smugglers died. A couple cried to declare three of their companions had been killed.

Agent Kurtz rubbed the stubble on his square jaw to assess the ragged group. He squatted on the deck and smiled at Mariela who was cradling her son.

"What the hell happened out there?" Kurtz had to shout over the engines, "To your boat?"

The men and women blinked, unsure what he was asking.

Ruiz leaned toward the group to interpret, "*Que le paso a tu bote?*"

The group looked at each other, anxiety returning to their eyes. Several hoarse voices exclaimed, "*El monstruo!*"

Two elderly women added, "*Monstruo de Cojimar!*"

Agent Kurtz frowned at Ruiz, puzzled. "What are they saying?"

Ruiz turned to him. He shifted his jaw to consider his words. "They're saying it was a..." He paused, "A sea monster."

Chapter Three
The Winter White House

Key West

"Which is precisely why we're putting together this little expedition," Agent Kurtz announced to the five others. He spread his fingers on one hand and raised his voice, "This was the fifth incident in six weeks. What makes this one different? Innocents were killed. It's our job to do something about that."

With Agent Ruiz seated at his side, the four others nodded with pensive frowns. They sat around an antique table with a brass sign on the wall that declared, "Joint Interagency Task Force."

Kurtz huffed like a frustrated parent. "If we learned anything last night, it's that we can't do it by ourselves. Which is why I've reached out to civilian experts." He squinted out the window's plantation blinds. "If she can find us in our little paradise."

⁓

The quaint Key West neighborhood was a unique mix of Victorian and Bahamian-style homes, with gingerbread lattices and wrap-around porches. The designs had been inspired by the settlers' diverse ports of origin: New England, New Orleans, and the Bahamas, and splashed with the pastel pinks and yellows of the Caribbean.

Almost hidden within the Easter-colored wonderland was a sign that announced, Key West Naval Station —Truman Annex. The former Fort Zachary Taylor, built in 1845, was converted into the Naval Station Key West until its closure in 1974. Nuclear submarines had been docked at the base during the Cold War, then decommissioned as the vessels grew too large.

The station was sometimes called the Truman Annex because President Harry S. Truman considered it his Winter White House in 1946, where he spent 175 days of his presidency. During his island getaways, decisions were considered, and State of the Union addresses prepared.

Agent Kurtz loved to joke that America could've been a more peaceful and progressive nation if all its presidents were forced to spend time ruling from the rejuvenating island.

Beyond the annex gate, a road led past the fort's beach to the building that housed the Joint Interagency Task Force. The JIATF's mission was to provide an operation for the detection and deterrence of drug smuggling operations. It was an alliance of military and law enforcement, including DEA, Coast Guard, and Immigration and Customs Enforcement, working under the umbrella of Homeland Security to prohibit the flow of illicit drugs into the US.

To assist the pursuit, the US Drug Enforcement Agency assigned two full-time members to the JIATF: Resident Agent in Charge Curtis Kurtz, originally from Key West, and his younger partner Agent Ernesto Ruiz, a transplant from Chicago.

The conference room's mahogany table had once served military brass and at least one president, discussing world-altering decisions. For the current crisis, the six men sat behind laptops with a fifty-inch monitor on one wall. The only throwback to the past was cigar smoke whirling under a paddle fan. Smoking had been prohibited in all federal buildings since 1997, but things seemed to progress differently on an island that was only ninety miles from Havana.

Agent Kurtz sat at the head of the table with Ruiz at his side serving as their A.V. expert. On one side of the table was a tanned, middle-aged agent from Immigration and Customs Enforcement (ICE) in black khakis. Opposite him sat two mid-thirties Coast Guardsmen who appeared pleasant but solemn in their navy-blue uniforms.

The only man without a uniform sat at the far end of the table. He was large and appeared bored. He wore a black t-shirt that strained to cover his immense crossed arms. He had a shaved head and chiseled features that fit his humorless expression.

The youthful Ruiz addressed the men, "We tracked the vessels last night from the port in Mariel, just west of Havana." He spoke with a slight Spanish accent, accentuating the words. He looked up at the monitor as he projected satellite imagery. "Both boats belonged to known narcotic smugglers."

"No surviving suspects to interrogate," Kurtz chimed in as if rehearsed. "And not enough of the boats left to track their origin."

Ruiz projected an image of the migrants huddled on the bow of the interceptor. "Last night's load included Cuban nationals. We didn't know the smugglers were going to add human cargo. They're our only surviving witnesses."

"Witnesses?" The sunbaked ICE officer scoffed, "If you trust third-world laborers who believe in sea monsters." He stressed the term, hoping the others would chuckle along.

"Show respect, Randy." Kurtz glowered, "Those poor souls paid five years' salary to risk their lives to come and live in your neighborhood." He raised his brows, poignant. "Not all of them survived."

Randy looked down at his calloused hands, silenced.

Agent Ruiz spoke with optimism to get back on course, "I'm not sure about sea monsters, but what if it was some sort of rare whale?"

Groans from around the table, from the Coast Guard agents to the large man with crossed arms.

"You boys have been around." Kurtz frowned at the cynics, "You remember Grodin, our last analyst. He was traveling thirty knots in a Sea Ray when he hit a manatee last year. It flipped his boat, a total loss. Grodin nearly met his maker."

The senior Guardsman, Newstreet, gave a warped grin, "You think the smugglers hit manatees last night…twice?"

"No!" Kurtz barked. "Just illustrating we must consider all possibilities."

"2019, Sea of Japan," Ruiz interjected, reading from his laptop, "Eighty people were seriously injured when a ferry hit a large whale."

Newstreet dipped his head as in *really?* "So, we're running with the whale theory?"

"Just have a goddamn open mind!" Kurtz swooshed his hands. He pointed to each man, "You might know everything about your field. But not everything about everything—"

The rattle of the doorknob paused the debate. Everyone turned to see a pleasant Latina analyst peek in.

"Pardon me, agents," she smiled at Kurtz. "Dr. Arrison has arrived. And she's brought an assistant."

"Two of them?" Kurtz seemed surprised. He shrugged, "Then round up another chair and let 'em in." He turned to the men. "My esteemed guest should be a breath of fresh air to you dinosaurs. Help us sort through some new possibilities."

The Coast Guardsmen rolled their eyes. The large aloof man shook his head and lit a fresh cigar.

"Be nice." Kurtz scolded them. He turned to the ICE agent, "Randy, you're making fresh coffee for our visitors."

Chapter Four
A Proposal for the Professor

Kurtz stood to greet his guest. A mid-forties woman entered, conservatively dressed for the tropics in slacks and a linen blouse. He extended his hand with a wide smile, "Ah, perfect timing as we babble about whales and krakens. Appreciate you coming down."

The blonde woman gave a faint smile, but her brows didn't soften. Kurtz would describe her as appealing but serious. She was fit like a swimmer and had a tan as if she worked outdoors.

"Hello, Agent." She maintained a staid expression. "A pleasure to finally meet."

Kurtz motioned to the men. "Gentlemen, this is Professor Patrice Arrison. She's with the FSU Coastal and Marine Lab. We're lucky to get her on short notice."

The men nodded. The Coast Guard officers glanced at their watches.

Kurtz noticed a young man following Arrison who looked like a student. He was in his early twenties with a stylish haircut. His slim jeans and flannel also seemed out of place in the Keys. Kurtz gave a single nod and the man just smiled, appearing timid.

"Sorry for being late." Dr. Arrison addressed the men, "Not many planes flying from the panhandle to the southern-most point." She winced at the cigar smoke with an exaggerated cough.

"I apologize, ma'am," Kurtz fanned smoke towards the door. "Maybe Key West isn't as caught-up as we should be."

Realizing the young man was quietly standing there, Dr. Arrison casually introduced him. "This is Chandler, my TA."

"TA?" Ruiz looked up. "Tech analyst?"

"No," Arrison replied. "Teacher's aide."

Kurtz noticed the young man seemed bothered by her description.

Dr. Arrison warmed somewhat, placing a hand on Chandler's shoulder. "In addition to oceanography, he also studied Latin American mythology. That might assist with some of the assertions I read in your witness statements."

Kurtz offered them seats. Chandler opened a laptop beside Ruiz. Dr. Arrison sat at his side. Agent Randy wheeled in a coffee cart, placing a carafe on the table.

As everyone settled in, Kurtz looked at Chandler. He felt bad for the kid. He seemed submissive to the professor as if he'd been told not to speak.

"I'm Agent Curtis Kurtz, DEA." Kurtz smiled at Chandler. "I'm rabbi to this young man, Agent Ruiz. We're all members of the Joint Interagency Task Force."

Agent Ruiz pleasantly nodded to Chandler and Dr. Arrison.

Kurtz motioned to the ICE agent with a passé mustache. "Randy here is Customs Enforcement. His job is to stop anyone trying to enter our borders who might do us harm. Traffickers or terrorists trying to enter through Cuba. You get the picture."

Chandler didn't blink. He looked at Arrison with eyes that asked *are we in the right room?*

Kurtz nodded to the other side of the table, "These two gentlemen are officers Roberts and Newstreet with our esteemed Coast Guard. These guys have been around a long time; know their stuff. They're our primary supplier of boats and choppers."

The men gave quick smiles, then looked back down at reports.

Kurtz looked at the large, chiseled man at the far end. "That gentleman is Mr. Ned Landa. He's a former Marine, Force Recon. A contract employee, invited today as an armaments expert."

Arrison tensed as if hesitant of the man's inclusion.

"So, you're a dream team of experts?" Chandler asked in a gentle voice.

Dr. Arrison cringed at his words, embarrassed.

"Absolutely." Kurtz winked at the kid, "We're the best there is."

"Hold a second," Arrison lifted a finger with a fixed jaw, "An arms expert?" She grimaced towards Ned Landa. "I was told this expedition was for potentially-rare marine life."

The surly Landa mocked, "Ma'am, this taskforce isn't a Green Peace holiday for fish-huggers. Did Kurtz tell you every destroyed vessel belonged to known smugglers?"

"However, Ned," Kurtz interrupted in a raised voice. "The reason the fine doctor was invited is because we have no incendiary evidence that any weapons destroyed the boats."

"That's true," Agent Ruiz added. "In every case, we found no accelerant residue."

The monitor was filled with photos of the collected boat wreckage. Shards of fiberglass and frayed life jackets had been placed on a surface and tagged. Some of the debris appeared charred with fire damage.

Dr. Arrison and Chandler leaned forward to study the images.

"In *every* case, we found no incendiary or chemical evidence," Ruiz continued. "If the boats had been destroyed by any sort of missile, bomb, grenade, or bullet, there'd be signs."

Newstreet asked, "What about shrapnel, pieces of metal?"

"What if saltwater washed away any chemicals?" Roberts offered.

"No," Ruiz shook his head. "There'd still be traces. And zero metal debris."

Landa raised his voice, "Narcos tested cellulose bombs that don't leave shrapnel."

Ruiz glared, "The only reasonable conclusion is the vessels hit objects."

Kurtz cleared his throat so all could hear. When the men looked at him, he turned to Dr. Arrison. "As you can see, these boys are very passionate about their jobs." His smile faded, "Which is precisely why there's a need to investigate both sides."

16

Ruiz projected a navigational chart of the eastern Gulf. "The only things confirmed are: six high-speed vessels have been destroyed. No evidence of a bomb or weapon hitting any boat."

"They didn't strike rocks or a reef." Roberts studied the screen, "They'd be on the charts. We're very familiar with that circuit."

"Only one common denominator," Ruiz aimed a laser pointer at the chart. "Every vessel was a suspected narcotics smuggler. They all occurred in this triangle between the US, Cuba and the Bahamas." He highlighted six dots on the map within a triangular area.

Gawking at the screen, Chandler reached for the coffee. His hand knocked the carafe over, drenching the table. "Whoa!" he cried out, returning the carafe upright. Steaming coffee saturated several of the men's reports. "My bad! I'm so…sorry," he stuttered.

Arrison recoiled, mortified. "What'd you do?" She scolded him like he was a child.

Newstreet cursed under his breath and handed over napkins. Ned Landa openly laughed.

"I apologize," Arrison formed a smile. "Fortunately, Chandler is much more book smart."

Chandler looked at her, instantly hurt. His jaw opened as if about to speak but said nothing.

Kurtz sensed the unease between the two. "Don't worry, son." He helped wipe the table and attempted a chuckle, "Hey, fresh coffee smells better than cigars, am I right?"

Chandler withered in his seat. Dr. Arrison pinched the bridge of her nose.

When the room calmed, Kurtz looked at Chandler. He wanted to show the kid some respect, perhaps involve him as a peer to the others. "So, tell me Chandler, how might your… Spanish mythology studies help our predicament?"

Chandler's eyes widened at the query. He sprang to life, plugging a cord from Ruiz's laptop into his own. He stammered, eager. "I… we… read the survivor's account of what they'd witnessed."

The screen filled with an illustration that appeared to be from a textbook. It was an exaggerated drawing of an enormous shark in a lagoon, jaws gaping, with villagers fleeing.

"Your witnesses said '*El Monstruo de Cojimar*.'" Chandler transformed into a capable lecturer. "That's a legend from Cojimar, Cuba that dates to 1945. Locals claim it's a prehistoric-sized shark that terrorizes the area."

The men studied the image with skeptical brows.

"There are similar tales between here and South America." Chandler continued, "*Massacooramaan* is a legend from Guyana. A large water creature that attacks boats, dragging its victims underwater before consuming them." The image displayed an illustration of a beast toppling a small boat, and fishermen screaming.

The agents glowered at each other. Someone mumbled, "Really?"

Chandler didn't pause, "In Peru, *Yacumama* is an enormous serpent, destroying anything within its path—"

"What he's trying to say is," Arrison disrupted in a raised voice, "Myths are usually rooted in fact. Ancient people saw whales, giant squids, and so on, and labeled them as monsters." She rotated Chandler's laptop to type.

Chandler pursed his lips and sat. The spotlight had been yanked away.

Dr. Arrison addressed the room, "Your witnesses described a whale-sized beast with a large tusk like a unicorn. That's an almost perfect description of a narwhal." The screen displayed a large gray whale breaching the surface with a spear-like horn protruding from its head. "The problem is, they're only found in arctic waters."

Her grin faded when she turned to Kurtz, "Nothing in your emails mentioned smugglers. Chandler and I flew six hundred miles because rare humpbacks were spotted off Miami Beach. There have been historic migrations of whale sharks, the largest fish in the world, some over forty feet. Both could easily destroy small boats, especially if traveling at high speeds."

Landa audibly sighed. He gathered his folders as if he'd seen enough.

"Then it's decided!" Kurtz slapped the table, causing Chandler to flinch. "This will be a balanced pursuit." He continued with animated hands, "Could be large marine life. Could be a cartel weapon or turf war. We will move ahead to learn more."

Arrison and Chandler sat erect at his outburst.

Kurtz motioned to Newstreet. "The Coast Guard has graciously offered a vessel for our pursuit. Thank you, sirs." He then pointed to Arrison, "Professor: we require your expertise for any unique marine life we might encounter." He pointed to the end of the table, "Mr. Landa will be aboard to identify any signs of assault or weaponry. We'll have two Guardsmen to pilot—"

"Only five people?" Landa bellowed, "And two of them are a professor and a kid? What if *we* are targeted?"

Dr. Arrison stood upright, incensed. "This voyage is quickly changing from your request to the university. I'm not going to be destroyed in some armed military vessel!"

Chandler's jaw went slack at the thought.

Kurtz raised his hands. "There won't be any attacks. Our radars can see twenty-five nautical miles. We'll have eyes on any vessel that enters the triangle."

Arrison was slow to sit back down.

"If we see anything even possibly hostile, we'll have an interceptor and choppers on 'em like the cavalry." Kurtz looked into Arrison's eyes. "Think about it: hundreds of boats are out there every night without problems. If you don't encounter any marine life, I'll take you back out tomorrow during daylight. The boat's got a sonar fish finder. I'll make your trip worthwhile."

Arrison gazed out the window, contemplating his words.

"The truth is, Dr. Arrison," Kurtz stiffened, his tone more direct. "If you no longer want this rare and unique opportunity, the University of Miami has a wonderful Marine Science professor who'd love to fill in. I called you first because you have an excellent department and my husband's son went to FSU."

Arrison went deadpan at the warning, dumbstruck. Chandler looked at her, awaiting a response. The others watched in silence.

Kurtz looked at his Tag Heuer. "Our boat departs at 22:00 hours tonight from our Sector Key West Station." He turned back to Arrison, "We'd love to have you aboard, but we need to know now."

Chapter Five
Bridge from the Old World

Professor Arrison entered the pink Key West taxi at 8:45 p.m. She sat in the front passenger's seat, believing it'd give her some sense of control. Chandler placed their equipment in the trunk and then sat in the back.

During the grinding ride down the motel's musty elevator, Arrison had hardly spoken. The motel hadn't helped her disposition, though it was free, directly billed to Agent Kurtz.

The King Conch motel was not one of the glamorous resorts on the beach, nor a quaint bed-and-breakfast found in historic Old Town. The hotel faced a four-lane US-1 in an area northeast of the city, referred to by locals as New Town. A clustered area with bumper-to-bumper tourists lining up for every fast-food chain, cookie-cutter franchise, and an anemic mall anchored by a deserted Sears.

Ironically, less than a mile away was the storybook side of Key West as seen in people's imaginations, art, and films. Vibrant Victorian homes, lush tropical gardens with vines of pink bougainvillea, and cobblestone roads leading to raw bars on the water.

But it wasn't going to be one of those kinds of trips. Agent Kurtz's request through the university had not allowed time for recreation or deliberation. They offered to pay for a roundtrip flight, two nights at the King Conch, and a meal per diem of forty dollars per day. Certainly, no Florida lobster or stone crabs anytime soon.

The truth was —and despite anyone's assumptions— Professor Arrison didn't receive many travel opportunities. People presumed the title "Marine Biologist" meant a jet-setting career exploring the high seas. However, her salary and duties with the university didn't allow for extravagant international travel. And though her job was in Florida, the university was located nearly an hour inland, and her marine lab was situated on a marshy backwater called Sopchoppy. Not exactly a carefree expert with the Seven Seas as her playground.

So the offer from Agent Kurtz to travel to Key West had been compelling, considering the marine opportunities the trip might provide. That was until Kurtz clarified the more ominous details during their briefing.

Kurtz's ultimatum had left her with two choices: Decline the opportunity and fly back home to explain to the Vice President of Research how everything fell apart, which had required a substitute professor to cover her duties, and reimbursement to Kurtz for the hotel, flights, and food. Or she could enjoy a boat ride off the coast of Key West in hopes of encountering unique marine life —while trying to not get caught in the crossfire of a cartel's turf war.

"He did say we could go out again tomorrow," Arrison mused aloud as the cab entered the congested US-1.

"I bet their fish finder's better than ours," Chandler offered from the backseat. "It's Coast Guard sonar."

Arrison smiled back at Chandler but didn't respond. She wasn't necessarily looking for a conversation. At least the taxi driver wasn't looking to chat either. The driver was sixtyish with spiked hair, wearing a pro-vegan t-shirt and earbuds, humming to her own tune.

Arrison folded down the visor to look in the mirror. She sighed to realize her tired, forty-three year-old eyes, jade with silk threads of red. She'd slept only five hours in the past twenty-four. Maybe her sun-streaked hair and moderate tan would offset the absence of any make-up.

She and Chandler had done little to prepare for this excursion. There was no need for anything but a ponytail for a boat ride in the dark with three grizzled military guys. Arrison wore matching khaki shorts and shirt over her long, slim form. Chandler looked like a college student on an off day with cargo shorts, flip-flops, and a faded denim shirt with his sleeves rolled up.

Their cab merged right onto the Palm Avenue Causeway, a bridge that branched off from the mainland. Dr. Arrison gazed down to see docks thriving with tourists and fishermen despite being almost 9:00 pm. This made her feel more confident; it was true that boats traveled every night without any danger.

As the causeway returned to land, the lively vacation town was suddenly an industrial area with boatyards, scrubby expanses that looked like former airfields, and signs for military housing.

Chandler told her they were going to Trumbo Point, which was built in 1912 to accommodate a shipping port, and now housed several bases including the Naval Air Station and the Coast Guard. He was known to methodically research their destinations and recite what he'd learned whether anyone asked him or not. Chandler had an *eidetic* or "photographic" memory, which could be both a blessing and a curse.

The cab turned right on Mustin Street, a narrow road that ran along the water to her left. Arrison gazed out to see illuminated piers with impressive Coast Guard vessels. *Which vessel is ours?* she wondered.

"Did you know the laundromat next to our hotel is famous for Cuban sandwiches?" Chandler asked from the back. "So, I got us," he rattled paper bags, "a thermos of Cuban coffee and two *medianoche* sandwiches. *Medianoche* means midnight." He continued to babble," It's made with pork, ham, Swiss, pickles–"

"Chandler," Arrison interrupted. She turned to face him. "I know you're nervous."

"No…" He paused with a childlike expression, "What do you mean?"

"We both know what's at stake with this entire trip." She smiled, "I– we—need this opportunity. It could change everything." She looked into his eyes to gauge his understanding, "You know what I'm talking about."

Chandler nodded.

The cab stopped at a gate attached to a white cement wall that stated, UNITED STATES COAST GUARD — SECTOR KEY WEST. A uniformed officer approached their car. Arrison located her identification and took Chandler's driver's license and handed both towards the driver's window.

The guard took the cards and examined each.

Arrison noticed a small sign on the gate that declared, PROUDLY SERVING THE US MILITARY. She swallowed, suddenly parched. Arrison wondered if they were being used as a tool for the military, rather than invited for her marine knowledge.

"Here you go, Professor," the guard returned the IDs. "Go through the main building to access the docks to the rear." He added, "You're right on time."

Chapter Six
Meeting *Abraham Lincoln*

"If your program loses funding, can't you just pursue something else?" Chandler asked as he removed equipment from the taxi's trunk.

Arrison scowled, "Of course not." Before she could launch into a lecture, a young female in a navy-blue uniform approached.

"Welcome, Professor." The ginger woman smiled with dimples. "I'm Cadet Ireland with the Coast Guard." She brought a cart for their gear. Chandler loaded two black cases that looked like suitcases, two scuba tanks, and mesh bags containing dive masks and fins.

Chandler blushed just being near the cadet, mumbling, "Thanks, I got it."

Ireland led them through a two-story main building designed without any flair and painted chalky white. Arrison guessed it had been built practical and solid for any storm threats.

Chandler's inquisitive nature emerged. He asked the cadet, "Tell me about this station."

Ireland recited like a tour guide, "We have a 55,000 square-mile responsibility, stretching to Cuba and the Bahamas." She continued as they walked. "Our duties include search-rescue and assisting law enforcement with anti-narcotics efforts." She smiled at them, "Like what you two are doing."

Chandler and the professor traded an uneasy glance.

They exited the rear doors to face the harbor. The marina had wide piers with lights revealing imposing patrol vessels and 150-foot response cutters.

"Which boat's ours?" Chandler asked.

Ireland grinned, "Only vessels under sixty-five feet are called 'boats.'" She pointed to various vessels. "We got forty-seven-foot Response Boats and the larger Island-class cutters. I'm not sure which is yours."

Ireland halted. "This is far as I go." She motioned to the center of three piers. "Straight ahead, slip B-11. They're waiting for you." She nodded, turned, and was gone.

Arrison and Chandler inhaled the salty breeze. A silent moment acknowledging it was time to proceed.

"I was just saying," Chandler spoke gently as he pulled the cart. "If your curriculum is no longer funded, maybe you can pursue something new."

Arrison's brows tensed. "I'm not like your friends, changing degrees every other year."

His face wilted. "What do you mean?"

"I can't just float around subject to subject," she sniped. "I've devoted over twenty years to my profession—" She stopped mid-sentence and took a breath.

Chandler fidgeted with the cart's handle, unsure how to react.

"I'm sorry." She paused to capture his glance. "That wasn't fair for me to say that. I know I've been challenging. I've just been emotionally distressed."

He smiled.

She leaned an inch closer, "If we can document any new migrations or any rare species that have drifted this far south..." She looked up, searching for words, "Or just anything *unique*, it could change everything for both of us." She looked into his eyes. "Do you understand?"

Chandler scanned the ground and nodded.

❧

The large Ned Landa stood with Coast Guard Officers Roberts and Newstreet on the pier. He was dressed for the night in paramilitary black cargos and another tight t-shirt. He took one last puff of his illicit Partagas cigar and flicked the butt into the water.

Roberts carried twenty extra pounds that gave him a moon face. He motioned towards the building, "Here comes that professor and the kid."

Newstreet turned. The senior officer was trim with a face that showed little emotion. "The doctor seems all right," he shrugged.

Landa chuckled, "Doesn't her name 'Arrison' sound like arrogant?"

Roberts smirked, "Why are they really here?"

"Kurtz told me," Landa glanced over his shoulder, "she's here to appease the animal rights wackos. If dead whales wash up with boat injuries, it looks like we're doing something about it." He flashed a deceitful grin, "And if anyone were to attack us, we have civilians aboard. Bigger penalties for the smugglers."

Roberts' eyes bugged, "Let's hope it is just whales."

Newstreet tapped his foot on a five-foot rectangular case at Landa's feet. "I need to know any heavy arms you're planning to bring aboard."

Landa eyed the container, "Kurtz loaned me his FIM-92 Stinger. We don't care if the cartels are annihilating each other." He cocked his head, "Just keep it off our shores, you know?"

They turned to see the professor and her assistant approach with gawks of disbelief.

Arrison pointed, "Don't tell me that is our boat."

"Yes ma'am," Newstreet turned to his pride and joy. Moored between two imposing cutters was a thirty-two-foot aluminum boat. "Our Port Security Boat. Twin outboards, center console. The open deck should have enough room."

Arrison froze to assess the boat. It looked like a toy in comparison to the surrounding vessels. It was shaped like an inflatable boat but was bare aluminum as if someone had forgotten to paint it. There was no cabin for any possible shelter or bathroom.

"Don't you worry," Newstreet motioned to the bow, "We got a .50-caliber gun on the front, along with two M60 machine guns."

"She's our sixteenth Port Security Boat, so we call her the *Abraham Lincoln*," Roberts beamed.

"What happened to the other fifteen?" Chandler mumbled.

"How can we complain?" Landa dipped his head to Arrison. "We got the taxpayers to fund your little field trip."

She took a sharp breath, ready to scold the pompous man. Before she could utter a word, Newstreet shouted.

"21:20. Everyone aboard!" Newstreet ordered. "Off to the dark unknown."

Chapter Seven
Under Way

As the professor seethed, Chandler remained observant. He noticed they didn't even have a gangplank to board the *Abraham Lincoln*. Newstreet had to grab a rail to pull the boat close enough to the dock for them all to board.

Ned Landa insisted that he board first, carrying a large case. Newstreet helped Arrison aboard, then helped Chandler hand over the professor's equipment. Roberts was already at the center console. Landa proceeded to the front of the boat, which was fine with Arrison since it was the farthest point from her seat in the stern.

Chandler stored their gear which included cameras to capture footage of creatures too large to bring back to the lab. One case contained a Canon digital camera with an underwater housing, and another held a baton-shaped hydrophone for underwater sound recording.

Dr. Arrison kept one camera on a strap around her neck. Chandler held onto his phone which had a decent camera. He shuffled the narrow path to the stern with two paper bags to a seat next to Arrison.

Roberts passed out life vests to everyone. The professor and Chandler readily fastened theirs. Ned Landa refused to wear his, babbling how he was an "expert swimmer" with the Marines. Roberts moved to the console to throttle the engines. Two cadets on the dock helped with the ropes. With everyone settled in, the *Abraham Lincoln* idled west towards open water.

Regardless of how many boats Chandler had been on, the scent of diesel made his stomach sour. He purposely hadn't overeaten; their last meal was at a McDonald's on US-1 three hours earlier. Arrison had chosen the restaurant to contain expenses. Chandler ordered a McFish, so it'd seem like a seafood meal in Key West.

Everyone on the *Lincoln* seemed occupied with their tasks. Newstreet and Roberts stood at the controls. Landa remained on the bow, examining whatever gear he'd brought aboard.

Chandler looked to his left to watch the coast roll by. The shore was filled with marinas and historic structures. It was nearly ten o'clock, so the lights of Old Town's bars and cafes glimmered. The Half Shell Raw Bar and Turtle Kraals, with their illuminated dockside tables, passed a hundred yards away. Chandler heard faint laughter and hollering from happy crowds. If he concentrated, he wondered if he could hear any live bands emanating from the saloons of Duval Street.

Chandler could only dream of such places. As an introvert with a limited social existence, he'd never experienced the night life in a popular city. He'd never even been invited to bar hop with fellow students. His classes and responsibilities consumed most of his days, combined with an almost paralyzing anxiety of the opposite sex.

Making things seem more lifeless, the *Lincoln* didn't play any music, and no one onboard spoke. He looked at Arrison who just smiled and looked out at the horizon. But Chandler knew that smile; she was equally uneasy about the evening.

The *Lincoln* increased speed between Sunset Key and Mallory Square to head south towards the open Gulf. There was only a mild breeze and the stars sparkled in the cloudless sky.

Chandler wondered if it was the cliché calm before something else. Perhaps something dreadful. Were there armed criminals targeting boats? Immense whales crushing small vessels?

The undisputed fact was people had lost their lives. *At least these men are armed,* Chandler supposed. From what he could see, they were heading farther away from land, towards an even darker horizon.

With the lull of the engines purring and no one speaking, Chandler pulled a banana from his bag. When Roberts turned to him, he froze.

"Where'd you get that?" Roberts exclaimed.

"My banana?" Chandler frowned, confused. "Our motel has a breakfast bar thing."

"Never bring bananas on a boat!" Roberts scolded. "It's bad luck."

"I thought that was only for fishing?"

"No, it's for sinking too," Roberts retorted.

In a single move, Dr. Arrison took the banana and threw it overboard. She then stood to approach the controls. Chandler watched his banana drift away.

Dr. Arrison approached Roberts at the console. She always felt more in control if she understood the logistics. He turned to her with a polite nod.

"So, you're a marine biologist?"

"Yes," Arrison had to grasp a rail for balance. "But that title is pretty general."

"So, there are specialties?" He seemed genuinely curious.

"There are titles depending on what we do." She had to shout over the mounting wind. "An ichthyologist studies fish; a cetologist studies whales; a microbiologist studies tiny organisms. I guess I know just enough of each discipline to teach at a university level."

Roberts bumped up the speed. "I specialize in navigation; Newstreet in seizures." He looked at her, "So what's your objective tonight?"

Arrison smiled, "My goal is to study marine life in their natural environments. Not in tanks, aquariums, or textbooks."

She looked out to gain her bearings. The lights of Key West twinkled far in their trail. Their destination ahead appeared pitch-black. She hoped a quarter-moon to the east might help their eyes adjust.

"We're approaching the triangle, sixteen miles southeast. See?" Roberts tapped his screen. "Where every vessel has been destroyed."

Any warmth in her face drained with the reminder of their pursuit.

"Reminds me of the old Devil's Triangle," Roberts chuckled. "Remember that? Never solved that one!" He laughed and pushed the throttle forward.

⌘

Newstreet concluded a call on his radio, "I'll advise, over." He approached Ned Landa on the bow, who was examining his equipment. Packed in molded foam was a weapon that looked like an olive-green cannon. "Seems a little extreme for a whale."

Landa beamed like a child. "It's an FIM-92 Stinger." He lifted a tube nearly five feet long. "A surface-to-air missile with infrared. It can be fired from vehicles, choppers, and maybe tonight: boats."

Roberts kneeled, curious. "How do you fire it?"

"Shoulder-fired with a range up to 4,800 meters." Landa lifted a shaft and handgrip. "The launch tube is fitted with a gripstock."

Newstreet raised his brows, "How do you fire that without torching my boat?"

"No worries," Landa showed the base of the missile. "It's launched by an ejection system that pushes it a safe distance before fuel engines kick in."

"Listen," Newstreet checked over his shoulder, "I just got the call." He spoke close to Landa's ear, "The intel spotted a triple-engine, heading north out of Manzanillo right now."

Landa stiffened, back to business. "I'll be ready if anyone targets a biology cruise with a teacher and a kid." He gave a quick wink.

The *Abraham Lincoln* followed the horizon as the ivory moon slid west at a snail's pace.

Chandler remained in his seat, staring at his cellphone. He listened through earbuds and watched other people's travel videos. He'd huff and groan when the reception faded. Chandler would stand and loop his phone in the air in hopes of regaining a signal.

Ned Landa remained up front, turning his head left to right to scan the horizon like a cyborg. Roberts and Newstreet took turns with the controls, alternating chores, and smoke breaks.

⌘

At nearly 1:00 am, Chandler yawned and opened a bag of food. He

31

pulled out a small thermos and offered Arrison a drink.

"Café Cubano," he whispered as he poured her a small Styrofoam cup. He lifted two sandwiches wrapped in foil. "Cuban sandwich?"

"Do they have mayonnaise?" Arrison wrinkled her nose. "How long have those been unrefrigerated?"

He shrugged and decided to try his. It tasted fine; maybe the tangy mustard hid any spoiled mayo taste. As he listlessly ate, the only sounds were the drone of the engines and the hypnotic lapping of waves. If he hadn't been chewing, he believed he might fall asleep. Until he heard Newstreet's voice.

"We got *nada*," Newstreet uttered into his radio, "I'll give it 'til 03:00. Otherwise, return to port. Over."

"Copy," a garbled voice responded.

Dr. Arrison approached Newstreet like a diner complaining about overdue food. "Excuse me, have you been using your fish finder?"

He frowned, "You talking about our sonar?" He pointed to a monitor, "It'll pick up large marine life or approaching schools of fish." His radio crackled.

"*Lincoln*, come in." It was Kurtz's voice. "Suspect vessel is now southeast, two nautical miles. Twenty-three degrees North, eighty-one degrees West. Over."

"This is *Lincoln*, copy," Newstreet reacted fast. "We'll attempt visual—"

"Suspect vessel?" Arrison interrupted. "You've been tracking a boat this entire time?"

Chandler's jaw stopped, mid-chew.

"Cut the lights!" Newstreet ignored her. "Southeast, two-zero knots."

"Copy," Roberts replied. All lights instantly darkened on the boat.

Despite the darkness, Chandler could see the men move in a flurry. Newstreet joined Roberts at the con. Landa lifted binoculars on the bow.

"What's happening?" Chandler whispered.

Arrison didn't reply. She turned her head to each man.

"Vessel approaching south-southeast," Roberts announced from the glow of his screen.

Arrison and Chandler turned to study the horizon, anxious.

"Yep, got 'em," Landa responded. "I'd say, two miles."

Everyone looked in the direction Landa was aiming his binoculars.

There was a pause in the rolling blackness. A menacing calm as the men seemed to be waiting for something. Arrison and Chandler squinted to see whatever was out there.

Chandler spotted a light shimmering on the horizon. At first, it was a faint flicker, but then became distinct. "A boat," he tapped Arrison, "There!" With the swaying hull, it was hard to keep his eyes on the light.

Everyone was silent as if holding their breath. Nothing but the relentless slosh of water.

A sudden flash made everyone gasp. A plume of orange painted the sky, then a thunderous boom a second after the flash. The boat on the horizon had exploded.

"They're hit!" Roberts bellowed, "And something's heading our way!"

Chapter Eight
Scaling the Spine

Chandler covered his ears. Professor Arrison's body locked, riveted with fear.

"I got a large reading, closing fast," Newstreet shouted.

"Do we engage?" Roberts exclaimed.

"I see no other vessels..." Newstreet scanned the area with his binoculars.

"Maybe a long-range weapon?" Landa lifted the stinger from its case.

Roberts dashed to the .50 caliber gun mounted on the bow.

Arrison and Chandler were paralyzed with confusion. They crouched low as if hiding.

Landa adjusted his infrared binoculars. "Impossible..."

"What do you see?" Roberts retorted.

"It's like a...rogue wave," Landa continued to focus. "Are those... eyes?"

Arrison aimed her camera towards the faraway flames. Chandler aimed his phone's camera. They clicked towards the darkness.

"Jesus," Newstreet's face glowed from his sonar. "It's massive; it's no whale!"

Landa snapped the gripstock onto the stinger and inserted a

battery unit, allowing just one shot. He lifted the weapon onto his right shoulder. Roberts was at his side, preparing the .50 caliber.

Newstreet shouted, "I haven't given orders to fire!"

Arrison could see a spew of water in the distance. She blinked faster, aiming her camera at whatever was racing towards them. "Is that spray coming off an enormous fin?"

"A fifteen-foot fin?" Chandler's voice trembled. They jolted as Roberts fired the .50 caliber. Newstreet joined them on the bow with a handheld M60 machine gun. They fired into the water towards the approaching enigma.

Landa struggled to aim his weapon in the chop. White spray was visible in the blackness. The eyes and enormous fin became more distinct as it raced within fifty yards.

With an earsplitting blast, Landa fired the stinger. The missile launched forward, hurling him ten feet back onto the deck.

Arrison watched the rocket miss its target. It detonated underwater with a muted thump and a blinding flash in the clear sea. Within that light, she saw the silhouette of something massive. *Dear God—*

The *Lincoln's* bow shattered upwards. Both officers were thrashed as if struck by a locomotive. The crumpling metal was deafening. Arrison clutched Chandler's shirt.

The remaining hull capsized. Arrison was heaved overboard. The sensation was like being launched from an enormous seesaw into darkness. "Chandler!" she shrieked.

She splashed into the water. It was colder than she'd imagined, like a million needles. As she descended, her obscured vision recognized portions of the hull sinking. Her lungs burned; she hadn't taken a breath when they were hit. She needed to swim towards the surface, but with the churn, she didn't know which way was up. She kicked towards an orange glow.

Arrison breached the surface and drew in a long breath. Radiant embers rained down like sparks. Choking smoke filled the air and flaming wreckage bobbed on the surface.

She called out, "Chandler!" Waves slapped her face, burning her eyes. She spun, clutching her life vest and treading water. "Chandler!" Her voice became hoarse.

A faint, fretful voice responded, "Where are you?" It was Chandler.

"I'm here!" She splashed towards his voice. The swells seemed four to five feet. "I'm coming." A strong current pulled her away from the flaming debris which meant less light.

As she crested a wave, she could see Chandler's head and orange vest bobbing in a trough between swells. "It's me!" She shouted, "Are you okay?"

Though coughing, he beamed at the sight of her. He reached for her with both arms. They embraced for what seemed an eternity, a grip of survival instinct and an unsaid affection.

Chandler pulled back with red eyes, "Are they all dead?"

She didn't answer. She turned to see the wreckage farther away. "The current's too strong. Look for anything we can grab."

In the rolling darkness, they couldn't see any debris to swim towards.

"Whatever did this," there was a fracture in his voice, "what if it's under us right now?"

Arrison looked down into the black water. She hadn't considered any ongoing threat other than drowning. "Kurtz will send help."

Under her feet, she did feel a churning undercurrent. Her imagination raced with possibilities. *Too large to be a shark or a whale. Maybe a school of humpbacks?*

It was difficult seeing over swells that seemed infinite and darker than before. As they labored to stay afloat, they were surrounded by the unsettling hush of lapping waves.

A faraway voice called out from the dark, "*I found your whale.*"

They perked up and turned in search of the voice.

Arrison called out, "Who is it?" Her voice seemed lost in the expanse.

The voice shouted again, closer. "I'm up here."

"It's Landa's voice!" Chandler exclaimed. With renewed strength, they splashed towards his voice. Arrison kicked harder, pulling Chandler by his hand.

She saw a figure in the gloom ahead, but it seemed to be above the water.

Like a mirage, Ned Landa appeared forty feet away in the darkness. It was him, with his broad shoulders and a black t-shirt. Through her salty tears, it looked like he was crouching above the sea.

As they swam within twenty feet, Arrison saw waves breaking against a surface below Landa's feet. He stood like a beacon, either on the water by magic or on an unseen deck.

Arrison and Chandler swam to him. Landa leaned to help them out of the water. He pulled Arrison by her hands, up a black slope until she was out. He then gripped one of Chandler's arms and lifted him in a single move and dropped him next to Arrison.

They both panted, hands on their knees, to catch their breaths.

"I was flung overboard." Landa huffed, "The two officers are dead."

Arrison nodded, solemn. She didn't like the man, but he had just saved them.

Chandler looked at the black surface they were standing on. He stomped with his bare foot. "Is it metal? A platform?"

Arrison looked down. The ground felt solid like concrete. "A jetty wouldn't be this far out." She followed it with her eyes to see it fade into the darkness. It was a narrow path about ten feet wide. Waves sloshed against inclines on both sides. She stepped forward to see the path stretch well beyond a hundred feet.

"A buoy platform?" Chandler studied their surroundings.

"It's too long," Landa replied. "Too big for a shipping container."

As Arrison cautiously walked, she looked up to distinguish a tower at least twenty feet tall protruding from the deck. It looked like a steel triangle with sharp, angular edges. She gasped, "Is that the fin we saw?"

Landa's eyes looked at the deck, to the fin, and back to the deck.

At the base of the tower, Arrison saw glowing circles on each side, three feet in diameter. "Are those portholes?"

"They look like eyes," Chandler mused.

"Oh no..." Landa became rigid. "It's a narco-sub."

Chandler frowned, "What's a narco—?"

Their world turned black before anyone could utter another word.

Dark figures pulled hoods over their heads from behind. Before the three could resist, they were shot with 50,000-volt electroshock weapons. With three sizzling bursts, the intruders dropped like marionettes.

PART II
THE *NAUMTSEV*

Chapter Nine
Captives

A silent abyss of complete darkness. Then blurred, nauseating streams of light.

Muted voices drifted in and out. Echoes in melodious Spanish shifted into harsh Slavic words. Then an abrupt silence as if something had been slammed shut.

Nothing made sense, like a hallucinogenic nightmare.

With a sharp gasp, Dr. Arrison's eyes sprung open. She shouted, "Where am I?"

She sat upright, clammy, and breathless. Her fingers tightened to grasp the floor, but it was cold steel. The space was dark, and the air smelled like burned motor oil.

As her eyes adjusted, the confining space looked like a ten-by-six-foot cell. There was no light except what seeped through a vent on the door. She looked down to realize a body was on the floor beside her. "Chandler!" she shrieked.

She seized him by his shoulders. "Are you okay?" Frantic, Arrison checked for a pulse and lifted his lids. His eyes rolled to her. She smiled with glossy eyes. "It's me."

Chandler labored to sit up. He held his forehead as if in agony and squinted at the gritty bulkheads. The walls were steel with large rivets and rust stains. In a raspy voice he asked, "Where are we?"

A voice behind them replied, "We're in a sub."

They turned to see Ned Landa in the shadows. He was hunched on a bench and breathing heavily.

"A sub?" Chandler gently stood.

"Yes," Landa barked. "A submarine. I should've known. It was too dark." He covered his face with both hands.

Arrison moved closer to him. "Are you okay?"

"I'm fine," Landa snapped. "I'm not good in tight spaces."

"You're claustrophobic?" Chandler gaped, naïve. "Aren't you a Marine?"

"It'll pass," Landa shouted. He lowered his hands to see them standing over him. He took a breath to explain, "We're in a sub. The white whale of the DEA, a narco-sub."

Landa saw their bewildered faces. "Drug dealers, narco-traffickers, have begun using submarines for smuggling. They're usually homemade pieces of crap that are barely seaworthy." He looked at them, "The ultimate fear is they get their hands on a Soviet sub."

Arrison mocked, "You think this is a Russian sub?"

Instead of responding, he pointed to a stained sign by a pipe. Arrison and Chandler leaned closer to read it. It was written entirely in Russian script.

Dr. Arrison's face went blank, stunned. She closed her eyes to recall her dream. "I heard voices, but they were Spanish." She turned to Landa, "Maybe Cuba's attacking?"

Chandler shook his head, "I heard Spanish too, but I think it was Colombian, not Cuban."

Arrison balked, "How could you possibly know that?"

"Remember Lina Gomez in reef lab?" He dipped his head, confident, "She was from Bogotá. I heard a voice say '*que pena.*' That's how Colombians say, 'I'm sorry' instead of *lo siento.*"

Arrison frowned to consider the inference. "Who's apologizing to us?"

Chandler patted his pockets, "My wallet's gone, and my phone!" He looked at Arrison, "Our cameras!"

Arrison's hands sprung to her waist. A pouch where she'd kept her wallet, phone, and identification was gone. "Where's our belongings?"

"They took all our stuff," Landa replied without moving.

Arrison glared, "These people robbed us?"

"So we can't communicate with anyone." Landa rubbed his temples. "My guess, they're running our backgrounds right now."

Chandler exhaled under his breath, "So we have nothing."

Dr. Arrison slouched against the wall with fears greater than a missing wallet. Who were their captors? And more significantly, what were they going to do to them?

In the pause, she realized there was a mechanized vibration from the floor. But was that proof it was a submarine? She'd done research on barges and cargo ships with the same feel.

Arrison studied what little she could see. The cell was tarnished, but it seemed clean. There was no disturbing evidence of any prior prisoners, such as blood or worse.

Are we hostages? She quivered at the notion. Were there modern pirates in the area, like Somalia who kidnap and demand enormous ransoms? She then questioned the bleak reality; *would the university even pay for us?*

She looked at the men, "Do you remember being thrown in here? Or see any of them?"

Chandler shook his head, weary.

"No," Landa replied. "I suspect we were drugged as well."

There was a clank at the door like a lock was turning. They tensed as it creaked open to reveal the silhouettes of two men. They were dressed in black and aiming pistols.

"Face the wall," a guard shouted with a thick Spanish accent.

Landa studied their guns. "Latinos aiming Russian Makarovs." He sneered, "Well, that proves that."

The larger guard kicked Landa off his bench with a grunt.

Arrison and Chandler froze. Though Landa was strong, he scowled from the floor, electing not to strike back.

The guards had them stand with their noses to the wall. The men, who appeared Hispanic, said little. They handled Landa with force and were more humane to Arrison and Chandler. They bound their wrists behind their backs with cable zip-ties.

Blocking the light, a third figure appeared in the doorway. The three turned to see a man. Though difficult to see, he was tall and trim.

"Who are you?" Landa shouted, brazen.

The man spoke with a serene Russian accent. "I am *Nikto*. I am the captain of—"

"You're a murderer!" Landa bellowed.

The man, Nikto, paused as if assessing him. "I am not a killer of innocents. I target my former employers, and anyone who commits acts of war." He enunciated the words.

"What act of war?" Landa taunted. A guard jerked him back by his wrists.

Without responding, Nikto shouted to the guards in flawless Spanish, "*Tráelos conmigo.*"

The guards shoved the three to exit the chamber.

Chapter Ten
Eternal Guests

Ned Landa was slow to follow this Captain Nikto into a dim corridor.

Landa had to duck his head under the door's threshold to follow the man. The hallway was poorly lit and narrower than the inside of a subway car. There were horizontal pipes a foot in diameter and a steel-grated deck. The walls were gray and government-issue beige. It looked like an abandoned power plant.

Landa was first in line, walking five feet behind Captain Nikto. Chandler was behind him, with Arrison to the rear. The guards loomed close behind.

He tried to conceal his anxiety, not from their predicament, but from the enclosed space. He monitored his breathing, *inhale... slow, and out...* The air was stale with a faint scent of diesel. Though perspiring, Landa tried to remain tall and vigilant.

He realized they were walking at a slight incline as if going downhill. This supported his submarine theory. If this were a ship, they'd be sinking. The passageways had handrails, but they couldn't use them with their hands bound. He glanced back at Arrison to see how she was coping. She was quiet, but her eyes darted with fear. Landa whispered, "Stay close."

"Face forward!" a guard shouted with a thick accent.

Landa turned back to Nikto who was stepping through a partition. The entryways had rounded corners with locking doors to seal the compartments from each other. Bulkheads every thirty feet would make it difficult to run from these captors, nor was there anywhere to go.

Despite advertising he was an expert at military equipment, Landa's career had never included working on a submarine. However, he had studied the US versions and he'd toured a nuclear sub, the USS *Seawolf,* at Fort Lauderdale's Port Everglades. This vessel's corridors appeared the same, except for sporadic warning signs in Russian.

Captain Nikto turned the hatch wheel on a door. "Follow me." He pointed down. "Mind your step."

Professor Arrison entered the room behind Landa. She immediately noticed it had a higher ceiling. The space was larger, twenty feet wide by twenty-five feet long. She guessed the walls were the same steel bulkheads, but they'd been covered with scarlet drapes. The ceiling-to-floor fabric looked like velvet curtains for windows that weren't there. Gold-framed oil paintings and antique maps adorned the walls between the drapes.

Arrison stepped beside Chandler and Landa. The two guards entered behind them and sealed the door. All three looked around, studying their surroundings.

In front of them was a long, ornate dining table on a Persian rug. Above it hung a crystal chandelier, gently swaying at a forward angle. The whole room looked like someone's incongruous attempt to make an industrial room homey by filling it with items from an estate sale.

Captain Nikto walked to the far end of the table and turned. For the first time, they could see him. The man was in his late forties with prominent cheekbones, a neat beard, and silver at his temples. He wore black fatigues and a turtleneck, the same uniform as the guards. Though he was striking, he was pale as if he hadn't seen the sun in months.

"This is the wardroom." Nikto spoke with his Russian inflection, "The officers' mess hall."

Arrison noticed Nikto glancing up at a specific painting to his left. Above a fireplace mantle was the portrait of a beautiful Asian woman with a faint smile. The painting appeared contemporary, unlike the other antiques. She was curious about the connection.

Nikto shouted to the guards, "*Corta tus enlaces. Déjalos aquí.*"

The guards lifted blades from their sheaths. Arrison and Chandler tensed but realized the men had been ordered to cut their binds. With single swipes, they severed the cables behind each of their backs.

"I apologize for the binds." Nikto spoke with an aristocratic flair. "I must recall my terrestrial manners."

Nikto sat at the head of the table and narrowed his eyes at Landa. "It was an act of war because you attacked my vessel. Our receivers identified your missile locked on *me*." He raised his voice, "Your officers fired heavy weapons at *me*. Acts. Of. War." He spat the words and waved his hand, "Take a seat."

Arrison, Chandler, and Landa glanced at each other, hesitant. The guards stepped forward from the shadows, so the three promptly took seats at the table. Landa sat across from Nikto as if to stare him in the eye. Arrison and Chandler took seats on each side.

Nikto pulled a silver cigarette case from a pocket. He tapped out a cigarette and lit it. After a pensive inhale, he spoke. "The injured refugees were a truly regretful mistake. They were not supposed to be on board that vessel." With solemn eyes, he looked at Arrison, "Did any perish?"

"Yes," Landa shouted. "You murdered three innocent migrants." His voice was indignant. "One couple married sixty years and their granddaughter."

Silence. Nikto's face went blank. He glanced up at the swaying chandelier. "That will never happen again." His eyes became glassy with emotion. "Which is why you are here now, very much alive."

"Where are we?" Chandler asked with the purity of a child.

Nikto turned to him and smiled at his poise. "You are aboard my vessel, the *Naumtsev*—"

"A Soviet Akula-class submarine," Landa interrupted. "The quietest in the fleet." He crossed his immense arms. "So, Captain

Nikto, did the cartels abduct you? Or just old-fashioned greed to sell out your country?"

Nikto flashed a lethal smile. "Mr. Ned Landa," He peered into his eyes. "You are a former engineer-mechanic for the Marines. And now a self-proclaimed armaments expert."

"Once a Marine, always a Marine," Landa snapped.

Nikto frowned. "Not when you are dishonorably discharged for dereliction of duty." He continued without flinching. "You are divorced with two outstanding IRS liens. You are nothing more than a hired contractor, hustling to sell your opinions."

Landa fumed. His face turned red.

"Conversely, I am elated to have a marine biology professor aboard my vessel." Nikto smiled at Arrison. "Dr. Patrice Elaine Arrison. You are even more striking than your faculty portrait."

Her mouth fell open, lost for a response.

Nikto continued, "I am sickened to see your funding cut by your university due to dwindling respect for marine studies. My partner was also a scientist."

They watched him look again at the painting of the Asian woman.

"She modified this vessel for research," He gave an expressive pause, "After I brokered its sale to my previous employers."

"Cartels don't do research," Landa growled. "They were your previous employers. Did you steal this sub and now attack the hand that fed you? Committing international crimes—"

"I am free of any land-based society," Nikto's shout reverberated within the room. "I do not obey its rules, and I ask you never to invoke them in my presence again."

Chandler's gentle voice emerged from the clamor, "What about us?"

Nikto turned to him. His face softened at his innocence. "Mr. Chandler Arrison. A university senior and Student Chapter President of the High-Functioning Autism Society. You have done good things. You, sir, are a true leader."

Chandler blossomed at the unexpected compliment. Arrison also smiled.

Nikto nodded toward Dr. Arrison, "If you are anything like your mother here, I will show you things your eyes cannot imagine." He soaked the word with mystery.

Chandler smiled at his mother.

"Read between the lines, folks." Landa shattered their moment. "He's saying we're prisoners."

Confused, Chandler and Arrison turned to the captain.

Nikto gave an elegant shrug. "You have my word as a gentleman I will never harm you. I am in dire need of a mechanic, and I would truly relish having a marine expert onboard." His eyes hardened, "But I cannot have anyone betray my existence."

Before anyone could interject, Nikto leaned to Arrison with a hypnotic gaze, "What if I show you what lies six hundred meters beneath *Guanahacabibes*?" The strange word rolled fluently off his tongue.

Chandler's eyes widened. He turned to his mother.

She gasped for words. "Two thousand feet below…" Her eyes fluttered around the room. "The Guanahacabibes Peninsula? That's been shielded by Cuba for over sixty years…"

Nikto uncurled a roguish grin, "I assure you the *Naumtsev* is not limited by imaginary borders."

Chapter Eleven
Witness from the Clouds

Key West

"Officers Roberts and Newstreet were very dear friends." DEA Agent Kurtz tried not to crumble behind his lectern. "I can't believe they're gone," He paused to gather his emotions.

"Hell," he continued with glassy eyes. "Newstreet's boy Jackie feeds our cat when Lyle and I travel." He thumbed over his shoulder, "Roberts' wife Becca caters our holiday dinner-dance every year." He sniffled, "They will be sorely, sorely missed."

The room was hushed. There were more eyes on him than before in the JIATF conference room. His task force had expanded with additional officers from multiple agencies and local law enforcement.

Kurtz blotted his eyes with his thick forearm. "Unlike our deceased Guardsmen, we have not recovered the bodies of contractor Ned Landa, Professor Arrison, or her son Chandler." He shook his head and exhaled, "And he's just a kid."

&

Kurtz had been tirelessly working. Thirty minutes earlier, he'd had to provide a status to the press. Rather than a full-blown press conference, it was to a reporter he'd known for years from the island's only newspaper, the *Key West Citizen*.

"Immediately after we received the *Lincoln's* mayday, we appointed a mission coordinator to run search-rescue. Right now, we got an MH-60 Jayhawk and a forty-five-foot response boat searching." Kurtz had spoken to the reporter from the steps of the Truman Annex. "We're keeping tabs on the missing persons' odds of survival."

The Latina reporter frowned from her old-school notepad, "How are their odds calculated?"

"I'm not a techy, Tania, but its software called a survivability model. We plug in various factors such as water and air temp, the person's approximate height and weight, garments they wore, etcetera. The program tells us how long the person is likely to stay alive."

"They're still flying out there now?"

He nodded, "To maximize our probability of success, our choppers are flying V-shapes over a large circular area. A radius of 149 square miles so far."

Kurtz sighed and rubbed his weary eyes. "Sadly, it's the coordinator's job to decide when to give up. We give it an extra day before an official suspension, so we can do our best to notify next of kin." He shrugged, "We have no info on any other family members for the professor and her son."

⁂

In the annex conference room, extra chairs had been arranged to accommodate five additional people invited to the task force, including Navy, Border Patrol, and local sheriffs.

Seated in the front next to Agent Ruiz was a quiet Navy officer. She was mid-thirties and appeared pleasant but bookish, with short hair and thick glasses. She meekly raised a hand.

"Has the vessel been recovered yet?" the woman asked.

Kurtz shook his head. "It was 11,000 pounds of aluminum. Straight down. Too deep for any salvage hunts on my budget."

Agent Ruiz clicked a key on his laptop, "This is the *Lincoln's* last broadcast." The wall monitor displayed an audio waveform.

A garbled, panicked voice sounded, "*It's massive; it's no whale!*"

Ruiz played the recording twice. The roomful of officers gazed, wordless.

"I'd like you all to meet Officer Cynthia Engel." Kurtz motioned to the female Navy officer. "She's a Navy Intel Officer who's way smarter than me. We're lucky to pry her away from her desk in DC. Welcome Officer Engel."

"Thank you." She nodded to the men and women. Kurtz bestowed his podium to Engel, and Ruiz attached controls to her laptop.

Engel straightened her glasses. "As Agent Kurtz said, I'm a Navy Intelligence Officer, rated IS —Intelligence Specialist—and my job is to collect and interpret data." Her soft voice seemed unaccustomed to presenting to larger groups. "We analyze photographs, prepare charts and maps to help explain strategic situations." Her voice trailed as she shuffled her notes.

Engel looked up, realizing the room of eyes upon her. "I'm rarely invited to the field. This is a first for me. My husband and I were at Disney when I received your call, only a forty-five-minute flight. So, here I am." She rolled her shoulders.

The screen was filled with a file image of the *Abraham Lincoln*. "Regrettably, with the destruction of your Port Security Boat, all cameras were lost. Any video went down with the ship. The waterproof cases you recovered contained cameras that hadn't been used."

Ruiz and Kurtz pursed their lips at the luckless facts.

"But the young man, Chandler Arrison, had his cellphone," Engel continued.

"You recovered his phone?" Ruiz blurted, "How?"

"No." Engel paused at his outburst. "But he used it frequently on the boat." She cocked her head with drama. "It seems his phone automatically uploaded images to his cloud account before the accident."

"Photos might be in his account?" Ruiz blinked to process. "But we can't access them."

Engel lifted a finger to indicate she wasn't finished. "Our analysts in

DC have contacts with the Bureau who work closely with cell carriers. To get an order to access the images, we don't need a warrant if the data's 'relevant to an ongoing criminal investigation,'" Engel used air quotes. "I was able to demonstrate your attacked boats and deceased officers met the standard."

Her audience sat erect, instantly more engaged.

"My analysts were able to retrieve these photographs." The screen filled with images that appeared black and useless. Engel scrolled through them to enlarge a particular photo. Two tiny blurred white spots came into view.

"It appears to be an object in the foreground with a discernible wake." Engel brightened and highlighted the image. A stream of gray looked like foam from a triangular object. "Note the two spots that could be mistaken as eyes."

The officers squinted to see what she was referring to.

Engel superimposed a digital outline over the image. "We enhanced the exposure to reveal this." She pointed to the screen, "An approaching dark shape like a whale but much larger. If you notice in the foreground, it appears to have a sharp, bayonet-like nose."

Kurtz gasped, "Jesus Christ, it's a—"

"Narco-sub," Ruiz finished his sentence.

The room muttered with skepticism.

"That was my first guess." Engel typed and the screen filled with file images of narco-subs. "The only drug-related submersibles seized to date have been home-grown. Built by inexperienced craftsmen hired by the cartels."

One image showed a small submarine in a murky river that looked like it'd been spray-painted camouflage. "These were seized off the coast of Colombia." Engel showed another slide of Colombian police opening a hatch on the deck of a vessel smaller than a school bus. "They're typically fiberglass, barely seaworthy, under forty feet in length."

Engel projected highlighted dots on the recovered image: three points in the foreground and two on the horizon. She turned to her rapt audience. "Based on the field of view and reference points, our analysts calculate this object's length at over 350 feet."

Kurtz and Ruiz winced as if she'd misspoken.

"The largest whales are a hundred feet, and the US doesn't have any missing submarines." Her voice became somber, "But a Soviet Akula-class sub is 375 feet long, with stealth equal to ours."

"Are you serious?" a female deputy laughed.

"It's possible," another officer scowled at her. "A Russian sub was sited off Virginia in 2018."

"A Yasen-class Russian sub was tracked off the east coast in 2020," a DEA agent added.

As the room debated, Kurtz's voice resounded, "Commies aren't attacking us, folks." He stood to reclaim the room. "This thing targeted five drug traffickers. This is a turf war in our backyard."

"This is a national security matter," the ICE officer snapped.

"It's DEA if it's from Colombia," Kurtz sharpened his eyes. "Especially if we're speculating a cartel acquired a real sub. Cartels do only one thing: traffic narcotics." He looked at the quiet Engel, "I'm guessing there are very few ports to hide one of these things."

"Yes, correct," Engel stammered. "Only certain seaports would be deep enough to accommodate an Akula-class."

"Ernesto," Kurtz turned to Ruiz, on a roll. "Is Raul still taking your calls at the embassy in Bogotá?"

"So far." Ruiz bobbed his head.

Kurtz looked at his audience, "How could someone buy and hide a 375-foot steel monster?" He thumbed to his junior partner. "Agent Ruiz has contacts with the Colombian National Police. If a cartel achieved the improbable, there will be a shitload of witnesses."

As the room paused to grasp their proposition, Kurtz added, "I can't keep this from the press too long; a school will be looking for their professor."

Chapter Twelve
Glaza Na Mir

The Caribbean Sea

Professor Arrison opened the steel door. She looked like a new person, rested, and refreshed. Her green eyes were clear, and her long blonde hair was still damp from a shower.

"I trust your quarters are suitable?" Captain Nikto asked from the threshold with hands behind his back. Despite her tall, svelte form, he was respectful, keeping his eyes locked on hers.

She gave a guarded smile, "I don't feel like I'm on a submarine."

"That is my goal," Nikto replied. "This is my home."

ↄ

When a crewman had been ordered to take Arrison and Chandler to their quarters, she presumed it'd be another cell. To her surprise, her cabin was over ten by ten feet with a plush single bed. She guessed it was originally designed as an officer's quarters. The floor was covered with faux wood planking and an Oriental rug. The walls were burgundy, with framed art and shelves adorned with nautical trinkets such as a compass and antique books. Installed in the corner was an acrylic mini-shower, reminiscent of those found in cruise ship cabins.

And the water was magnificently scalding. She washed away untold hours—or days—of grime, salt, and stress. Laid out on her bed was fresh clothing: black slacks and a turtleneck, the evident uniform of the crew. Not her first choice of style, but Arrison was in no position to complain.

She was further comforted knowing Chandler had been given a cabin next to hers that was similarly appointed. She didn't know or care where Landa had been taken.

As the hot water ran over her scalp, Arrison finally had the peace to close her eyes and reflect. There was a looming distress that hadn't been clarified: "what" exactly was Nikto going to do with them? Was Ned Landa correct, they were essentially prisoners? As the cliché goes, if Nikto wanted them dead, he could've done so. But he had literarily saved them from the sea.

Arrison wondered if there was some maritime law that would require Nikto to release them at the next port. Or were they hostages to leverage something out of the US government?

Or —Arrison opened her eyes— what if Nikto really could show her undersea discoveries like Guanahacabibes like he had promised?

She tried to envision the possibility. *That could change everything,* she imagined. The impact alone on her profession; it would save her career and resolve thousands of years of conjecture.

Her shower and pipe dreams were cut short by Nikto's knock on her cabin door.

Arrison felt uneasy standing alone with the captain. The officers' quarters were on the second deck, near the center of the vessel, according to Nikto. He explained halls on a submarine were called passageways. In the housing area, they appeared less mechanical than in other areas. The passageway that connected their quarters was decorated to appear more elegant, painted bronze with stainless fixtures and handrails.

Arrison crossed her arms, slightly chilled. "Where's Chandler and Landa?"

Nikto smiled, "Your son wished to see our control room. That is where we pilot the *Naumtsev*." He pointed to the ceiling. "It is directly above us near the heart of the vessel."

Arrison looked up, hesitant. "I don't want him in anyone's way." She didn't like the idea of Chandler away from her side, especially within the mazelike bowels of a potentially hostile vessel.

"Not at all." Nikto paused with pensive eyes. "Your son is naturally curious. He is gifted. You should be proud."

Arrison's posture softened. She wasn't accustomed to hearing praises from strangers. "And where's Ned Landa?"

Nikto gave a tight smile. "Mr. Landa is resting in his quarters."

ↄ৲ↄ

Ned Landa beat on his cell door with both fists.

"Let me the hell outta here!" His shouts echoed within the small chamber. He'd been returned to his original holding cell, with the same single vent for light and a small bench. He decided to sit in the center of the room, close his eyes and practice deep breathing.

At the very least, he'd been allowed a three-minute shower in the crew berthing area on the third deck. He'd take any triumph he could get from these criminals.

An hour earlier, a guard had directed Landa along a humid passageway filled with pipes and ducts. They reached a companionway with steps leading down to the next level.

How many decks, passageways and steps does this thing have? Landa mused. It was futile trying to memorize his way around. He was told the crew berthing area was below the wardroom, undoubtedly smaller and more confining.

The crew berthing was congested with rows of stacked bunks. The area smelled like sweat, and the lights were dim as if to mimic night. Landa heard men snoring, and he received confused glares from men lying in their bunks or playing cards. The men appeared either curious or annoyed that a stranger was in their space.

Next to a metal commode was the shower. It was a stainless-steel casket that looked like an old-school phone booth. In a thick accent, the guard told him he had one minute of water; he could then lather for a minute; and then one minute to rinse. "Three minutes! *No mas!*"

Landa was concerned about the claustrophobic stall, but he closed his eyes and inhaled. *Only three minutes.* He silently counted down to help pass the time. The water was icy, but the wash was invigorating over his shaven scalp.

Crewmen loomed outside the shower, muttering derisive comments in Spanish and Russian. The guard tossed Landa a small towel that felt like burlap and he was given a black uniform. Landa guessed from the men's faces they were upset how an American outsider was stealing their precious bath time.

Since he was now outfitted like the crew, Landa presumed he'd be forced to do some hard labor to prove his worth. Instead, the guard led him straight back to the holding chamber.

Landa groaned in the gloom of his cell. He didn't know if it was night or day. At least he was alive, and this Nikto had no interest in torture or physical threats, yet.

He tried to analyze their predicament with logic. A drug cartel had somehow obtained a Russian submarine. While they were carrying out their nefarious plans, they'd stumbled across three outsiders and chose to bring them onboard. From a tactical standpoint, Landa understood why Nikto said he couldn't release them back into the world. It would give away his presence. No criminal would do that.

Logical or not, this didn't help his dilemma. He huffed, *we're stuck forever on an enemy nuclear—*" His chest tightened at the sudden realization: if this was an Akula, it was a nuclear submarine with nuclear weapons.

He stood upright, eyes flickering to recall his warfare training. *The Akula would have at least eight torpedo tubes to handle RPK-2 nuclear-armed missiles.* His breathing hastened. *Weapons could include twenty ballistic missiles armed with nuclear warheads.*

Ned Landa was trained to never display anxiety or fear in front of others, but he could alone in a dark cell. *We're trapped in a steel nuclear coffin that could annihilate half the planet.*

The fear of drug dealers suddenly seemed insignificant. And what were these narco-terrorists now doing to the kid and Professor Arrison, the only female onboard?

❧

Dr. Arrison's jaw dropped as they entered the cavernous room.

"This is my grand parlor," Captain Nikto waved his hand theatrically across the room. He seemed strong and graceful as he pointed.

Arrison looked to her right. The room was at least forty feet long and thirty feet wide, tapered to span the base of the forward hull. It looked like a larger version of the extravagant wardroom. She looked up; the ceiling's painted pipes looked like brass steampunk.

"These furnishings have been in my family for five generations," Nikto smiled.

Arrison observed neoclassical furniture, velvet couches, with Victorian armchairs in the corners. The floor was covered with red Persian rugs. She inhaled to smell a faint aroma of smoldering incense.

Nikto looked up at wood paneling and crown moldings. "Colombian craftsmen required six months to outfit this room." He illustrated with his hands, "They had to disassemble the fixtures, bring them on board one item at a time, then reassemble them here."

Arrison had never been lost for words, but the room appeared entirely inconsistent with what she'd envisioned for a cold war military vessel. The walls had a slight creak as if the paneling had been attached to uneven bulkheads. It sounded like she was on a wooden schooner.

"This is where I come to meditate, study my journals," Nikto paced the length of the room, "And play my Steinway. The crew enjoys it over the speakers."

To her left, she tapped an ivory key on a grand piano that appeared priceless. Along a draped wall, she was drawn to an oil painting. In earth tones, it depicted a beach with rough waves and a sailboat.

"You have a good eye." Nikto approached with a humble grin. "Yes, that is a Van Gogh. *View of the Sea at Scheveningen*. Stolen in 2002 by my previous employer." He nodded over her shoulder. "There is a Monet over there."

"Stolen by a previous employer?" Arrison asked, dubious.

He shrugged, "A man who believed he could have everything he

59

desired. He was wrong."

Arrison realized the glint in his eye came from light at the far end of the parlor. She moved to her right to see the source of the pulsating aqua light.

"My god…" she exhaled to behold eight-foot circular windows, one on each side of the parlor. She dashed towards the glass, eager to experience the view. Her face glowed from the undulating radiance.

In the crystal-clear water, she saw a sprawling reef pass thirty feet below. She looked up with a wide smile to see sunlight from the distant surface. A school of yellowtails swirled by with light glistening off their scales.

"These are my Iris windows. Named after my mother." Nikto approached over her shoulder. "My, *glaza na mir,*" he elegantly pronounced in Russian. "My eyes onto the world."

Arrison had her nose to the glass like a wide-eyed child at an aquarium. "I didn't think submarines had windows this large."

"My Irises are one of a kind. Developed by my former partner." Nikto knocked on the curved glass. "The sphere is the strongest shape to endure extreme pressures. Eighteen centimeters thick of polymethyl methacrylate. Its strength-to-weight ratio is equivalent to carbon steel."

Arrison flinched as a large stingray skimmed the window with its gray wings and white belly.

Nikto added casually, "The Irises can close for combat."

Arrison instantly wilted. *For combat?* An abrupt reminder of their predicament. She turned to face him with any pleasure drained from her face.

"What are your intentions with us?"

Nikto shifted his jaw to consider a reply, but they were interrupted by a female voice.

"How many of them are dining? Two or three?" a girl asked with a Spanish accent.

Arrison turned to see a stunning Latina with long black hair. She appeared about twenty years old with large brown eyes. Though she wore a turtleneck and slacks on her slim form, she didn't seem like one of the crew.

Nikto locked as if her intrusion hadn't been anticipated. "Dr. Arrison, this is my ward, Pilar."

The young lady gave a faint smile. With a glance, she scanned Arrison as though she hadn't seen another female—or visitor—in some time.

He replied to Pilar in abrupt Spanish. Arrison tried to understand the words.

Pilar gave a nod and exited.

Arrison asked, "What'd you tell her?"

"I said, 'two for dinner. Dr. Arrison and her son. I am not certain of the third.'"

Arrison paused with a nod. "She's beautiful. Is she related?"

"No." With a side glance, he selected his words, "She is the daughter of my prior employer in Bogotá." He looked at her, "He understood she is in a safer world here."

Arrison frowned at the bizarre response. *A safer world than what?*

Chapter Thirteen
The Chamber of Babel

A tall, gangly officer had been dispatched to escort Chandler to the *Naumtsev's* control room.

"You call me Pavlo," the man offered in a thick Russian accent.

Chandler just nodded, bashful. Interaction with strangers was not his forte. The pale man had a wispy attempt at a goatee and seemed pleasant.

"Follow me." Pavlo led Chandler along a passage. The man had to hunch to step through entryways.

Chandler guessed he and Pavlo were about the same age. He tried to envision the different world and upbringing the man must've experienced. Chandler realized his studies had never included that part of the world or anything political. This made him more curious.

"Where are you from?" Chandler asked in a monotone.

"Vladivostok," Pavlo uttered.

Chandler didn't understand the word. So, he tried, "What's your job here?"

"Sometimes navigation. Sometimes helmsman or copilot." Pavlo warmed slightly, "We are not many, so must do many jobs."

They approached a companionway and Pavlo led him up a stairway to the first level.

"This is the Operations Compartment," Pavlo muttered, helping Chandler up. "Here in the control room is where we operate the *Naumtsev*."

Chandler scanned the room, disenchanted. It was nothing like his cabin or the wardroom. The walls were steel panels that were either beige or mint green. The fifteen-by-ten-foot area was cluttered with controls, some on the ceiling. The walls were filled with innumerable dials, knobs, and switches. Though the room was dim, Chandler had to squint from the fluorescent light revealing a haze of cigarette smoke.

He had never seen a place that still allowed smoking. Seven crewmen chattered with a dissonance of Spanish and Russian voices. They sat behind laptops and monitors that appeared a decade old. The men were either pale or olive, making it easy to determine who was speaking which language. They glanced at Chandler, but kept busy with their tasks, garishly blowing smoke towards the ceiling.

With a thick accent, Pavlo described the room. The bulkhead to their right was for navigational equipment and GPS receivers. On the forward portside corner, there were chairs for the ship's control station. The seats were for a helmsman and planesman, who used steering wheel-type controls to adjust the rudder and diving planes.

"That is the EOT," Pavlo pointed to a round dial at the helm. "On US ships it stands for," he squinted to recall the term, "Engine Order Telegraph. If the captain orders the helm to accelerate, the EOT is a direct throttle for turbines." He pointed up, "Sometimes you hear alarm bells."

Pavlo described the opposite wall as the weapons control. Chandler hesitated at the sobering reality the vessel was armed. He saw a large red switch and he wondered if the "fire" control was big and red like in the movies.

In the center of the room were two periscopes that pulled down from the ceiling. Chandler looked up, trying to imagine their current view. Hundreds of miles at sea? Or near a coast, if so, friend or enemy?

His eyes were drawn to a panel filled with red and green lights like a Christmas tree.

"Hull Opening Indicator Panel." Pavlo pointed to the lights, "Every hatch, vent, or exhaust has a red light if open. We are not safe to dive until all lights are green."

A little man with round glasses approached fast. "Greetings," he smiled with crooked teeth. He was bald and his glasses made him appear goggle-eyed.

Pavlo introduced the man, "This is Dmitri."

Before Chandler could react, Pavlo switched to rapid Russian to speak to the man. Chandler felt excluded, so he just nodded his head.

To appear harmless to the American boy, Dmitri smiled as Pavlo spoke to him.

"Captain Nikto said to show this boy around," Pavlo said in Russian. "But he asks many questions."

Dmitri chuckled. "Nikto said we can answer all their questions because they are never leaving!"

Chandler looked back and forth between the men, puzzled at their exchange.

After Pavlo turned to exit, Dmitri smiled at Chandler. "Welcome to the *Naumtsev*," he spoke with decent English. "You call me Dmitri. I came with Nikto from Severodvinsk." He motioned for Chandler to follow him to seats behind a communication station.

"Do you guys only speak Russian?" Chandler asked.

"Half the crew speaks Spanish. Men who came from Colombia," Dmitri pointed to a clique of men. "The rest Russia or Ukraine. To avoid confusion, we try to use English for navigation, like pilots and air controllers. We might reply aye to the captain instead of *da* or *si*."

Chandler skimmed the overwhelming controls, "What's your job?"

Dmitri bobbed his head to consider an accurate answer. "Sonar and I am the data communication specialist."

"Are you a hacker?" Chandler blurted, shameless.

Rather than being offended by some crude stereotype, Dmitri smirked. "I am the best." He checked over his shoulder, "You recall the two American elections?" He winked.

Chandler expelled a sharp laugh then stopped, unsure if he was joking.

℅

Ned Landa's solitary confinement was disrupted by the squeal of his cell door. He opened his eyes to see the figure of Captain Nikto, alone with no guards.

"Greetings Mr. Landa," Nikto gave a scant smile. "Would you care for improved accommodations?"

Landa stood with tight fists. "I want off this coffin before someone's navy —or cartel— sinks it."

"Fair enough," Nikto remained serene. "If you are indeed a mechanical expert, I need your assistance. If you succeed, you may disembark at the next port."

Landa was thrown by the offer. He squinted, "What do you need?"

℅

Chandler became much more comfortable in the control room. Since he didn't smoke, Dmitri offered him fruity Colombian bubble gum called Bon Bon Bum. He was seated with a set of headphones around his neck at an array of monitors next to Dmitri.

"If there's no Wi-Fi, how do you communicate?" Chandler fidgeted with the headphones.

"On land, Wi-Fi is transmitted using radio waves." Dmitri spoke with a cigarette dangling, "But it does not work through salt water."

Chandler frowned, "Submarines are cut off from communication using ordinary radio frequencies."

"*Da.*" Dmitri raised a brow, impressed. "We can surface and raise an antenna above sea level, but that would disclose our location." He tapped a monitor. "So I use communication buoys I call C-Buoys."

Chandler's eyes flickered, "How's that work?"

"Okay," Dmitri spread his hands to illustrate. "If Captain Nikto asks me to search for any reports of our vessel, I launch a C-Buoy. They are round, the size of your American basketball." He reached for a switch. "With this control, I launch the C-Buoy from the forward hull. It ascends, tethered to the ship with a thin fiber optic cable."

With a mind that functioned visually, Chandler would imagine things as if they were occurring before his eyes. He could see a small orb ejected from the *Naumtsev's* hull like a cannonball. It would swiftly rise, trailing a long string like a child's balloon. It'd finally breach the surface to bob along the whitecaps.

"It has a small antenna," Dimitri pantomimed with his little finger. "I can create a secure link with the iridium satellite constellation," he struggled with the pronunciation. "That is a series of satellites used for data coverage, cellphones and so on." He looked at Chandler. "After a data dump of information to the ship, the buoy is scuttled."

"Scuttled?" Chandler shrugged.

"The buoy self-destructs. From the base, barbs spring up like a scorpion tail." Dmitri snapped his hands shut like a Venus flytrap. "The ball breaks and the C-Buoy sinks." He swiped his hands together, "No evidence."

Chandler blinked at the vision.

Something caught Dmitri's eye. He focused on his monitor as the screen filled with unintelligible Russian code.

"What is that?" Chandler squinted. "Data from above."

"*Zatknis!*" Dmitri exclaimed. He lifted a finger to shush him.

Chandler watched the strange code roll across Dmitri's screen, reflecting in the man's glasses. The man's eyes twitched as he read.

Dmitri tapped his earpiece and uttered, *"Kapitan, u menya yest byulleten."*

With no knowledge of Russian, Chandler's mind raced through a spectrum of possibilities based on Dmitri's tone and posture. None of which were positive.

Chapter Fourteen
Enter the *Cyclops*

Dmitri's words blared over the grand parlor's speakers in Russian, "Captain, I have a bulletin."

Having just arrived from Landa's cell, Nikto stood beside the man at a large Iris window.

He replied in Russian, "This is Nikto, what is it?"

Oblivious to the foreign words, Landa remained engrossed by his spectacular view of a passing reef.

Dmitri spoke fast, "I tested a vulnerability in the DEA's VPN server—"

"Just tell me the message," Nikto interrupted, stepping away from Landa.

"The US claims it was a capital offense to kill servicemen."

Nikto tensed his brows to understand the context.

"The Coast Guard vessel. Their two officers are dead." Dmitri continued in Russian, "Our three guests are also presumed dead."

Nikto squeezed his eyes closed. With Landa occupied at the window, Nikto struggled to conceal a wave of emotion. He ran his fingers over his beard.

"A capital offense means punishment by death," Dmitri added, solemn.

Nikto smoothed his sweater and took a breath. "It is of no consequence. We will not be returning to the United States anytime soon."

"What the hell's going on?" Landa's voice boomed. Though he was irritated with the captain's ongoing discussion in Russian, he was referring to something outside.

Nikto realized he was pointing out the window. He returned to Landa's side to look out.

In their translucent view, the vessel was stationary above a reef thirty feet below. Landa pointed to the remains of a demolished boat resting on the seafloor between two coral beds.

"We are temporarily anchored," Nikto stated with a shrug.

Landa huffed, "I'm talking about that boat; what's going on out there?" The sunken vessel appeared to be a thirty-foot Avanti power boat that had been shattered in two. It looked like a recent incident based on the clean condition of the boat.

"We will check the vessel for anything worthwhile," Nikto dismissed with his hands.

Before Landa could respond, he froze at what he saw. Coming into view was a black minisub, slowly maneuvering from under the *Naumtsev*. It was tubular, approximately fifteen feet long. On its front was a large, single dome window.

"That is the *Cyclops*," Nikto stated. "A prototype mini-submersible."

Astonished, Landa watched the small sub progress towards a gaping hole in the sunken boat's hull.

"It was designed using the same schematics as the sub that explored the Titanic," Nikto smiled with pride. "It can accommodate four men and dive 3,000 meters with a 1,000-kilo payload. Its observation dome is made of borosilicate glass."

To Landa, it looked like a high-tech version of minisubs he'd seen in deep-sea exploration journals. "Whose boat was that?"

"It was an enemy vessel," Nikto replied with no explanation. "As you can see, one arm is in need of repair."

Landa looked out to see the *Cyclops* had two robotic arms under its observation dome. But only one folded out, as the other arm hung limp.

"It's left grappling arm is inoperative," Nikto shrugged. "Entirely useless."

Landa pressed his face to the glass, attempting to focus. His view of the boat's hull was obscured by swaying ribbons of seaweed. As the *Cyclops* hovered closer to the boat, it forced the seaweed aside.

He gasped at what he saw: countless small white bricks spilling from the boat's hull. The *Cyclops* extended its right arm and the claw began to collect the bricks, dropping them into a net under its dome. The sub looked like a giant crustacean feeding from the seafloor.

Landa felt a shiver at the base of his skull realizing what he was witnessing.

"My crew is small, less than fifty men with limited disciplines," Nikto said. "No one trained in robotic or hydraulic repairs." Nikto looked at Landa, "Can you repair the arm?"

Landa turned with a vacant expression. He mumbled, "I've repaired pneumatic cylinders. That seems similar."

Nikto stood erect. "If you repair the *Cyclops'* arm, you may depart the next time we surface."

Landa took a last glance at the minisub collecting the white bricks. "I'll do it." He turned back to Nikto, "I want out of here. The sooner the better."

℗

Dmitri wiped his brow, exasperated by Chandler's endless questions.

"How far can the *Naumtsev's* fuel last?" Chandler asked.

Dmitri took off his glasses and huffed. "With enriched uranium, we can circumnavigate the globe many times without refueling."

"How?" Chandler challenged.

Dmitri responded with lively hands. "Fission in a reactor generates heat. That produces steam. That turns a turbine for electricity." He took a breath, "The *Naumtsev* is self-sufficient up to thirty years."

Chandler paused to process. "What about oxygen and water?"

Dmitri lit a new cigarette. "We do not come up for air unless venting for emergency. Machines called scrubbers remove carbon dioxide from the air. Oxygen generators extract oxygen from seawater and distillation makes clean water from seawater." He blew smoke at the ceiling, "Air is always breathable, and clean water forever—"

Dmitri was mercifully interrupted by whispers from the crew. They looked over to see the men murmur in Spanish that someone was entering the room. "*Tranquilo. Ella está entrando!*"

Puzzled, Chandler turned. He gawked at the unexpected vision of a young female. As if his senses had abruptly slowed, he saw dark hair floating around an angelic face. Though petite in her uniform, she had curves that entirely conflicted with the unsightly male crew.

"She is Pilar," Dmitri uttered under his breath.

She walked straight to Dmitri and spoke English with a Spanish accent, "Nikto says the guests should rest in the parlor before dinner." She gave an obvious glance towards Chandler.

He locked onto her large mocha eyes. He felt a surge down his spine like a static shock.

Pilar also paused, but with furled brows at the ogling stranger.

A few crewmen began whistling, with lewd catcalls in Spanish.

Pilar glared at them and scolded in rapid Spanish, "*Haz tu trabajo o le diré a Nikto que te corte en cebo de tiburón!*"

The men instantly turned back to their systems, silenced.

Chandler was captivated by this spirited lady. He whispered to Dmitri, "What'd she just say to them?"

Standing three feet away, Pilar replied, "I told them to do their jobs or I'll have Nikto cut them into bait for the sharks."

Chandler's face beamed. He'd never been mesmerized before.

Pilar flashed a coy smirk in Chandler's general direction and exited the room.

Chapter Fifteen
The Dinner Bell Chimes

Professor Arrison and Chandler stood alone in the grand parlor. Gazing out an Iris window, they shared a rare moment of silence, from either the hypnotic shimmer of the water, or contemplating the day's events.

Earlier, they'd been told they should "retire" to their quarters to "refresh" for dinner. Such a formal request seemed odd from a group of supposed narcotic smugglers.

Arrison had climbed up—and Chandler climbed down—companionways to meet in the middle on the second deck.

Chandler had relayed everything he'd learned in the control room. His mother had absorbed every word, finding it truly fascinating.

"Oxygen and water forever?" she'd marveled. "Fuel that can travel the globe?"

Arrison had told him about the astounding views from the eight-foot windows in the parlor.

Each of them had returned to their quarters to prepare for dinner. They were told they could enjoy the parlor in the interim.

After they'd changed into fresh clothes—more of the same uniforms—they'd met outside her cabin. Arrison had memorized the path to the parlor: one flight of steps down, then forward toward the bow.

Chandler's reaction to the parlor had been equal to hers. With an awestruck grin, he'd observed every fixture. He especially liked an antique chess set and a large globe—until he saw the Iris windows.

He sprinted to a window, but rather than enjoying the view, he studied the brass molding around the glass. He recited under his breath, "Spheres are able to withstand the highest external pressure."

Side by side they gazed into the world of her cherished profession. After following spiraling schools of fish, it was time to deliberate.

Arrison glanced over her shoulder, then asked in a low voice, "If Nikto's telling the truth about Guanahacabibes, do you realize what that implies?"

Chandler bobbed his head, "I've read the myths." He looked at her, "But there's been no corroborating evidence."

"Because no one has ever had access," she countered. "They're not myths; they're actual theories." She looked out into the sea, conflicted. "What if this is our only chance to see it?"

"Do you trust him?" Chandler frowned. "Mr. Landa says Nikto's a thug and we're prisoners. But the captain seems—"

They paused to see Ned Landa enter the room. He shouted, "A room this size in the forward bow? They had to gut crew berthing. Nice priorities."

Arrison knew Landa was arrogant, but he seemed larger than in her memories from the night before. He was cleaned-up and wearing a uniform, but with short sleeves that were snug on his biceps.

She pointed outside and spoke to Chandler as if they'd been studying the view. "See that bright green flower design? That's ridged cactus coral."

"That means we're still in the Caribbean," Chandler nodded.

Landa approached their window. He looked down to see a reef forty feet below.

"Look at that goliath grouper," Chandler inhaled. "It's the size of Volkswagen!" The enormous, serene fish had a thick girth with brown and tan patterns.

Landa stepped between them to interject. "I know about fish." He pointed out, mocking, "That grouper, I'd cut into chunks and fry it up, served with malt vinegar." He pointed to the right, "See that school of yellow tail? It'd make enough sushi for an entire—"

"Cute, Mr. Landa," Arrison cut him off. "But the captain actually respects our studies."

Any humor in Landa's face vanished. "Nikto is no scientific benefactor. I saw firsthand what they're *really* doing."

Chandler paused at his tone. "What'd you see?"

"They got a minisub." He pointed out the window as if he could still see it. "They call it the *Cyclops*. It was launched from the lower hull."

Arrison's eyes flickered at the prospect, "A research sub?"

"Hardly," Landa chuckled. "They sent it down to a smashed boat, sunken on the seafloor. When the sub maneuvered closer, I saw the boat was filled with narcotics, white bricks of it, pouring out the hull." He spread his hands with drama. "He sinks the competition to steal their loads."

Arrison and Chandler tilted their heads at the notion.

Landa flashed an ironic smile. "He's just a drug dealer. Nothing more." He paused, "With a ship that could start World War III."

They flinched at a voice behind them. They turned to see Captain Nikto as if he'd been standing there all along.

"We have pulled anchor." Nikto gave a thin smile and turned. "Follow me."

∾

No one spoke as they hiked single file along the narrow passageway. They only had to climb one flight of steps to the wardroom on the second deck.

When Nikto opened the door, Arrison was hit with the aroma of cooking. A faint scent of garlic, wine and perhaps seafood, a smell she'd nearly forgotten from the mainland.

The captain took his seat at the head of the table. Landa sat across from him, with Arrison and Chandler on both sides. There was an extra chair beside the captain.

Nikto looked to his right and a smile filled his face. Pilar entered from a side door. Her appearance was even more striking as she wore a bright floral dress that contrasted with everyone's dark attire. She returned a faint smile to Nikto.

The captain gave her a once over. "Interesting, you are so dressed up."

Pilar shrugged, "So?" Her tone seemed insolent as she took a seat between Nikto and Chandler.

The captain turned to the three, "You must understand we have not had guests," He paused to recount, "Ever."

Pilar pursed her lips, indifferent. Chandler glanced at her and then back to his place setting. There were no sounds other than the tinkling of the swaying chandelier.

"Pilar is too modest to say, but she is quite a chef," Nikto tried again to draw her into a conversation. "She is a graduate of Moreno Escuala De Gastronomia, a culinary institute in Bogotá. She manages a team in our galley."

Pilar shrunk with discomfort. She raised her brows waiting for the topic to pass.

Nikto blinked, intolerant of her silence. "Why don't you tell our guests the *carte du jour* this evening?"

Pilar manufactured a smile, "We are starting with a wakame seaweed salad. Then Gulf oysters broiled with blue crabmeat; and sautéed Scallops in a chardonnay sauce."

Ned Landa gave a lopsided smile to Arrison, impressed.

They turned at the clang of a crewman rolling a serving cart. Plates of food were protected in silver cloche covers. A magnificent aroma wafted in from the galley.

"That'd be like thirty bucks in a fancy restaurant," Chandler grinned.

Pilar stifled a chuckle at his comment.

"As your American cliché goes," Nikto smiled, "the *Naumtsev's* food supply is very sustainable, considering we have 139 million square miles of ocean on our planet."

Pilar looked at Chandler. "Seafood tastes the same after a while."

She smirked, "I'd kill for a grilled *churrasco*. Rare."

Chandler beamed at her recognition of his existence. The best response he could assemble was, "I like steak too."

Nikto frowned like an exasperated parent. "Adolescents are the same around the globe, no?" He looked at Arrison, "I am just thankful she is not attached to any mobile phone, electronics or the Wi-Fi."

The conversation paused as the server presented plates of food before each guest. Everyone's eyes widened, with smiles to the server.

Arrison used the moment to absorb the subtleties. There was some tension between Nikto and Pilar. Perhaps comparable to any relationship between an adolescent and a parent figure, combined with different cultures and being sealed in an illicit submarine.

The girl seemed formally educated, graceful yet assertive, and clearly beautiful. Arrison couldn't imagine being the only female among an all-male crew of fugitives. But from observing Pilar's confidence, it appeared she could hold her own.

Arrison looked at her food as the steam reached her nose. Her mouth watered to behold large oysters on the half-shell, swimming in butter and lemon, with broiled lump crabmeat on top, and a drizzle of hollandaise on each. On a separate plate, sea scallops were the size of large marshmallows. They'd been seared with olive oil, wine, garlic, and cherry tomatoes.

She lifted a fork, eager. Such a meal would've been a luxury, even back home. Studying her plate, she realized Nikto's lofty speech about eating only from the sea couldn't be entirely true. The presence of tomatoes, lemons, butter, garlic, and wine meant the *Naumtsev* had to get provisions from somewhere. *But where and how often?*

Nikto raised a glass of Fangoria Cru Lermont, a Russian chardonnay. He waited for everyone to raise their glasses before toasting in Russian, "*Dlya nashego zdorov'ya i svobody i vechnosti, chtoby naslazhdat'sya imi oboimi.*" He smiled to interpret, "To health, freedom and an eternity to enjoy them both."

Arrison's eyes shot to Landa. *An eternity?*

Everyone began to eat. To Arrison, it was better than she had imagined. The seafood was fresher than any she'd tasted on land and she lived in Florida. Chandler seemed hesitant of his wakame salad, a bowl of neon-green seaweed with vinegar and sesame seeds. A silence fell over the room with just the sound of silverware and crystal glasses being refilled.

Landa gulped his third glass of wine in one draw. He wiped his mouth with a forearm, "I have to admit everything seems so perfect." He paused until he had everyone's attention, "On the surface." He cut his eyes to Nikto. "Do you mind if I ask a blunt question?"

Arrison and Chandler lowered their forks, anticipating what was coming.

"I expect nothing less." Nikto dabbed the corner of his mouth with a linen. "I am as transparent as Abaco waters."

Landa leaned forward, elbows on the table. "I'm not the PhD in the room, so maybe you can help me understand." He lifted a finger, "First, you're a traitor to your own country by somehow stealing an entire submarine." He raised a second finger, "Then you steal it again from your new business partners—who happen to be drug lords—to then rip them off."

All heads turned to Nikto. He leered with a venomous smile.

Landa plowed ahead, "But in reality, you've stolen at least twenty ballistic missiles with nuclear warheads, and a dozen cruise missiles with a range of 3,000 kilometers." He paused for gravity, "Some might define that as a terrorist."

Arrison and Chandler froze in their seats.

"You dare use the word terrorist?" Nikto's voice grew and his eyes blazed. "With Pilar as my witness," he pointed at her face, "I jettisoned every torpedo, missile, and warhead. Gone!"

His words echoed within the small room. He'd reacted as if 'terrorist' was the most profane word in any language.

Chandler's voice broke the silence, "Where'd they all go?"

Nikto turned to the boy. "The Pacific. The Mariana Trench, the deepest in the world. Seven miles, 11,000 meters. Unreachable from terrorists as well as your nations."

Pilar gave a solemn nod.

Nikto continued with flailing hands, "I stole this vessel—as you so simplify—for a very precise reason; they took something from me!"

Arrison saw him look up again at the oil painting of the stunning Asian woman.

"My partner Kana. She was the scientist." Nikto looked back at the three. "The cartel had partners in China for their precious opioids," he uttered with sarcasm. "And their disgraceful fentanyl labs."

Arrison and Chandler reacted to the abrupt shift in subject.

"I met Kana. She was chosen like an asset, to retrofit the Akula," Nikto continued with disdain. "The cartel sourced their technology, to improve its smuggling, its speed," His voice softened. "Kana's intellect was more attracted to exploration than drug trafficking. I shared her vision. We fell in love."

Silence. The guests studied the portrait of Kana, painted with an ill-fated smile. Nikto paused and smoothed his beard. Arrison knew she was seeing a different side to the man.

His eyes reignited. "The cartel believed she was modifying the *Naumtsev* for exploration rather than smuggling. Her design of the Iris windows, the *Cyclops*," He looked directly at Arrison. "So, they took her to ensure I fulfilled my duties."

Arrison's mouth opened, unsure how to respond.

"So, I seized something just as precious from them." Nikto turned to Pilar.

Pilar said nothing. Her lip quivered, with large glistening eyes.

Chandler gazed at her with confused empathy, then to his mother.

After an uneasy five seconds, Landa spoke, "With all due respect, Skipper, I want no part of your cartel feud. But I will repair your *Cyclops*." He pointed a finger at Nikto. "But then I get to I walk at the next port. As you promised."

Pilar scowled with confusion. She turned to Nikto and uttered furious Spanish, "*Les mentiste? No hay otro puerto. Nuestro combustible dura treinta años!*"

"I speak Spanish you idiots." Landa's lips drew into a snarl, "My mom's Cuban!"

Chandler darted his head between them, "What did she say?"

"I called Nikto a liar!" Pilar crossed her arms, "There is no next port. Our fuel can last thirty years." She cut her eyes to the captain with contempt.

Before anyone could react, all five jumped at a deafening alarm. Yellow lights flashed above the doors. Nikto dashed to the door to shout into a speaker, "What is the crisis?"

"*Kapitan*," Pavlo's voice responded in frantic English. "There is a coolant leak in the reactor compartment! Men are trapped!"

Nikto spun to his guests, "Stay here." He opened the door and rushed out.

Landa bolted upright, almost tossing his chair. "Screw that," he muttered as he dashed out the door in Nikto's trail.

Chapter Sixteen
The Heart of the Beast

The captain jogged the passageway with Landa ten feet behind him. Unlike the wardroom, the corridor became more industrial the farther they walked. Crown moldings and brass fixtures were exchanged for pipes and gritty ducts.

"Where are we headed?" Landa asked, working to keep up.

Nikto glanced back, irritated he was following. "Engineering." His accent was more pronounced, "Reactor control."

Landa needed the handrails for the incline. The relentless alarm was piercing. There were flashing lights every thirty feet. Below the lights were yellow signs with the red trefoil design, the universal radiation warning symbol.

Great, Landa groaned. He was a prisoner on an enemy submarine, led by an egocentric drug lord of the deep, and now marching into a radioactive crisis. *Which way will finally do me in?*

Landa quickened his pace. He was trained to combat any emergency, despite any personal consequence.

They walked a straight path, which meant engineering was on the same deck towards the stern. They halted at a steel door. Nikto swiped a badge from his hip across a security pad. The *Naumtsev* seemed to be a hybrid of cold-war technology with modern upgrades. Nikto's tale of China retrofitting the vessel with advanced technology made sense. He watched the captain open the door.

The reactor control room was small, ten-by-ten feet, and stifling hot. It had steel bulkheads with the same flashing alarms. It smelled like the nearby diesel auxiliary engines.

Landa wasn't a nuclear engineer, but he knew the reactor was the heart of the vessel's propulsion and electrical systems. It was basically a sophisticated tea kettle. The reactor got hot, which heated water in its core. The resulting steam powered the propulsion turbines, which turned the propellers for motion and the generators for electricity. The pressurized water would then recirculate back to the reactor for the process to repeat.

If the reactor room was anything like those in US subs, it was adjacent to the reactor, separated by a shielded door. The nuclear reactor would be housed within a three-story silo, accessed with ladders and catwalks.

When Nikto entered, two engineers stood at attention, oily and scared. They wore dosimeters that looked like thermometers around their necks to measure the level of radiation. The men saluted and shouted, "Kapitan!" Landa was unable to read the radiation levels.

Nikto and Landa looked down to see a crewman sprawled on the deck and shouting in Russian. His leg was crushed under the steel door to the reactor. The pail, clammy man was writhing in pain, clutching his leg below the knee.

"Aleksei, report!" Nikto shouted to a lead engineer.

The man had wet bangs in his face. "Kapitan, there was a leak in the reactor." He panted, "They went in to contain it. The door then closed!"

"It is a shielded door," Nikto shouted to Landa over the alarms, "designed to drop as a safeguard."

The crewman screamed in pain. When Landa saw a pool of blood under his shin, he dove forward to attempt to lift the door. Nikto crouched to join him. Together, they labored to grip the bottom of the thick door. It wouldn't budge.

"If we contain the leak in the cooling circuit," Nikto grunted to lift again, "we can stop any spreading risk."

The two men struggled to lift in the confining space as the engineers monitored the radiation. The injured man released a deep, guttural groan with fading stamina.

Landa studied the cluttered room. He shouted to Aleksei, "Give me that pipe wrench and that toolbox!" The captain watched, curious.

The engineer frowned at the large American but pivoted to hand him an enormous thirty-six-inch wrench of solid steel. The second man slid him a toolbox the size of a large brick.

"Make a lever!" Landa shouted, frustrated with the men, "Do you understand?"

He wedged the wrench under the door like a crowbar. He lied on his side and shoved the toolbox under the wrench like a seesaw. With one foot, he pressed the box closer to the door.

The men wiped their eyes, fixated on whatever Landa was attempting.

"Use the box as a fulcrum." Landa's perspiring face grew red. "A fulcrum!" Angry with their delay, he thrust down on the wrench with both arms. The men understood; they joined him to push down on the wrench as Landa kept pressure on the box with his foot.

After a minute of unyielding effort, the door lifted an inch, just enough to pull the man's leg out. Aleksei pulled the man back by his shoulders, freeing his leg from the door.

The steel door then fell closed with a resounding boom.

Landa shouted at the men, exasperated, "Do you even know basic mechanics?" When he looked up, he was shocked to see Aleksei pointing at the door with a trembling finger.

The man stammered with horror in his eyes. "Ivan is still in with the reactor!"

Nikto froze at the realization a man had been trapped inside. Dread transformed his face as he gazed at the sealed door. Landa looked at the men, equally perplexed.

Captain Nikto turned to Aleksei. "The only way to override is to shut the primary circuits?"

"Da, Kapitan," Aleksei nodded. "If we do, auxiliary will slow us to ten knots. And we need to surface to ventilate."

Nikto's eyes ricocheted, gauging all consequences. He looked at Aleksei, "Shut the primary circuits."

With an audible *clank, clank,* the door to the reactor was manually ratcheted open. Two figures wearing yellow radiation protective suits appeared in the doorway. With their large helmets, they looked like cosmonauts.

They looked down at the steel-grated catwalk encircling the radioactive core. Face down on the deck was Ivan Popov, their chief engineer. His hands were locked in claw-like grips at his temples as if he'd been in agonizing pain. His face was scarlet with oozing blisters.

It had taken too long to open the door.

☙

Hunched in a chair, Captain Nikto kneaded his forehead at his desk.

Landa sat across from him. With no words, he watched the man brood. He looked away to observe the captain's study. It smelled like pipe tobacco. The office was small, but richly appointed with antiques including a model sailing ship also called the *Naumtsev.* There were framed maritime charts and black and white portraits of, presumably, relatives from Russia.

Growing fatigued, Landa crossed his arms. Nikto's desk was covered with unfolded charts. A pewter tray held a crystal decanter and two glasses. The only item that seemed out of place was a flat-panel monitor.

"We suffered a loss of coolant." Nikto murmured as if speaking to himself. "Aleksei said it was a leak in the primary circuit. Cooling of the core had been reduced." He shook his head, "That's what Ivan had been repairing, to save us all."

Landa just listened, allowing the man the consolation of grief. He was staggered how empathetic the man seemed towards his crew.

Nikto took a deep breath, emerging from his gloom. He reached for the two glasses and poured something clear from the decanter. He handed one glass to Landa. With glossy eyes, he lifted his glass to make a toast. He recited a lengthy quote in Russian.

He looked at Landa to translate, "May misfortune follow you the rest of your life, but never catch up."

"Russian wisdom?" Landa studied his glass.

"Irish." Nikto gave a thin smile, "My mother."

Landa warily sipped his drink. It was vodka, bitingly strong but smooth like iced water. He nodded and finished his glass.

Nikto's monitor illuminated. It was live video of Pavlo from control. *"Kapitan, ty zdes'?"*

The captain turned to his screen and replied. "Outcome? In English."

Onscreen, Pavlo swallowed before replying. "Captain, regretfully Officer Ivan Popov was exposed too long. He was pronounced dead. Dr. Yuri is testing the other men for sickness. Results will take time."

Nikto shrunk hearing what he already knew. He shaded his eyes with a hand. "Status of the *Naumtsev*?"

"The leak can be repaired. But we need time," Pavlo implored. "We do have a safe harbor off Haiti, only fifty nautical miles—"

"That will take five hours on auxiliary!" Nikto barked, exasperated.

"Da, Kapitan," Pavlo nodded. "We will need to vent."

Nikto pinched the bridge of his nose. "Make it so. Launch a C-Buoy to scan for any sightings." He turned off his monitor before Pavlo could reply.

Landa remained silent to digest the exchange. From Nikto's mannerisms, it didn't seem there was any ongoing radiation threat to the people onboard. He knew venting was usually done to bring in fresh air through a snorkel mast, while any potentially contaminated air is expelled through a different duct. The *Naumtsev* still needed to surface, and they knew of a safe harbor, whatever that meant. *Could this provide a window to escape?* Landa wondered.

He watched Nikto drink another shot with a thousand-yard stare.

"I knew Ivan Popov's family." He paused to relive the moments. "I went to Kuznetsov Naval Academy with his father in Saint Petersburg.

Young Ivan volunteered for my crew, and I was honored to have him." Nikto gave a melancholy smile, "He followed me from Severodvinsk, all the way to Colombia." His smile faded.

Landa fidgeted with his empty glass.

Nikto's expression hardened, "Ivan and my entire crew agreed to follow me—essentially committing treason—because they agreed with my ideals." His brows tensed. "And I have now failed him. Dead." His tone underscored the word.

Landa inhaled to respond but had nothing that would pacify the man. Nikto sat upright and paused as if studying him.

"Mr. Landa, you saved a man's life tonight. If radiation had leaked beyond that seal..." He didn't need to finish his sentence.

Landa squirmed in his seat. "I did what anyone would do."

Nikto flashed an ironic smile. "To you I am the villain." He motioned to the room, "Do you realize I lock myself in this very room to weep? I can admit that now." He nodded with a shrug. "Any time a blameless dies. Whether they are defenseless refugees or my crew."

Despite his usual impulse, Landa remained quiet. He reached for the decanter and poured two more drinks.

"I'm no saint." Landa handed the captain a glass. "And I'm not fascinated by fish like your other guests." He drank the vodka in one toss and looked at Nikto. "Your man said we're surfacing off Haiti."

Nikto narrowed his eyes, "Briefly."

Landa put down his glass. "That gives me five hours to fix your minisub."

Chapter Seventeen
Things that Swim with a Neon Glow

Chandler's hair was in disarray and his eyes were half shut when he opened his cabin door. The person facing him on the opposite side made him stiffen.

He stared, speechless, at the lady who was not his mother there to wish him good night.

At nearly midnight, Pavlo had assured Chandler and his mother there was no further emergency. He'd claimed the alarms were a drill, and Mr. Landa was working with the captain.

They'd been told it was midnight, because neither of them had any idea of the hour. They had no phones or watches, and the ship had no clocks. The concept of time was like that of a windowless casino.

Chandler's brain felt like it was at least midnight. It had been difficult to stay awake after dinner, and he needed to recharge after the events of the prior twenty-four hours, or could it have been longer considering time zones and so on?

His mother had retired to her quarters. She'd wanted to read a few of Nikto's journals and to write entries in a diary the captain had given her. She seemed very swept-up by the captain's stories and promises.

Chandler was alone in his cabin. His bare feet felt a mechanical vibration through the floor. He'd looked around his room; it was homey, and the bed appeared comfortable, but there was no television or any form of amusement other than a deck of cards. With his given predicament, he'd let his exhaustion take over. He was asleep within minutes.

Until someone meekly rapped on his door.

It was that awkward moment where you forget where you went to bed. In the unfamiliar space, he'd stumbled towards the door and shouted, "I'm comin' Mom."

When he'd opened his door, wearing only a t-shirt and boxers, he'd needed a second to comprehend Pilar's large brown eyes gazing back at him.

She was still dressed for the evening, with her long hair on one shoulder. She cocked her head with a poised smirk, "I want to show you something, or do you have to ask your mother?"

Pilar led him down one flight of steps, and forward towards the bow. Chandler barely had time to pull on his clothes. She walked six feet in front of him and said little. Chandler had no idea where they were going, but somehow felt safe with this exquisite stranger.

"Do you like the grand parlor?" Pilar asked in a soft Spanish accent.

"Yeah," he replied. "I love the Iris windows."

She grinned over her shoulder. "*Bien.*"

They entered the parlor. The room was almost completely dark. The only sound was the slight hum of the *Naumtsev*'s engines.

"Is there a light switch?" Chandler asked.

Pilar gave a half smile, "We won't need it."

Chandler was further mystified when she pulled him into the room by the hand. His eyes adjusted to ambient light from several art lamps. She proceeded towards a bookshelf. He watched her strike a match to light a stick of incense. She placed it in a brass ashtray and pulled him towards a window.

The aroma from the incense was sweet but spicy, and Chandler couldn't help but associate it with the air floating from her hair. She mentioned wanting to show him something, but the large circular windows revealed nothing but black.

"But it's night out." He checked over his shoulder as if they'd broken into a museum. "Should we be here?"

"*Tranquilo,*" she cooed with a grin. "It is okay. Captain Nikto is busy with some radiation concern."

His eyes went round. Pilar then pulled him down to sit beside her, cross-legged on a Persian rug two feet from the window. She turned towards the glass, waiting for something.

He looked out the window, confused. "There's no light. It's darker than in here—"

"*Shhh,*" Pilar touched his lips with a finger. "You will see."

"See what?" he replied. Either Pilar or the room smelled great.

"You must be patient," Her voice was soothing. "There is no instant gratification in nature."

"You been talking to my mom—" His mouth fell open mid-sentence and their faces glowed.

Outside their window, swirls of blue lights appeared within the darkness. The pinpoints of light twinkled and spun like a million blossoming stars. The radiant sapphire cloud was at least twenty feet in diameter.

"Bioluminescent life forms," her white smile was visible. "They are called dino—"

"Dinoflagellates," he finished her sentence, awestruck. "They're beautiful." They watched the lights shimmer and bloom like slow-motion fireworks.

"They illuminate because the *Naumtsev* is upsetting their shallow home," Pilar whispered.

Chandler replied without blinking. "They emit light when the water around them is disturbed."

They shared a moment of silence, engrossed by the show.

"Look!" Pilar pointed. A school of pulsing illuminated jellyfish drifted by with long, irradiated tendrils. Alternating blue, pink and purple, like neon.

Chandler watched the serene, pulsing creatures. Their translucent bodies were like prisms, emitting rainbows of light.

"Comb jellyfish." Pilar added softly, "They scatter their light through their cilia."

Chandler cocked his head like a fascinated puppy. "In the 17th century, Spanish explorers tried to close-off a bioluminescent bay in Puerto Rico. But the warm water made the dinoflagellates multiply. The bay glowed even brighter. The settlers thought the lights were—"

"The work of the devil." Pilar turned to him, "Sometimes things are not what they seem."

When he turned to her, their faces were closer than he'd anticipated. Chandler said nothing, not because he had nothing to say, but because he was distracted by the lights reflecting in her eyes. She returned his smile and looked back out.

Chandler and Pilar remained on the floor, staring out at an undersea galaxy.

∽

Ned Landa followed the captain down two flights of stairs, which was one deck lower than he'd been. It had to be the bottom of the vessel, probably some oily dungeon where Nikto wanted him to slave-away.

The captain paused at a large secure door. He pressed a switch and the door slid open, along with a second set of doors behind it.

Landa had seen double doors like this, usually used to shield against extreme pressures. When the second set opened, the chamber illuminated. It was bright white and metallic, unlike the rest of the ship. Nikto continued inside and Landa followed, cautious.

He was immediately hit with the briny scent of seawater. The chamber was thirty feet long and spanned the forty-foot beam of the ship. It was spotless, with modern mechanical fixtures like a space station.

"This is the moon well." Nikto motioned for him to enter.

Landa looked left to see the *Cyclops* hanging by a crane system. The fifteen-foot minisub was positioned above a large mechanical door on the floor that appeared wet. The salty aroma made sense; this was where they'd launched the *Cyclops*.

"This is a pressurized and floodable chamber," Nikto affirmed. "My divers and the *Cyclops* can submerge and reenter at any depth." He motioned to the door beneath the sub. "The drop point has double doors. The well is waterproof; the inner is pressure resistant."

Landa raised his brows. "You said divers?"

"That's what those are for," Nikto motioned behind Landa. "I call them ADS: atmospheric dive suits. State of the art."

Landa spun to see high-tech dive suits hanging on the wall. His eyes examined the suits. They were gray metal, with dome helmets and thick jointed arms and legs. The suits looked more like nine ghostly astronauts hanging on the wall.

Though the suits were remarkable, he wasn't stunned. The Navy and Marines had similar ADS suits. They were heavy, designed for the user to walk upright on the seafloor. Landa had never worn one, but he knew they were used for military deep-sea operations, including search missions and crash-site recovery for water and aircraft.

The suits were atmospheric, meaning they required almost no compression or decompression. The users didn't need to be a professional diver; they could just suit-up and maneuver on the bottom of the sea with a 180-degree view.

Despite all that, the thought of wearing such a confining suit gave Landa unease. He turned back to Nikto standing beside the *Cyclops*. "The room's pressure can be adjusted?"

Nikto gazed at the four corners of the room as he spoke. "If we dive to 600 meters, the pressure would be sixty-times greater than the surface." He stepped closer to the minisub. "When the *Cyclops* is docked, the moon well's pressure—as well as the pressure of the *Naumtsev*—is maintained at one atmosphere to mimic the surface."

Landa turned to absorb the room. His eyes twinkled like a kid in a toy store. There were work benches with power tools. Bins contained replacement parts, cables, and hand tools. He stepped beside Nikto to study the sub's inoperative arm.

The *Cyclops* was suspended eight feet above the deck by steel cables attached to a winch. Beneath the *Cyclops'* dome window, its left arm hung limp. Landa reached to inspect the grappling arm and claw. It was stainless steel, and the pistons confirmed a hydraulic system.

"I've never worked in robotics." Landa looked at Nikto, "But it appears its mode of actuation is a basic hydraulic cylinder."

"So, you can restore it?"

"If you give me access to your tools," Landa nodded. "And two men who can speak English."

Without replying, the captain turned to a panel on a wall. He pressed a switch and began to utter quick Russian, presumably to summon men to assist.

Landa noticed the wall behind the *Cyclops*. It had a square opening, protected by steel bars like a vault. He stooped to look inside.

He closed his eyes, disheartened by what he saw. *Nothing's changed.* Despite the captain's noble sermons, Nikto was nothing more than what he'd already predicted.

Inside the vault were countless stacks of bricked narcotics.

PART III

HUNTING OF THE SNARK

"He had bought a large map representing the sea,
Without the least vestige of land;
And the crew were much pleased when they found it to be
A map they could all understand."

—*The Hunting of the Snark*, Lewis Carroll

Chapter Eighteen
The Emissaries

Buenaventura, Colombia

The air tower at Gerardo Tobar López Airport cleared the King Air 350i for landing.

Arriving from Key West, the pilot of the approaching plane confirmed, "Cleared to land runway two, King Air One Kilo Charlie."

The pilot's announcement didn't wake Agent Ernesto Ruiz. He'd dozed off with Kurtz's heartbreaking words echoing in his mind. *The professor and her son were enjoying a normal life in Tallahassee before I called them. And now they're dead.*

Ruiz had been with Kurtz when he'd made the gut-wrenching call to suspend the search for missing Professor Patrice Arrison, her son Chandler, and consultant Ned Landa.

Though people could survive in waters above seventy degrees for days, they'd ultimately succumb to thirst or exposure. Their life jackets had been curiously recovered intact, and there were no missing rafts from the *Lincoln* they could have used. After the Coast Guard had spent days searching over one thousand square miles, Kurtz had reluctantly made the call.

Ruiz knew the worst part for Kurtz: it had been his idea to hire civilian experts for their investigation. That was rarely done by the DEA. *Now look what I've done. I've killed three innocents and two guardsmen,* Kurtz's emotional words lingered.

The King Air 350i was the finest of Beechcraft's twin-turboprops. It could accommodate eleven occupants in its plush leather seats, with a maximum range of 1,800 nautical miles. The plane was registered to a Daniel Rice with KYC Research, a Kentucky coal firm. However, "Daniel Rice" and his coal were fictitious creations of the US Drug Enforcement Agency.

The plane had been a confiscated drug plane, and the pilot was from the DEA's Aviation Division, a small but vital unit of the agency. The division, also known as its "Air Wing," could move special agents to remote jungles or track drug-carrying vehicles within a moment's notice.

The JIATF in Key West had obtained DEA approval to use the plane. Agent Ruiz and Navy Intel Officer Engel were eager for this delicate opportunity.

Despite Agent Ernesto Ruiz's boyish appearance, he'd made countless high-level calls, risking stepping on many toes to arrange the meeting. His senior partner, Kurtz, liked that quality about him, repeatedly grumbling, "You remind me of a better-looking me twenty years ago."

~

When Ernesto Ruiz had originally transferred to Key West from his hometown of Chicago, the DEA had approved the move based on his Colombian heritage.

The DEA's footprint in Key West was small, just a few agents on the taskforce. Their primary South Florida office was in Miami, three hours north. Nevertheless, Ernesto had eagerly applied. Though he loved Chicago, it sounded more exciting to chase smugglers on the Gulf versus low-rent dealers on the south side, and he'd always dreamt of Christmas on a beach.

Though the agency would never select applicants based on heritage, when Agent Kurtz had learned Ruiz could speak multiple dialects of Colombian Spanish, his transfer was fast-tracked.

Kurtz had become a mentor to Ruiz. In his first year alone, Ruiz had been involved in multiple investigations tied directly to his ability to connect with key individuals within the Bogotá embassy and the Policia Nacional de Colombia, the National Police of Colombia.

Currently, "Project Devil's Triangle" was no different. The project was named after the mysteriously vanishing and sunken vessels within a triangular region between Bermuda, Puerto Rico, and Miami. The seven —thus far— boats had been destroyed within a similar triangle.

The lead theory Kurtz and Ruiz had agreed upon was the likely existence of a narco-sub, used by a cartel to destroy their competition. But when Navy Intel Officer Engel suggested it could be a black market Russian nuclear sub, the concept seemed unachievable, or was it?

Applying the forensic rule of inclusiveness—to follow all leads—Kurtz had agreed to check with their Colombian counterparts for any evidence that could prove or refute Engel's theory. In Kurtz's eloquent words, the presence of a 375-foot Russian sub at any port would create a shitload of witnesses.

∞

"Prepare for landing." The pilot's voice over the P.A. roused Ruiz from his rest. "Approaching Geardo Tobar López Airport in beautiful Buenaventura."

Ruiz looked over at the only other passenger on the plane, Navy Intel Officer Engel, seated across the aisle. Her face was glued to her window. She seemed excited about travel, especially the thought of visiting another country. She'd mentioned more than once her job usually involved staring at reports while seated in a cubicle all day.

"You saw my timeline on the Bogotá cartel?" Ruiz asked.

Engel turned with a tranquil smile. "I did." She looked back out the window.

Ruiz thought Engel was pleasant but academic. She was feminine, with no need to rely on make-up. Her hair was short and uncomplicated with any time-consuming style. She wore appealing slim glasses, but they were noticeably thick, so certainly not a fashion accessory.

"Your report didn't include anything about Buenaventura itself." Engel gave a timid grin, "I haven't been out of the country since Cancun when I was in college."

"No fiestas on this trip." Ruiz smiled. "Buenaventura means 'good fortune,' which is sort of ironic. Its large port is their primary industry, with access to many rivers used for commerce." He pointed to her folder, "Many of those narco-subs you showed us were seized in these rivers. They're used to move narcotics to the port."

Ruiz paused. There was a darker side of the city he needed to explain, but the plane jostled, and its landing gear audibly engaged.

Engel turned back to her window to watch the lush countryside rise to meet the plane.

In the middle of a grassy meadow, the one-story airport was not much larger than an American chain restaurant. Its mustard-yellow walls and terracotta roof stood out against a backdrop of emerald-green mountains.

As with most small international airports, Ruiz and Engel had to exit the plane using stairs and then walk across the tarmac to its Customs office. For safety reasons they did not wear any uniforms. Ruiz was casual in a denim shirt and aviator Ray-Bans. Engel wore khaki slacks and a blue blazer.

Thankfully, Customs was quick with only two passengers. Ominous-looking military police stood at the doors, wearing full camo, and carrying immense Colombian ACE assault rifles. Ruiz simply nodded at the men as they walked by.

He'd explained to Engel the goal was to play it low-key. He gave a few pleasant nods and spoke only in Spanish to the Customs officials on behalf of Engel and himself.

As they exited the building, a black Denali SUV pulled up in front of a queue of VW cabs. Engel tensed as if it were the cliché mob vehicle, but Ruiz knew it was their driver.

"It's Pascal, local DEA," Ruiz explained.

Engel dodged shady cabbies to follow Ruiz. "We have American DEA here?"

"Yes, Bogotá." He paused to greet the large driver who stepped out of the SUV. The man was also dressed in casual clothes. They exchanged pleasantries in Spanish, and Engel was advised they should get moving. She and Ruiz climbed inside, and the truck exited.

Seated in the back, Engel wanted to clarify, "Our DEA can work in Colombia?"

"Yes," Ruiz slid on reading glasses and opened a folder. "The closest office is Bogotá. We have a working relationship with the Policia Nacional." He frowned with a shrug, "But we can't make arrests or any seizures. So it's about relationships and trading intel."

Engel nodded, absorbing the information. "Kurtz mentioned the port wasn't safe."

He looked at her, somber. "It's considered the most dangerous port in the world. Buenaventura has been called Colombia's deadliest city."

Her eyes widened behind her glasses. "Why'd we fly here and not Bogotá?"

Ruiz unfolded a map and pointed to its northern coast. "Buenaventura has Colombia's only port that's deep enough to dock an Akula-class."

She pulled the map close to her face.

"Most deep-water ports are twenty-five to thirty feet deep, even for cruise and cargo ships." Ruiz flashed a smirk, "But this port is over fifteen meters, nearly fifty feet deep."

Engel nodded, "So if a cartel could ever obtain a submarine that size, it could only have come here."

Ruiz winked.

Chapter Nineteen
Catching Smoke

Officer Engel attempted her best poker face. She was accustomed to having all the facts, and rarely comfortable asking people for answers. Was it normal to be distressed—after not flying outside the US for fifteen years—if she'd just landed in Colombia's deadliest city?

She looked outside her window. Crooked dirt roads wound up the grassy hills. Their street was paved, but heavily potholed. On the right side of their truck, green pastures with barbed-wire fences rushed by. On the left, shacks and rickety cafes with ancient Coca Cola signs.

"We're going to the Distrito Especial de Policia." Ruiz handed her a memo, "Buenaventura's police department."

She scanned the report and nearly choked. "The department that was bombed last year?"

"Evidently." Ruiz chuckled. "That was tied to protests or something."

That didn't make her feel better. He handed her another file.

"The Bogotá cartel controlled the port." He pointed to a mug shot of a handsome fiftyish man with thick hair "The cartel boss, Don Ricardo Salazar, was arrested and jailed four months ago."

Engel studied a spreadsheet. "From his assets, it's conceivable he had enough money to purchase a black-market vessel if there ever was such a thing."

Ruiz shrugged, "Military vessels are your department. My job's narcotics."

She paused to look at him. "How long do we have to make our point?"

Ruiz lifted a finger. "The Policia Nacional has given us one hour." He gave an iffy shrug, "Attorney General Martinez promised he'd stop by. We've helped him many times."

Engel looked out her window, her insecurities surfacing. "So, I'm presenting to bureaucrats whose first language isn't English."

"Please use layman's terms and as little technobabble as possible." He raised his brows, "And try to be convincing."

જ

Their SUV pulled up to Buenaventura's Distrito Especial de Policia. They stopped at a guard gate where uniformed men with rifles approached all sides of the truck.

Engel tried not to appear nervous. She studied the building's two-story curves. It looked like it had been planned as modernistic, but the feds settled on gray cement walls that were now stained. With overgrown grass and barbed wire, it looked post-apocalyptic.

The guard finally uttered something in Spanish, and they drove through the gates.

Agent Ruiz and Officer Engel were escorted to a small conference room on the second floor. It was government-bland, only twenty-by-twenty feet and smelled like cigarettes. An archaic projector was on the table and a screen had been pulled down for Engel's presentation.

She looked at her watch. It was seventeen minutes past the hour.

"They're on Colombian time," Ruiz exhaled under his breath.

Engel huffed. She'd been taught there was no excuse for bad punctuality.

Six men finally entered the room as a tight group. They all had holstered semiautomatics and wore camo fatigues.

"Colombian National Police," Ruiz whispered. "Not military, but they combat illegal drugs."

Engel nodded. She stood beside the projector like a teacher. The men didn't acknowledge either of them as they sat around the conference table, chattering to each other in Spanish. There was a sudden quiet as a man in a tailored gray suit entered the room.

"*Buenas dias*, Fiscal General Martinez." Ruiz approached the man with a firm handshake. The man had silver hair and a red pocket square that matched his tie. Ruiz turned to Engel, "This is Attorney General Martinez, and this is Engel, an Intel Officer with the US Navy."

Martinez maintained a staunch frown as he gripped her hand. He said nothing to either of them. She wondered if Ruiz had overstated his relationship with the attorney general.

With everyone seated, Engel was ready to begin. It was already 10:27 am, and they only had until 11:00. She stood beside the screen and Ruiz remained seated at her side.

"Good morning, eh…" she paused, "*Buenas dias*."

"I'll handle the Spanish." Ruiz rolled his hand, "Just go." He turned to speak quick Spanish to the men.

"They read your memo," he said to Engel. "So just dive right in."

Engel forced a smile, feeling slighted as well as rushed. She clicked a remote to project a satellite photo of a sprawling port. "This image was taken above Visakhapatnam Port in India four years ago." She pointed, "Note the long, dark cigar shape here."

She paused to allow Ruiz to interpret. His version was noticeably shorter. The men squinted at the screen to discern what she was referring to.

"That object is a Russian Typhoon submarine," she continued. "Russia has leased Typhoons to other countries such as India. They're usually retired vessels, leased for ten-year periods for between three and five billion dollars."

The men frowned and nodded.

Her slide changed to a close-up of an enormous Typhoon sub. "Just last year, India signed another ten-year lease for a nuclear sub they call the *Chakra III*. It was also a decommissioned sub that had been sitting useless in Russia's port town of Severodvinsk."

Ruiz translated, and again it seemed suspiciously shorter. He looked at Engel. "I think they're curious what this has to do with them."

"I'm getting to that," she whispered. She turned to the men. "We call it Typhoon-class, but in Russia it's called *Akula* which means shark. It's the quietest nuclear vessels in their fleet."

She paused at a clamor from the door. The men turned to see a man wheeling a coffee tray into the room. The men all seemed excited, with "Ahs" and "*Muy biens.*"

Engel's presentation came to an abrupt stop as the men poured themselves China cups of coffee. They muttered and chuckled to each other as they clanged spoons to stir their cups. She watched them turn their backs to her with zero respect.

In a firm tone, she plowed ahead. "Twenty Akula-class subs were planned, but only fifteen built, that we know of." Ruiz translated into Spanish and she projected a chart with fifteen Akulas. "Out of those fifteen, only five are known to still be active."

Martinez and the men finally settled, appearing to follow along.

"According to Russia, only three Akulas were retired and reportedly scrapped." Engel made air quotes. "They allege some decommissioned subs were scrapped to make other vessels. One was reportedly destroyed by fire. Others lost to the perils of the sea—whatever that means— without any proof they were scuttled." She paused for Ruiz to translate.

"My point," Engel looked at the men to conclude, "with only five out of fifteen subs still in service, it's conceivable a 48,000-ton, nuclear-armed Soviet sub can just go missing."

The men began to quietly debate each other in Spanish. With a pensive nod, the attorney general turned to Ruiz to give an animated lecture in Spanish.

Curious of his reaction, Engel watched Ruiz rub his eyes, frustrated. She whispered to Ruiz, "What'd he say?"

He huffed, "Attorney General Martinez is reminding us that his mission is to combat drug trafficking, not to track Soviet submarines."

With dwindling patience, Engel turned to Martinez with a raised voice, "We are willing to waive Don Ricardo Salazar's extradition." She articulated her words to compensate for not knowing Spanish. "If he cooperates with our investigation—by just answering a few questions—the US will not pursue any extradition from Colombia."

A hush fell over the room. Engel instantly regretted how she'd spoken to the man. She hoped the silence was more about her brazen conduct than the content of her offer.

Martinez gave a tight smile and fidgeted with a gold pinky ring. He then spoke in clear, intelligible English. "That means nothing to me."

Engel halted, not entirely understanding.

"You wish to question him about buying submarines?" Martinez continued, "For Salazar's crimes, narcotics, extortion, kidnapping, and murder of children, he will serve decades in La Modelo prison." He cocked his head for gravity, "He will not be alive when we are finished with him for any extra...dition." He mocked the word.

෬෩

"That was it?" Ruiz roared in the back seat of the SUV. He pounded his fist on an armrest between him and Engel. "That was our one play! And now it's gone?"

Engel didn't dare respond. She inched farther away from Ruiz. She didn't feel physically threatened, but she knew she was responsible for their meeting coming to a screeching halt.

"I-I wanted to cut to the chase," she finally stammered. "Considering our reduced timeframe."

Ruiz didn't look at her. He released a gruff sigh and put his aviators back on. "All we had to do was hook him with just enough curiosity."

"Is there any other way we can question Salazar?" Engel looked out to see harried pedestrians just inches outside her window. "Some way to find out what he knows?"

Ruiz wiped his face with both hands. "The US has no power to thrust our implausible investigation on their number-one convict."

At a stop light, Engel watched locals buying fruit from booths. Barefoot children were shouting for coconut popsicles from a vendor. One shop that sold cellphone cases had an obsolete Kodak sign. She realized different places and experiences meant nothing. People were essentially the same, with similar wants, needs and desires.

"We have zero leverage." Ruiz continued to groan.

Engel noticed a handsome young father on the sidewalk. He wore a faded Disney t-shirt, and he hoisted his toddler daughter onto his shoulders. The girl laughed and played with his hair.

Engel cocked her head with a new idea. She checked her file and turned to Ruiz.

"Doesn't your drug lord Ricardo Salazar have a wife and child?"

Ruiz's entire body froze. He turned to her as his mouth curved into a smile. "He certainly does."

Chapter Twenty
Ladders and Chutes

The West Indies

Freshly dressed for the day, Dr. Arrison leaned over the wardroom table to study a navigation map.

She sipped her coffee—a dark, earthy variety from Indonesia—and tried to visualize their track, southeast from the Keys to the islands of Hispaniola. *Roughly 700 miles*, she calculated in her head. *So today would be…*

Arrison turned at the sound of someone entering. Ned Landa ducked through the doorway wearing fresh clothes and a smug smile.

"Mornin', Professor." He stepped beside her to see what she was doing.

"Mr. Landa," she nodded. "The gentleman in the galley can bring you breakfast or coffee." She looked back at her map.

He made a sour face. "If all their food comes from the ocean, how do you do breakfast?"

She shrugged, "They brought me a shrimp and grits with a cream sauce that was excellent, and crab cake Benedict on an English muffin and hollandaise."

He narrowed an eye, "How'd they make grits and an English muffin from the sea?"

"Kelp flour. I asked the same thing," Arrison replied. "They grind flour from dried seaweed. It's common in Asia, filled with nutrients, with lower fat and calories."

"I'll stick to coffee," he grumbled.

Arrison had to squint to scan the chart. "I never appreciated online maps until now..." She paused when Landa touched her shoulder. She turned to see his focused eyes.

"A man died last night." He checked over his shoulder and spoke low, "A mechanical accident. Did he even tell you?"

She went pale. "Someone died?" Her eyes skimmed the room at the startling news.

Landa nodded. "We're surfacing off Haiti to vent for a repair." He leaned close, "I'm leaving. I don't care if it's Haiti or the Dominican Republic, but I'm gone." He captured her glance. "Come with me."

She stepped back. "I can't just...leave," she stammered. "Nikto promised to show us an extremely significant—"

"This is our chance!" Landa hissed. "Forget your big *National Geographic* opportunity."

They stopped and awkwardly stood upright to see Captain Nikto enter the room. He was groomed and dressed for the day. Arrison was surprised to see Chandler and Pilar following in his trail.

"*Dobroye utro.*" Nikto smiled at Arrison with his morning greeting. "Aside from Mr. Landa and myself, I trust you had a restful evening?"

Chandler and Pilar traded a glance. When she grinned, he blushed.

Pilar approached Arrison to see her map. "We are here," she tapped a coordinate with a finger. "Islands west of the Republic of Haiti. We have a safe harbor."

"They are not interested," Nikto moved between them, "in the minutiae of our navigation." His expression hardened at Pilar as if she were revealing too much.

Landa glared at Nikto. "What makes a harbor 'safe'?"

The captain tightened his jaw, then conceded, "It is a moon-shaped cay. An island too small for most maps, with a deep lagoon invisible from three sides. It is abandoned, a hundred years ago it was used for measles patients."

Pilar grinned at Chandler, "He also added signs warning of dengue fever."

Nikto's eyes blazed again at girl.

"How long are we surfacing?" Landa asked.

"Less than an hour," Nikto replied, eyeing him. "We can conclude our repairs and bring fresh air into the vessel through the mast."

"What about your casualty?" Landa's tone was vilifying, as if to expose the news.

The captain blinked. "It is true." He turned to Arrison for full disclosure. "There was an unfortunate incident last evening. A man sacrificed his life to save this vessel, and our lives."

Chandler, Arrison and Pilar inhaled, distraught at the revelation.

"What happens to his body?" Chandler asked.

Nikto gave a poignant smile. "He is being preserved until we can perform a proper burial. In approximately twenty-four hours."

Arrison glanced at the map, perplexed. "Where in twenty-four hours?"

"Under Guanahacabibes. Just as I have promised." The captain turned and exited the room.

⁊

Nikto entered the control room. Several crewmen with cigarettes stood at attention.

"*Dobroye utro. Buenas Dias.*" Nikto greeted them in both languages as he approached Dmitri at the comm station.

"Reports of our existence?"

"None. Since Key West, 1,200 kilometers," Dmitri replied.

"Very good." Nikto folded his hands behind his back. "Periscope depth; do not broach."

"Da, Kapitan," Pavlo replied, seated as helmsman.

In the center of the room, the periscope handles lowered with a hydraulic hiss. Nikto grasped the controls and pressed his face to the eyepiece.

With the sunrise, he had to squint. He adjusted the focus and range to observe a clear morning above the surface, with calm two-foot seas. He rotated the periscope 360-degrees, confirming no other vessels. Just the one small island directly ahead.

"Isla Moustique, two kilometers," Pavlo announced.

"Make preparations to surface," Nikto ordered.

"Aye," a diving officer confirmed. "Secure ventilation. Shut bulkhead flappers."

"Open main induction when ready and no surface alarm." Nikto inhaled, content, "Proceed, four knots."

☙

It was a pastel dawn with pink and azure skies. The surrounding Caribbean was calm, with a golden sun edging the eastern horizon.

The immense *Naumtsev* breached the surface with a gentle trail in its wake.

If there had been witnesses, it would appear to be an enormous prehistoric shark or swordfish. Stretching from the *Naumtsev*'s bow was a thirty-foot bayonet nose of serrated steel. Its modified sail looked like an immense dorsal fin. To its rear, the aft rudder was its sharp tail.

If a boater ever attempted to report the 375-foot monstrosity, they'd be dismissed as either inebriated or delusional. That was precisely the plan.

The *Naumtsev* idled south towards the small, lone island.

Nikto lifted the periscope and turned to Dmitri to speak privately in Russian. "Please call Dr. Yuri up to the bridge. I'm heading up."

"Da, Kapitan," Dmitri nodded.

"Where are our guests?"

Dmitri adjusted his glasses. "Dr. Arrison is studying journals in the parlor. Mr. Landa is in the moon well with the *Cyclops*."

"Please call Dr. Arrison to join me at the bridge." Nikto then asked, "Where are the kids?"

Dmitri shrugged, "Staying out of the way."

❧

Pilar swiped a security badge to proceed through a hatch, then up a ladder. She moved quickly with enthusiasm. Six feet behind her, Chandler struggled to keep up.

"Why does Nikto forbid us to go here?" He huffed in the narrow passageway.

"You will see," she replied with a mischievous grin.

They entered an industrial area with bulkheads, pipes, and a steel-grated deck. Chandler thought it smelled like oil lubricant, and it was noisier than the other areas of the vessel.

"This is the torpedo room," Pilar stopped in front of a wall with multiple hatches.

Chandler paused to study the circular hatches. He counted at least eight torpedo launch tubes, and each was less than two feet in diameter.

"They are called breech hatches." She unlatched and turned a wheel to open one.

Chandler moved closer, "But Nikto got rid of the torpedoes."

"With the missiles gone, it created room for cargo." She opened the door, revealing a dark, vacant pipe. "Nikto uses them for hidden storage."

Chandler half-grinned, intrigued. When he looked inside, it was dark and seemed endless.

"There are three hundred pounds of coffee beans in this one from three continents." She moved closer to his face. "Can you smell it?"

Her warm breath on his ear made his spine tingle. He inhaled to smell an intoxicating mix of coffee beans and her spicy fragrance.

Chandler reached to open a second hatch, enthralled. "What else does he keep here?"

"I found champagne, bottles of vodka," she placed her hands on his back to peer inside. "Last week I saw a large bundle covered in foil. I opened it to find fifty pounds of Belgian chocolate."

He turned to her with pure wonder, "That'd be incredible."

Pilar pulled an emergency flashlight from a wall and tossed it to him. "You go in that tube. I'll look in this one."

"What?" Chandler fumbled to catch the light. "Go inside these?"

"Why not?" she replied. "It's not too tight. Mr. Landa said Navy SEALS have exited through torpedo tubes."

I'm not exactly a SEAL, Chandler wanted to reply. He shined his flashlight into the narrow tube. It was dark and metallic and he couldn't see the other end.

He heard Pilar open another hatch. He turned to see her climb into a tube, face first. "It is easy!" She shouted, "You do that one!" Her voice echoed the deeper she climbed.

Chandler froze. Within seconds he tried to consider all conceivable outcomes. He didn't think he was claustrophobic, but who would voluntarily enter a tube the width of a garbage can, with no light, forty feet underwater?

"Chandler, I think I see something," her voice resonated from deep inside the tube.

He squeezed his eyes closed to rationalize. Would Pilar consider him a coward if he didn't go in? He was an experienced scuba diver, including night and cave diving, which were considered terrifying by some. *This isn't much different,* he supposed. *And what could be in these tubes?*

Chandler opened his eyes with a renewed vigor. He took a deep breath as if diving into a cold pool and climbed into the torpedo tube.

After computing any imaginable consequence, he concluded, *what could possibly go wrong?*

Chapter Twenty-One
Foiled Curiosity

"This way," Captain Nikto motioned for Professor Arrison to follow him.

With a good sense of direction, Arrison knew they were mid-ship, on the upper-most deck. The bulkheads and ceiling were darker and more confining.

Nikto stopped at a ladder. "We are below the *Naumtsev*'s sail," he explained. "The tower you had described as a fin."

She looked up to see the ladder lead up a shaft. "What's on top of the sail?"

"The bridge." He started up the ladder. "Where I control the *Naumtsev* while surfaced."

We're on the surface? Her heart fluttered with mixed emotions. She longed to see open sky and breathe fresh air. But she also craved to experience so many of Nikto's undersea promises. She grasped the ladder and looked up to follow the captain.

At the base of the shaft were two dome portholes on each side. She had to squint from the blinding blue light flooding through the windows.

"Careful, please." Nikto implored. "The steps can be hazardous."

She found it amusing how considerate Nikto could seem. Was that a trait of a merciless drug lord as Landa had suggested? Or, like her, was he truly a scholar of the sea?

Arrison climbed, cautious. The shaft was about five feet in diameter and twenty feet high. It was welded steel with safety lights every few feet.

When Nikto reached the top, he opened a circular hatch. "This way. Careful."

She looked away from the sunlight leaching from the hatch. The roar of a nearby shore echoed within the shaft. Arrison continued to the top and Nikto reached to help her out.

Arrison gripped handrails to stand behind a four-foot partition. Her first impression was nothing short of exhilarating. It looked like they were flying since they were twenty-five feet above the water. She had to squint at the cloudless sky. Seagulls squawked and swooped over the cobalt-blue water. When she inhaled, she could taste salt in the back of her throat.

"This is the bridge." Nikto lifted binoculars to study the horizon.

When Arrison gazed down at the sub, her smile vanished. It was a sobering reminder she was standing on the monster that had attacked them. The sail she was standing on had been modified to look like a twenty-foot dorsal fin. It was connected to the hull with a sharp edge like an upright hatchet blade. The two portholes below were designed to look like eyes.

The vessel stretched before her seemed even larger in daylight. It was flat-black, probably coated in a material to avoid reflecting light or radar. At sea level, a long steel spike extended from the nose of the bow. It was at least thirty feet long, with a jagged edge that pierced the waves like a lance. *That's how it destroys boats.* Her stomach roiled.

She flinched when Nikto touched her shoulder.

"There." He pointed to a small island a half-mile ahead. "Our destination, Isla Moustique." Nikto put his arm around her to point out to sea. "See those mountains far to the east?"

She turned to see a hazy mainland on the horizon.

"That is near Port-au-Prince. We will maintain our distance here."

Arrison had been to Haiti once before with an FSU group that had helped victims of Hurricane Matthew. She was aware they had a coast guard, but unsure how far they patrolled.

Arrison turned back to the approaching small island. It appeared crescent-shaped and less than a mile in diameter. "You said it's uninhabited?"

"Yes," he nodded. "It has a deep-water lagoon, protected on three sides."

The *Naumtsev* idled into the mouth of the inlet. In the clear aquamarine water, Arrison saw channel markers, bent by prior storms. She then saw rusted metal signs on posts with some sort of warning symbol. As they got closer, she could see the warnings displayed an image of a mosquito with the words, WARNING DENGUE FEVER.

Nikto noticed her reading the signs. "I also posted the dengue warnings in Spanish and French." He smiled, proud of his deception.

The captain lifted a mic from a control panel. His amplified voice echoed from within the ship, "Attention off-duty: we will have a steel beach. Only thirty minutes."

Arrison gave a half-smile, "What's a steel beach?"

"You will see. Something for morale and vitamin D."

ᥱᎥ

Pilar crawled within her dark torpedo tube. She pushed with the soles of her shoes, while pulling herself forward on the slick surface. She moved one foot at a time in the tight diameter. She paused to aim her flashlight in front of her.

"I might have found something." Her shout resonated. The flashlight beam revealed a small wooden case the size of a shoebox. "It says Havana on it."

She didn't hear Chandler respond. He was either too far away for her to hear, or he hadn't heard her at all. *Or he passed out from fear,* she chuckled.

It was hard to open the box with both hands in the tight space. When she cracked the lid, she sighed as if it were a consolation prize.

"Cuban cigars." She shouted, "*Hoyo de Monterrey.* Do you like Cuban cigars?" She heard no reply other than the echo of her own voice.

Chandler was not as calm. He guessed he was half-way into his tube. It was almost unbearable. The sides were tight against his shoulders. It was dark and smelled like WD-40. But there was a gnawing curiosity that kept him moving.

He tried to crawl forward using his fingers, but the surface was too slick. The echo of his breathing sounded like amplified stereo. Like cave diving, every few feet he'd pause to take a meditative breath to focus on his task.

Chandler shouted, "What?" He thought he heard Pilar say something. She didn't reply, which made him feel even more alone.

When he aimed his flashlight in front of him, the light shimmered off something that looked like foil. He smiled and shouted, "Did you say foil could be chocolate?"

No response. With renewed interest, he inched deeper. The foil-wrapped bundle appeared larger than he'd imagined. He shouted again, "What do you think it is?"

*

On the bridge, Nikto pointed out features of Isla Moustique. "The center of this lagoon is over fifty feet deep. Dredged for smuggling ships years ago."

The *Naumtsev* entered the lagoon, bordered by a semicircle of tropical foliage. With no inhabitants, the shore was just a sliver of white sand. Vegetation had overrun the landscape.

A portly, older officer with white hair climbed onto the bridge. His eyes seemed surprised to see Dr. Arrison with the captain.

Nikto introduced her. "Dr. Yuri, this is our guest, Professor Arrison." He turned to her, "Yuri is our Medical Officer. He came with me from Severodvinsk."

The humorless doctor gave a small nod.

Nikto asked, "Do you mind if I speak Russian? Dr. Yuri knows limited English."

"Go ahead," Arrison shrugged and turned back to the island.

Nikto spoke quick Russian to Yuri, "Do you have the results on our engineers?"

"Da, Kapitan." Yuri replied in gruff Russian, "There is no evidence of radiation poisoning. The men have no symptoms, no decrease in white blood cells. The men are healthy."

"That is wonderful," Nikto exhaled. "And Leonid's leg?"

"We were able to save it," Yuri replied. "The door fractured his tibia. I gave him a plaster cast." He paused with a slow shake of his head, "Ivan was not so fortunate."

Nikto's face withered, solemn. "Did you stow Ivan's body somewhere absolutely secure?"

"Of course," Yuri dipped his head. "His body is wrapped and protected in Mylar. Stored away, safe and dry from any curious eyes."

೮೨

Chandler inched closer to the foil-wrapped bundle. His chest ached as it seemed harder to breathe. He wondered if his oxygen was being depleted within the narrow space. With short breaths, he shimmied closer to the foil, now just two feet away.

He inhaled to shout, "It's something big! Pilar?" There was no answer.

With the flashlight in his left hand, he stretched his right arm to reach the bundle. He still couldn't touch it, so he squirmed closer. When his fingers could finally feel the foil, he placed the flashlight in his mouth so he could use both hands to peel back the wrap.

"I'm takin' a look!" He muttered with the light clenched in his teeth.

Chandler crept closer until his face was inches away. He pulled back the foil, trying to aim the light with his mouth. It reminded him of opening a foil-wrapped turkey at Thanksgiving. "I still can't see…" he huffed. He craned his neck and adjusted the light until he could finally see.

His eyes bulged, mute with horror.

Gazing at him from the foil was an inflamed, blistered face. The corpse had milky red eyes that were locked open. The man's head was wet with oozing sores.

As Chandler opened his mouth to scream, the flashlight fell out. The bulb turned off when it struck the surface. It was dark again and he could smell the sour corpse. He dry-heaved to vomit.

"It's a body!" Chandler finally roared. He flailed his arms, trying to scurry backwards like a crab. Acid crept up his throat to puke, but he gnashed his teeth to hold it in.

"Pilar, it's a body!" His shriek echoed.

Pilar climbed out of her hatch holding the box of cigars. She moved closer to look into Chandler's tube. It was too dark to see. She wondered why he wasn't using his flashlight.

She heard a muffled shout. Uncertain if she'd heard correctly, she replied, "Did you say it's a bottle? Of what?"

Pilar teasingly closed his hatch, covering her mouth to contain a chuckle.

Chandler's tube went pitch-black. *Someone closed the hatch. I'm locked in with a corpse!* He cried out in pure panic, exhausting his remaining breath, "Pilar!" Fighting to contain his nausea, his whole body trembled to wiggle towards the opening.

Light flooded the tube as the hatch opened. Hyperventilating, Chandler peeked over his shoulder to see Pilar's grinning face.

She tugged his legs out of the opening. He clambered to pull himself out. Chandler finally stood, hunched and dripping with sweat.

He scowled when he realized her impish grin. "Did you close the hatch?"

She gave a demure shrug. "I was just being playful."

Through labored breaths he pointed to his tube, "Do you realize what's in there?"

"You said a bottle?" She batted her large eyes. "Anything good?"

Chapter Twenty-Two
Piraty!

Alone in the moon well, Ned Landa had already completed the repairs to the *Cyclops*.

He never admitted he was finished, pretending he needed more time. His team in the Marines used to tease him, comparing him to Scotty from *Star Trek*, if a job required four hours, he'd tell the team leader he needed eight.

The minisub's arm had been a simple repair. Previous crewmen had replaced a hydraulic fluid tube incorrectly. They'd used a tube that was too wide which decreased the pressure, and they never bled the line to remove air. Landa completed the repair in less than two hours.

It was ironic the *Naumtsev* had nuclear engineers who didn't know how to do minor hydraulic repairs. He guessed it was like asking a NASA engineer to bake a cake. Whatever mutinied crew Nikto had assembled came with a limited bag of specialties.

The repair provided perfect cover for Landa to be alone. Two men had been assigned to assist, but when he worked without ever speaking, they finally left out of boredom.

Landa was now by himself in a first-class workshop. Sensing the waves gently rocking the vessel, he knew they had surfaced. *Let's get off this barge,* he grinned with a gleam in his eye.

On a wall near an extinguisher was an emergency kit. He opened the box to find a small life vest with a water-activated locator beacon. The vest was neoprene and folded to the size of a small book. The emergency beacon was designed to transmit a signal to locate the user.

Landa stuffed the life vest in his waistband. He left the beacon behind; he didn't want to be located by anyone onboard the *Naumtsev.* He hit the switch to open the door and exited the chamber.

ↂ

The massive *Naumtsev* idled in the center of the lagoon.

From the top of the sail, Dr. Arrison estimated the cove was the size of a football stadium. The vessel began to slowly rotate clockwise so it would face out for an easier departure.

As the sub turned, Arrison watched the shoreline pass by. It was an untouched utopia of tropical flora. She spotted orchids, coconut palms and sea grape trees. Absolute paradise.

Her trance was disrupted as Nikto made an announcement through the PA.

"Off-duty: you may disembark through the forward and aft hatches," his voice boomed. "Steel beach, three-zero minutes." A bell rang three times.

Uncertain what was happening, Arrison saw a square hatch open on the bow. She turned to see another hatch open near the stern. Crewmen began to file out of the ship and onto its narrow deck like marching ants.

It took Arrison a second to realize the men were either shirtless or in t-shirts and wearing bathing suits or boxer shorts. Some carried towels. The pale men grinned up at the sun like they hadn't seen the sky in months. They laughed with spirited shouts to each other.

Arrison blossomed into a smile when she saw the first man dive into the water. Two others followed with childlike cannonballs, and the rest leaped with excited howls. They swam and splashed like children. They used rungs on the side of the vessel to climb back onto the deck to jump again or lounge on towels for sun. *A steel beach,* Arrison finally understood.

When she turned to Nikto, he had the widest smile she'd ever seen on the man.

☙

The passageways were empty as Landa marched up three flights of steps. With the life vest stuffed into his pants —along with small binoculars and two bottles of water— he continued forward towards the bow. He finally saw several men standing in the rear of a queue.

When he saw an intense glare above them, Landa realized it was the open hatch. The men were waiting to disembark, wearing shorts and t-shirts. He casually entered the back of the line.

Landa almost chuckled; it was easier than he'd planned. He had been debating how to escape, and now Nikto was encouraging his men to disembark for sun and swimming.

He shuffled forward, patient. No one spoke to him and that was fine. He climbed the steps leading to the *Naumtsev's* deck. He couldn't contain a liberated smile as he squinted at the blazing sky. Landa never realized how much he'd missed something as simple as the sun.

The *Naumtsev's* hull provided a long black path above the waterline. Mixing with the men, he looked up to see the towering sail and the aft rudder behind it.

He studied his surroundings. The vessel was anchored in a circular lagoon. The closest shore was fifty yards to the right of the vessel. It would be an effortless swim. The island looked like Fiji. *Too good to be true,* he tried not to laugh.

The narrow deck was congested with crewmen, jumping in the water or seated on the hull. The chaos helped Landa blend within the crowd. He kept his head down when he walked under the sail, knowing the captain was certainly on top. He continued towards the stern.

A tall bulging Russian stepped into his path. He growled, *"Tvoy pervyy raz?"*

Landa didn't understand. He assessed the man who was roughly his same size. His bare, muscular torso was scribbled with tattoos. But

118

whether he'd win or lose in a tussle didn't matter; Landa didn't need any undue attention. He decided to just smile and shrug.

The large man loomed closer. In broken English he uttered, "I say, this is your first steel beach, eh?" The man gave a warped smile and then dove into the water.

Landa exhaled with relief and proceeded towards the rear. The rudder was easily fifteen feet high and had been modified to look like the creature's tail. The rudder contained the vessel's sonar array, which used hydrophones to detect sounds from outside sources.

Landa dashed into the shadow of the rudder. He crouched and looked back to see no one looking in his direction. On top of the sail, he saw silhouettes of the captain and a second person with long hair. *A female. It's Arrison,* he surmised. They were both looking forward.

Timing was critical. He slid on his belly down the curved hull to drop into the water without a splash. The sea was warm and clear. Immersed with just his eyes above water, he confirmed no one had seen him. He took a deep breath, submerged, and swam towards the shore.

℘

Arrison and Nikto shared a moment of quiet as they enjoyed the view. Arrison relished the warm sun on her face as she watched a school of yellow striped sergeant-majors in the translucent water. The captain watched over his men like a contented lifeguard.

Nikto lifted a radio, "Pavlo, this is Nikto."

Pavlo's voice replied, "*Da, Kapitan.*"

"Repair status."

"Aleksei is preparing the last weld between the turbine and—"

"We dive at 09:30." Nikto shouted with an irritated shake of his head. "Not a minute more. *Ponyal?*"

"Understood Kapitan. Over," Pavlo replied.

Nikto turned to see Arrison's raised brow. He grinned, ashamed he'd lost his composure. "Improvised repairs can be challenging."

"I get it," Arrison smiled to relieve the man. She looked out with a wistful tilt of her head at the thought of going ashore. It looked like a five-star island resort she could never afford. But there was nowhere

119

onshore to go. And possibly more to see beneath this world.

೦೦

Ned Landa crawled out of the waves and onto an overgrown beach. His wet clothing felt like forty extra pounds. He slogged behind an overturned palm without looking back. He crouched out of view and checked his pockets to confirm his binoculars, water, and life vest.

He needed a moment to catch his breath. Looking out at the *Naumtsev*, he could still see men jumping and swimming. He didn't see any heads looking his direction.

The profile of the immense vessel did look like a fierce, spiny monster. Landa was surprised to find himself sad about leaving the professor and her son behind. But he had given her a chance, and despite Nikto's deceitful motives, he was relatively sure he wouldn't harm them. He took a final glance at the *Naumtsev*, knowing it'd be his last.

Landa hiked inland. The jungle became darker the farther he trudged. The air smelled like damp earth after a rain shower. The faint hollers of the *Naumtsev*'s men were exchanged for squawks of wild parrots and the buzz of mosquitos in his ears. Landa wished he had a machete as he stepped around vines and dense cabbage palms.

To his surprise, he came upon a small clearing. It was an area that had been hacked clear by someone. There were stained wooden crates around a pit that had been used for a bonfire. He paused to breathe and study the camp. There were crushed cans of Prestige beer in the dirt. It was evident the island wasn't always uninhabited. Probably used by kids to party around a fire.

When Landa looked ahead, he saw the shimmer of the sea through the branches. Revitalized, he jogged along a path. It was indeed the ocean, just fifty feet away. He'd already reached the other side of the narrow peninsula. He smiled to absorb his view of freedom.

Landa stood on a rocky ten-foot cliff that faced northeast. He lifted binoculars to confirm a hilly mainland on the horizon. It was the west coast of Haiti.

"What do you think?" he asked himself. "Five miles?"

Landa was a certified advanced-level swimmer, courtesy of the Marine Corps. Aquatic Intensity Training required swimming 250 meters while wearing sixty pounds of gear. The notion of floating in a life vest, in heavily-traveled waters off Haiti, wasn't intimidating.

A sudden glimmer caught his eye. Landa aimed his binoculars to see a reflection from a small boat's windshield. His pulse quickened as he focused on the vessel. *How can I signal them?* He needed to get to them before the *Naumtsev's* radar picked them up.

As the boat cruised closer, Landa could see it was a small skiff, less than eighteen feet long. Then he noticed a second boat behind it, almost identical. He debated, *is this a good thing or terrible?* The Naumtsev might pick up their motors soon.

With the boats now approaching a hundred yards, he could see they appeared shabby with stripped paint. He could make out the figures of four men on each boat. *Haitian fishermen...* But he didn't see any poles or rigging. His breath halted at another possibility.

The thin men were carrying immense AK-47 rifles. They were not fishermen.

Landa lowered his binoculars with dread. "Pirates..."

He instantly dropped behind a bush. He peeked out to see a man standing on the bow to scan the island with binoculars. As the man rotated, he stopped, looking directly at Landa's location.

Landa paused as his mind raced. *Did he see me?* He had zero weapons. *Do I run? Take cover? Return to the Naumtsev?* He looked back out through the leaves.

The man on the bow aimed his AK directly at him. Then he fired.

Chapter Twenty-Three
Statues Fell at the Hand of God

Bullets struck palms above Landa with cracking *thwacks.*

Sprawled flat on the ground, he squeezed his eyes closed. He peeked out to see the men in both boats pointing and aiming guns his direction.

Three...two...one! With an internal countdown, he inhaled and sprung up to race inland through the brush. An obstacle course of coiled vines and dense growth slowed his pace.

Another burst of bullets peppered the branches above him. Twigs rained down.

ᘓᘐ

"Those are shots!" Nikto shouted, "Get down!" He shoved Arrison down by her shoulders so she was shielded by a partition.

Nikto lifted his radio, "Dmitri, report!"

Dmitri responded immediately, "Kapitan, three vessels. Could be pirates. Two small boats and perhaps a mother ship."

Nikto gnashed his teeth. He lifted his mic for the PA. "Emergency: all aboard! All aboard!" His amplified voice resounded within the lagoon.

The crewmen on deck looked up, confused. Some were still splashing around the perimeter of the *Naumtsev*.

"All aboard! That is an order!" Nikto repeated in Russian, "*Vse na bort! Teper'!*"

Nikto turned to see Arrison cowering, petrified. "We will be fine," he assured.

Her voice quivered, "Pirates, in the Caribbean?"

He huddled closer. "A coast with political and economic crisis can spark anarchy." He stood upright to see his men climbing aboard. He repeated into the PA, "Now! All—"

A spray of bullets sparked on the titanium just feet away. It sounded like clanging pots. Arrison screamed with hands over her ears.

"Go below!" Nikto barked as he opened the hatch. He looked the direction of the gunfire to see two small boats approaching the mouth of the lagoon.

❧

Landa heard the echo of shots as he ran, but it was no longer behind him. The rocky cliff was no place to dock, so he knew the boats were proceeding to the lagoon. *Which means,* he huffed, *they'll see the Naumtsev.*

He reached the clearing that had been a camp. He squatted behind wooden crates to catch his breath. In that instant, his psyche flashed to recall what he knew about piracy in the region.

Reports of piracy had increased in the waters between Honduras, Nicaragua, and Haiti. Economic crises were exploding between the countries, sparking chaos. As the rules of law failed, recent incidents had included robberies of merchant vessels and attacks on yachts.

Landa was jarred by another burst of gunfire. When he focused on a crate inches from his eyes, he saw "7.62 x 39 mm" stamped on the wood. It was the type of bullets used by AK-47s. He sprung upright; the boxes were ammunition crates. *This is the pirates' camp!*

He sprinted towards the lagoon with a new sense of urgency. He snaked through the trees until he saw the white sand of the beach. The sporadic crackle of gunfire was closer. Were the scrawny pirates actually attacking an armed nuclear vessel?

Landa found the same overturned palm on the beach from moments earlier. He panted, relieved, to see the *Naumtsev* had not departed. The last of the crewmen were scurrying into two open hatches. He looked to his right to see the two pirate boats blocking the mouth of the lagoon. They began to cruise towards the sub, firing their assault rifles as they moved.

Through his binoculars, Landa noticed a larger fifty-foot vessel a hundred yards behind the pirates. Though he hoped it was the Haitian Coast Guard, it looked like an old shrimp boat. He could see several figures on its deck. When he focused, he could see they were also carrying rifles. He'd heard stories of smaller pirate boats launching from mother ships.

Landa's breaths hastened, conflicted. He felt helpless as he watched three pirate boats targeting Nikto's vessel. He knew it'd be impossible for the scavengers to do any real harm, and the *Naumtsev* would certainly submerge and flee any minute.

So what about me? He tightened his jaw. He couldn't survive against a dozen armed men. Could he get back to the sub before it departed only to be held captive by a different set of criminals? Landa watched the last men dash into the sub with the hatches closing behind them.

Within seconds, two pirate skiffs pulled alongside the *Naumtsev*. The pirates leaped from their boats to climb onto the hull. All eight men were shirtless and barefoot. Some wore rags on their heads, and all of them carried AK-47s. They shouted to each other in creole, seeming desperate to find the hatches. Frustrated, they began to aimlessly shoot at the titanium hull.

Landa had to decide. He'd already been seen and was unarmed. There was nowhere to hide on the small island. He was no expert at computing probabilities, but it seemed he had a better chance of survival if he could get back to the sub, versus fighting the pirates on his own.

He stood and bolted towards the water.

❧

Captain Nikto charged into the control room with Arrison at his side.

"Kapitan, eight men are on the upper hull. Heavily armed," Dmitri declared.

Nikto watched a monitor above Dmitri's head. Shirtless armed men were scurrying on the *Naumtsev's* hull. They appeared to be searching for any hatch or vent.

Incensed, Nikto barked, "Prepare to dive."

Pavlo turned from his console with wide eyes. "Kapitan, Aleksei reports the welds require ten more minutes." He swallowed, "Ivan was our lead engineer."

Nikto glared at being questioned. Before he could respond, Dmitri shouted.

"They are damaging the hull." Onscreen, the pirates began to fire at the vessel's aft rudder. "They could destroy our sonar array!"

Nikto scowled as if his own offspring were being attacked. He tightened his eyes, "Auxiliary voltage to the deck mesh."

Pavlo exclaimed, "That's 115 volts, two amps—"

"Make it so!" Nikto snarled, furious of his distrust. "*Seychas!*"

Pavlo turned back to his console. Though Arrison was terrified of the armed men, she was speechless at the captain's outburst.

❧

Landa struggled to swim in his waterlogged uniform. He panted between unrelenting strokes. He squinted in the salt water to see the *Naumtsev* still thirty yards away. He pushed harder.

Through the water he heard shots that seemed closer. He looked up to see a man with a rag on his head firing his gun at the aft hatch. When the wiry man turned, he gazed directly at Landa in the water. The man's eyes widened, and he shouted in creole to his cohorts.

Landa halted, treading water. The other men looked his direction and aimed their weapons. He inhaled to dive but froze at what he saw next. Landa was stunned and then aghast.

Sparks spewed at the pirates' bare feet. Their perspiring bodies stiffened like boards. Wisps of smoke rose from their glistening scalps.

125

The *Naumtsev's* deck was electrified with 115 volts from its auxiliary engines, carried through a fine wire mesh that covered the hull's rubberized anechoic plating.

The netting was energized with a surge of milliamperes. The captain knew, at sixteen milliamps, the assailants would be unable to move. Their bare feet would remain locked on the netting without any ability to jump overboard. A hundred milliamps would then deliver muscular contractions and lung failure. At 2,000, their hearts would stop with scorched internal organs.

The entire power surge lasted three seconds.

The pirates' eyes rolled up into their heads. Smoke floated from their locked jaws. All eight men fell onto the deck like statues.

જી

The surge caused the lights to flicker off in the control room. With a mechanized hum, the lights resumed. Arrison, Nikto and the entire crew were riveted to the video screen. No one spoke as the image revealed the eight fallen bodies.

Arrison turned to Nikto with wide, misty eyes. The man who ostensibly shared a passion for the sea, and seemed to care so much for her security, stood rigid with a vacant expression.

With a fragile voice she asked, "Did we just watch those men get executed?"

Chapter Twenty-Four
The Nature of a Scorpion

Chandler and Pilar sat cross-legged on the torpedo room floor. When the lights went out, the abrupt darkness made him gasp.

Pilar placed a hand on his shoulder. Within seconds, the lights flickered back on to the relief of a pale, clammy Chandler gripping a bottle of vodka. From their hazy eyes and her lipstick on the rim, it was clear they'd been passing the bottle for some time.

She tried to rationalize, "Where else could they have stored Ivan's body? You wouldn't want him kept in the food coolers."

Chandler convulsed at the image. She snatched the bottle out of his hand and took a swig. The lights dimmed with the faint hum of the diesels.

Chandler looked up, "What's going on up there?"

✑

Feeling like her legs were giving out from anxiety, Arrison took a seat in the control room. Captain Nikto huddled over her with blazing eyes.

"They were savages." He stressed the word. "I've seen their damage. They kidnap women and children. They assassinate prisoners if ransoms are not paid." He leaned closer, "I've seen what they've done to women."

127

Still in shock, Arrison rolled her eyes up at the man.

"Kapitan, the mother ship is approaching," Dmitri announced. "They are firing weapons."

Nikto spun towards the monitor to see the larger pirate vessel less than a hundred meters away. It continued to face the *Naumtsev* as if it were a foolish game of courage.

He lifted his radio, "Aleksei, weld or not, we must dive!"

A hectic voice replied, "We haven't tested the seal—"

Nikto cut him off, shouting into the PA. "All departments: rig for dive."

"Rig for dive," Pavlo confirmed. "Depth two-zero meters as we exit the lagoon. We need more depth."

Nikto nodded, "Move and we'll get our depth. Open main vents."

"We have a green board." A man checked the Hull Opening Panel, "All hatches sealed."

Pavlo turned to Nikto, "All rigged for dive except for engineering."

Nikto's face reddened. He shouted the venerable command, "Dive, dive, dive!"

The *Naumtsev* churned forward in the lagoon. The pirates' bodies were strewn across the deck or drifting off the edges.

Ten yards to the side of the sub, Ned Landa labored to swim. He glanced through the froth to see the *Naumtsev* begin to lunge forward. It was like swimming towards a dock that started to move away. He threw his arms forward and kicked with pure adrenalin to reach the vessel.

Dmitri leaned towards his monitor and wrinkled his nose. "Who's that in the water?"

"Dead pirates," Pavlo retorted.

Dmitri zoomed the image and adjusted his glasses. "It's a man. In uniform and he's swimming." He shouted over his shoulder, "One of our men!"

Nikto stepped over to study the screen. "No." He sneered, irate. "It is Ned Landa."

Arrison sprung from her seat to see for herself. Onscreen, the view was from a camera on top of the sail. To the right of the sub, a figure dressed in black was splashing towards the *Naumtsev*.

"Hatches are sealed." Pavlo looked to Nikto, "Full stop?"

Nikto paused, deliberating. It took three long seconds to utter, "No."

Arrison gasped, "You can't just leave him!"

"He wanted to return to land," Nikto's eyes raged. "He belongs with savages!"

◈

Landa swam within ten feet of the *Naumtsev's* side. His progress was slowed by a rolling wake from the vessel. Though the sub was cruising no more than four knots, it created significant waves. Landa's shoulders ached, and his legs burned, churning with every ounce of his dwindling energy.

Advancing within two feet, his blurred eyes saw a handgrip on the hull. As if coiled against an imaginary wall, Landa exploded forward, lunging for the rung. His right hand slipped off the wet handle. But like a windmill, his left arm revolved to grasp it as tight as a wrench.

Landa struggled to hoist himself up. His biceps flexed to climb one rung at a time up the curved hull. Only a five-foot width of the deck was still above water. Breathless, he reached the top of the hull and crouched. He gulped air and coughed salt water from his lungs.

As the *Naumtsev* picked up speed, Landa gazed forward to gain his bearings. He stood in a crouched position, with the sail and bow many yards ahead of him. Water was rising on both sides. He franticly searched to find the aft hatch, only to confirm it had been sealed.

◈

The crew gazed at the monitor as if riveted by a movie. They watched Landa give up on the aft hatch, to then hike towards the bow in a desperate search for any way in. The man was like a rat on a sinking ship.

Arrison looked at the men, horrified. "You're going to watch him panic until he drowns?"

Nikto clenched his jaw, frustrated. He refused to reply.

Onscreen, Arrison saw Landa balancing on the center of the hull, water climbing on both sides. "Someone, please." she implored.

"Kapitan," Pavlo interjected, "Too late to open the bow hatch unless we stop."

"We will not stop!" Nikto shouted.

Arrison turned to the captain with eyes that plead for him to reconsider.

"Kapitan!" Dmitri exclaimed. "The pirate vessel is firing a .50 caliber."

She stared, unflinching, into Nikto's eyes as he made fists at his sides.

After an excruciating moment of silence, Nikto barked, "Open missile door twelve!"

Pavlo frowned, confused by the command.

∽

Landa shuffled towards the bow, water approaching two feet on both sides. He cowered as .50 caliber bullets smacked the hull twenty feet away. He dropped to his belly, realizing it'd do no good if one of the massive shells ricocheted through his flesh.

He peeked through his fingers to see the pirate boat approaching. The old shrimp boat had outriggers used to launch their skiffs, and a .50 caliber gun mounted on its bow.

I should've known, Landa groaned. Of course, Nikto wouldn't let him back onboard. He guessed the vessel had cameras somewhere, and they were undoubtedly watching him search for a way in. *They're probably laughing.* Nikto's final snub, now the *Cyclops* had been fixed.

Water was rushing towards him as the *Naumtsev* gradually submerged. The pirates would fire again, and even if he jumped overboard with his life vest, he'd be a floating target. He could hide behind the sail, but that'd only add seconds. *It's just a matter of time.*

Ned Landa hadn't seen his daughter in a year and hadn't been to church in ten years. But he prayed. He squeezed his eyes closed, wishing he'd taken so many different paths. Despite his transgressions, he would die an honorable Marine's death.

Water was now touching his thighs on each side. There was no need to hold his breath. *Let's get this over with.*

His eyes sprung open at a mechanical hiss. Like a mirage six feet away, an enormous eight-foot rectangular hatch opened. It took him a second to process it was a vertical-launch missile door, *but Nikto doesn't have any missiles.*

With no deliberation, Landa jumped to his feet and dove into the hatch, headfirst. The hydraulic door closed behind him with a mechanical thud as the vessel submerged.

ᘓ

Adjacent to the torpedo room, Pilar led Chandler to the missile compartment. It was equally industrial, with upright shafts for missiles that weren't there.

Chandler was thankful she was guiding him by the hand. The effects of the vodka seemed stronger than what he'd read.

"This area's okay, but…" He had a slight slur. "Can we go back to look out the windows?"

They flinched at an abrupt thud and a muffled shout above them. Void of any rational concern, Pilar hit a switch on the ceiling.

When the automated door opened, Ned Landa toppled out, falling six feet to the deck, followed by several gallons of sea water.

Sprawled in a puddle, Landa looked up with a bleeding lip. Momentarily dazed, he gave a crooked smile, "Hi-ya kids. Stayin' outta' trouble?"

ᘓ

Captain Nikto leaned forward on a handrail to glare at the monitor. Dead ahead was the approaching pirate mother ship.

"We got our depth," Pavlo announced. "Twenty-one meters."

As if waiting for a precise moment, he growled, "Ramming speed, four-zero knots."

"Four-zero knots," Pavlo confirmed.

Arrison remained seated. Her emotions were depleted, and she was in no position to beg for anything more. She was grateful Landa was back onboard, and Chandler was reportedly safe.

She knew what was coming next. Arrison looked down for any sort of seatbelt, but there were none. She gripped a rail next to her and looked up at the monitor.

A seagull's view would have witnessed a 375-foot serrated monster swimming six feet beneath the clear emerald sea. Though submerged, its sharp sail sliced through the surface. Its bayonet nose was concealed just below the waterline.

The monster sped directly for the pirate's fifty-foot boat. Men scurried on its deck, shouting and pointing at the beast, bewildered. A man fired the .50 caliber machine gun.

The *Naumtsev* impaled the boat like a lance. In a single move, the impact thrust the bow skyward as the hatchet-like sail split the boat down its center. The shattered halves collapsed, and the *Naumtsev's* steel spur struck the boat's gas tanks.

When the spark ignited the fuel, the *Naumtsev* was fifteen feet beneath the surface. Its fin and tail vanished under a deafening sphere of fire.

There was an unnerving silence in the control room. Arrison watched the crew resume their duties as if it were just another day at the office.

She looked at each man, searching for any shred of sentiment.

Nikto stood firm in the center of the room. He finally spoke as he turned towards the door, "I will be in my office. Alone."

PART IV
OCULAR PROOF

"A hundred suspicions don't make a proof."
—Fyodor Dostoyevsky, *Crime and Punishment.*

Chapter Twenty-Five
The Pry Bar

Guanacaste, Costa Rica

The gorgeous estate overlooked thirty miles of pristine Pacific coastline from an altitude of 2,000 feet. The two-story home was Spanish Colonial, and its landscaped grounds included an orange grove and a horse pasture. The backdrop was green-swathed volcanoes to the east, and the azure sea to the west. The owner called it her *el cielo en la cima del mundo*. Heaven on the top of the world.

The homeowner had chosen to live alone. Aside from its splendor, the house had been selected because it was far from any potential neighbors. After all she had endured, she craved solitude.

The owner put on a silk robe as she stepped out of her marble bath. With such privacy, she played her *cumbia* dance music at full volume throughout the spacious home. Singing along to the harmony, she combed her long dark hair while studying her face in the mirror. As an early-forties Latina, she tried to preserve her smooth skin by avoiding the sun when she could. She was proud of her cheekbones, and her body was toned with age-appropriate curves. She'd been called stunning in a previous life. Today there was no need for heavy make-up or glamorous clothing in her private heaven on earth.

She looked up at a skylight to see a pink dusk. Grooving to the music, she swayed to the back patio door to enjoy the sunset. Maybe some wine on the balcony.

When she opened the blinds, she released a bloodcurdling scream. Looming in the window was an ominous figure in all black. His helmeted face jerked towards her.

She spun to dash to the closest exit, a French door at the end of a hall. As she rounded the corner, an identical figure stepped into view behind the glass. The nightmarish troop lifted a gun and tapped it on the glass. Clutching her robe, she sprinted towards the home's front doors. Her screams were dampened by the pulsing music.

When she opened the tall oak door, a third black troop blocked her path, aiming an AR-15 assault rifle to her face. She froze in her tracks, unable to breathe with short gasps.

She didn't realize the troops were with the *Unidad Especial de Intervencion*, or Special Intervention Unit, an obscure Costa Rican Special Forces Unit. They were part of the Intelligence and Security Directorate, which reported directly to the Minister of the Presidency.

The mostly peaceful Costa Rica didn't have any army or military forces. It did, however, maintain a police force to keep public order within its borders and surrounding territory.

The woman gasped with panic, clasping her robe in fear of being assaulted. She saw two black SUVs at the base of her driveway. The armed troop stepped back as a stocky man in a gray business suit approached. The man was bald with a staunch frown. He lifted a hand for the soldier to stand down.

The woman calmed slightly, realizing the man was dressed too conservatively to be from any cartel she'd ever known.

He stopped two feet in front of her. The troops lowered their weapons and maintained a perimeter behind him. The man finally spoke without any pleasantries.

"You are Mirta Salazar, yes?" he asked in Spanish.

Shock crossed her face. "No, I am Lina Negroni," she stammered in Spanish. "Visiting from San Jose—"

The man cut her off with a raised hand. "I am with Attorney General Martinez's office in Bogotá." He raised his thick brows, "The same man who gave you your new name."

Her lip quivered. She sounded rehearsed as she repeated, "I am Lina Negroni, visiting from San—"

"You are Mirta Salazar, wife of Ricardo Salazar," the man interrupted with a raised voice. "Do you wish to confirm with a physical examination?"

Mirta looked at the ground and shook her head.

The man continued, "Our agreement states you shall continue to cooperate with any of our investigations, at our request." He flashed a sinister smile. "Or you can join your husband in La Modelo prison."

Mirta became flushed. As she searched for a response, she glanced at the wall inside her door. In a gold frame was a portrait of a beautiful girl, a near clone of herself. It was the face of Pilar, her missing daughter, when she was about fifteen years old.

She looked into the man's eyes. "What is it you need?"

∽

The door opened to Professor Arrison's quarters. Light from the corridor created a bright sliver across her bed. Chandler entered her room with Pilar at his side.

He approached his mother and touched her arm. "Mom…wake up," He spoke in a low voice, "You gotta' see it."

Arrison's eyes opened. She sat upright, blinking to discern the figures of her son and Pilar. "Are we there?"

"Yes," Chandler smiled. "And it's incredible."

Chapter Twenty-Six
The King's Garden

Gulf of Cazones

Professor Arrison located the grand parlor in record time. One ladder down, then forward towards the bow. When she entered with Chandler and Pilar, she noticed the lights had been dimmed to allow the large windows to take center stage. Armchairs had been arranged in front of each window as if they were opera boxes to witness something amazing.

To her right, she was surprised to see Captain Nikto and Landa seated together at the window. She assumed he would be furious at Landa for attempting an escape. Had they reconciled in some way? Landa probably accepted responsibility to curry favor from the captain. Just so he can escape again.

"Good morning." The captain noticed her arrival with a smile. He pointed to a copper samovar in the center of the room. "We have fresh-ground Sumatra coffee from the Sunda Islands for our show this morning."

Arrison skipped the coffee and proceeded to the opposite window. The three sat and scooted forward, inches from the eight-foot circular window. Their faces were illuminated by the view.

Twenty-five feet below, they saw a vibrant reef teaming with tropical fish. Traveling less than four knots, Arrison watched enormous orange starfish glide by that were over a foot in diameter. Soaring yellow elkhorn coral nearly grazed the ship.

"Where exactly are we?" Arrison asked.

Nikto walked over to join them. "I call this place *podvodnyy ray.* My undersea Eden." His eyes sparkled, relishing the view. "I can only reveal we are somewhere between Jardinas de la Reina and Cayo Piedra."

The reef was bursting with colors more vivid than any Arrison had seen. Red, orange, and purple corals. Undulating ribbons of lime-green kelp. Lustrous schools of yellow tail. The clarity and colors gave the reef a surreal quality.

"I know about Cayo Piedra." Chandler looked at Pilar, "It was Castro's secret island."

"As in Fidel Castro?" Landa approached with a mug of coffee.

Chandler nodded. He looked at Nikto, "Captain, can you at least admit if we're somewhere near the Bay of Pigs?"

Nikto raised his brows at the question. "Very well. We are indeed sixteen kilometers from Bahia de Cochinos."

Chandler turned to Landa, "Castro had a private island because of the Bay of Pigs invasion."

Landa dipped his head, "How is that?"

"The US's attack on Cuba in 1961 was a disaster. Our boats didn't know about the shallow reefs. After the failed assault, Castro came out to explore the entire region. He asked a local fisherman to give him a tour. That's when he discovered Cayo Piedra, a small island ten miles off the coast. Known only to locals."

"So, how is it Castro's secret island?" Landa smirked.

"He loved it so much, he took it for himself," Chandler shrugged. "Castro ordered his men to build him and his wife an enormous house overlooking the coast. Their own private island."

"While his citizens suffered in poverty," Pilar scoffed, "Castro was in a hammock in paradise."

Landa grinned at her, equally cynical.

"It is true," Nikto conceded. "Only Castro's personal yacht was allowed in these waters." He waved towards the reef. "Imagine exploring all of this with no other humans."

The guests turned their attention outside. Arrison and Chandler gasped and pointed at lobsters over two feet in length. There were at least a half dozen red and brown Caribbean spiny lobsters. They crawled carefree on the seafloor, never knowing human predators.

Landa chuckled, "At Joe's in Miami those tails would be five hundred bucks a piece."

"This is the result of the US's attack. No humans allowed." Nikto watched from over their shoulders. "Closures from you're abhorrent COVID-19 made the waters of Venice crystal-clear within weeks. Imagine waters that haven't been touched by man for six decades."

Chandler nodded in a daze. "The fish and lobster were like the king's deer."

∽

To Arrison, this dreamlike playground was entirely conceivable. She'd read about the other location Nikto had mentioned, Jardinas de la Reina. The untouched area was a sprawling reef stretching over two-hundred kilometers. Cuba's political isolation over the past sixty years had created an astounding marine preserve.

Arrison tried to envision how the Caribbean would have appeared without man's destructive touch. The brightest color she'd ever seen on a reef in Florida was from a sunken Budweiser bottle. Castro's paranoia about his citizens escaping by sea had inadvertently preserved the entire region. The waters were off-limits, no commercial fishing, no human visitors. The much-speculated Utopia of the Caribbean had existed all along, just off the shores of Cuba.

"How much longer can this exist?" Nikto added with a critical tone, "Without chemical runoff from golf courses? The inevitable algae blooms."

Their attention was drawn to the window as two goliath groupers swam by, each over five feet in length and easily six hundred pounds. Their spotted bodies against the vibrant backdrop looked almost psychedelic.

"Whoa!" Landa shouted. He pointed at enormous clams over three feet in diameter. "That'd feed an entire platoon!"

Arrison's mouth dropped to see a bed of massive clams. "*Tridacna*, colossal clams?" The clams were the size of suitcases, with deeply furrowed shells and incandescent royal-blue patterns. Some shells were ajar like enormous jaws waiting for prey. Arrison looked at Nikto, "That's impossible, they only exist in the South Pacific."

"And extremely endangered," Chandler added.

"Precisely why I transplanted a colony to this garden," Nikto stepped closer. "The waters and temperature closely resemble their indigenous homes. Some are a hundred years old. Legends say they have swallowed divers whole." He looked at Arrison with a raised brow, "You should see their pearls; the size of billiard balls."

Landa's eyes went round at the notion.

"The irony of a nation that does not progress," Nikto gave a bittersweet smile. "It creates a revitalized world right off its shores."

Arrison turned to him with an inquisitive frown. "So, this isn't Guanahacabibes."

"Not yet." He touched her shoulder. "Soon. Very soon."

❧

Dr. Yuri was ready for his dreaded but necessary chore.

At the captain's direction, he played "Yaroslavna's Lament" from Alexander Borodin's opera *Prince Igor*. The Russian aria played softly through the *Naumtsev*'s speakers. The haunting words invoked images of the hero's wife as she appealed to the forces of nature—the wind, the sun, and the waters—for her husband's enduring safety.

As the evocative melody drifted through the corridors, Dr. Yuri chose two crewmen to assist. The men remained solemn as the elder doctor led them into the torpedo room.

Dr. Yuri paused in the chamber to locate the proper hatch. He nodded at his two assistants. It was time.

The wrapped corpse of Ivan Popov was gently removed from the tube. The men were methodical, treating their fallen comrade's body with reverence. Dr. Yuri noticed the Mylar wrap around Ivan's face had

141

been moved. He shuddered, praying the vessel didn't have rats.

The body was placed on a stretcher, and the two men carried it out of the torpedo room. The stretcher was carried delicately down two stairways, back to the infirmary. They placed the body in the medical bay, ready for the next task. The mournful music fit the mood.

Under the direction of Dr. Yuri—who required a few nips from his flask—Ivan's body was prepared according to maritime tradition. It was wrapped and sewn in a shroud of sailcloth. The only omission from 18th century custom was the last stitch was historically sewn through the deceased's nostrils to awaken a man mistakenly in a coma. That would not be needed for poor Ivan.

The men then carried the swathed body down to the *Naumtsev's* lowest level. Yuri entered the moon well and the men placed Ivan's body on the deck under the *Cyclops.*

The opera played on.

৩

Though Arrison could never grow tired of looking out the window, she had a gnawing impatience. Considering the approximate time she'd woken up and how lunch had been served with Nikto's rigid itinerary, she estimated she'd been in the parlor over four hours.

Four hours at forty knots, she made a few calculations. Forty knots was approximately forty-six miles per hour. A brass compass in the parlor showed they'd been traveling due west. *That's almost two hundred miles west of the Bay of Pigs.* She jotted that in her journal.

Arrison looked up to see Chandler and Pilar returning from wherever they'd been. Arrison smiled; she liked Pilar, though there was a sadness about her. Nikto had said she was the daughter of a former business partner, and she was now in a safer world. The girl seemed to smile more around Chandler, and she'd never seen her son so exhilarated by another person. It had all been books and journals until, she withered, *until our captivity.*

Their predicament was a concern that would not go away. Were they passengers or prisoners? A passenger would have a final terminus to disembark. Did they? Nikto had sworn he'd never allow them to betray his existence. Would that allow any exceptions? Landa's attempt to escape had been almost disastrous.

In the states, she and Chandler were certainly missing persons, undoubtedly presumed dead. But she had to admit there was no real sense of urgency. They had no other family or relatives to contact to assure they were safe. Were her students worried or upset?

She had to admit Nikto's tour of his domain was fascinating. Castro's private reefs were a dream come true and would have a significant impact within the marine community. Couldn't Nikto see the benefits of sharing the coordinates with her colleagues? The research possibilities were boundless. More people could witness untouched nature.

Nikto would certainly say, "People are precisely the problem!"

Arrison found herself somber when she should be excited. What would be their fate? She turned to the other Iris to see Pilar and Chandler standing close. Arrison's own romantic life had flourished and concluded with no regrets. But what did it mean for them? Pursue their relationship while confined underwater for the rest of their days?

Arrison turned at the sound of Landa and the captain entering the parlor.

Nikto smiled, "I have confirmed the *Cyclops* is fully repaired." He approached Arrison at the window. "Thanks to Mr. Landa's fine craftsmanship."

Landa forced a smile. "Took longer than I thought."

Pilar and Chandler joined them. All five gazed out the window to see it had grown darker. Fish were just scarcely defined shadows. The solar rays diminished by every degree of depth. Arrison had watched the view slowly fade from aqua, to navy-blue, into ink black.

"We are now between Guanahacabibes and the Yucatan peninsula." Nikto remained behind them. "Approaching 600 meters."

"That's impossible," Landa chuckled. "The max depth for Navy subs is around 250 meters."

Nikto gave a smug grin. "That is the depth your militaries admit, but the true depth is classified. The *Naumtsev* has an outer hull of titanium, over a pressure hull of two-inch thick high-tensile steel."

That hushed Landa, who had no choice but to accept his words. He turned to Arrison and Chandler, "What's this Guana-haca-whatever you two been going on about?"

"It's just a myth," Chandler chuckled. "An area that's—"

"Been inaccessible for decades," Arrison scowled at Chandler, troubled by his lack of faith. "You think it's a myth? It was reported in *National Geographic* and the *Washington Post*."

"The theory was reported," Chandler retorted.

"Be your own judge," Nikto remained diplomatic. He touched a switch on the wall and called out, "Dmitri, floodlights, please."

At his command, lights ignited outside the windows. Arrison looked out to see spotlights shining down from the *Naumtsev*. Since there was nothing for the beams to reflect off of, the lights gave the water the appearance of milky fog.

Chandler and Arrison cupped their hands to the glass, waiting for anything. Nothing but twirling particles of plankton.

"What? "Landa shrugged, "I don't get it."

After an eternal pause, light revealed a surface beneath the vessel. All five craned their necks to look down. Through the haze, a surface the color of sand appeared, but it was flat as if it were paved. It was the width of the *Naumtsev*, and there were seams every five yards like immense slabs had been laid to form a path.

"It looks like a road." Chandler spun to his mother, "Like the Bimini Road in the Bahamas."

"What's Bimini Road?" Landa grumbled.

"North of Bimini there are flat formations underwater that appear manmade," Arrison explained. "Archeologists theorized it was an ancient road. But a UM study dated the slabs to be over 3,500 years old. Thousands of years before the earliest known inhabitants."

The three visitors huddled close to look out the window. The *Naumtsev's* spotlights continued to illuminate the bizarre, flat path. It continued downward like a ramp, deeper into the darkness. Coral rocks came into view that looked like symmetrical blocks lining the path.

"Mom, look!" Chandler exclaimed. Through the blur, the path appeared to be obstructed by several stone columns resting on their sides. As the view cleared, the columns appeared too perfect to be random formations. They looked like crumbled pillars, two feet in diameter and twenty feet long. When the *Naumtsev* slowed over them, lights revealed engravings down their length, with pedestal bases. The fallen columns were unquestionably manmade.

Wonder softened Landa's face. He turned to Pilar. "What exactly are we seeing?"

She tilted her head with a grin. "It's the road to Atlantis, Mr. Landa."

Chapter Twenty-Seven
Beyond the Pillars of Heracles

"The theories are true?" Arrison's voice was an octave higher.

Nikto just smiled. "As first suggested in 1951, then confirmed by sonar in 2001. Symmetrical structures and pyramids of stone. You are among the few non-communists to witness it for yourselves."

Just hearing the word aloud gave Arrison goosebumps. *Atlantis.* It even rolled of the tongue as mysterious, exhilarating, and preposterous. Landa and the rest would consider her as respectable as a UFO fanatic. She didn't care.

Then again, they were equally fixed to the window. Her stomach stirred with anticipation. In her profession, she wasn't qualified to have an intellectual debate about the existence of Atlantis. But she had read volumes about undersea discoveries that fueled speculation.

After Captain Nikto had promised to take them to Guanahacabibes, she'd reviewed every journal in his library, including a book about symbols found in Cuba's Punta del Este caves depicting the demise of Atlantis.

Scientists were taught to regard coincidences as inherently meaningless. But weren't there too many auspicious discoveries to dismiss the notion entirely?

As Arrison leaned towards the window, a torrent of research engulfed her memories.

ↁ

In 2001, deep beneath the Yucatan Channel off the coast of Guanahacabibes, experts uncovered what appeared to be a lost city. Sonar equipment aboard a research vessel detected what appeared to be roads, pyramids, and other structures at a depth of 2,200 feet.

They had been mapping the ocean floor of Cuba's territorial waters. Remote sonar equipment had sent back footage of linear stone features and large stone blocks, with edges worn by the sea.

The discovery ignited theories about the presence of Atlantis, as described by philosopher Plato more than 2,350 years earlier.

Arrison had taken Philosophy in college. Her first exposure to the notion of Atlantis was reading Plato's description of the mythical island.

According to Plato, Atlantis was an island empire founded by Poseidon, god of the seas. Zeus unleashed "earthquakes and floods" that submerged Atlantis between 8570 BC and 9421 BC.

Following Columbus' landfall in the Bahamas in 1492, explorers discovered stories from the natives about a flood that had divided a larger landmass, killing the residents and leaving behind the many islands that remain today. They described "fire falling from the sky."

Based on the parallel accounts, had some cosmic event caused a catastrophe in the Caribbean? Was it tied to the destruction of a city called Atlantis?

Plato had described Atlantis as an east-west positioned island approximately 600 by 400 kilometers in size. To the north, were "mountain ranges," while the southern end was at sea-level.

Arrison had to admit Cuba's topography was an almost exact description of Plato's Atlantis.

Furthermore, the Punta del Este caves of Cuba were filled with petroglyphs of concentric circles and geometric shapes that are thousands of years old. Archaeologists theorized the drawings reflect a cosmic catastrophe, such as a comet, which had devastated Atlantis.

It wasn't just decades-old conjecture. Revered modern periodicals discussed the same information.

Kevin Sullivan, a Pulitzer Prize-winning correspondent for the *Washington Post,* described Cuba's deep-water findings, "The videotape, made by an unmanned submarine, shows massive stones in oddly symmetrical square and pyramid shapes in the deep-sea darkness… Smooth, white stones are laid out in a geometric pattern. Like fragments of a city, in a place where nothing manmade should exist."

Arrison never dreamed she'd be witnessing the edifices with her own eyes from mere yards away.

৫১

"So why have I never heard of it?" Landa chuckled. "It'd be the top story on every news."

"Think about it, Ned." Arrison didn't back down, "Sixty years of communist rule. Castro had no resources to research. Do you think he'd share with the world what he possessed in his private backyard?"

"Mom," Chandler called out.

She turned to see him gawking out the window. She joined him to see the spotlights revealing a structure that looked like a crumbled Grecian temple. The lights followed its form to expose a triangular pediment atop leaning columns, laced with a thousand fish.

Chandler pivoted to Nikto's bookshelf to take a well-worn book, *Cyphers of Punta del Este.* He flipped to a page to show the others.

Pilar and Landa turned from the window to see the book opened to a page with black and white photographs. They showed drawings on a cave wall, sketched by primitive man.

"These petroglyphs," Chandler spoke fast. "They depict a cataclysm, destroying Atlantis."

The others leaned closer to observe. Arrison pointed to a drawing of a circular swirling pattern like a spherical maze. Landa seemed more interested than she'd predicted.

They turned back to the window. The *Naumtsev's* lights slowly zigzagged to behold stones assembled in the shape of a large pyramid.

Arrison was wordless. As the lights traced the structure upwards—

ascending above the *Naumtsev*—she estimated the height at almost a hundred feet. Unlike the smooth pyramids of Egypt, the sides had a tiered design like Mayan structures. Though it was streaked with growth, the deliberate design was indisputable.

"My god..." was all Landa could utter.

With tears in her eyes, Arrison turned to Chandler. "Your father would have loved this." She gave a bittersweet smile.

Chandler returned the smile with quaking lips. "He would have."

Dmitri's voice rang from the intercom, "Captain: we have reached our destination."

"Drop anchor," Nikto replied aloud. He turned to the four, "Time to suit-up for a special memorial."

Chandler's eyes widened. "Suit up?"

Chapter Twenty-Eight
Slumbering Sentinels

Captain Nikto led Pilar and the three guests into the moon well.

It was Arrison's first time seeing the moon well. She knew research subs that had smaller versions of the same thing, a floodable chamber to allow divers and equipment to move between the sub's interior and the water. As with most innovations on the *Naumtsev*, it was beyond what she could have imagined.

Arrison's eyes were drawn to the most prominent thing in the room: the *Cyclops*, hanging from its hoist. It was almost identical to minisubs that could dive two miles below the surface. She'd seen a documentary about director James Cameron's sub, the *Deepsea Challenger*, which had completed the deepest solo dive to the bottom of the Mariana Trench, nearly seven miles deep. Arrison felt like a high school violin teacher gazing at a Stradivarius.

Chandler walked straight to the dive suits hanging on the wall. He beamed, "These are like a cross between an astronaut and Iron Man."

"Indeed," Nikto smiled. "ADS exosuits, atmospheric dive suits." They were gray metal with maroon joints on the arms, legs, neck, and torso. Chandler compared his hand to its hefty mechanical glove.

"Light-weight aluminum alloy," Nikto explained. "Divers can work safely to depths of 700 meters and still have flexibility with unique rotary joints for delicate work."

Arrison stepped closer to study the details. "Pressurized?"

"Yes. The same cabin pressure as the surface. No danger of decompression sickness or nitrogen narcosis."

Chandler tapped the helmet's teardrop-shaped globe face mask, "An almost perfect 180-degree view."

"Reinforced acrylic with integrated lights." Nikto nodded. "The wearer need not be a skilled swimmer." He smiled at Arrison and Chandler, "But it would help."

Their heads turned to see two crewmen enter. One was fully suited aside from his helmet.

"These gentlemen will help fit the suits on each of you." Nikto spread his hands, "It is as easy as walking in a park."

The thought of diving wasn't daunting to Chandler. Thanks to his mother's vocation, he'd been a PADI-certified advanced open water diver since he was eleven.

The crewmen were methodical, applying the suits to each of them. They stepped into the suits, which were sealed in the back by an assistant.

"The helmet is the last thing installed before the diver enters the water," the crewman muttered in a thick accent. Each diver had to adjust their helmet's neck ring. Once locked, each diver had to inhale to create a suction on the neck ring, indicating a proper seal.

When Captain Nikto, Pilar and the guests were fully dressed, they were led by four suited crewmen to a platform beneath the *Cyclops*.

Chandler froze. There on the deck was a wrapped corpse, bound in a tight linen. He knew it was the dead body from the torpedo tube. His anxiety subsided, knowing it was the crewman who had died trying to save the *Naumtsev*. Nikto had explained this outing would be a ceremony to bury the man.

They stood on the platform, suspended over the well by steel cables as thick as a man's thumb. Chandler looked down at the floor. It was a lattice of grated steel so he could see the door beneath it.

All nine divers were a snug fit on the platform. Ivan's wrapped corpse was added to the floor. Nikto nodded to a crewman who hit a switch. A motorized winch began to lower the platform.

Chandler awkwardly bent to look below his feet. The well door opened like an elevator door on the floor. He whispered on his voice-activated mic, "This is it."

☙

Ned Landa estimated the *Naumtsev* was anchored twelve feet above the seabed. Floodlights lit the barren landscape below. Curious fish flurried away as the platform carrying the divers descended.

The stage landed on the seafloor with a small cloud of sediment. Nikto and Pilar were the first to step off. Then the four crewmen, who carried the wrapped corpse on a stretcher like pallbearers. Landa followed, along with Dr. Arrison and Chandler.

Landa tried to calm his breathing. He looked up in his dome helmet. It looked like night skies above him, with just the glimmer of fluttering plankton. To his sides were structures set against a backdrop of black. The 180-degree view looked like a virtual reality game. The open vista suppressed any feelings of claustrophobia, though the suffocating darkness was menacing.

He wondered if this was how it felt to walk on the moon. Everyone looked like they were moving in slow motion. Despite the suits, it wasn't difficult to walk. The weight was balanced by its buoyancy. Landa looked down to see his heavy feet create a trail of disturbed sand. When he looked up, they were dwarfed by ruins that were inconceivable.

Captain Nikto and Pilar led the group, aiming powerful spotlights. As they hiked the path, their lights revealed immense leaning columns that seemed suspended with vine-like flora. Thirty-foot-tall formations had the unequivocal outlines of human statues. Shadows of large fish slithered away from the light, back into their ancient homes.

Landa didn't know anything about Roman or Greek or even Aztec history, but the seaweed-covered ruins looked like every photo he'd ever seen on the subjects. Some structures were several stories in height.

The columns had ridges down their length. Their triangular tops had etchings that had to be ancient words.

Grasping the entirety of what he was seeing, he realized he was within an entire city, not just random relics. Their straight path had been a central road. Streets branched off to other structures with their roofs open to the sky. Temples had fallen when their columns crumbled to the earth. Something had annihilated this prehistoric city.

He understood why people like the professor found it fascinating, but he felt like he was walking in a sunken ghost town. He could imagine the black, beady eyes of unknown sea creatures watching them from ancient windows.

Landa took a deep breath. He needed to focus on marching in a straight line behind Nikto. When he turned to the four geared crewmen carrying the body, he noticed one man had a speargun attached to his back.

Why does he get a gun? Landa wondered. He checked the darkness above him. *Do I need a gun?* Behind the dome of his helmet, his face perspired, and he could hear the echo of his own breathing.

"How much farther?" Landa asked into his mic.

"The temple structure, just ahead." Nikto's voice crackled through his headset.

Pilar looked at him with a tranquil smile. "Just breathe Mr. Landa."

ↇ

Dr. Arrison and Chandler walked together, relishing the moment. She felt a sort of déjà vu; her stomach had the same butterflies as when her parents had taken her to Disney World for the first time as a child. After reading so much about it, there it was. What she beheld was so overwhelming, she tried to view her surroundings as an academic.

As her eyes became attuned to the shapes, the lights revealed the base of an Acropolis. To her distant right was the outline of a Parthenon. All of it dormant at the foot of a pyramid with tiered steps. Where the streets had certainly accommodated thousands of inhabitants, they were now forsaken, aside from nine walking divers.

The sceptic in her knew she'd never really be able to confirm this was some version of Atlantis. At the least, it was a sunken ancient metropolis. Nikto didn't allow cameras, so she'd have to rely entirely on her journal entries with approximate coordinates and sketches. Perhaps after the burial, he'd take her inside some of the structures.

"Mom, an oarfish," Chandler's voice announced through static.

She turned to see an enormous fish weaving its way through a row of columns. "It looks like a silver serpent!" Arrison exclaimed. The oarfish was a rare deep-water fish she'd never imagined seeing in its natural environment. It was at least twenty-five feet long, with large eyes and a dorsal fin that ran down its length. It was the longest bony fish alive, and with occasional beachings after storms, the oarfish had been responsible for "sea serpent" sightings.

Pilar approached with her light to track the creature, only to see its shimmer vanish within a structure, like a fish hiding in a vast aquarium's castle. As her light wandered upwards, it exposed the towering statue of a woman.

Arrison, Chandler and Landa stopped in their tracks to behold the effigy. Though its edges had been worn by time, the figure was at least thirty feet tall, and curved in the classical female form. Its face gazed eerily down at them.

"Who do you think she was?" Landa uttered.

"A woman of some great import," Nikto's voice responded. "Perhaps a leader."

With all beams on the statue's face, Arrison studied the shape. Was it some ruler or queen of Atlantis? Though her traits were faded, the woman had symmetrical features, with wide eyes and full lips.

As the lights moved on, the figure was both beautiful and unnerving, looming over them in the blackness. When the lights brightened its base, it revealed a carved pattern. Arrison gasped to see it was the circular, swirling design that looked like a spherical maze.

"It's the same pattern from the Cuban caves," Chandler declared.

He was right. It was proof of some connection. Landa touched the chiseled symbol, genuinely fascinated. The lights then faded to their right as the captain and his team proceeded on their course. The guests hastened their pace to catch up.

Chandler led the three. But as the lights converged on a rectangular area five yards ahead, he halted in his tracks.

"Mom...Captain." Chandler stammered. "There are..."

"Yes," Nikto turned to the three. "They are the sentinels of Atlantis."

In their path were a dozen sharks, eight to ten feet in length. But they were frozen in place, motionless, eerily suspended five feet above the sand as if tethered by invisible cords. Unlike stone statues, their gills were moving.

"They are sleeping." Nikto stepped between a pair of ten-foot sharks. "Certainly, Professor Arrison knows the discovery of sleeping sharks off the Yucatan."

Arrison's eyes blossomed with recognition.

"They are Atlantis' loyal guards." With outstretched arms he added, "If you are cautious, they will let you pass."

Chapter Twenty-Nine
A Perilous Procession

Twenty-two years earlier, Patrice Arrison had helped organize a dream trip she'd be unable to attend with the love of her life.

As a Marine Science student at her alma mater, Florida Atlantic University, she'd been asked to plan a dive tour of Mexico's Isla Mujeres to observe the legendary sleeping sharks. She and her newlywed husband Michael had been counting down the days for the unparalleled adventure.

They'd never had an official honeymoon because of school and monetary constraints. When the class sponsored the trip, it was a godsend, a dream destination, infinitely better than a weekend in Vegas.

Patrice and Michael had met at FAU, and their mutual passion for marine sciences had been an instant attraction. "There's no logical reason to wait to get married," Patrice had said to Michael. They'd been sharing an apartment in Deerfield Beach and spent every weekend diving out of Hillsboro Inlet. Weekdays were spent studying for class or nuzzling on the couch to watch old Jacques Cousteau videos featuring adventures on the high seas.

"That'll be us one day," Michael had promised. They were married six months later at Boca Raton's City Hall. He wore an untucked Tommy Bahama, and she wore a white backless sundress with a golden French braid. She felt feminine and pretty. Both sets of parents paid for dinner at the Mai Kai in Fort Lauderdale, show included.

One evening, the radiant couple watched *The Undersea World of Jacques Cousteau's* special, "Sleeping Sharks of the Yucatan." Cousteau's vessel, the *Calypso*, traveled to Mexico to investigate the discovery of sharks who retired to deep-water caves to sleep.

When their department announced a trip to Isla Mujeres to study the very same sharks, it had been a perfectly timed miracle.

Until Patrice was diagnosed with another miracle: she was pregnant.

After strange bouts of seasickness—and she never got sick on boats—a visit to FAU's clinic confirmed the unexpected blessing. They projected she would be in her third trimester at the time of the dive trip. Patrice wasn't permitted to travel.

She pled for Michael to go without her, to witness the sharks for himself. "How can you miss this exceptional opportunity?" she'd begged.

Michael had unwaveringly refused, stating he wouldn't miss the birth of his child for the world.

❧

Twenty-two years later, that child was standing next to her, 600 meters beneath the sea, somewhere in the proximity of the Yucatan, staring at sleeping sharks.

Arrison became almost teary eyed within her dome. She looked at Chandler, six inches taller and thirty pounds heavier than she was. He'd become a remarkable man, and they were together, both petrified and amazed. Michael would have been honored.

She took a brazen step closer to the sharks. They were a mix of reef sharks and deep-water bluntnose sharks. "No one knew sharks slept."

Landa didn't move. "I thought sharks had to always keep moving."

"So did most marine biologists," Arrison replied. The closest shark to her was six feet away. It was a thick, eight-foot bluntnose shark with six gills, a rare creature usually found at deep depths.

"Scientists theorized sharks had to continuously move to keep water flowing through their gills." Arrison stepped closer. "Until a group of reef sharks—the most dangerous species to humans—were discovered sleeping in the caves off the Yucatan."

The sharks hovering in her path made sense. Nikto had said they were somewhere between Guanahacabibes and the Yucatan. They were in the correct vicinity, at a sufficient depth.

Arrison approached the shark. She'd only seen bluntnose sharks in deep-water photographs. It had characteristics of prehistoric sharks. She noted the species' girth and muscular body. Its snout was blunt and wide, and its jaw hung open. She bent forward, within twelve inches of the beast's gaping mouth to see six rows of serrated teeth the size of arrowheads.

"Mom, please." Chandler implored. Landa equally glowered, tense.

"Don't worry," Arrison whispered. "They're out cold." She leaned closer to stare into the shark's large eye. It was the size of a lime but appeared white, rolled up into its skull.

"The depth produces a euphoria similar to nitrogen narcosis," Nikto explained from several yards away.

Arrison stepped back to absorb the entire herd. "Aren't they gorgeous?"

"That's not the first word that comes to mind," Landa mumbled.

The sharks were about six feet from each other. Some faced the team head-on, while others had their flanks exposed, creating a perilous obstacle course. There was no other way around them.

"The goal is to not wake them." Nikto motioned for his men to resume their trek. His crewmen coiled around the beasts as if accustomed to the task. Arrison followed in their path, and then Landa. They tried to step directly into the tracks of the preceding men.

Before Chandler could move, Pilar tapped his arm. He turned to see her mischievous grin inside her dome. She stretched her arm to gently stroke a shark's tail as if it were a game.

"Are you insane?" Chandler exclaimed.

Her finger paused within a centimeter of the tail. She winked and turned to follow the others.

Like a maze, the nine wound a path through the sleeping giants. Fortunately, Ivan's corpse was strapped to the stretcher. The crewmen had to gently roll the stretcher to the side to navigate around a curve of eight-foot sharks.

Landa held his breath to step sideways through a lane of parallel sharks. He rotated and shuffled slower through a passage of two more beasts.

Arrison and Pilar were more graceful, with arms outstretched to loop their bodies around two sharks that were perpendicular. Chandler followed in their steps, focused and precise.

As Nikto and his team approached the last shark, Landa tensed to see a man's speargun almost graze its massive tail. He calmed when the men finally exited, unscathed.

Landa completed the course with Arrison, Chandler and Pilar close behind. Relieved, Landa's deep sigh was heard by all.

"This shrine is our terminus," Nikto pointed up at a triangular pediment resting on six slanted columns. Its roof was open to the night sky of the sea, with a bed of untouched sand underneath.

Landa watched the crewmen remove equipment from each other's backs. They assembled an underwater dredge and two folding shovels. The men worked fast to extract sand. They used a pry bar to unearth rocks and ancient conch shells. Landa saw they were digging a trench about seven feet long and three feet deep. Nikto remained on one side of the trough, while Pilar and the guests watched from the other.

Landa stepped back as a cloud of silt drifted his way. When his boot struck something, he turned to see a stone barrier that must've been part of a wall. His peripheral vision caught a sudden sparkle. He looked down and saw nothing, guessing a spotlight had flashed past him. Seeing the glimmer again, he bent to notice the remains of a tall broken urn. He nudged it with a glove to see it filled with shells.

Curious, he leaned closer to rake his hand through the shells. With another yellow glint, he froze at an epiphany: only one metal will never tarnish after centuries underwater.

Gold. Only pure 24 karat gold.

159

He looked up to confirm no one was looking in his direction. The others were occupied watching the crewmen dig. He then stirred the shells, sifting away eons of sediment. Without blinking, Landa halted at what he beheld: a mound of gold coins. Hundreds of them.

With his pulse escalating, Landa lifted a coin towards his face. His helmet illuminated a rough, circular piece of gold. *Dear god!* he almost exclaimed. The coin had been engraved with the same circular swirling symbol as on the statue.

"Mr. Landa," Nikto's voice boomed. "Won't you join us?"

Landa turned and dropped his hand to his side. Nikto's view was blocked by the others; he hadn't been seen. "Yes, of course." Before anyone could turn, he scooped a handful of coins and dropped them into a side compartment of his suit.

While walking to join the others, his mind raced at what he'd uncovered. *What would be the value? Solid gold on top of the historical significance? How many did I grab?* Landa wondered. With the clumsy gloves, it was probably only five or six coins.

The four crewmen lifted Ivan's corpse. Landa tried to appear unruffled as he stood beside Arrison and Chandler, but his mind continued to spin. If he announced his discovery, Nikto would either claim it all, or insist it not be touched, with some pretentious speech. *Will I have a chance to go back to the urn?* Landa wondered.

He fought to contain a grin in his helmet. What he'd found would extinguish his crushing debts. *Finally, a fresh beginning.* But his enthusiasm waned; the value would mean nothing if he never saw home again.

When he watched the men lowering Ivan's corpse into the trench, the reality of the moment took root. This was a funeral. Of an innocent sailor, just doing his job. This man —Ivan Popov— would forever be buried under sand and coral in his Atlantean grave. Gold or riches meant nothing 600 meters below the surface.

After the crewmen covered the mound, they stood beside Nikto. With all nine divers encircling the grave, Nikto began a solemn sermon in Russian. He paused after each line so Pilar could translate into English.

"Hark, now hear the sailors cry," Pilar recited gently. "Smell the sea and feel the sky…"

Nikto continued in Russian, his eyes closed.

"Magnificently let your soul and spirit fly."

"*V mistiku…*"

"Into the mystic."

The nine paused with reverence.

The currents pulled a cloud of silt away from the excavation. Particles of sand swirled and drifted until it reached a dreaming shark.

Its large eye twitched.

Chapter Thirty
The Zombie Horde

The divers drew in deep breaths to shed the weight of the moment. It was time to return to the *Naumtsev*.

As two crewmen led the way, Arrison and Chandler gazed up, absorbing their surroundings as if etching it onto their memories.

Before Landa could return to the gold, Captain Nikto approached. Landa gave him a nod, "Your man buried deep enough from the sharks?"

"It is not the sharks I fear," Nikto remained stoic. "His body will be safe from men."

The nine reentered the maze of "zombie sharks," as Landa had named them. Two crewmen walked as leaders: then Chandler, Arrison and Pilar, with two crewmen behind them for protection. Captain Nikto and Landa brought up the rear.

Landa had to concede there was no going back to the urn. The coins he'd taken would have to suffice. He wondered if Arrison had any idea of their approximate coordinates, *in case we're ever able to return.* He halted any fantasies to focus on their hike. There was a sense of relief seeing the *Naumtsev's* lights smoldering through the gloom, just over fifty yards away.

The crewmen navigated the maze of sharks easier than when they'd arrived. There was no stretcher to carry, and everyone followed by stepping into the existing footprints. It was like charting a path through a wax museum of monsters.

Landa cringed as Chandler's arm nearly grazed a shark when he pointed at something. Arrison pushed his arm down, along with a few terse words. Pilar then pretended she was going to stoop *under* a shark as if playing limbo. Nikto scolded her in Russian. No one seemed as daunted by the zombie sharks the second time around.

The first two crewmen exited the maze. They turned to assist Arrison, Pilar and Chandler. Landa could see their smiles inside their domes. They were back on Atlantis's spectral boulevard that led straight to the *Naumtsev*.

"Fifty meters ahead," Nikto commanded, pointing forward. "Let us move along."

"I'm doing the best I can in this suit of armor,'" Landa countered. "Seems faster going back."

A Russian crewman in front of him turned, "You are expert soon, eh?"

When the man rotated, Landa saw his speargun protruding from his back. As if every detail were suddenly clarified, he could foresee what was about to happen. The spear slanted two feet above the man as a shark loomed just twelve inches over his shoulder.

Before Landa could warn the man, the spear jabbed the shark. When the man kept walking, the barbed tip raked its tail, pushing the entire fish like bumping a canoe.

The shark flinched at being roused. Its eyes rolled open, white to black. It thrashed its powerful tail, knocking the crewman off balance. Landa lunged to help the man.

Arrison, Chandler and Pilar turned at the commotion. They saw a ten-foot bluntnose erratically flail, dazed by its abrupt awakening. Like bodyguards, the crewmen escorts pulled the three back, away from any threat.

Nikto and Landa bent to help the man who'd fallen. In his

cumbersome suit, the man was lying on his back like a helpless beetle.

The floundering bluntnose bumped two reef sharks, waking them. Their eyes rolled open, and they began to wallow in confusion, each waking two more like dominoes.

"*Speshite na korabl'!*" Nikto exclaimed in Russian. "To the ship!"

The captain's words resounded in everyone's headsets. Landa and Nikto labored to pull the man up. Landa was infuriated how slow he could maneuver in his suit. More sharks swirled above them like a nest of riled hornets.

"Go now!" Nikto shouted to the men standing with Arrison, Pilar and Chandler. "That is an order!" When he pointed towards the ship, a circling bluntnose shark bit his upper arm.

Landa turned at Nikto's startling cry. The shark clenched its jaws on the captain's arm above the elbow. Landa instinctively turned, knowing a speargun was still on the crewman's back. With no time to explain, he tried to unfasten the gun.

The shark continued to chomp with a vice-like grip. It swooshed its head, heaving Nikto back and forth. "Leave me!" Nikto screamed. "*Ostav'te menya!*"

With his glove's thick fingers, Landa fumbled to unfasten the gun. He blanched at another guttural roar from Nikto. He looked up to see the shark sawing its head from side to side to tear the man's arm off. So far, the metal was too thick.

"Red tab," a crewman mumbled, his accent almost unintelligible. "Push the red tab!"

Landa understood. He pushed the tab on the man's back and the gun released.

"Go to the *Naumtsev*!" Nikto bellowed. "Now!" He choked on his words as the powerful beast lifted him a foot off the sand. Three more sharks swirled closer, drawn to the turmoil.

As Arrison hiked towards the *Naumtsev*, she quaked at another ghastly scream from Nikto. She couldn't look back with crewmen on both sides, wrangling them towards the ship.

"That's the captain!" Chandler exclaimed. "We have to help!"

"Negative," a voice crackled in their headsets. It was Dmitri from control. "Get the guests to the platform. We'll send tranquilizer spears."

Pilar looked at Arrison and Chandler, "These men were ordered to protect you."

Clashing voices of panic resonated in their helmets. Nikto screamed again and Landa yelled something about a speargun.

Arrison could see the ship's platform twenty yards away. Trying to move in her suit was like running in molasses. To her side, Chandler was attempting to look back. Pilar remained oddly quiet about Nikto. Was she so used to sharks and threats that she was confident of his safety? Or did she despise the man?

Arrison's world had abruptly swung from the relics of Atlantis to a race for their lives. She'd desperately wanted to explore the temples, but a maternal instinct consumed her. This was about her son's safety. She tugged him by his hand.

She'd lectured to students how sharks rarely attack people. Usually cases of mistaken identity, where a human is perceived as an injured fish. But she also understood their volatility. They were in the sharks' domain, with an unfamiliar deep-water species, awakened by reckless trespassers.

"If he uses a speargun," Chandler panted. "It'll make things worse."

He was right. A wounded fish among a dozen sharks would cause a blood frenzy.

Spotlights illuminated the sand twelve feet below the *Naumtsev*. The dive platform was hanging below the well. As the vessel aimed its lights towards the sharks, the crewmen ushered the three onto the platform.

Watching in horror, Arrison could see a cyclone of sharks surrounding a blur of four men. Nikto was hanging by his arm from a beast sweeping him back and forth like a mop. The largest man stepped back; she could tell it was Landa. He aimed a speargun towards the erratically moving target less than eight feet from him. Landa fired a single shot with a muffled thump.

"He got him!" Chandler shouted.

It was a direct hit to the shark's abdomen. Its jaws released Nikto, who dropped to the sand. But Arrison knew a single barb wouldn't kill a ten-foot bluntnose. She also knew what would happen next.

"Run!" Arrison roared.

The shark flailed above Landa like a cut worm. A trail of red spewed from its white belly. With Arrison's shouts echoing in his helmet, he knew they had to move fast.

He and a crewman helped Nikto to his feet. Inside his dome he could see Nikto's shocked, distressed eyes, certainly a side of the man few had seen. When he hissed at being pulled, Landa saw an enormous bite mark on his left arm. The suit's aluminum alloy had saved him, but the metal had been perforated by countless teeth.

The men huddled together to proceed towards the *Naumtsev*. The lights of their destination looked like an eternal twenty yards away.

"They're sensing the blood!" Arrison's voice warned.

Slogging as fast as they could, Landa glanced back to see the horde swarming around the wounded bluntnose. The sharks seemed crazed by the scent, looping in wild patterns through a scarlet haze.

A reef shark was first to take a bite from the injured shark's stomach. Then a second shark, and then a third joined in. They feverishly competed to rip chunks of flesh from the carcass. In the mayhem, some nipped at each other. The swarm looked like piranha attacking a drowning calf.

"That won't last." Arrison cried. "Hurry!"

Landa and a crewman helped Nikto walk. They struggled to trudge in a straight line towards the ship. With their heavy suits, the muck felt like quicksand. Landa prayed the sharks would remain occupied tearing each other apart. They needed a few more minutes.

Arrison felt her entire body ease as the men arrived, but it was not over. Nikto's face was ashen in his helmet. He had a half-circle imprint on his arm, eighteen inches across.

For the first time, Pilar's face appeared pleased to see the captain.

A crewman helped the men onto the platform as another stood ready at the controls. They assisted Nikto first, and then Landa. When the final crewman stepped aboard, he gave a thumbs-up to the man at the controls.

Nikto barked, "*Vverkh!*" With a muted grind, the platform began to lift.

"His suit!" Arrison exclaimed. She touched Nikto's elbow joint. "His ADS was punctured!" A high-pitched torrent of bubbles spewed from a tiny hole with a stream of red.

"He's bleeding," Chandler affirmed their worst fear, "And he'll decompress."

Arrison looked towards the sharks. Lights revealed a fading cloud of crimson. Their rage was slowing as the injured shark was now just a shredded skeleton. Its spine drifted from the scene as smaller fish moved in for their turn to peck at the bones. The remaining sharks circled, frustrated and ravenous.

"Can this thing go any faster?" Landa shouted. Cables lifted the platform at a snail's pace.

Arrison stood close to Nikto, feeling powerless. Her effort to cover the injury with a glove couldn't stop the bubbles or wisps of blood.

She drew in a sharp breath when she looked over his shoulder. A large bluntnose seemed to look right at them. It withdrew from the herd to swim towards the *Naumtsev*.

"No." Arrison groaned. She knew sharks were drawn to vibrations. The platform was creating a mechanized thrum and Nikto was bleeding.

"One's coming this way!" Chandler shouted. The shark was swimming fast, uncompromising. Other sharks turned in their direction, also curious.

Five more feet. Arrison looked up to see the well's light getting closer. The platform was already seven feet above the seafloor.

Confined on their stage, everyone's eyes were fixed on the sharks. The bluntnose was now ten yards away. Its iridescent green eyes studied the nine humans stuffed on the platform. Four more sharks raced in its trail, competing for the prize.

"This rail's not gonna' do us any good," Landa grumbled, gripping the guardrail enclosing the platform.

The well door was now three feet away. In the clear shimmer, they could see the silhouettes of crewmen looking down, waiting for them.

Chandler and Pilar instinctively raised their arms, hoping to be plucked to safety.

Four sharks—each over ten feet long—surrounded them, circling in a tight orbit, evaluating how best to tear them apart. The remaining throng approached close behind.

Arrison saw Nikto look at his arm. They caught each other's glance, accepting his blood was wafting towards the beasts.

"We're in!" Chandler voice blared. A shadow surrounded them; it was the rim of the well door. They were seconds from the cool air of the *Naumtsev*.

Boom came the first jolt under their feet. A massive bluntnose rammed the bottom of the platform. Arrison and Pilar screamed and sprang back. Through the grated floor, they could see the shark butting its large snout into the metal.

Landa kicked down with his boot in vain. Then another shark smashed its scarred nose into the platform's mesh.

"No sudden motions!" Nikto shouted with feeble authority.

Sharks jarred the floor from two sides like charging bulls. Everyone stomped or hopped to dodge the mouths grinding under their feet. A husky reef shark attacked from the side, nearly swallowing an entire corner of the platform. Above its gaping mouth, its black eye rolled, curious and angry. Landa stomped down on its nose.

Arrison looked up. *Two more feet and we're—* She recoiled at a nails-on-chalkboard screech. She looked down to see a jaw scraping the edge of the platform. The shark's three-inch teeth grated against the metal, unaffected by its bleeding gums. The platform trembled like an earthquake.

All nine divers rose above the waterline. Their helmets had entered the sub, though they continued to stomp and kick.

Crewmen rushed in to help them off the platform, ladies first and then the captain. Around the open edges of the stage, teeth and fins continued to scrape and splash.

After everyone had exited, the winch lifted the platform out of the water. The weary divers collapsed to the deck to remove their helmets. Two men assisted Nikto with his suit.

The well in the center of the room was still churning with sharks. Black eyes and the slosh of overlapping tails. Their mouths made wet, snapping sounds at the waterline.

"Seal the well!" Nikto commanded, his vigor returning.

A man hit a switch and the double doors closed as fast as a mousetrap. So fast, a single shark was trapped in the ship. It had been above the door when it sealed. Everyone was stunned to see an eight-foot reef shark violently flapping on the sealed door like a caught marlin. It made a wet barking sound, flailing in a puddle of seawater.

One crewman grabbed an electric prod. Another lifted a spear gaff.

Chandler watched the shark, breathless. He looked at Pilar and Nikto, "What are we going to do with it?"

༄

A silver tray was served showcasing a long, thick filet of a solid white fish, garnished with lemon and chives.

Pilar smiled with her hands clasped behind her back, "Filet of *tiburón*, prepared with a Chilean sauvignon blanc, butter, scallions, with a touch of cream."

Chapter Thirty-One
Coastal Comrades

Professor Arrison was less hesitant to eat shark than Chandler and Landa. They winced with sour expressions when she tasted her first forkful.

"Exceptional," she nodded at Pilar. It was thick and meaty like swordfish, but slightly sweeter. Since the meat had a fine marbling, the meat was moist. She knew it was an alternative to eating swordfish, due to that fish's troubled sustainability. And Pilar's rich wine sauce was decadent.

Chandler and Landa listlessly raked their fork through kelp that had been seared with olive oil and garlic. Pilar had lied to the men, calling it sea spinach.

Exhausted, no one spoke as they ate. Pilar took her seat between Chandler and Nikto. The captain used his right arm to refill their glasses with a 2014 Momento Verdelho, an African chenin blanc. He gave just a humble smile, with no toast, wearing a sling on his left arm.

☙

After their dive, Arrison had insisted she go with Nikto to Dr. Yuri's cluttered medical bay. Thankfully, the *Naumtsev*'s outdated x-ray machine had revealed no broken bones. The doctor confirmed he'd suffered severe contusions on his left humerus, causing heavy bruising. The aluminum of the ADS had saved his arm. The only open wound was a one-inch gash above his elbow. Yuri used a Russian version of Liquiband superglue to seal the cut, and Nikto was given a sling to immobilize his arm. Nikto had little to say during the exam, humbled at being damaged.

No one had wanted to eat dinner after the harrowing day, but the captain incessantly preached they would have one formal meal a day in the wardroom. He believed dressing up for a proper meal was good for morale.

But the day hadn't begun as harrowing. The submerged ruins that could have been some version of Atlantis were a scientist's dream come true. The evidence from multiple sources seemed promising, but she'd departed without any tangible proof. Just a nebulous proximity, and perhaps sketches she would draw in her journal.

But we are alive. She looked at Chandler. They were both safe to tell the tale.

Nikto blotted his mouth and cleared his throat to break the silence, "There is an old Russian saying, '*Nikogda ne budite spyashchuyu akulu.*'" He stared as if everyone should understand.

Chandler took the bait, "So, what's that mean?"

"Never rouse a sleeping shark."

The guests glanced at each other, mute.

"That was my attempt at a joke." Nikto's lips lifted into a weak grin.

Everyone exhaled collective chuckles. It was the first time Arrison had seen any suggestion of humor in the man. She wondered if it was Nikto's way of deflecting the discomfort of being injured and vulnerable in front of his guests and crew.

The entire room seemed to unwind. Unseen speakers played a beautiful piano piece by Russian composer Tchaikovsky. Nikto explained it was "*Valse Sentimentale in F minor*, a sentimental waltz."

Everyone drank and ate more heartily. Arrison's entire body relaxed and she found herself laughing more. Pilar bullied Chandler and Landa to try the shark. They did, and each loved it with an extra helping.

"I could've stayed on that road to Atlantis forever." Arrison mused while sipping her wine. "It was like every fantasy of my entire career."

"I'll never forget what it felt like seeing it for the first time," Chandler nodded.

Landa shrugged with mouthful of food. "To me, it was like the Grand Canyon. Fun to see once, but then you're like, I'm good."

Nikto eyed the man as he took a bite of fish, "You saved my life today, Mr. Landa."

Landa paused at the unexpected comment. He almost seemed to blush, "It's only because I can't pilot this thing alone." He motioned to the vessel around him. "The manual's in Russian."

Pilar and Chandler laughed, undoubtedly aided by the wine.

Landa raised his glass towards Nikto. "You saved me in Haiti, so I guess we're even."

The captain narrowed an eye. "I recall saving you twice."

Landa paused to recall. He shrugged and downed the last of his wine.

To Arrison, Nikto seemed like a different man. Either it was the wine, or perhaps a new humility. He'd nearly been killed on his own expedition, ironically, to a funeral. He had been seen pale and nauseous behind his helmet, even unable to walk. He'd required the help of a civilian and his men to survive.

She wondered if this new captain would have a more compassionate perspective of the world above. Would all lands above the sea still be the enemy?

"Patrice." Nikto poured her another glass.

She looked at him, thrown by his use of her first name.

Though weakened, he leaned toward her with an entrancing smile. "Atlantis was just the beginning. I can promise you many, many more wonders. The Sao Miguel pyramid, deep under the Azores of Portugal, Cleopatra's lost kingdom off the shores of Alexandria." He smiled. "All, if you simply remain by my—"

"Kapitan," Dmitri's voice blared from the intercom.

"This is Nikto," he barked at the wall.

"We picked up an approaching vessel," Dmitri spoke fast. "A *Stenka*-class patrol."

Landa stiffened, back to business. "Stenkas are Russian boats built for Soviet Allies, Cuba."

"We are near Cuban waters," Nikto replied. "So, I am not shocked."

"But Captain," Landa frowned, grim. "Those vessels carry anti-sub torpedoes."

❧

Captain Nikto entered the control room like a cyclone, pointing and shouting orders in all directions. The three guests and Pilar followed like an entourage. In the tight space, they remained on the sidelines as Nikto pulled the periscope from the ceiling.

"Status?" Nikto shouted.

"Single vessel, less than four nautical miles," Dmitri responded, monitoring the sonar through headphones. "Approaching from due north, perhaps Cienfuegos port."

Nikto growled at the inference. "Why did you not see it sooner?" He gripped the periscope's handles and pressed his face to the eyepiece.

Landa and the others remained quiet. Though weapons were his specialty, he tried to remain silent to let the captain and crew handle the situation.

"One boat." Nikto expounded as he looked through the periscope. "Gray, less than forty meters in length. It is indeed from the Fuerzas Armadas Revolucionarias."

Landa knew that meant the Cuban navy. It had existed since the overthrow of the Batista dictatorship in 1959. They were still a lethal force, with vessels and weapons provided by the former Soviet Union.

Though Landa still considered Nikto his abductor, he also didn't want to get sunk by a torpedo. "Captain," he stepped forward. "The Stenka's primary anti-sub weapon would be the SET-40 torpedo."

Nikto was silent as if he already knew the information.

"It's old, Russian. Designed back in the sixties." Landa was succinct, "Non-nuclear, but a high explosive. It can't go faster than thirty knots, or dive more than 200 meters."

"How do we know if they see us?" Arrison exclaimed. "Or aims at us?"

"Subs have sensors," Landa replied. Though he had no experience with submarine sonar, his Marine training included radar tech courses. He had a basic understanding of how sensors can tell if you've been spotted by the enemy.

Sonar uses sound waves, usually underwater. If an enemy approached—such as this Cuban boat—it might have its detection systems set to a wide spread to scan a large area. With a wider spread, you can time the gaps between each time their beam hits you.

If the beams suddenly drop to a narrow focus, your adversary may have spotted you. They might be attempting to focus directly on you. Time to move fast with a defensive maneuver.

Landa recalled a perfect analogy: If you want to see someone in the dark, you shine a flashlight at them and look for the light to bounce off them. However, if you're the person whom they're aiming at, it's obvious when it's shining directly at you.

"Kapitan," Dmitri spoke up. "The Stenka is now less than three miles."

"If it's a communist boat," Chandler asked aloud, "why would they consider us an enemy? We're in a Russian sub."

Landa paused, it was a good question.

"You must remember," Nikto adjusted his scope, "Russia is still Cuba's chief creditor." He stepped back to look at the guests. "If they do identify us, they will surely believe the Motherland is simply conducting drills off their coast."

"They've locked on our position!" Dmitri exclaimed. A red light flashed above the receiver.

Nikto closed his eyes, dismayed by the boat's stance. He hung his head and sighed as if he'd endured enough for one day.

"Ramming speed captain?" Pavlo didn't blink.

"Affirmative, ahead four-zero knots," Nikto ordered. He looked at Arrison like a child having to explain, "They targeted us first!"

She scowled, furious with his command. Any farfetched hopes of Nikto becoming non-aggressive, or even peaceful, had been doused.

She glared to recapture his gaze.

Nikto ignored her and gripped a rail at his side. The floor vibrated with the hum of the accelerating engines. He finally spun back to her, defying her emotions.

With no words, her jade eyes pled for any sense of compassion. Arrison would never verbally debate the man in front of his crew. She cocked her head with eyes that implored, *is there any other way?*

With a granite frown, Nikto refused to look away. His steely eyes locked onto hers. At her unyielding refusal to blink, he huffed and bent at the knees.

"Cancel Attack!" Nikto snarled, furious.

Pavlo and the helmsman turned to him, mystified.

"They just fired!" Dmitri bellowed. "Torpedo locked on our position."

Nikto seethed, "Launch countermeasures. Dive, dive, dive!"

℗

Dusk embraced the indigo waters between the Cayman Islands and Cuba. Twenty meters below the surface, Nikto had brazenly plotted a course ninety miles south of Cienfuegos naval base. And now he had been seen.

He knew the imminent torpedo was a deadly equation of time and distance. His order to increase speed would create more noise, further confirming their position to the enemy.

From the *Naumtsev's* forward bow, tubes launched an array of countermeasures. Some rapidly ascended, spewing bubbles. Others hovered at a designated depth in a concerted effort to confuse the oncoming missile.

The *Naumtsev* employed two types of countermeasures. One involved drum-like devices filled with compressed air that would form a wall of bubbles. To the enemy's sonar, it would sound like propeller churn from an accelerating submarine, a large but false target.

Nikto's vessel also launched ADC (Acoustic Device Countermeasure) decoys, also designed to mislead the torpedo. With tiny propellers, the rocket-shaped decoys hovered vertically at a pre-selected depth. They emitted acoustic signals to deceive the torpedo.

At the very least, Nikto needed the countermeasures to add precious seconds so he could dive beyond the torpedo's abilities.

The *Naumtsev*'s steel skeleton squeaked and groaned like the Cold War sub it was. The deck sloped forward at a near thirty-degree angle. Everyone in the room had to grasp the rails around them.

Arrison tensed. It was like the entire room had just crested the highest drop of a rollercoaster. The soles of her shoes struggled to grip the floor. The wall panels hummed, rattling her teeth.

"Torpedo closing, 1,500 meters," Dmitri announced.

"Emergency deep!" Nikto ordered a crash dive maneuver. "Flood negative." An alarm rang for the crew to return to their stations. The Chief Engineer would flood the forward ballast tanks. "Forty-five-degree on the stern plane."

Coffee mugs and ashtrays tumbled to the deck. Water rushing into the ballast tanks sounded like a freight train. Arrison's arms ached, clasping the rails to stay in place. She turned to Chandler, whose eyes were wide with anxiety. Pilar gripped his hand.

"Torpedo eight-zero-zero meters."

"Prepare for impact!" Nikto roared. He hissed in pain to unbend his injured arm to hold a rail.

Twenty meters below the surface, the countermeasures created a screaming wall of bubbles. The illusion filled the space previously occupied by the *Naumtsev*. Nikto prayed for any deviation in the course, no matter how minuscule.

The fifteen-foot torpedo, delivering eighty kilograms of explosives, raced towards them.

After decades of practicing maritime mathematics, Nikto tried to calculate. At 700 meters, with the torpedo's current speed, a deviation of just one degree would create a lateral error of fifty feet away from the target. The *Naumtsev* was diving at a rate of four feet per second. *Is it enough?*

A muffled boom reverberated. A thrumming jolt resonated through everyone's hands holding the rails. When everything went black,

Arrison knew it was over.

But the control room's lights flickered back on. No one blinked or made a sound.

The deck began to level, and the engine's deafening drone eased.

Arrison inhaled with immense relief to see Chandler smiling at her. Pilar grinned beside him. Landa looked at them with a bewildered gaze.

More curiously, the entire crew resumed their duties without pause. Nikto rubbed his eyes and readjusted his sling. The room remained unnervingly quiet.

Dmitri whispered to Nikto, "Detonation was fifty meters above, Kapitan."

He replied in a low voice, "Take us to two-five-zero meters. Rig for quiet. All nonessential, do not make a sound."

Landa chuckled, "God bless fifty-year-old weapons."

"Silence," Nikto hissed. "We've been reported. Planes may be on the way."

Arrison found herself smiling at Nikto. Without being patronizing, her entire face said, *I'm proud of you.*

Nikto didn't return the smile. He turned away, indignant. His ashen face looked like it had aged a year in the past twenty-four hours. He finally groaned, "I have had enough of this hemisphere."

The captain approached the helmsmen. "Plot a course due east. To our much more grateful recipients."

PART V

THE BOUNTY

Chapter Thirty-Two
Looking for Mr. No One

Bogotá, Colombia

The witness, forty-three-year-old Mirta Salazar, sat rigid with anxiety. Across the table, two plump Colombian attorneys in black suits spoke over each other, barking orders.

Mirta's large glossy eyes didn't know which man to look at. She looked like she might cry.

∽

An hour earlier, Navy Intel Officer Engel had to visit a boutique in her Bogotá Marriott to purchase another business outfit. She and Agent Ruiz's trip to Colombia had been approved for only three days, including travel. With this new opportunity to question a witness, a drug lord's ex-wife, Ruiz attempted to get approval from the DEA to extend their trip. When Kurtz denied his request, Engel contacted her commander in DC.

With Engel's geeky passion—eager with a theory of a rogue Russian submarine—her boss had chuckled with skepticism but agreed to the extra days. Unknown to Ruiz, she'd been ordered to report any findings directly to her commander.

Ruiz's attitude had begun to decline. He kept grumbling about how his investigation was being hijacked by the Navy. Engel had no time for such trivial concerns. She missed her husband and son and was in a strange country for the first time. Though travel was exciting, she'd much rather be home, conducting an investigation from her desk.

Navy Officer Cynthia Engel lived and worked in Suitland, Maryland, a community in Prince George's County. Though it sounded rural, it was one mile from Washington DC. Her office was at the Nimitz Operational Intelligence Center. Their mission was to provide intel to support Navy fleet commanders and national officials.

Engel's role was to assist in the collection and dissemination of intelligence information. For such a significant job, few knew her work was done almost entirely from her cubicle in Maryland. After she'd completed her sea rotations, travel was infrequent. And she enjoyed working in solitude until she received the unique request to assist the DEA in Key West.

ɷ

The night before meeting their new witness, Engel studied her file on Mirta Elena Salazar. She was the ex-wife of narcotics kingpin Don Ricardo Salazar. The woman had been transported back to Colombia from her new life in Costa Rica. Her ex-husband had been arrested four months earlier and jailed at La Modelo prison, one of the worst in the country. The capture had made international news, second in significance after Mexican kingpin Joaquín "El Chapo" Guzmán.

Mirta had been married to Salazar for twenty-two years. Upon his arrest, Colombian prosecutors granted Mirta full immunity in exchange for her testimony. With her help, Don Salazar was further charged with extortion, kidnapping, money laundering, and arms trafficking.

The well-educated Mirta Salazar had negotiated two requests. She wanted a fast-tracked divorce. And she wanted a new life, far away in their Witness Protection Program.

Ms. Salazar's demands had been fulfilled. She was granted a divorce, and though her dream was to live in America, she was relocated to

Guanacaste, Costa Rica with a new identity.

According to Engel's records, the Salazars had a daughter, Pilar. Engel found it curious there was no mention of her. The girl would be approximately twenty years old. She guessed the girl could've run away, wanting no part of the family humiliation, if she was alive.

Engel removed her glasses and made a few notes. She needed concise questions for Mirta since they'd been granted only one hour. The meeting had been arranged after her superiors leaned on the US Ambassador in Colombia. The prosecutors reluctantly agreed, believing they'd already squeezed Ms. Salazar of any useful information.

After El Chapo's illustrious escapes in Mexico, Colombian officials refused to allow Engel or Ruiz to meet with Ricardo Salazar under any circumstance. They vowed he'd "never see another human being." Engel hoped his ex-wife might have the same information she needed.

With a *ding* of her laptop, Engel received an email she'd been waiting for. She'd requested a rush job from a fellow analyst in Maryland. Engel had contacts at the Department of Justice, which happened to be the parent department of the DEA. She'd learned the DEA could share intelligence with other agencies in the event of a parallel investigation.

On a hunch, Engel requested records containing thousands of phone calls. Though they'd been placed in a workable spreadsheet, it was going to be a long night.

∽

After noisy streets packed with busses and bicycles, Ruiz and Engel arrived at the Fiscalía General de la Nación, the General Prosecutorial Office of Colombia at 11:00 am. The gray, boxy building was Attorney General Martinez's office in Bogotá.

Ruiz wore a new shirt and tie, and Engel had purchased an ivory blouse and navy skirt to match her blazer. She hadn't packed her service blues since she hadn't been on an "official" trip when they'd flown to Buenaventura.

A frumpy receptionist escorted them to a conference room that had two guards at the door. Inside the small room, they were surprised to see Mirta Salazar already seated at a table, facing two standing men.

They were shouting at her in Spanish, and she appeared scared.

"They're meeting her without us?" Ruiz whispered, irritated.

It was the first time Engel had seen Ms. Salazar in person. Despite the mood, she was beautiful, with wide cheekbones and golden-brown eyes. Her hair was pulled back into a conservative ponytail. The only thing marring her face was a scowl at the two attorneys trouncing her with questions.

"What's going on?" Ruiz boldly asked the men, "We haven't begun?"

The men looked at him with pompous hands on their hips. The larger man responded in rapid Spanish. With a wave of his arm, she and Ruiz were told they could have two seats beside Ms. Salazar. Unable to follow the conversation, Engel felt excluded.

She sat to Mirta's right. She flashed a feeble smile at the woman. Mirta simply studied her, undoubtedly curious why they were there. Ruiz continued to argue with the two men.

Engel noticed the room had a table in the corner with coffee and a tray of *pandebonos,* a Colombian cheese pastry that she'd devoured almost every morning while in the country.

She awkwardly pointed to the tray of pastries and smiled at Ms. Salazar, "You want some?"

Mirta frowned at her with a slow shake of her head.

The two attorneys resumed their lecture to Ms. Salazar like a firing squad. Engel watched the exchange with no clue what they were saying.

Ruiz whispered in Engel's ear, "That guy just told her, 'If you wish to keep your life in Costa Rica, you must tell us anything you have not yet revealed.'"

It appeared the men enjoyed bullying the fragile woman. They were sweaty and their suits were a size too small. Mirta Salazar's glossy eyes kept widening.

Ruiz pointed to the other man, "He's warning her if she's holding back information, he'll void the entire deal she signed."

An emotional Mirta Salazar finally cried out, "*Me estás ladrando como perros!*"

"What'd she say?" Engel whispered.

"She said they're barking at her like dogs."

Engel shamelessly reached to touch Mirta's shoulder. She asked her in clear English, "Ms. Salazar, would you be more comfortable speaking just to me? Privately?"

Mirta turned to her like a savior amidst the horrid men.

Ruiz looked at Engel with a baffled grin, "You can't just walk out with her…"

"We're the ones who asked for this meeting," Engel replied so the men could hear. "There are more guards in this building than the White House. They can follow us. I just need fifteen minutes."

The attorneys chuckled. The larger man exclaimed in English, "She is our witness. You are just visitors here."

Engel shot back, "I have a very narrow line of questions." She raised her palms, pretending to have a sudden idea. "Let's call the ambassador at the embassy and the Attorney General at his daughter's birthday party. They can come in and decide for us."

The men frowned at each other, tongue-tied. Ruiz looked at Engel like she'd lost her mind.

✂

"How did you know I speak English?" Mirta Salazar asked Engel with no trace of an accent.

Engel sipped her espresso and placed the cup on the café table. "You have a master's degree in accounting from the University of Miami. You lived there for seven years. You worked for two years at a Cheesecake Factory even though you went by a different name."

Engel had been granted precisely fifteen minutes alone with Mirta. The building had an enclosed courtyard, with a small coffee bar for employees. The ladies were permitted to use the piazza, though armed guards watched them like hawks from each corner.

Ruiz had been furious he wasn't permitted to join them. "This is my investigation," he'd bawled. Engel had promised to share any pertinent information after calling her superiors.

Engel had purchased two espressos with her last few pesos, and they sat at a café table within the blue-skied courtyard.

"You were your husband's bookkeeper for nine years," Engel continued. "You knew the names and locations of most of his business associates." She moved her saucer aside and leaned forward. "You already got full immunity to tell me anything, but I don't work narcotics."

Mirta blinked, staggered by her level of information. "You are not DEA or law enforcement?"

"No," Engel smiled. "I'm an analyst with the Navy. I sit at a desk with my Tupperware reading spreadsheets all day."

Mirta frowned, bewildered. "How could I ever help a navy?"

Engel pulled a folder from her bag. "They gave us fifteen minutes; we already wasted five. I'll talk fast and get straight to the point."

Still perplexed, Mirta looked down at a stack of prints.

"The DEA began its investigation into your husband four years ago," Engel lifted a spreadsheet. "They tracked his calls. They couldn't listen to the content, but they could track the locations." She handed Mirta the document.

"Okay?" Mirta narrowed her eyes at the report.

"There were thousands of calls between Central and South America and the US," Engel slid her finger down the page. "But within those thousands of calls, there are thirty-one from your husband to a phone connected to a cell tower in Severodvinsk, Russia."

Mirta's eyes imperceptibly widened.

"Have you ever heard of Severodvinsk, Russia?" Engel feigned confusion, "It stands out because it's a strange word."

"I don't know." Mirta shook her head. "He had contacts in Eastern Europe with his heroin labs." She shrugged, dismissive.

"I don't think that was it." Engel's face became grim. "Severodvinsk is a very specific town, only known for one thing: it's Russia's largest shipyard for submarines."

Mirta looked up, caught in Engel's gaze as if ensnared in a web.

"Do you recall any of your husband's associates who were Russian?"

Mirta's eyes began to water. After an uncomfortable pause she replied, "He despised the Russians. But there was one…"

Engel remained quiet, hoping silence and caffeine would keep her talking.

"My husband never used real names with me," Mirta dabbed an eye with her hand. "I was just his bookkeeper. He always used code names."

"Who's the Russian you're talking about?"

Mirta doubled over and covered her face with her hands. She sniffed back a tear, "A man who I never want threatened."

Engel paused, baffled. She'd struck a chord with the woman who suddenly seemed terrified. "Why? What was the man's name?"

Mirta took a deep breath and wiped her nose. She sat upright like she'd made some resolute decision to talk. "The name he used was easy to recall. It was Nikto."

"Nikto?" Engel frowned as she jotted the word. "Does that mean something?"

"No one," Mirta replied, firm. "It's the Russian word for 'no one.'"

Engel wasn't sure how this detail fit the larger picture. But Salazar seemed to confirm her husband had worked with a Russian in a town that built submarines. "Why do you never want this man threatened?"

Mirta's face agonized before replying, "He took something very valuable from us so my husband would never try to find or destroy him."

Engel was now even more puzzled. *Never try to destroy him?* What had this Mr. No One taken that was so valuable? With the clock ticking, she decided to leap straight to the point.

"Was it a Russian submarine?"

Chapter Thirty-Three
Fractures in the Iris

The Atlantic Crossing

In the parlor, Pilar and Chandler stood together at a large Iris window. They smiled as they watched immense hundred-foot blue whales swimming alongside the *Naumtsev*.

The vessel was cruising fifty meters below the surface. When the morning sun brightened the royal blue water, a pod of four massive whales joined the vessel for a sunrise race.

"*Ballenas azules*," Pilar cooed. "The largest animals on our planet. Is that true?"

Chandler's jaw hung slack as he watched the blue-gray giants. They gracefully arced up and down, just yards beyond the window. He replied, "Not even a dinosaur was larger than an adult blue whale." They had long, torpedo-shaped bodies with lighter undersides that were visible when they rolled to the side.

"They're playing with us." Pilar touched the glass.

"I never thought I'd see one in the real world." He put a hand on her shoulder to look out. They gasped when a whale swerved closer, equally curious. Its large black eye seemed to study them before the animal rolled under the ship to the other side.

They reminded Chandler of seeing dolphins racing alongside their dive boats. This appeared to be the same game, but these mammals—and vessel—were almost twenty times larger.

When Pilar looked at Chandler, her entire face beamed to see his natural joy.

℗℗

On the other side of the parlor, Dr. Arrison and Ned Landa watched the whales through the opposite Iris. Arrison studied them, captivated and curious. Landa smiled but was equally engaged in stirring his coffee.

"I've never seen blues this size," she remarked. "Highly endangered and poorly misunderstood. We must be in the very deep Atlantic."

"Captain says we can maintain forty knots," Landa replied while gazing out. "So, what's more than two days at forty knots?"

"That's about forty-six miles per hour," Arrison squinted to calculate, "Forty-six times twenty-four hours is…1,104, so we're well over 2,000 miles."

"Over halfway across the Atlantic." Landa leaned towards her and lowered his voice, "Did he tell you where we're headed?"

She shook her head, "He said east. To his 'recipients'?"

"What's that mean?" Landa's face hardened, "Drug buyers?"

His blunt words made her wither. She stepped away, closer to the window. When she looked out, it was just blue. The whales had gone under the ship. She felt a sadness not seeing them. They'd fled the same moment Landa had spoiled her bliss.

"Patrice…" He looked over his shoulder and moved closer, "Nikto loves to remind us how he saved our lives. He shows us cool stuff. Ancient ruins… fish… fancy food… But it doesn't change the fact he's still a narcotics dealer." His tone darkened the words.

She looked at him, dismayed with his approach.

"Let's not forget," he focused on her eyes, "we are here against our will."

Arrison frowned to weigh his words. She had deliberated about their situation every night as she struggled to sleep in a windowless cabin. Yet every morning, she awoke to a new discovery.

She replied, calm, "Do you realize I've learned more in six days than twenty years in a lab or classroom? If I were to go home today, it'd be to a two-bedroom condo off I-10 in Tallahassee."

He shook his head with a derisive chuckle. "Confinement within freedom."

"What's that mean?" she winced.

"We freely walk his ship. I can go from one end to the other, up and down the ladders." He pointed to her, "You're free to study. You have access to his entire library. He's even given you blank journals." He flashed a bitter smile, "We just have no freedom to leave."

Arrison huffed without a response. With the silence, his words loomed. Her eyes were pulled back to the Iris. She wanted to be part of the blue aquatic vista. With the curved glass, her view was almost 180 degrees.

She crossed her arms. "I don't necessarily see things the same way as you."

Landa expelled a laugh, incredulous. "I'm no shrink, Professor, but this is textbook Stockholm syndrome."

She recoiled, "Do you even know what that means?"

His smile vanished. "Feelings of trust or emotions for your captor."

"You're the sociopath," she exclaimed, "with delusions of grandeur."

"Have you heard of a 'sub psycho?'" Landa raised his voice. "Some sailors go crazy the first week underwater. Hostility, obsession, paranoia…"

She glared, "Have you analyzed yourself?" She stepped into his space. "A dishonorably discharged Marine? Charged with dereliction of duty?" She stuck a finger in his chest. "What'd you do? Probably hit someone."

With an ominous quiet, Landa looked down at her finger, then back up at her. "What'd I do? I tried to run. Just like in Haiti, and just like now."

"You run away from tough situations?" She fired back with a crooked smile, "Good luck in a sub fifty meters underwater!"

She watched him stare, fuming. There was an unsettling pause before he replied.

"My sergeant ordered me to march ten miles. He thought I was being a wise ass." Landa's voice was startlingly calm. "I was just excited. My ex-wife was going into labor."

Arrison halted, hushed by his words.

"She was high-risk. Diabetes. And forty miles away, so I refused to march." A caustic mile creased his face. "So, I ran. AWOL. To see the birth of my only daughter. That's the order I disobeyed. That's why I was discharged."

Staggered, Arrison's knees felt weak. She took a seat on an armchair beside her. With no quick retort, she realized she didn't know anything about the man. He was crass and arrogant, *and he's a father?*

His story of being there for his daughter was evocatively like her late husband refusing to miss Chandler's birth. Saving her from crafting a rueful response, Nikto's voice rang from the speakers.

"Good morning," his voice was tranquil. "We have live audio you may enjoy."

The speakers began to play whale songs. Hauntingly beautiful vocalizations from the whales echoed throughout the parlor.

Arrison smiled, lost in the sounds. "Only the males sing like that."

Landa sat beside her, perhaps part of some unspoken truce. "What are they saying?"

"No one's sure." She shrugged, "Their songs can be heard over sixty miles. It may help with pair-bonding."

"So, they're calling out for buddies?"

"Something like that."

❧

At the opposite window, Chandler gawked, enthralled by the whale's mournful melodies. "Isn't it remarkable?"

"Nikto's still trying to astound you," Pilar ridiculed. "I guess it's working. He's as sincere as a politician."

Chandler's smile vanished, confused by her manner. "Do you hate Nikto or something? You only say negative things about him. Isn't he like a father figure?"

She turned, abrupt. "He is not a father!" Her accent was more pronounced, "You have no idea what I have endured." She leered, "But you could never understand."

"Is that so?" Chandler frowned, insulted. "I watched my dad wither away to nothing before I was ten. I have a perfectionist mother who thinks autism means I can memorize everything." He raised his voice, "There's no excuse for anything less than a 4.5 GPA. 'Just memorize the textbooks,' she says. And with her all-consuming career, eighty-hour work weeks are expected."

Pilar didn't blink, stunned by his anger.

"Look at your life here," he pointed out the window. "You essentially travel the globe. Seeing the wonders of the world in an undersea cruise ship."

Pilar gasped and then stiffened. She bellowed, "Nikto kidnapped me so my father would never try to destroy the *Naumtsev*!"

Silence. Chandler's mouth opened and then closed.

Her face reddened. "Nikto said I would have a better life underwater than on land as the child of a drug lord!" Her words were amplified within the chamber.

Chandler stood silent. Pilar didn't budge. They slowly turned to see Arrison and Landa gaping at them. They'd heard the entire outburst.

Landa asked, "So why's he dealing thousands of kilos of stolen narcotics?"

Arrison's mouth fell open at his tactless question.

Pilar spun and stormed off towards the parlor's rear door. Chandler scowled at Landa and marched out the side door.

Landa shrugged at Arrison, "What'd I say?"

༄

Chandler stomped into the passageway of the third deck. He was hit with the unmistakable scent of the crew's berthing racks. He did not attempt to greet the men who were reading or playing poker on their bunks. He continued up to the next deck.

He'd never been so embarrassed, confused or upset. He'd been told his entire life he was "always happy" because of his ubiquitous smile. But he had wavering emotions like anyone else.

It was evident his mother's undersea world was her sole passion since his dad died. Her pursuits had stolen precious hours from him, barring her from ever truly knowing him. He wasn't a klutz, he wasn't a coward, and he wasn't a parrot that could recite everything he'd ever read.

Then there's Pilar, he groaned. He'd angered the only female he'd ever developed an affection for, and she'd shredded him in front of the others. *Who —or what—is she? A kidnap victim? A drug lord's daughter?* Was Mr. Landa correct, they were all trapped in a criminal's narco-sub for the rest of their days?

Anxieties collided in his psyche as Chandler climbed the stairs to the operations compartment. At least Dmitri might've launched a new C-Buoy with fresh news. He craved any distraction.

The level was darker, with colder AC to protect the servers. The smell of cigarette smoke meant men were working. As he rounded the corner into the control room, he saw the backs of Captain Nikto and Dmitri standing at the comm station.

A curious intuition stopped Chandler from making his presence known. He quietly approached the men. Perhaps they were monitoring the whales. He heard faint voices from a speaker. A man's voice and then a woman's.

He stopped, it was the voices of his mother and Landa. They were still speaking to each other in the parlor.

His mother's voice said, "I don't do this much, but I apologize about before. I didn't know those things about you."

Landa's voice responded, "Don't judge a book, right?"

Chandler's eyes flickered. *Is Nikto spying?* He was listening in on both of them. For how long? *Did he hear what Pilar called him?*

The captain turned. Without any reaction, he peered into Chandler's eyes.

"Mr. Arrison," Nikto's mouth smiled but his eyes did not. "Why don't we go for a walk? In a forest, just you and I."

Chandler stepped back. "A forest?" he stammered, "We're surfacing?"

Nikto replied, "We are not."

Chapter Thirty-Four

The Commandeers

Somewhere over Cartagena

Officer Engel sat in a posh leather seat in the King Air 350i. She felt the armrests and looked around, admiring the interior of the DEA aircraft.

She usually flew on one of the discount airlines that made you pay for water or pretzels. And that was once a year if they were lucky. With her husband Chuck's insurance agency, he could rarely get away. Their son Sean had just started middle school, and he loved to visit theme parks. Their trip this year had been cut short by the call from the DEA.

Bogotá, Engel grinned to herself. She wanted to show Sean her passport stamped "Colombia." Chuck would be amazed how she'd handled a conference room full of loud bureaucrats. *Nothing like that back at the office,* she mused.

And the opportunity with Mirta Salazar seemed promising. She'd agreed to speak but had only offered kernels of information until her demands were met. Things were looking good.

Engel shrunk in her seat with a thought. Would her superiors be able to work with the DOJ to grant Mirta immunity in the US? And then —not to get ahead of herself— how much evidence would she need to persuade them to contact the Commander of Submarine Force Atlantic? At last count, they had thirty-two subs that could help look for a possible rogue.

Possible rogue, she huffed at her own words. The Navy would never allocate precious resources for an analyst's fantasy about an illicit Russian submarine covertly cruising the Atlantic. At the office, she was just a five-year employee who was in charge of her team's coffee club. Even the security guard at her office could never remember her name.

She gazed out the window at distant clouds. *How can I get tangible evidence?*

"Gotta' love DEA travel," Ruiz declared as he shuffled down the aisle. He was holding two green bottles of Coca Cola.

"It is comfortable," Engel smiled. "I fly Spirit once a year to Epcot so we can see all the countries."

Ruiz bobbed his head, "This King Air was courtesy of the Sinaloa Cartel. Got it three years ago in a federal asset-grab." He chuckled, "There was actual blood on the carpet by the mini-fridge, but they got it up." He handed her a bottle, "Try this Mexican Coke, it's way better than American. They use cane sugar instead of syrup, or something."

Ruiz and Engel sat together, again the only passengers. He tapped his bottle against hers for a job well done and they sipped their drinks.

"Just hung up with Kurtz." Ruiz was animated, "He is juiced! He's checking NCIC right now for anyone who's ever used the alias 'Nikto'."

She frowned, puzzled. "If this Nikto is Russian, I plan to reach out to Interpol. Maybe beg for records from Russian Armed Forces."

Ruiz looked at her like he'd sucked a lime. "He's a drug dealer," he inflated the words. "If he was ever tied to the Bogotá cartel, Kurtz will find him. Believe me."

Engel cocked her head with a curious blink. "You do realize this is no longer a DEA matter."

His jaw dropped with a smirk, "Our witness—who was the wife of a cartel boss—says her husband was approached by a Russian wanting to sell him a narco-sub."

"A nuclear sub," she countered.

"Cartels only do one thing: distribute narcotics," Ruiz lectured, patronizing. "They don't care how it's powered."

"A rogue nuclear sub is a national, no, an *international* security threat," Engel corrected. "According to Salazar, Nikto has no interest in drugs."

"If she's talking so much," Ruiz crossed his arms, "why'd he steal a sub, twice?"

Engel hesitated, equally frustrated. "Something terrified Nikto." Her vague conjecture had an air of dread. "Ms. Salazar refuses to say more unless she's granted protection in the US."

Ruiz stared at the seat in front of him to digest her words. He turned, "This needs to remain quiet."

"I must report to my command chief," she shrugged. "Maybe then work with Sub Force Atlantic to locate—"

"Locate?" Ruiz forged a laugh. "You're gonna' find a sub in 41,000,000 square miles of Atlantic? From your desk in DC?"

She slouched at his jab. Engel knew she had zero credibility with this man. She wanted to prove her expertise could surpass the abilities of rash agents using boats and guns. She collected her thoughts and turned to him, cool.

"I can search Coast Guard witness reports that fit the profile." She was succinct, "Then I cross-reference satellite imagery for those dates. With those events, I can use predictive tracking to forecast its possible course. Our vessels can then use passive sonar to listen—"

Ruiz stood, mid-sentence, to move three rows in front of her and sit. Without speaking, he looked out the window like a pouting child.

Engel almost chuckled, *that's it? That was all it took to shut him up? Rational strategies?* She involuntarily grinned. With her job, it was all data and statistics. She rarely had verbal debates with other humans, yet alone brash egotists.

Her smile spread wider. She liked how it felt and, evidently, she was good at it.

Engel slid over to sit by the window. She gazed down to see the infinite blue sea. According to the pilot, they'd flown over Cartagena, now over the Caribbean for their route home.

Studying the field of blue stretching to the horizon, she wondered *where are you?*

ↄ

Ned Landa entered the moon well, alone. When the lights came on, he paused to confirm no one else was in the chamber. He looked up to see the only security camera was aimed towards the *Cyclops*.

He approached a locker beside the hanging dive suits. He squatted to the lowest bin and opened it. Reaching past wadded rags, he felt an ADS dive glove. He glanced over his shoulder and pulled it out.

He tilted the large glove until six gold coins jingled into his hand. With a scoundrel's grin, he lifted one until it glinted in his eye. He studied the two-inch diameter Atlantean coin with the unique swirling symbol. His brows twitched at the possibilities. *What's this worth?*

He flinched at the hiss of the doors. He sprung upright and turned to see Captain Nikto facing him from the threshold. At his side were Chandler and two crewmen who appeared equally surprised to see him.

"Mr. Landa," Nikto stated with narrowed eyes. "May we help you?"

Still holding the glove, Landa folded his arms. "I'm more comfortable around tools than marine biologists right now."

"Then you are in luck," Nikto remarked. "I need some work done on a C-Buoy rack." He turned to the crewmen, "Please show Mr. Landa to the racks."

Landa swore under his breath at the arbitrary command. He wasn't Nikto's servant or even a paid worker. But considering what was concealed in his hand, he chose to cooperate.

The captain turned to Chandler, "Let us now suit-up for our stroll."

Chandler's eye twitched, equally flustered by the man's orders.

Chapter Thirty-Five
Little Farm in the Big Woods

Somewhere in the North Atlantic

The dive platform slowly descended from the moon well. Unlike the last walk, the sea was brilliantly illuminated. With the *Naumtsev* anchored at a shallow hundred feet, solar rays painted the turquoise water with shafts of light.

Also unlike the previous excursion, the platform held only two divers. Geared in their ADS exosuits, Captain Nikto and Chandler stood alone. No weapons and no escorts.

Chandler abandoned any sense of alarm when he realized their surroundings. His gasp echoed and his eyes darted to absorb the scenery. It was truly a forest.

"A kelp forest," Chandler broke the silence. "We're off the west coast of Africa?"

"Correct," Nikto replied, stoic.

Before them, towering "trees" of kelp created a true jungle. Their stalks soared a hundred feet above the seafloor. Some trunks were ten inches in diameter. Like true trees, their stalks were brown, and their lofty fronds were bright green. Some were accented with red blooms of color. When Chandler looked up, the silhouetted stalks looked like slow-motion palm trees.

"This forest stretches over 150 kilometers." Nikto stepped off the platform.

Chandler absorbed the scene as he walked. The soaring expanse of seaweed appeared as dense as the Congo Rain Forest.

"Follow me," Nikto moved towards the stalks.

As far as he could see, the forest swayed in unison, back and forth like a choreographed waltz. Almost overwhelmed, Chandler didn't know where to begin. He was torn between darting off like a child to play in the woods or stay in place to study the forest as a whole.

He and his mother had visited a kelp forest exhibit at an aquarium in Monterey, California. They compared the kelp to a redwood forest. The stalks grew vertical due to air-filled bladders, giving the plants a woodland appearance. Its thick fronds sprouted from bulbs near the surface. They provided shelter and food for thousands of species of plants and animals.

"It is one of the most productive ecosystems in the world," Nikto uttered. "A complex habitat for rock lobster, abalone, sea cucumbers, and almost every fish."

Chandler's eyes followed a stalk down to its base. Unlike real trees, the kelp didn't need roots to extract nutrients from the soil. It obtained all the nutrients it needed directly from the water. The stalks were anchored to the rocks through a root-like structure called holdfasts.

He trailed ten feet behind Nikto. When they walked through a gate of trees, the light dimmed from the canopy. The water felt five degrees colder. He never considered what it'd be like walking into the labyrinth. The darker it became, his excitement ebbed into apprehension.

"We come here to restock our rations." Nikto didn't look back as they walked. "A nursery for more species than one can count."

Intrigued, Chandler looked down at the ground. Though rocks were carpeted with vibrant flora, he didn't see any sea creatures. Turtle grass swayed. There was coral and shrubs of red algae. The floor was speckled with abandoned clam and conch shells.

"You see nothing." Nikto watched him skimming the seafloor.

"But a thousand eyes are watching you right now."

Chandler's brows leaped at the thought. He bent to look closer at the ground around his feet. A shaft of light brought a new focus. There was suddenly life everywhere. A camouflaged octopus slinked between rocks. Lobsters' antennae protruded from behind a sea fan. Reef crabs the size of his hand skated across staghorn coral. Yellow Goby fish swirled past his ankles.

He smiled at the tapestry of busy creatures. With his attuned eyes, everything seemed to move. A bustling community of life; each species interacting and gathering food. Chandler stepped back as a shimmer of blue and yellow angelfish rushed by like a passing train.

"A sea dragon!" he gasped. Rising above the grass, he looked into the eyes of a rare seahorse-shaped creature. The two-foot sea dragon was red and purple, with long fins and wing-like fronds. Chandler wished he had his mother—or camera—with him.

His reflexes compelled him to duck when a six-foot manta ray glided over him like a kite. "Whoa, Captain." When he turned, Nikto was gone. He called out, "Captain?" Nikto was nowhere in sight. Nothing but the infinite, swaying jungle.

He had to keep moving. "Captain Nikto?" His gasps increased inside his helmet. He had to twist in the bulky suit to meander through the trees. Like a house of mirrors, everywhere he turned looked the same. Chandler wondered if he'd been abandoned as some sort of test. Even in his suit, he felt eclipsed by the underwater wilderness.

In his paranoia, the sea life somehow appeared more hostile. The ground was carpeted with crabs, like giant insects, with their pincers raised to attack. An orange moray eel the size of a man's leg slithered past his waist. When Chandler turned, he saw a three-foot lemon shark chase and devour a clownfish. He spun the other direction.

Using his hands to separate trees, he pressed forward. "Captain?" He continued to shout, hoping the frequency would remain in range. He saw a shimmer of light through the stalks ahead, perhaps a clearing with a broader view.

When he stepped beyond two stalks the size of coconut trees, he found himself gazing down at a breathtaking undersea valley. Columns of light brightened the area as if it were divine. He smiled to see four divers wearing the same ADS suits. They were from the *Naumtsev*, marching into the vale.

"Remarkable visibility today," Nikto's voice blared.

Chandler nearly leaped out of his suit at the voice. He turned to see Nikto standing at his side. With the pulsing shadows, the captain blended perfectly with his surroundings. Relieved but unnerved, Chandler wondered if he'd been there all along.

"Time to check our crops." Nikto stepped into the valley.

Chandler thought he still seemed incensed. He didn't smile and there was zero warmth from the man. But there was no choice but to follow.

The water's clarity was extraordinary. Sunlight showcased the area from thirty yards above. The valley was nestled between underwater dunes. Wooden traps rested on the sand; some had ropes pulled vertical by round glass floats.

Nikto's divers spread out. Some carried poles, while others had shovels or nets. The men went about their work without any regard for Nikto or Chandler. From their actions, it looked like they were performing routine tasks.

Nikto finally spoke, "If you pledge to follow me, and remain with me, you will never be lost again."

Chandler scowled to interpret his words. He didn't like his foreboding tone. Was he referring to him being lost in the kelp? Was he speaking metaphorically about remaining with him on the *Naumtsev*? "Never be lost again" sounded like some religious zealot.

Before he could respond, they approached a diver emptying a square trap.

"Stone crabs." Nikto motioned to the large brown and orange crabs. They had enormous claws the size of pears. "We take just one claw from each to preserve the species."

They proceeded to a patch of sea grass to see a man pulling South African crayfish from a rectangular trap. The lobsters had beautiful rust-colored patterns and no claws, but their meaty tails were over a foot long.

"This way," Nikto muttered again. They observed two divers harvesting short stalks of seaweed using hoes. "Baby kelp. Much more tender."

Chandler attempted a smile. "Your favorite sea vegetable?"

"It is indispensable," Nikto retorted. "Ten times more calcium than milk. Rich in antioxidants, including vitamins A, C, and E."

Chandler watched the men, now fascinated. "How many ways do you serve it?"

"Sautéed. Dried into chips. Ground into flour for pasta, a thickener for soups." Nikto looked at Chandler, "Even ice cream from that machine you and Pilar abuse so much."

It was the first time he'd heard Pilar's name in hours. Chandler hadn't seen her since their argument in the parlor. She'd marched off to parts unknown of the vessel, while he had made the mistake of bumping into Nikto. *Am I on trial with some overprotective father-figure?*

The man still wasn't smiling. Nikto turned and walked, implying he should follow. Beyond a ridge, Chandler was comforted to see the blur of the *Naumtsev* hovering in the distance. He continued to follow like an admonished child, watching the kelp forest pass to his left. To his right, a diver was collecting abalone from a reef.

"I need to know your intentions." Nikto's words were sharp.

"Intentions?" Chandler slowed, "With Pilar?"

"No." Nikto spun, his eyes laser-focused. "Your plans. Your intentions. Both you and your mother's."

Chandler opened his mouth, but nothing came out.

Nikto placed a hand on his shoulder. It felt like it was to keep him from fleeing.

"Do you consider me a depraved narcotics dealer?" Nikto paused an eternal three seconds. "Or a terrorist?"

Chandler shrunk in his suit. "I'm…not sure I under—"

Nikto lunged within inches of his helmet. Their visors nearly touched. "I need to know you and your mother's allegiances by sundown." He didn't blink. "And we are *very* far from your home."

⌘

"I refuse to be given ultimatums," Professor Arrison exclaimed, furious. She crossed her arms and paced the floor of her quarters.

Chandler and Landa were crammed in her cabin. They were gathered at the foot of her bed, shouting in whispers.

"What if they're listening to us right now?" Landa hissed, thumbing to the walls.

"I checked the room," Chandler replied. "The air vent, closet, and all corners. I think it's safe."

"You're a surveillance expert now?" Landa snapped.

Arrison scowled. "That's more than you've done."

Landa gave a bitter laugh, "I told you on day one, he's a drug trafficker." He raised his voice, "Then I witness his stolen stash myself twice!" He looked at Chandler, "How much evidence does a scientist require to prove a hypothesis?"

Chandler didn't respond. He stuffed his hands in his pockets, defiant.

Arrison's jaw clenched as a hundred cruel responses spun in her head. But she said nothing. Had she been so blinded by Nikto's hospitality and marine discoveries that she'd been ignoring the truth?

She studied Landa and her son. Their postures seemed indignant, which was completely out of character for Chandler. They scowled, waiting to attack each other's words.

A new thought entered her mind: perhaps this is what Nikto wanted. To create turmoil so they'd have to choose sides. Was this some sort of emotional manipulation?

Arrison took a breath to change course. "Maybe they can only hear us in the parlor." She turned to Landa, "I hate ultimatums, but I can't align myself with a drug dealer. I haven't witnessed any evidence of that."

"Jesus!" Landa bellowed, "I'll show you his stash myself!"

Chandler turned to his mother. "When Nikto looked at me, his eyes were like those sharks' eyes. I didn't like what I saw."

They jerked their heads towards a voice. It was the intercom.

"Dr. Arrison and Mr. Chandler," It was Pavlo's voice. "Please come to the control room."

Arrison and Chandler locked eyes; they had never considered the intercom.

Landa shouted, "What about me?"

There was a pause. "The C-Buoy rack is incomplete," Pavlo replied. "We require your assistance. I will send an escort."

After the intercom went silent, Landa pointed at the wall. "So, how'd they just know we were all in here?"

Chapter Thirty-Six
Turning Tides

Côte d'Ivoire — The Ivory Coast

Twenty meters below the surface, large missile doors opened on the bow of the *Naumtsev*.

After an initial discharge of bubbles, three teardrop-shaped bundles were launched. The four-foot-diameter parcels ascended like an underwater race for sunlight.

When they breached the surface, CO_2 cylinders instantly inflated the bundles into fourteen-foot rafts. Each of the three skiffs were constructed of military-grade PVC vinyl and could accommodate six people. The boats were navy-blue for low visibility and came with compact six-horsepower outboard engines.

Two larger bundles were then launched from the *Naumtsev*. Due to the weight of the five-foot bales, small round floats were required for buoyancy. They bobbed to the surface, held in place with cargo nets.

છ

As commanded, Dr. Arrison and Chandler stepped into the control room, timid and silent. A half-dozen men were at their stations while

Captain Nikto stood at the periscope. When he turned, he wasn't smiling, but his face didn't seem angry.

"I would like you both to accompany me for my *dobrovol'chestvo*." He rubbed fingers together to recall the word, "Charity work."

Arrison and Chandler looked at each other. It was the last word they had expected.

With a rolling surge of water, the imposing *Naumtsev* surfaced. Jagged yet graceful, the sea beast glistened in the midday sun with only its spine and fins visible.

From the forward hatch, eight crewmen appeared. They stepped along the hull to tie-up the rafts. Four men hoisted the large bales into two of the boats.

After a man radioed the all-clear, Captain Nikto, Dr. Arrison and Chandler emerged from the hatch. Gazing up at the radiant sky, Arrison and Chandler followed the captain to the lead boat. Crewmen helped them aboard and untied the ropes.

Six of the men climbed aboard the boats carrying the bails. The two remaining men joined the captain to pilot the lead boat.

As soon as the last man's foot stepped off the *Naumtsev*, the sub sunk back into the sea. Though its huge fin and tail were last to disappear, the vessel was soon gone without a wake.

Like a calculated drill, surfacing and boarding the skiffs had taken just eleven minutes.

⸎

Arrison was seated next to Chandler in the rear of Nikto's raft. She looked straight up, soaking in the noon sun like a sponge. Chandler was occupied watching the men maneuver the boats. Whatever Nikto's cryptic "charity work" meant, intuition told her there was no need to fear for their safety. She squinted at the horizon to study their surroundings.

"Land!" Chandler shouted as he pointed east.

With the *Naumtsev* gone, Arrison turned to see a lush, tropical coast about two miles away.

"Captain," Chandler had to shout over the breeze. "West Africa?"

"Côte d'Ivoire," Nikto replied with a decent French accent. "Closer to the border of Ghana."

Though he again avoided giving an exact location, Arrison tried to envision it on a map. The Ivory Coast and Ghana were halfway down the length of the continent, closer to the equator. Located near Togo and Nigeria, she guessed it was a poor nation. Otherwise, she knew nothing of its people, political or economic issues.

The three boats sped towards the coast. Nikto's boat took the lead as the two boats carrying the bundles followed in a triangular formation. Their small but powerful motors raced over the two-foot swells.

Too noisy for conversation, Arrison watched the captain. He stood on the bow, leaning into the wind like George Washington crossing the Delaware.

She tried to remain cool to absorb the scenery. The warm wind was humid, somewhere in the mid-eighties. As they got closer to land, she could see tall palms and tiny structures like shacks on the beach. She didn't see any larger buildings to indicate any hotels or commerce.

Studying the shore, something caught her eye to her left. She turned to see a small boat speeding towards them. *Other people!* Arrison almost exclaimed out loud. *Are we being returned to civilization?*

"A boat," Chandler shouted, but he was pointing to their far-right.

Arrison turned to see a second boat, also ten or fifteen feet long. Its bow pounded the waves as it approached. When she narrowed her eyes, her face went gray.

"They have guns!" Chandler roared. He half stood, rigid.

Arrison covered her mouth to realize the gangly teens on the boats were holding large assault rifles. Unlike their attackers in Haiti, she knew the perils of the African coast. Both boats were charging over the swells like missiles.

"Pirates!" Chandler yelled to the captain. "Both sides!"

Nikto didn't flinch. He turned with a tranquil smile, "We are fine. They are our escorts."

☙

Ned Landa didn't care what everyone else was doing. He was fine being away from Arrison and Chandler and even the girl Pilar. They all seemed brainwashed anyway. He had his two favorite things: tools at his disposal and the solitude to work alone. And at the press of an intercom, he could have lunch brought to him anytime.

He sat, sprawled on the torpedo room floor. He'd single-handedly built an entire C-Buoy rack, and now had to attach it to the bulkheads so it could withstand extreme angles.

The C-Buoys that were launched to the surface for satellite communication were the size of volleyballs. A rack that once held countermeasures had slots the same diameter as the buoys but were long like a giant wine rack. Since the buoys were small and round, he adjusted the rack so the buoys could be stored in cradles like bowling balls at his favorite alley back home.

Landa smiled at his handiwork and wiped his hands with a rag. His pleasure faded, realizing he was happy about his craftsmanship without thinking about the devices themselves. This was not a job; it had been a command. And C-Buoys were machines to help his captor.

His stomach growled, now feeling like a traitor. Maybe he'd order lunch. The chef said they had fresh dolphin, or called mahi-mahi in the Pacific, or *dorado* in South African waters, or *lampuka* in the Mediterranean. He'd have to figure out where they were to know how to order it. He balked at the absurdity of his day.

When he stood to stretch, he looked at a workbench to see a C-Buoy that had been damaged during the last emergency dive. Landa peered over his shoulder and an eyebrow shot up. Ever since dissecting a frog in high school, he realized he could understand how things worked by taking them apart. *And this is how they communicate with the outside world?*

Landa leered like the Grinch. His lunch would have to wait.

☙

Chandler didn't sit back down in the raft until Nikto waved at the approaching skiffs. The shirtless young men lowered their weapons and waved back. Their skiffs circled them, and then led Nikto's three boats towards shore.

Chandler looked at his mother. She shrugged, equally puzzled.

The boats slowed as they came within twenty yards of the beach. Chandler could see a smattering of locals standing on the sand. They appeared to be children. When Nikto gave a broad wave to his arrival party, the kids all waved back.

Arrison also gawked at the scene. Chandler couldn't help but grin when he saw wide smiles on the kids' faces. They ran towards the surf to wave the boats in.

They know him, Chandler realized. From the kids' reactions, it appeared they knew Captain Nikto. They weren't frightened by the arrival of three boats carrying eleven foreigners.

Chandler's smile vanished when he saw the condition of the shore. The water was carpeted with plastic and debris. An accumulation of water bottles, plastic bags, toy parts, even medicine bottles. The waves on the beach were mere sloshes of water, burdened by the weight of the trash.

Fixated on the refuse, Chandler nearly lost his balance when the boat abruptly stopped in the shoal. The children ran towards them with happy splashes. They were gaunt and barefoot, and shouted in a language he didn't understand.

To his far-right, Chandler noticed weathered tombstones just twenty feet from the water. Some slabs were overturned, leveled by the elements. He wondered who would build a cemetery so close to shore.

The young men who looked like pirates helped pull the boats onto the sand. Glistening with sweat, they were muscular but wiry. They didn't smile as much and shouted to each other in a foreign language.

Captain Nikto hung a satchel over his shoulder. He was the first to step ashore as his pilot helped Arrison and Chandler onto the beach. His crewmen tended to the bundles in the rafts.

Nikto turned to the children with raised arms. They encircled him as if he were some deity. He grinned and spoke to them in their native tongue.

"I thought they speak English in Ghana," Chandler whispered to his mother. "I don't know what that is."

Nikto reached into his pockets to produce handfuls of candy bars. He tossed them to the smaller children, and they all laughed and jabbered "Nikto!" with delight.

The captain turned to the men helping his crew. They were pulling the bales off the rafts and onto the beach. He shouted in their language with a tone that seemed more businesslike. The men nodded, then whistled to smaller boys to roll wooden carts to them.

Nikto turned to Chandler and Arrison. "This village is *Mohamé*." He pointed towards a murky waterway that spilled into the sea. "West Africa's rivers flow into the Bandama River. Then here." He scowled, "Imperiling my sea." He spoke with scorn for the sludge polluting his entire universe.

"What's that language?" Arrison asked.

"It is Akan," Nikto replied. "Indigenous, spoken by tribes in the southern regions. I speak Akan to show respect, just as I speak English to you."

Nikto spread his hands on Chandler and Arrison's shoulders. "There is someone I want you to meet in Mohamé." They began to walk inland.

Beyond a scrubby path, Chandler could see an assembly of shacks fifty yards away. He took a quick glance back towards the beach. The men were unloading the bundles into two wagons. When he saw what they were unpacking, he tried not to gasp.

The men were stacking white bricks. The bricks Landa recognized as narcotics.

Chapter Thirty-Seven
The Last Elder of Mohamé

"The village of Mohamé is one of the last of its kind." Nikto ushered Arrison and Chandler down a red-dirt path. "Those huts shelter the families, with a fence around the community they call a *kraal.*"

Chandler studied the village. Igloo-shaped huts had thatched roofs. Nikto explained the walls were made of woven branches plastered with an orange clay. Some sheds were plywood and bare aluminum panels. Outside their doors, large bowls were filled with the day's fresh water. Baby goats freely wandered the red sand that appeared neat as if it had been raked.

Children ricocheted between homes with excitement. They were all barefoot, and some wore secondhand t-shirts with outdated logos for "Blockbuster" and "Sports Authority."

Chandler paused his stride to see more shirtless young men holding rifles. They roamed the corners of the wooden fence like guards.

From one of the huts, a small person ambled on the path to meet them. Chandler presumed it was a small girl, but as she got closer, he realized she was a tiny, ancient woman. She was draped in a bright red garb and had a shriveled face that had to be over eighty years old.

Captain Nikto approached her and uttered *"Ete sen"* with a respectful bow. He then smiled with a traditional handshake.

"Ete sen, Nikto," the woman replied in a croaky voice. Her mahogany face gave a pruned smile.

Nikto turned to Arrison and Chandler, "This is Sewaa, an elder of Mohamé."

Timid, Chandler stepped forward to shake her hand. It felt small and fragile but had a strong grip. Arrison gave a timid tip of her head and then shook her hand.

"Elders maintain values and traditions of the tribe," Nikto explained while they greeted her. "They teach new generations."

Sewaa simply blinked at the guests.

"This is for you," Nikto reached into his bag to produce a bottle. "Peach schnapps, your favorite." He handed Sewaa the bottle.

The woman clutched it with both hands and pulled the bottle within inches of her eyes. Her entire face creased into a smile.

"Tell her, 'Nice to meet you,'" Arrison offered, hesitant.

"She hails from Ghana," Nikto replied. "She speaks English."

Seeing the men with rifles, Chandler blurted, "Ask her about the pirates."

Arrison winced at his graceless question.

"The men you call pirates," Nikto looked at him without any shame, "are Mohamé's coast guard."

ဢ

The four entered the wooden gates of the village. Nikto helped Sewaa walk by gently guiding her arm. Arrison and Chandler followed close behind.

Arrison thought the air smelled more pleasant than she'd expected. A scent of dry earth with a breeze of a wood fire and perhaps sage.

Chandler's eyes analyzed the structures, "The huts look almost new."

"Mohamé has been rebuilt four times," Nikto replied.

"From fires?" Arrison imagined with dismay, "Attacks of some kind?"

"A sort of attack, yes. From the sea." Nikto's voice became solemn. "Thanks to your climate change." He groaned the words.

"Coastal erosion?" Chandler guessed, "From global greenhouse emissions?"

"Yes," Nikto replied, sharp. "West Africa's coasts are most at risk. The rising waters will wash away Mohamé's shore by the end of the decade." He turned to Arrison, "In this village, three-quarters of its residents have left. The sea swallowed precious farmland. The school's playing field. Their only cemetery."

The tombstones on the beach, Arrison now understood.

Sewaa startled them by speaking up, "The sea wants to even take our dead." Though her voice was frayed, it was powerful. "Our elders for a thousand years. Gone forever."

Arrison and Chandler had no response. The place did seem to have limited residents, just a few kids and the young men. Was it inevitable that inhabitants of such villages ultimately move on to more modern towns?

Two teenage girls wearing colorful *kanga* fabrics emerged from a hut. They assisted Sewaa back inside as if they were handmaidens. Nikto, Arrison and Chandler remained in the sandy courtyard. They sat at a round wooden table that looked like it had been a giant spool for cable. Nikto lifted a bottle to fill three small glasses.

"Palm wine." He slid the glasses to Arrison and Chandler. "It is called *nsfufuo* in Ghana. Produced from the sap of palm trees."

Arrison examined her cup. The wine was white and cloudy. When she took a sip, it had a flavor between beer and a grape white wine. Though it was lukewarm, it was good.

Nikto rubbed his eyes with both hands and released a weary sigh. He seemed exhausted as if multiple events were taking their toll. Arrison wondered if he ever got frustrated of appearing virile all the time to so many. The weight of the world.

"In villages such as these," Nikto muttered, "anyone older than you has had more life experience. They are respected." He motioned to a young man gazing at his cellphone. "Knowledge here used to not be from technology. New generations know more about the outside world. So, the elders are dying out. Soon to be extinct."

"Dying out?" Chandler asked.

"Sewaa is sick." Nikto looked squarely into his eyes, "She is dying."

The three turned to see the young ladies escorting Sewaa to the table. They helped her sit next to Nikto, and then placed wooden bowls of food on the table.

Arrison smiled when children ran by chasing a ball. They were laughing, happy, but what did their future hold? She noticed two of the boys kept coughing. The more they ran, the more violent their coughs.

"Enjoy land food while you can," Nikto announced as he passed a bowl. "These are spiced yams they call *mpotompoto*. A delicacy."

When Chandler reached for the bowl, Nikto touched his arm.

"Use your right hand to receive items and to eat." Nikto gave a half-grin, "In this culture, your left hand is considered your 'toilet hand'."

Arrison almost chuckled but paused when she saw Sewaa. The woman cringed as if gored with a sharp pain.

Nikto sprung upright to help her. He whispered, asking if she was okay. The old woman dismissed him with a swoosh of her hand. She took a meditative breath and the pain seemed to subside.

When Sewaa looked up, she saw Chandler gawking at two armed young men. They had blank expressions and carried large AK-47s.

Sewaa pursed her lips and spoke, "The men you call pirates were once our fisherman."

Chandler looked at her, tongue-tied. "Fishermen, ma'am?"

"Mohamé once had many fishermen." The wizened woman became animated, speaking with her hands. "Before your nations came to steal from our waters. London, Paris, Spain…all dine on our fish. Our African fish."

"With no laws, many ships came here," Nikto added. "Cargo ships, cruise ships, and commercial fishing vessels came and took all the fish. The villages could no longer feed their families or earn." His eyes narrowed, "The ships dumped their waste. Fuel, oil, mercury."

"Our babies become sick!" Sewaa uttered in a hoarse voice. "So, our fishermen must fight back." Her words were fierce for a woman so delicate. "These are no pirates."

Arrison and Chandler sat dumbstruck. As a visitor from a first-world society, Arrison somehow felt culpable.

All four turned at a commotion. Boys were pulling the two wagons from the beach. For the first time, Arrison saw the mounds of countless white bricks, precisely as Landa had described.

"I know, I see it," Arrison whispered to Chandler after he nudged her with his elbow. She decided it was time to solve the dispute.

She cocked her head at Nikto, "What are those bricks?"

He didn't flinch. "They are kilos of cocaine and pure heroin."

Arrison felt numb. She had no sharp response. She was shocked, but why did it feel like a betrayal? Nikto had never made any promises about his moral character.

She felt a paralysis similar to the time Michael had been diagnosed with cancer. Her husband, Chandler, and her career had been her entire world, and her first love had been ripped from her.

She scrunched her face, *Nikto's nothing more than a grandiose drug dealer?* She turned to Chandler. His eyes revealed dismay like hers. Ned Landa had been right all along.

She'd grown fond of the captain. His discoveries, his devotion, and his passion for the oceans. This revelation felt like a death. The death of a fantasy. The man she had imagined was gone.

Nikto remained at the table, completely unflustered. The way he continued to speak, remaining so pragmatic, made him seem even more callous.

"Notice the clean, white color." Nikto pointed to the wrapped kilos, "Heroin from Colombia tends to be brown, chalky. Heroin in Europe is also brown, from Pakistan, Iran," he uttered those places with disdain. "However, white-powder heroin is more refined, pure. It is from Southeast Asia." He waved a hand, dismissive. "The powdered junk sold in the states has fillers or contaminants, sugars, and poison."

Chandler and Arrison sat mute, staggered by his words.

Sewaa groaned, hissing through her teeth. She doubled over, clutching her stomach.

Nikto shouted towards the hut, "Ladies, please! *Boa! Mesre!*" The two maidens instantly appeared. They approached Sewaa to help her stand.

Nikto placed a gentle hand on Sewaa's back. He leaned to her to whisper something. With trembling brows, he watched the ladies lead her away.

"Will she be okay?" Chandler asked with empathetic eyes. "Where's she going?"

"She is going to a home." Nikto plopped in his seat and looked heavenward. "In Abidjan, the closest city."

"Her family's home?" Arrison asked.

"She has no family," Nikto replied. "A home for the dying. You call it a hospice."

Arrison had an instant gush of emotion. Michael had spent his fragile last days at a hospice. She'd remained by his bedside, watching the disease ravage his body. Arrison's eyes began to well with tears. She flinched as Chandler put his arm around her.

Their moment was severed by the hacking of a ten-year-old girl. With a hand to her chest, she forcefully coughed several yards away. She then skipped away as if it were commonplace.

"Many more will become sick." Nikto saw the distress on Arrison's face. "Whether it's from the dumped poisons or something else," he raised his palms. "It will never be proven." He pointed inland, "They also have an infirmary for children."

Chandler and Arrison gazed into each other's eyes, grateful for what they had. They'd had no exposure to the afflictions of such remote worlds. These people's challenges were only footnotes in any mainstream news.

She paused with a frown. This revelation didn't seem to absolve Nikto from his menacing vocation until he spoke again.

"For patients in chronic or acute pain, opioids are an absolute godsend," Nikto declared.

Arrison turned to him. She had to recalibrate to grasp his words.

He continued, almost clinical, "Opium drugs force brain cells to release neurotransmitter chemicals such as dopamine and serotonin. They are key to our pain management system."

Her brows flexed, trying to fit his words to the circumstance.

"Opium-based drugs can be used to treat almost every type of pain," Nikto shrugged. "From headaches to the havoc of cancer."

One of the handmaidens approached from the hut. She dipped her head to Nikto and spoke in a soft voice. "Sewaa is resting." She turned to Arrison, "She wants you to have this. From one leader to another." She extended a hand holding an ornamental necklace.

Arrison took the jewelry, grateful, "Thank you." The indigenous necklace was a cord of leather, decorated with shells and mother of pearl.

"Sewaa knows you are also a leader." The maiden smiled at her, "It will bring you strength and enlightenment." She turned to Nikto, "Our offerings to you will be loaded on your boats."

"*Medaase,*" Nikto placed his hands together in praise. "Thank you." He bowed his head, "Unfortunately it is time for us to depart."

Nikto turned to Arrison and Chandler. "I will meet you at the skiffs. I'm going to say farewell to Sewaa."

"Will she be, okay?" Arrison asked, fully aware of the answer.

Nikto's eyes were misty. "This is the last time she and I will see each other. In this world."

Chapter Thirty-Eight
Sunset Bar & Grill

Arrison and Chandler stood on the shore while Nikto's men loaded the skiffs with stuffed burlap sacks given to them by the locals.

Chandler looked south to see the scattered tombstones of Mohamé. Some were now just ten or fifteen feet from the surf. Some had to be hundreds of years old, sandstone with edges rounded by age. A few were still upright; others tilted in their return to earth. He wondered how much longer Mohamé's people had before their entire existence would be erased.

When Chandler inhaled, there was a sulfuric stench from rotting seaweed. He wrinkled his nose, seeing the place for what it was. What had been a mysterious and enthralling African coast, was now immersed in decay and despair. Because of his compassion for their hardships, Chandler felt guilty about how he just wanted to leave.

☙

Captain Nikto ordered everyone back onto the skiffs. After a flurry of good-byes in two languages, they headed seaward. Nikto was again with Chandler and Arrison in the lead boat.

Arrison held her necklace in the lashing wind. It was a tangible memento of the place and people she'd encountered. If village elders were considered spiritual or mystical, perhaps it would truly empower her with enlightenment. She gave a somber grin at her imagination.

The three rafts were loaded with a variety of the area's crops. Bags were labeled yams, sugarcane, or cocoa beans. Nikto had stated Ghana was one of the world's largest producers of cocoa. They'd also loaded several bunches of bananas that were still green. It was no longer a mystery where the *Naumtsev's* galley got its terrestrial ingredients.

Is it payment for what Nikto gave them? Arrison considered. That didn't seem commensurate. *Heroin for groceries?* Her shoulders tensed at the reminder that she still needed answers. No longer intimidated by the captain, she leaned close to speak to him.

"So you supplied that town with stolen narcotics?" She made the word revolting.

Nikto nodded, unshaken. "Not just a town, but an entire region of similar villages."

Arrison glowered at his response. "Thousands of kilos of opiates to help people in pain? At infirmaries?" She gave an animated shrug. "You had enough to supply…Florida."

He flashed an ill-timed smirk at her comment. "There are two opioid crises in the world." He looked at her, "One is the plague of abuse, which is truly abhorrent. The other is how the world's poorest nations have no access to morphine for pain and the dying. The US, Canada, and Europe consume ninety percent of the drugs like candy. In poor nations, terminal patients with just weeks to live cannot access opioids for their tormenting pain."

Nikto paused to tell the pilot to proceed on their course. He then kneeled beside Arrison with sober eyes.

"Not all is for the sick," he conceded. "In the world's poorest nations, narcotics are treated like gold. Those kilos may as well have been stacked bars of gold bullion."

Her eyes fluttered at the perspective. "But it's still drugs. How could you with children everywhere?"

"Granted," Nikto nodded, "I will not see the poor souls who may succumb to abuse." He lifted a finger, "But I did see the faces of the children we just fed. Do you realize that load was enough to purchase medication, clothing, shoes, and nourishment for thousands?"

She slumped at the concept, "Thousands?"

"Not just here," Nikto pointed south and east, "Angola, Namibia, Mozambique…some of the poorest nations on the entire globe."

Arrison blinked into space, "These people aren't your only recipients."

Instead of a reply, Nikto stood to give a final, outstretched wave to the children onshore.

Chandler clutched his mother's shoulder to point in front of the raft. It was the *Naumtsev* surfacing and it was indeed ominous. From within a churn of foam, its serrated snout and green porthole eyes lurked at their arrival like a gigantic crocodile's head.

৩

The crewmen threw ropes to men standing on the *Naumtsev's* hull. The rafts were tied in place, and a procession of men began to unload the provisions like a relay.

Arrison and Chandler sat on the hull to absorb the last precious moments of open sky and warm sunlight.

She watched Nikto, standing with his men, smiling, and giving orders in each of their languages. She wasn't convinced yet of the man's integrity. As an academic, she condemned any sort of drug trafficking. *But he's helping children and the sick?* She debated with herself, *maybe thousands?* The locals had embraced him like a savior.

Having heard Nikto's entire speech, Chandler was mute on the matter, undoubtedly weighing all scenarios.

"Remember that documentary about Pablo Escobar?" Chandler asked close to her ear.

She almost choked, "The Colombian drug lord?"

"He built schools, hospitals…even churches for the poor," Chandler replied. "Locals loved him."

"He was a sociopath and a killer!" Arrison snapped. "Escobar did those things to buy respect." She lowered her voice, "Nikto told us drug lords took someone he loved…" She looked towards Nikto with his men. "I think they did something horrible to him," she mused. "Something terrified him."

Before Chandler could respond, the captain approached with a white smile.

"Enough sorrow for one day." Nikto shouted with outstretched arms, "Let us now celebrate life." He turned to his men to announce, "A steel beach with all the food the crew can eat!"

The men applauded and cheered his name.

ๆ

As the gilded sun neared the horizon, the *Naumtsev*'s crew was spread across its hull. Shirtless and wearing shorts, the men howled and dove into the sea. Some climbed the aft rudder to do flips from fifteen feet. A joyous clamor of Spanish and Russian voices filled the air.

Arrison had watched two men attach stainless steel grills to the deck. A chef was preparing thick steaks of tuna and split lobster tails the size of footballs.

Wearing a t-shirt and borrowed men's boxers, Arrison sat on the hull's incline with her feet in the water. The grill hissed with steam as the chef painted the tails with butter. She inhaled the sweet fragrance of grilled seafood.

A blender whirred to her right. A man was dropping fresh bananas into a large industrial blender with a bottle of Tapanga rum from South Africa. He shouted, "*Daiquiris de plátano!*" The scent, sounds, and mild breeze were sublime.

Arrison turned to locate the captain. He was standing at the base of the sail with his crew around him as if telling them a story. Nikto wore a black tank top that revealed a lean body, more chiseled than she'd imagined. She had never seen the captain so jovial or relaxed.

The men burst out with laughter at some punchline. Nikto slapped them on their backs and lifted a bottle of vodka. He shouted a toast in Russian, "*Dlya zdorov'ya!*" He took a deep swig and passed the bottle to the next man.

Was this finally the real Nikto? Arrison could tell he was happy, perhaps satisfied a crucial mission had been completed. Was this the equivalent of sailors coming into port for rest and recuperation?

If that's the case, Arrison's eyes gleamed, *where to next?* She recognized a new sensation: she was no longer anxious about their fate.

As she looked towards the stern with a distant gaze, Nikto captured her glance. When she realized their eyes were connected, he grinned.

She paused, then waved at the man with a demure smile.

ↄ

"Where'd everyone go?" Landa grumbled to himself. Whatever they were doing topside, he needed the time to finish his objective.

He had walked straight to his quarters from the moon well. After he closed the door, he pulled a folded paper from his pants. He opened it to study his artwork. In pencil, he'd sketched a schematic of the inner workings of a C-Buoy. While in the torpedo room, he'd disassembled the damaged buoy to see what made it tick. He'd been methodical when opening and reassembling the orb so no one would know it had been disturbed.

Aside from tamper-proof security screws—which he was able to tamper with—dissecting its guts had almost been fun. He'd heard of similar buoys used for underwater mapping and tsunami forecasting. In addition to having air chambers so it could float, the ball had two components: an antenna to connect to satellites, and a mechanism for self-destruction.

Landa found its simplicity fascinating. The buoy was designed to perform its function—in this case communication—then scuttle itself to remove any evidence of its existence. A trio of sharp barbs were designed to spring up to puncture the orb. When water entered the buoy, it sank. The saltwater even destroyed the batteries to avoid emitting any traceable signal.

Reviewing his drawing, Landa studied four dry-cell batteries located in the center of the buoy. They powered an accelerometer that converted electronic signals and then provided power to the self-destruction barbs.

Landa stroked his jaw. *How can I use this to my advantage?* He was an armaments expert, not a techy. He didn't know anything about reprogramming circuits, nor did he have the tools. He couldn't just transmit "help" to some satellite.

His scribbled diagram and intersecting lines were almost overwhelming. *Where do I even begin?* He ran his fingers across his scalp.

As he was about to refold the paper, his eyes were drawn to the center of the sketch. *The batteries.* Everything requires power to function. A battery was also needed for the spring that triggered the puncture barbs. Landa squinted closer to his drawing, sure enough, a single wire led to the motor. *Occam's razor.* The simplest solution is usually the best.

Landa smirked. All he'd need was old-fashioned wire cutters.

❦

Chandler stepped away from his mother and Nikto. They were still seated, talking about every archeological marine myth on the planet as they ate lobster and skewers of grilled prawns. Chandler had plans to mend his own relationship.

He meandered through the crewmen waiting in the chow line. He gave a few bashful nods as he proceeded towards the bow. He looked up at the sail and back down at the hull to estimate a specific location several decks below. *I'm now center ship,* he established. He stomped forward, *fifty feet would be twelve paces.* He counted as he walked.

Pavlo had tipped him off that Pilar was reading alone in the parlor. He hadn't seen her since their quarrel, and he truly missed being anywhere in her general vicinity.

When Chandler believed he found the right spot, he gazed down at the hull. He took off his shirt, took a deep breath, crouched, and dove into the clear water.

❦

Pilar was sprawled on a rug, propped on an elbow to read. Draped in green silk pajamas, she wanted nothing more of the day. She relished her peace, with no desire to be with the sweaty crew splashing like imbeciles. However, she had been wondering about

223

one specific young man.

She had been upset with Chandler because he'd dared to call her out. And he'd been right; she was complicit in her dilemma. She should be fighting her captor with all her might, but she wasn't. She traveled the seas in luxurious comfort, with free rein of the vessel.

Why don't I hate Nikto? She fumed with conflicted emotions. Her brows softened at a possibility. Her fate would have been much worse if she'd stayed with her father. He was a criminal with lethal enemies.

But not my mother. Pilar's heart fluttered. She could envision her mother's luminous face. Her likeness would remain the same age forever because she'd never see her again. If her mother ever searched for her, it could lead the real enemies to the *Naumtsev*. The true evil.

Pilar shook off a sudden chill and looked down at her book. The Iris window provided a tranquil light. She was lying three feet from the glass like a cat curled in front of a fireplace. Curious fish hovered to see what she was reading.

She was enjoying Frank Herbert's *Dune* for the fourth time. A saga set on arid, dry land. No seas, boats, kelp, or sharks anywhere in sight. She had a rotating library of science fiction and American westerns, anything without oceans or submarines. Desperately needed escapism from the ugly facets of her youth.

As Pilar turned a page, she flinched at something beyond the book. She looked up to see a figure descending outside the window. *A seal? A porpoise?* Her brain raced through possibilities in a blink of an eye. Then she saw him.

Chandler was outside the window, upside down and grasping the glass like a tree frog. He flailed his pale arms to reach the center of the window. His cheeks were puffed, and his eyes were the size of quarters. With cupped hands, he pressed his face to the glass.

Pilar stood with a brilliant smile. Though he wouldn't hear her, she shouted, "Hello!"

Chandler waved at her. With a spurt of bubbles, he swam back towards the surface.

Pilar covered her mouth with a laugh, then she got an idea.

❧

Chandler stood alone in the parlor, wet and clutching a robe around him. With an eager grin, he waited in front of the same window.

Minutes earlier, he'd hopped out of the water, clambered up the hull, and had jogged to the parlor in record time. People who saw him probably guessed he had a personal emergency.

He panted to catch his breath. The parlor was cold and being wet didn't help. He pulled the robe tighter and there she was.

Pilar appeared outside the window, submerged in her silk pajamas. Unlike him, her strokes were slow and graceful. She seemed to float upside down, with her long hair suspended around her face. Her eyes were open, and her motions were elegant, with no indication she required oxygen.

Chandler was entranced. In the past weeks, he'd witnessed rare sea creatures, pirates, and even Atlantis. But there was one fabled being he still yearned to see. A mermaid.

Pilar's green silk flowed around her feet like a tail. She slid down the opposite side of the glass with a serene smile. With fluid motions, she twirled upright so their faces were aligned.

He was drawn to her, spellbound. Pilar placed her supple lips on the window. He closed his eyes and kissed the opposite side of the seven-inch glass.

After an eternal moment, he opened his eyes to see her gone. *Was it a dream?* In a stupor, he looked up to see a glimpse of the mermaid's tail swimming toward the surface.

PART VI

ULTIMA THULE

Noun. (*Latin*) – In classical and medieval cartography and literature, the term is the region believed to be the farthest point in the known world.

"Where no ships can sail."

—*Claudian*, Latin poet, 400 A.D.

Chapter Thirty-Nine
What Makes it Go

New London, Connecticut

At less than eleven square miles—half of which is water—New London was one of the smallest cities in Connecticut.

Located at the mouth of the Thames River, it was a seaport city on the northeast coast of the United States. In the early 19th century, it was one of the world's busiest whaling ports, along with Nantucket and New Bedford, Massachusetts. Times and commerce had changed.

ℯↄ

"Why do you have to go to New London?" Officer Engel's boss, Lieutenant Commander Gregory Law, asked while scanning an unrelated report.

Engel replied with veiled sarcasm, "How else can I get to the Naval Sub Base that's in New London?"

"In your role," Gregory scrolled through his phone as he spoke, "travel should be infrequent. Have you attempted Skype or Zoom or whatever?"

Engel huffed and sat on the edge of his desk. "Captain Berryhill

229

received my memo—with color images—over twenty-four hours ago. I haven't heard a peep. I need to present this in person."

Irked by his inattention, Engel said his first name, "Gregory." He looked at her. "I can get there in six hours. I'm offering to drive there myself."

"All right." Commander Law wiped his face with a hand. "But no pool car. You can expense a rental and no meal per diem!"

"Thank you, sir." Engel turned, triumphant.

"Listen, Engel," Gregory called out. He fidgeted with a pen, more pensive. "I haven't fully wrapped my head around what you've found. Please report to me right away what the captain and his men propose."

"Will do."

He shouted, "And please watch that matter-of-fact sarcasm thing."

☙

Engel left her house at 4:00 am to be at the Naval Submarine Base by 10:00 am. If she were fortunate enough to get an hour of their time, she'd be back home for dinner with Chuck and Sean. She'd texted Chuck a recipe, with his promise to make dinner two nights a week.

Engel had never been to the base, but she'd read about it. SUBASE New London was across the Thames River from its namesake city. Though in a tiny, unassuming town with a green bank along its river, the base was the US Navy's primary east coast submarine base. Some called it the "Home of the Submarine Force."

The base was now the home to sixteen attack submarines and the Navy's Basic Enlisted Sub School, an eight-week program that taught sailors about the rigors of undersea life.

Engel couldn't imagine being cooped up on a claustrophobic submarine, with zero comforts, no windows, and terrible food.

☙

"Tom, believe me," implored the silver-haired captain, "we want to do a July Fourth barbecue. But in this day and age, there are so many horse shit rules about booze."

"Captain," a lean Commander Hewson lifted a hand to interject,

230

"I promise we'll get back to the barbecue," He motioned to Engel seated beside him, "But we have one more agenda item. Officer Engel here, the analyst who drove from DC, so…" He raised his palms as if apologizing for her inclusion.

It was a dreary government-issue conference room—trapped somewhere in the mid-nineties—with an American and Navy flag shoved in the corner. Ten officers were seated around the conference table. They studied their guest with vacant gazes, then turned back to their captain.

"Ah yes, Officer Engel." The striking, sixtyish Captain Berryhill wore a hearing aid in one ear and seemed to shout everything. "Thank you, ma'am, for driving up. I understand you have something for our 'urban myths' folder."

A few chuckled, kissing up to their boss as they passed a box of Entenmann's donuts.

Engel bobbed her head with a smile. It wasn't the first time she'd been snubbed in front of others. Based on recent events, she was ready. As her daddy used to say about duck hunting, "There's no better ammo than being early and loaded."

"I know you've all read my report," Engel waived a paper copy in the air. "When I emailed it, the return receipts all said 'read.'" She grinned, "Not to be redundant, but I'll summarize for anyone who might've missed a few words."

On an old-school television monitor, her presentation appeared. Engel aimed a remote and the screen filled with a satellite image of a port.

"This is Buenaventura, Colombia." She remained behind her laptop. "This image was captured four years ago on July 8th. In the center, you can see an object that appears to be a submarine." The object was long and black, docked alongside a pier. "But no known subs were on the roster that day. We checked with Customs and the port captain. No submarine from any nation was on any lists or manifests."

She allowed a moment for the men to study the image. They were quieter and stopped passing the donuts.

"It's nine times larger than any narco-sub." Engel zoomed in to focus on the long object. "I don't need to tell you gentlemen it has the exact contours as a Russian Akula. A Russian sub would never dock in Colombia based on its diplomatic status. If it did so due to some emergency, the US would know about it within minutes."

Captain Berryhill's forehead creased, "How did no one catch this four years ago?"

"Satellite imagery flows nonstop, 24/7," Engel replied. "Our government has 154 satellites taking photos of everything, every day. But no one looks at every picture." Engel removed her glasses. "So, I searched precise dates based on calls between a cartel and a Russian broker. I found this on the week of July 8th."

The officers sat a little taller in their seats.

Engel gained an ounce of confidence. "Out of fifteen Akulas, only five are said to still be operational. If any are dismantled, the UN has no process to confirm." She zoomed even closer to the black sub. "This seems to document one was in a port operated by a Colombian cartel four years ago. Completely off the books."

The men blinked at the table for a moment as if solving equations in their heads.

"Even if that were remotely true," Commander Hewson asked with a crooked grin, "How's some narco scumbag going to pilot a 48,000-ton Russian sub?"

On cue, Engel projected a chart with a dozen black and white photos. "There have been twenty-five Russian sub captains since the Cold War." The image showed grainy photos of twelve men. "These twelve captains are either retired, reportedly went down with their vessels or AWOL. The Federation doesn't have resources to keep tabs on all their former officers."

The men squinted to study the portraits. They were all stern white men between forty and sixty years old. Aside from any facial hair, they all looked roughly the same.

"Anything new since four years ago?" Berryhill had his pen ready.

Engel pursed her lips with a nod. "There have been reported sightings that match. From various coast guards, all chalked-up as nonsense." She began typing. "But when I cross-reference the dates and times to satellite images…"

The screen filled with a Google Earth-type image of a dark cigar shape under the water.

"Thirty-one days ago," Engel narrated. "A shape was reported by a boater twenty-six miles south of Key West. Thanks to clear water, that shape is estimated at over 350 feet."

Before anyone could interject, she projected another satellite photo. Beside a small moon-shaped island was a long, dark shape with a white trail.

"Just over a week ago. Reported by fishermen to Haiti's Coast Guard responding to a sinking vessel. The victims gave a farfetched account of a monster-sized object. The authorities didn't believe them, but I pulled the satellite." She looked up at the image. "You can see a white plume behind the shape that appears to be a wake."

A few of the men took notes with brooding frowns. Engel closed her laptop and folded her hands. When all eyes were upon her, she continued.

"We have an intel department at Guantanamo." Engel maintained a smile, "Last week, we intercepted a transmission that Cuba fired a torpedo at an unidentified submarine and missed. Our hydrophones picked up the blast, south of Cienfuegos, which supports the claim."

"We don't have any subs in Cuba," Hewson exclaimed.

"Exactly," Engel snapped. "And Cuba only has a seventy-foot Delfin. So, it wasn't one of theirs."

"Why can't we just ask Russia if it's theirs?" Captain Berryhill shrugged.

Engel almost chuckled, "Why would a communist nation fire at a Russian submarine?" She smirked despite the man's rank. "We will ask their Ministry of Defense, but they'll never tell us the truth anyway."

The captain's face drooped like a hound.

"If a country ever 'loses' a sub, such as Argentina's missing sub in 2017 and Indonesia's in 2021, they ask for international help." Engel paused, "No one's declaring this one."

She displayed a map of the Atlantic with multiple highlighted dots. "With the attacks off Florida and the satellite sightings, we have nine points…" Engel turned to the men with drama, "Something—belonging to 'no-one'—is in your Atlantic."

After a second of silence, Captain Berryhill blinked. "Jesus H." He looked at Hewson. "Tom: order the Atlantic fleet to employ passive sonar?"

Hewson gave a measured nod. "That will hear anything propelled with a screw or engine."

Berryhill jerked his head to Engel with abrupt concern. "Do any of the unaccounted Russian subs still have weaponry?"

The men murmured and looked at Engel.

"Does that even matter?" She shrugged, stuffing reports back into her briefcase.

The room winced, bewildered by her glib response.

Engel stood. "Akulas use highly-enriched uranium for power, HEU," she explained as if addressing students. "Not the low-grade stuff found in power plants. HEU is what's used to create nuclear weapons. Whether they have weapons or not, the fuel from just one Akula could create a dozen nuclear warheads."

A mortal hush fell over the room. The men's eyes plead for direction.

Engel turned towards the door and smiled, "I'll let you get back to your barbecue."

The image of the twelve missing Russian submarine captains remained on the monitor. Unbeknownst to anyone in the room, a slender bearded man in the center of the screen now went by a different name: Nikto.

Captain No One.

Chapter Forty
The Court of King Neptune

The Gulf of Guinea

With a gorgeous copper dawn, 1,900 nautical miles west of Namibia, a small C-buoy bobbed to the surface. Its nub antenna connected to the iridium satellite constellation, a collection of sixty-six satellites circling at a low orbit of just 485 miles over the Atlantic.

Within minutes, the *Naumtsev* would download days of valuable information. The satellites were mostly used for cellphone data, GPS navigation and internet for news and weather. The buoy could then connect to the antiquated Russian Luch Satellite Data Relay Network, to read military hacks into US and international intelligence.

At times—and as a special treat—Nikto would allow the C-Buoy to link to broadcast satellites to download movies and television for the crew's library.

Dmitri monitored the influx of data from his comm station. Priding himself as an expert *khaker*, he had explained to Nikto how satellites were absurdly easy to infiltrate.

Most satellites were old, running on obsolete systems such as Windows 95. To the owning nations, it was more expensive to take down old satellites than to just leave them up. If a satellite were ever hacked, it'd be thorny for the countries to act without upsetting international relations. And the nations couldn't just send repairmen into space to diagnose the problem.

After a three-minute data dump to the vessel, containing more information than it could ever use for days, barbs sprang up to rupture the buoy. It filled with water and sunk without a trace.

Twenty meters below, the *Naumtsev* cruised on.

∾

Chandler was in bed, still reeling from the night before. And it had nothing to do with Africa.

Before midnight, he and his mother had been roused from their beds with blinding flashlights and earsplitting air horns. Chandler had thought it was a nuclear emergency.

When his eyes had adjusted, he saw his mother equally frightened. They were surrounded by a half-dozen crewmen with enraged scowls.

"You are to be on trial!" shouted a six-foot Russian.

With barely time to dress, Chandler and Arrison were shoved together and ushered down the passageway. They were steered so quickly, that neither could ask what was happening.

He looked at his mom. She shook her head. Chandler tried to imagine what they'd done. He'd spent most of the evening with Pilar. Had he broken one of the captain's rules?

Chandler had noticed Nikto wasn't there, nor Dmitri or even Pavlo. Just Colombian and Russian crewmen. *What if this is a mutiny?* His heart quickened.

They continued into a less-hospitable corridor. The lead man, a huge Russian in a tank top, kicked open a door that led to the crew's mess hall. The mob pushed Chandler and Arrison into the dark room and entered behind them.

He and his mother were in the center of an open space. The men slammed the door behind them and stood along the walls.

At the far end of the room, a row of men faced them like a firing squad. But they were seated in chairs. When a light turned on, Chandler was bewildered by what he saw. The men were wearing odd costumes and wigs like barristers. Was this some judge and jury?

The row of men stood. It took a second to realize Captain Nikto was in the center dressed in a "King Neptune" costume. Like a feverish dream, Nikto scowled, wearing a phony white beard, a crown, blue satin, and a cape. He held an upright trident. His chair was painted gold like a throne.

To Nikto's right, Dmitri was dressed like the devil in a vintage Halloween costume. A red hood on his head had horns and he held a pitchfork.

Pavlo stood to Nikto's left wearing a bear costume. All the outfits were frayed as if they'd been heavily used. Waking to the abrupt scene, with the retro costumes, was disturbing and made no sense.

"Why are we here?" Dr. Arrison shouted. She darted her head, terrified.

Chandler didn't like seeing his mother distressed. Some of the men behind them chuckled.

"You will not speak!" roared Nikto, gripping his trident like a sea god. From his throne, he eyed Arrison and Chandler like they were felons.

"You are both arrogant," Nikto growled, "to believe you are seaworthy enough to be here. To cross the prime meridian at precisely zero-degrees longitude and zero-degrees latitude?"

Chandler and Arrison went stiff, even more baffled. The nightmare was getting weirder.

"You are nothing more than pollywogs!" Nikto almost smirked saying the absurd word. "You only dream of being shellbacks!" His face contorted as if restraining a laugh.

Something triggered a memory. *Pollywogs? Shellbacks?* Chandler knew those words. *Zero-degrees latitude is the..."* He then saw Ned Landa in the corner. The man was grinning ear-to-ear with his arms crossed. More of the crew began to laugh.

Chandler released a heavy sigh. This wasn't a dream, and they weren't in any trouble.

Nikto burst into laughter. He pointed at them, and the men began to applaud.

Arrison looked at Chandler as it dawned on her as well. She covered her face with a grin.

This was a historic maritime tradition. An equator-crossing ceremony.

From the sides of the room, corks were popped on bottles of champagne. They sprayed Arrison and Chandler like fire hoses. With a wide smile, Pilar entered to turn on speakers playing electronic dance music.

The celebration had just begun.

Still hazed on champagne, Chandler had to recall his discussion with Nikto about the line-crossing ritual. It was a tradition from as far back as the 17th century to commemorate a person's first crossing of the equator. It was created to boost morale and as a test to confirm shipmates could endure rough seas.

The term "pollywog" —which is a tadpole— was used for anyone who had never crossed the equator. A sailor who achieved the feat earned the name "shellback." The costumes and court, including King Neptune, had been part of the tradition in almost every maritime culture.

Considering the *Naumtsev*'s position, it made sense. They were 650 miles west of the Republic of Congo, the coordinates for the prime meridian, zero-degrees latitude. The equator was 300 miles south of Ghana. Chandler's eyes widened with a delayed reaction: they had just crossed the equator at precisely zero-degrees latitude and longitude.

When he'd been studying alone in FSU's library just one month earlier, he'd had no clue in weeks he'd be crossing the planet at 0,0 degrees, in the Gulf of Guinea, while twenty meters underwater.

He looked up at Pilar standing over him. He now had a beautiful lady asking him to dance.

In his euphoric state, he felt like a different person.

ം

At 6:00 am GMT (Greenwich Meridian Time) Dmitri plopped in his seat with a second cup of coffee to review the C-Buoy data. Today's brew was an Ethiopian *Harrar* they'd picked up in Africa. It was spicy and full-bodied with an almost wine-like texture. He sipped with his eyes closed behind lenses fogged by steam.

He studied his monitors, deciphering the influx of information on three screens. Scouring for keywords such as "Russian submarine," revealed no news or sightings of their existence. International news appeared mundane; nations squabbling over borders or mocking America's leadership. A new tropical depression had formed on the other side of the globe, too far to be of any concern. No new pandemics. In other words, worthless news.

When Dmitri checked the data from the Russian satellites, he halted his lighter before it touched his cigarette. It appeared US Navy systems had been infiltrated. He squinted within inches of the screen to read the decrypted code.

His jaw fell open and his cigarette tumbled to the deck.

∽

Nikto slouched behind his desk. His office was his sanctuary to begin and conclude his days. Whether to chart destinations or grieve any past or present losses.

Smoking his pipe gave him comfort. His pipe was an heirloom from his father, made of carved whale bone called scrimshaw. This morning he had chosen a sweet pipe tobacco from their last visit to the Aegean islands off Greece, an area that few knew had excellent tobacco.

Despite a gnawing headache, he smiled. The line-crossing ceremony had been fun. He liked seeing joy on his guests' faces as well as his crew's. He blew smoke at the ceiling, realizing joy was less and less frequent. *Patrice Arrison brings me joy.*

He felt a twinge of guilt thinking about Patrice. He truly enjoyed her company, her intellect and passion. She was the first female who shared his desire for their undersea world. He felt guilty because Kana's portrait was staring at him. With her haunting smile, black silk hair and astute eyes. A photo he had taken himself while at their secret chalet near Buenaventura's port during the Naumtsev's renovations.

Would Kana approve of Dr. Arrison? Nikto wondered. They were both scientists; both beautiful and scholarly. They would have enjoyed discussing her innovations for sea exploration.

A glower creased his face like an imminent storm. Kana wasn't with him now because of him. *Gone because of our shared desires.* Don Ricardo Salazar hadn't trusted Nikto because of their romance. So, the cartel took her from this world. *It was all my fault.*

Then came the true terror his dreams could never elude. He squeezed his eyes closed. At least in the *Naumtsev*, he could escape them all for an eternity. Until every mile of the sea has been crossed.

He dabbed a tear with a sleeve. With a sudden knock on his door, he sat upright. He applied a thin smile and shouted, "*Voyditye!*"

Dmitri entered like a whirlwind. He closed the door behind him and turned, panting. "I received data from the *Luch* Relay." He took a breath and continued in Russian, "I read an order from the American Navy from a full day ago!"

Knowing Dmitri's flair for the dramatic, Nikto remained calm. "What is the crisis?"

Dmitri stepped closer, "Sub Force Atlantic has ordered its fleet to listen for a 'rogue submarine.'" He accented the term. "If that were my job, I would use passive sonar." He became animated, "Kapitan, if their entire fleet is actively listening—"

"Settle yourself." Nikto interjected, smoothing his sweater. "How certain is the data?"

Dmitri laughed, "US encryption is over a decade old." He shrugged at the simplicity. "If they employ passive sonar, they will hear any signature, any engine, propeller or pump noise from any vessel that crosses their path."

Nikto leaned his chair back on two legs with hands behind his head. "Demetrios, do you realize the Atlantic Ocean is over forty-one million square miles?"

"Kapitan," Dmitri straightened his glasses. "Their Atlantic fleet has thirty-two submarines."

Nikto's chair dropped upright. He squinted in a futile effort to calculate the probability of being heard by one of thirty-two vessels, spread within a definable space. After a pause, he reached for a brass globe on his desk. He touched the South Atlantic with a finger.

"As I see it, there is only one solution to avoid a fleet in the Atlantic." Nikto slid his finger down the globe. "We go to the Pacific."

Chapter Forty-One
Days of *Scheherazade*

Tropic of Capricorn

"How do you know we're going to the Pacific?" Arrison remained quiet, "The captain never discusses destinations."

The three guests stood together, encircled by an Iris window. After breakfast—a welcomed change of Ghana's oats and brown sugar—Landa joined Arrison and Chandler in the parlor. The Arrisons had been guessing their location by types of fish. From the parlor's compass, they knew the *Naumtsev* had been traveling south-southwest.

"I was working in the torpedo room," Landa explained in a whisper. "Two Colombians were yammering. They don't know I speak Spanish." Landa bent closer, "They were told we're heading to the Pacific 'as fast as we can.'"

"The Pacific?" Arrison scrunched her face, "Why the rush?"

Landa chuckled, "There's only one reason a fish jumps from one pond to another. If it's fleeing something…big." He paused, "I think there's a hunt for a hostile sub."

Arrison blinked at the ceiling. "The Pacific will take us a week."

"What about the Panama Canal?" Chandler countered.

"Too shallow to stay submerged," Landa shook his head. "Parts of the canal are just forty feet deep. This sub is seven-stories tall with the sailfin."

Chandler spun to his mother, "We'll have to go south of Argentina."

Landa was bothered by the boy's excitement. Had he missed the point entirely? Landa considered the news a bad thing. It created a diminished chance of being saved.

Arrison's eyes flared, "You think we'll see Antarctica? At forty knots, that'd only be…three more days."

Landa was confounded by their behavior. Despite their backgrounds, they'd once been peers, all prisoners of this Nikto. Now they were celebrating the possibility of more adventure?

He knew it was time to return to the torpedo room. More precisely, the C-Buoy rack.

⌘

Captain Nikto enjoyed playing the symphony *Scheherazade* by Russian composer Nikolai Rimsky-Korsakov through the ship's speakers. He explained Scheherazade was the beautiful bride in the Middle Eastern folktales, *One Thousand and One Nights*. In the fables, she told her husband one story per night. To sustain his interest, she wouldn't finish the story until the following night. She continued, night after night, hence the *1,001 nights*.

The silhouettes of the three guests stood at the bright Iris window. As the music played, the *Naumtsev* whooshed by forty meters beneath the surface.

The suite's first movement, "The Sea and Sinbad's Ship," fit their moods. Each of their stories were being doled out, one long day at a time. They were perpetually on the edges of their seats to await the destination of the following day. And the day after that.

⌘

Arrison used her days to write. Though she was no artist, she attempted to sketch Atlantis. The columns laced with fish, the towering statue of a female ruler, the circular symbols. With no cameras, the drawings would

243

have to suffice. With no exact coordinates, she wrote: "Approximately two hundred miles west of the Bay of Pigs."

She penned a heartbreaking account of her experience in Mohamé. The condition of their water, the children, the ill, the demise of their existence. For its location, she again had to guess, "Côte d'Ivoire, yet closer to Ghana."

Arrison paused at Nikto's music, hearing exotic swirls of eastern melodies. Would a day ever come where she'd have to prove her visits to such places?

What if I want to see more places?

❧

Chandler and Pilar sat close, legs touching on the torpedo room floor. They spent their days cooing and laughing, away from the humorless others.

"*Pasa la botella, por favor,*" Chandler asked in near-perfect Spanish. Pilar's daily lessons were paying off.

"*Muy bien,*" she smiled and handed him the champagne bottle.

The day's tube discoveries had included a case of Louis Roederer Cristal Brut 2008, Manchego cheese from Spain, Le Gruyère Swiss, and more cigars.

They enjoyed virtual picnics on the torpedo room floor. Though the deck was cold steel, Pilar told stories of the green rolling hills of Colombia, with a promise for a real picnic one day.

Chandler swigged the champagne, envisioning her words.

Pilar blew cigar smoke and wiped her lip with a thumb. She took the bottle out of his hand and placed it on the deck. She then straddled his slender waist.

Before he could gasp, she clasped his face by his ears. She pulled him close for an intense, passionate kiss.

By either the effects of the champagne, her alluring perfume, or her soft lips, Chandler didn't want to be anywhere else on the globe.

❧

Arrison was shocked how much Nikto revealed of their coordinates.

He invited her to his study to see his charts. Though the *Naumtsev* used electronic navigation, he said he enjoyed the feel and smell of paper, unfurled on his desk like ancient treasure maps.

"We are here," Nikto touched a latitude as they leaned over the chart. "Eight hundred miles east of Rio de Janeiro."

Arrison studied the map. They'd cruised a straight line from Ghana towards Brazil. South of Brazil was Uruguay, and then Argentina, supporting Chandler's guess at their route.

"We'll head south of Argentina, past the Falklands, and then 'round Cape Horn to the Pacific."

Her eyes widened, "Aren't the waters of Cape Horn the most hazardous in the world?"

Nikto grinned, "Not forty meters beneath the surface." He placed a hand on her lower back as he spoke.

For the first time, she didn't mind.

&

Ned Landa wished he had earbuds as he worked. He'd had enough of the captain's pretentious Russian operas. Knowing he was alone; he lifted a C-Buoy from its rack.

It was the next buoy to be launched. He rolled it over to expose its base. He opened the compartment as he'd done before. He simply located a red wire leading from the battery housing to the motor that operated the self-destruct barbs. With a single snip, he cut the wire.

Within minutes he reassembled the buoy and placed it back in its rack. He rubbed his weary eyes with a hand. There was nothing left to do but wait.

&

With the more frigid latitude off the coast of Patagonia, orca killer whales appeared beside the *Naumtsev*.

Chandler and Pilar were riveted, inches from the chilled window. Three beautiful mammals raced alongside the vessel just as the blue whales had done.

The graceful creatures were just as playful as their larger cousins.

They were glistening black with white patterns around their eyes and abdomens. They veered up and down, keeping up with the *Naumtsev's* speed.

Pilar rested her head on his shoulder. Nikto's piano seemed to complement the scene. But Chandler tensed when the music abruptly changed.

Curious about Russian composers, Chandler had asked the captain about *Scheherazade*. When Nikto had played the first movement, it was bold, with gravitas and ego. It was clear Nikto believed that about himself. In the tale, the music surged, like waves rocking the ship led by the fearless Sinbad.

When Nikto later played the second movement, it was exotic with Persian influences, hinting at adventures in faraway lands.

He had then enjoyed how the third movement was dreamier and romantic. Pilar liked its title, "The Young Prince and the Young Princess."

Chandler was now cold from the window. Nikto had begun playing the fourth movement. It had a different sound, frenzied and chaotic, suggesting violent waves.

When he had asked about *Scheherazade's* fourth movement, Nikto had flashed a devilish grin. "In the tale, the bold captain chooses to enter a raging storm. He ultimately crashes his vessel, overcome by a bronze warrior."

Nikto had shrugged, "That is simply the story. That will not be us."

❦

15,000 feet above sea level, a young Navy flight officer sat at his console. He had his chin in his hand, about to doze after a tedious day of training.

He flinched, eyes suddenly alert, fixed on his monitor.

"Commander," he uttered into his headset. "I think I found something."

Chapter Forty-Two
The Stain

Somewhere over the Gulf of San Jorge

The US Navy's P-8A Poseidon was flying far from its home, and not searching for anything in particular.

The twin-engine Boeing was the Navy's newest reconnaissance aircraft, loaded with state-of-the-art sensors for a wide range of missions. Its duties included shipping interdiction and anti-submarine warfare. It was armed with torpedoes and able to drop sonobuoys, expendable underwater listening devices.

Ironically, the Poseidon wasn't hunting for any submarines.

A US crew had just finished training the Uruguayan Air Force. They Navy had been invited to instruct Uruguay's military on weather forecasting and aeromedical evacuation.

After training in such a unique part of the world, with its rocky coast and deep-blue waters, the crew took advantage of the opportunity to run drills off the coast.

"You got something?" The commander replied in his officer's headset. "Can you be more specific? Over."

The young officer studied his monitor. The P-8A had workstations monitoring infrared multi-spectral sensors, with image intensifiers and laser rangefinders. The crew loved to boast, "We can read the insignia on a sailor's hat from 30,000 feet."

The man scratched his crew cut after reviewing his system.

His commander repeated, "So, what is it?"

"It's a…heat stain," the officer replied. "Metallic. Approximate depth…forty meters."

✧

"A heat stain?" Captain Berryhill shouted into his phone from his New London headquarters.

His office looked like it hadn't changed in decades. It had wood paneling and a mica desk covered in stacks of reports in a supposedly paperless workplace. It was after 6:00 pm and it was a miracle Berryhill was still at his desk. His team was at the local Applebee's for a retirement party, and they needed his credit card to pay.

He stood with a confused scowl. "What the hell is a heat stain?"

"It's a hydroacoustic anomaly," Officer Engel replied into her personal cellphone.

Despite the breakthrough, she remained seated in a lawn chair, wearing an MIT hoodie and sweatpants. The captain had interrupted her during her son's soccer game in Suitland.

Nothing was more important than attending Sean's sporting events even with the possibility of a rogue nuclear submarine prowling the seas. Seated in an open field, with a mild breeze and the smell of fresh-cut grass, was like heaven after hours staring at reports.

Engel had predicted Berryhill would call within seconds of getting the news. She had posted an alert through the Multiple Threat Alert Center for any anomalies suggesting an "unidentified hostile vessel." It was the equivalent of the Navy issuing an APB.

By doing so, she had nothing to lose. It could result in nothing, or something might be heard, seen or located. Engel had no idea the Navy had a Poseidon flying as far south as Uruguay, which made the report even more intriguing.

"Hello? You there?" Berryhill's voice howled.

Engel had a smirk of satisfaction. Everything she had warned them about was coming true.

"Just a sec' Captain." She enjoyed putting the man on hold. When Sean's coach called a timeout, she continued, "Did you notice it was one of our Poseidons that spotted it? That's pretty ironic."

"What's ironic?" Berryhill barked.

Engel wondered if he knew the meaning of the word. She replied, "In 2017, we sent two Poseidons to help Argentina search for their missing sub. When they found it, the radio operator reported the same thing: a heat stain."

Berryhill paused, his voice more austere, "Does it always mean a submarine?"

"Not at all. Thermal anomalies can come from large whales or magma flow. There are volcanic vents under Antarctica, not that far away—" She stopped to see Sean return to the field.

"Hello? Engel?"

She continued, "But according to the flight officer, this one sounded mechanical." Engel sprung upright to scream, "Go Sean! That a boy! Shoot it!"

Sean missed the shot, but his team cheered the effort. Engel sat back down and lifted the phone back to her ear.

"Let's just say if I were you," she crossed her legs, "I'd have all ears on your hydrophones."

There was a weary sigh from Berryhill. "You do realize, if we ID anything, it's my job to alert NATO Sub Command and maybe even the Senate Intelligence Committee."

"You are correct, Captain." Engel opened a can of Pringles with a thin smile. "That is your job."

❧

With snowcapped peaks in the distance, a fifty-foot fishing trawler swayed in six-foot seas. The battered boat's hull stated a home port of Ushuaia, Argentina. Scrawled under that was, *"Fin del Mundo."* The end of the world.

The village of Ushuaia had earned the title, "The end of the world" because it was located at the southernmost tip of South America, with nothing beyond but the barren Antarctica.

The vessel's exhausted crew wore rain jackets as they clutched the rails. They smoked soggy cigarettes, waiting for the day's last haul of king crab. The exporters of Ushuaia loved the giant crustaceans for their delicious meat and hefty profits.

A thick, bearded captain stepped out to holler, "*Tire de él!*"

A man hit a control and a winch pulled the ropes. The crew worked together to hoist nets from the icy water filled with immense crabs. The nets were dumped beside a conveyer to separate them by size.

A man exclaimed, "*Que es eso?*" He hit a switch to stop the conveyer. Within a pile of scurrying crabs was a circular orb the size of a basketball.

The captain stroked his chin, puzzled. At first, he thought the ball was a lost buoy. But this one appeared mechanical, with a small antenna protrusion and prongs folded at its base.

"Stand back!" the captain shouted to his men in Spanish. He'd heard tales about round explosive mines.

"Should I throw it overboard?" a crewman asked.

"No." He was the captain, but not the owner of the boat. He had to follow strict protocol. Whether it was a weather buoy, a toy, or something potentially dangerous, it had to be reported.

The captain shouted into his two-way, "Raul, call the PNA."

Chapter Forty-Three
Mountains of Emerald

Propped on an elbow, Captain Nikto cradled his face in his hand. He'd knocked over his glass, dribbling apricot brandy onto his desk. His eyelids fell until a vision made him smile.

It was the warm sun. He rolled over to look beside him. Within bedsheets, her silky black hair was swathed across the pillow. They were in their bed, in their secret chalet in El Palomar.

"Kana..." Nikto whispered with a smile. He reached to stroke her shoulder.

The golden dawn gave their sheets the hue of vanilla. A gentle breeze blew the curtains. Fragrant oleander from the garden smelled like apricot.

No human in the world knew they were there. Their secret chalet was just outside of Buenaventura. Their employer, Don Ricardo Salazar, didn't know about the place. It was close enough to the port, yet far enough for cleaner air and serenity. After paying the right people, it was their clandestine hideaway while overseeing the *Naumtsev*'s renovations.

The night before, a cargo ship from Shanghai had delivered the polymethyl methacrylate glass for the Iris windows, and the first parts of the unassembled *Cyclops*. It would be a long but rewarding week of graveyard-shift construction and more bribes for silence.

"What time is it?" Kana cooed in broken English, their only common language. She stretched like a feline and rolled to face him. Her smile made her almond eyes sparkle.

"Not yet seven o'clock." His face went slack, confused.

Kana began to cough. Soft at first, growing violent with convulsing gasps. Her eyes protruded and she gripped her chest, struggling to inhale with a rattling wheeze.

"Kana!" Nikto lunged to hold her by her shoulders. Her watering eyes locked onto his. With terror etched across her face, her mouth gulped to breathe.

Clutching her shoulders, Nikto roared, "What is happening?"

"It's me," Ned Landa shouted through Nikto's office door. "You invited me…"

After a pause, Nikto replied, "*Zakhodi!*" He corrected, "Come in!"

It was time for their nightly drinks. When Landa entered, the room smelled like apricot. He could tell the captain had been sleeping. The man was perspiring as if he'd been having a nightmare. He used his sleeve to wipe brandy from his desk.

"I am sorry. I must have dozed," Nikto muttered, seeming winded.

"Is a Russian who drinks vodka," The captain's words slowed, "Redundant or a cliché?" He laughed with a broad shrug, "Can something true be a cliché?"

With one eye closed, Ned Landa poured Nikto another shot of Kors Vodka. He was aware the George V-edition bottle was worth over $24,000. Landa had opted for a more understated Jack Daniels. He poured himself another double over ice.

With glazed eyes, Nikto took his glass and tossed it back.

Landa was not as hammered as his drinking partner and that was the plan. Despite Nikto's height, Landa was thirty pounds heavier and accustomed to Marine-style drinking. He could hold his own longer than his drunken comrade.

He'd almost begun to enjoy his evening cocktails with the captain.

But he had noticed Nikto was drinking more. And when he drank, he talked. Landa used the opportunities to gain information and to curry favor from his abductor.

Landa had three primary queries: how often the C-Buoys were launched, any safety threats onboard, and the *Naumtsev's* next destination.

Since Nikto was smug about his technical prowess, he answered the buoy question. They were launched every two days to access news, look for reports of their sighting, and to recalibrate their GPS.

As far as the ship's safety, Landa learned one troubling detail: when they'd tried to replenish the air, saltwater may have entered through the mast. If it did, it could have led to the battery compartment. His engineers were studying the situation, any short circuit could be critical. Though the *Naumtsev* was a modern sub with sophisticated upgrades, the skeleton of the Cold War vessel was showing its age.

Nikto remained tight-lipped about their destination and the reason for their change in course. With no ports anywhere in their near future, there'd be no opportunities to escape any time soon.

❦

"Hey, easy on the good stuff," Landa huffed when Nikto reached for another pour.

"Why?" Nikto smiled instead of being angry. "It is mine."

"Because I'm guessing we're quite a few miles from another port."

"So, it seems." Nikto wiped his face. "If only there were a hidden port in the center of the South Pacific." He motioned to the ceiling, "In our world of satellites, the days of uncharted islands are gone."

Landa weakened to pour two more glasses.

"Japan, during the war," Nikto resumed, rambling. "Deep in the center of the Pacific they planned to create an undersea sub station."

"Yeah right," Landa chuckled. "With World War II technology?"

"Imagine sunken cargo containers. Hundreds of them." Nikto spoke with his hands, "Twenty-foot-diameter pipes. All of it connected, sunken and pressurized." He squinted, envisioning his words. "Like an entire city. A place to hide." He gave a lavish shrug and lifted his glass.

253

Landa paused, intrigued by Nikto's assertion. Was it drunken words from a maniac? Or something else? A hidden submarine base seemed like nonsense, but he had read about others.

In 1994, a secret sub base had been discovered on Simushir Island, a sparsely-inhabited volcanic island between Japan's Hokkaido Island and the Russian Kamchatka Peninsula. When Russia had control of the island, they'd built a secret submarine base that was hidden until the fall of the Soviet Union.

But what about a base so deep? Landa mused. Nikto's description reminded him of the SEALAB projects from the 1960s. They were the Navy's experimental underwater habitats to test the capability of people living underwater for extended periods. Steel chambers were submerged over six hundred feet deep.

And there were other rumors. Engineers with the Navy's China Lake Ordnance Test Station created plans to construct an underwater base by excavating the seafloor. They proposed sinking a wide shaft to the seafloor that could be drained and used as a staging area. Tunnel-boring machines could create tunnels. For power, a small nuclear reactor could be installed like those already in use on bases in Greenland and Antarctica.

Landa wondered, *could there be any truth to Nikto's story—*

"Mr. Landa, are you still with us?" Captain Nikto had a sharp grin. "Perhaps you have had too much to drink?"

Landa blinked to clear the haze. He decided to shift topics.

"Captain," he paused, almost humble. "Patrice told me about the narcotics you gave that village for the sick to afford nourishment."

"My altruism shocks you? I have many other recipients. Cambodia, Liberia, Bangladesh…"

"I mean, you don't have a stellar résumé," Landa chuckled. "You steal a $2 billion sub from your own country to give to drug dealers then you double-cross them."

"Assumptions." Nikto had a thin smile, "It is an ugly word. I presumed you were a coward. I was mistaken." He shifted in his seat, "Have you ever considered I may be keeping the *Naumtsev* safe from parties much worse than I?"

Landa didn't have a response.

They were interrupted by Nikto's monitor. Dimitri appeared, speaking in hurried Russian.

"Kapitan," Dmitri uttered. "I have something that requires your attention." He knew the captain didn't want to be disturbed, but this was vital.

Nikto's face frowned at the screen, "Proceed in Russian."

Dmitri nodded. "I picked up a sound, it was a plane."

"An aircraft that concerns you?" Nikto cocked his head, "What variety of plane?"

This was Dmitri's specialty; matching acoustics with his index of signatures to determine types of equipment. A legitimate submarine could use its periscope or photonics mast to peek above, but the *Naumtsev* couldn't risk cruising that close to the surface.

"When I first detected the engines, I thought it was a commercial 737." Dmitri spoke fast, "As it got closer, I suspected it was an F-8 Poseidon."

Nikto almost spit his vodka, "We are far beyond the jurisdiction of a Navy plane."

"You are correct. But the plane made a transmission. It confirmed it was a Poseidon." He swallowed, "It reported to the US that it detected our heat signature."

Nikto recoiled from his monitor, "Our heat?"

Landa was growing weary of the men's ceaseless Russian banter. But from their demeanor, they seemed flustered. He knew the little man, Dmitri, was a communication expert. It was easy to surmise something from the above world was troubling them.

Landa swirled his glass of ice. When he did so, the captain turned to stare at it.

In that instant, Nikto switched to English, "The best place to cloak heat is…beneath the ice."

⁓

In the parlor, Dr. Arrison, Chandler and Pilar were enjoying a game of poker. It was too early for dinner, so Pilar poured glasses of an excellent red from Marqués de Puntalarga, a vineyard north of Bogotá.

"My mother taught me the hold 'em game from Texas," Pilar dealt the cards like a pro. "She said the casinos in Medellin were more extravagant than any in Las Vegas."

"I've never been to Vegas." Chandler grinned, "I'll take you one day."

Pilar beamed, but her face went slack. "Not unless there is an ocean at Las Vegas."

There was a silence at the blunt reminder of their plight.

When Chandler glanced towards the window he shouted, "Look!" He sprung out of his chair, "Icebergs!" The ladies rushed to join him.

The deep-blue water was illuminated by the dusk above. Just yards from the *Naumtsev*, the jagged bottom of an iceberg drifted by.

Like most of their recent encounters, Dr. Arrison had never seen icebergs in person. She'd always dreamed of seeing them from a research vessel. Pyramids of frozen white, looming on an arctic sea. With sparkling eyes, she would accept a view from below.

"Why are they blue-green?" Chandler's breath fogged the glass.

Arrison had noticed the same thing. Rather than white, the underwater peaks looked like enormous green jewels. "These are the bottoms that are rarely seen. Icebergs flip over when gravity tries to bring the bulk of its weight underwater. When that happens, people have witnessed the phenomenon of *blue glass*."

"What causes it?" Pilar studied the building-sized boulders.

"The emerald radiance is from centuries of pressure," Arrison replied, equally fascinated. "Air pockets have been squeezed out, buffering the crystals. Minerals frozen inside polish its blue and greenish tint."

The bottoms of the icebergs looked like inverted mountains of translucent turquoise.

"The cliché is true," Chandler tilted his head to look up. "The tip of the iceberg we normally see is just ten percent of the whole. Frosted with centuries of snow."

They stood in silence to watch the upside-down mountain range glide by. At less than four knots, the *Naumtsev* steered though the daring passage, pivoting right and then left.

Arrison was growing colder watching the bergs that dwarfed their vessel. "We must be near Cierva Cove," she guessed. "I read it's a majestic, isolated cove. The tail of Antarctica that stretches north to Cape Horn."

The three sprung back as the massive arm of an iceberg nearly grazed the glass.

"Do not fear," Nikto spoke from behind them. "Navigation has improved since the Titanic."

Arrison turned to see the captain standing five feet behind them. She hated when he did that.

"We are headed away from the bergs," he added. "Much deeper."

"Where are we going?" Chandler asked.

After a measured pause, he responded, "Under Antarctica."

Chapter Forty-Four
"Release the Kraken!" —Zeus

Under Thwaites Glacier

"That is not possible," Pilar shot back. "Antarctica is rock, a continent."

"You are correct, partially," Nikto tipped his head. "I should be more precise. We are going under Thwaites Glacier."

Chandler gave a broad smile, "I know about that glacier." He looked up out the window. The sunset was illuminating a ceiling of ice fifty yards above them, like an auburn glow on frosted glass. Pilar and his mother joined him to observe the sea's frozen ceiling.

"This glacier is the size of Florida." Chandler put his arm around Pilar.

"Climate change is melting a cavity under the glacier the size of Manhattan." Nikto's tone had an air of disgust, "Deeper than the Eiffel tower. This hollow space was half the size three years ago, thanks to global heating."

"No," Chandler shook his head, "It's melting from geothermal heat from volcanic activity. Thermal vents below are warming the water."

"How can you believe that?" Nikto frowned.

"You figured I'd leap to global warming because of my demographic?"

"Either way," Arrison declared, "If the entire glacier melts, it could raise the earth's seas by two feet." She looked at Nikto. "Thwaites Glacier is extremely unstable. Is this the best place for us to be?"

"An unseen cavity the size of Manhattan is the perfect place to be. It also allows us a pause to attend to maintenance items."

The four turned back to the window. As they plunged deeper, the bergs soared out of view. Chandler watched the water darken from a royal blue with good visibility to a murky indigo. When the ship's spotlights ignited, they revealed nothing but a vacuous abyss.

It was no longer his imagination; their breaths were becoming visible. He held Pilar closer, her rosy nose almost touching the glass. He asked, "Captain, how cold—"

They leaped back as if jolted by lightning. A massive purple squid appeared outside the window.

"*Calamar gigante!*" Pilar shrieked, leaping into Chandler's arms.

The squid's head had a five-foot girth and was over ten feet long. With slick, translucent skin and mauve spots, it was like a monster from a science fiction movie. A golden eye the size of a dinner plate peered through the glass.

Rather than cowering, Arrison beamed, "*Mesonychoteuthis hamiltoni.* The colossal squid." She put her hands to the glass, "This one has to be over fifty feet!"

The creature's long, thick tentacles swished by the window. It had eight spiraling arms and two longer tentacles with suction cups. It grazed the glass, swimming up and out of sight.

Chandler and Pilar dashed to the opposite window. He shouted, "It's coming down this side!" From above their window, sail-like fins on the squid's head appeared. The enormous beast descended the hull as if circling the *Naumtsev*.

"It's just curious." Nikto seemed unphased, "Not so large to affect this vessel."

Arrison wondered if she was the first woman—or even human—to see a colossal squid this size. Scientists knew they existed; enormous specimens had been observed closer to the surface, and they knew even larger varieties existed at depths unseen by human eyes.

For centuries, fishermen told legends of a massive sea monster, the kraken, with giant tentacles that could pluck sailors from their boats and drag them to the depths. It seemed obvious the colossal squid was responsible for kraken sightings.

She knew it was also called the Antarctic squid, believed to be the largest of the species. In photos, she'd seen bodies washed ashore by storms or caught in fishing nets with masses over 1,000 pounds. Colossal squids of this size had never been observed in their own world. *Until now,* Arrison grinned.

Scientists knew of their existence from the squid's sharp, indestructible beaks found in the stomachs of sperm whales. Their size indicated specimens over 1,500 pounds, with lengths over forty feet. Their eyes were nearly twelve inches wide, the largest of any known animal.

Its arms and tentacles had swiveling, claw-like hooks. Sperm whales have been observed with scars on their backs, caused by the hooks of the giant squids.

Arrison's smile vanished recalling her glimpse of the creature. A fifty-foot squid couldn't conceivably harm a 375-foot submarine. *Right?*

Pilar nuzzled into Chandler's shirt. His eyes remained fixed out the window, hoping for another glance of the illusive creature.

She spoke with warm breath on his ear, "Can we play somewhere warmer?"

He turned to her. When he gazed into her cocoa eyes, he was reminded of his blessed reality. "Where do you have in mind?"

"I know somewhere very private," she grinned.

ﱢ

Captain Nikto entered the control room and marched straight to Dmitri. "More aircraft?"

"*Da, Kapitan,*" Dmitri crushed out a cigarette. "Before the glacier, I picked up another set of turboprops. Sounded like four engines."

"Commercial?" Nikto's voice was more hopeful than true.

"Not this far south," Dmitri shook his head. "The US has been known to fly Lockheed LC-130s to Antarctica. It has four engines."

Nikto sighed, at his wits' end. The *Naumtsev* and her crew had been alone for a long time. No one tracking them; no one knowing of their existence. But in the past week an alert to the entire Atlantic fleet? Two planes in as many days? *The US claiming they've picked up our heat?*

After years crisscrossing the seven seas at his leisure, was it a coincidence these warnings had all begun after rescuing three trespassers? *Should I have killed...* He squeezed his eyes closed, ashamed of where his mind was wandering.

He could sense his men's eyes upon him, eager for his orders.

"We'll drop deeper, colder." Nikto turned to Pavlo, "*Tikhaya*, cut all nonessentials."

He gave the order for a silent running, a stealth mode of operation by eliminating noise. Unneeded systems would be shut down, their speed reduced to minimize propeller noise. Operation of the reactor would also be minimized. His plan was to drift and sink for the time being, far under the ice to cloak any residual heat.

"We will anchor until this subsides."

"Anchor?" Pavlo's face creased, "You do realize how deep we—"

Nikto shot him a fiery gaze, weary of the man's cowardice. "Take her down, Mr. Pavlo, or I will chain you to the anchor myself."

❧

Ned Landa used the downtime to enter the moon well. He'd already sabotaged three C-Buoys so they wouldn't self-destruct. They'd all been launched over the course of the past week, but he had no way to know their fate.

His breath was like steam as he blew warm air into his hands. He was curious of the drop in temperature, but knew the room was the closest point to the icy water, a meter outside the hull. Due to the salinity, Antarctic waters were below freezing, nearly twenty-eight degrees.

He confirmed he was alone and proceeded to a tool bench. The lighting over the desk would be sufficient as the *Cyclops* hung in the shadows behind him.

He opened the emergency kit from the wall. When he'd stolen the life vest at Isla Moustique, he'd left behind the rescue beacon. He grabbed the small device and sat at the workbench.

He studied the Personal Locator Beacon. It was yellow and the size of an old cellphone. It was a safety device used to alert search and rescue services in the event of an emergency. They were usually water-activated for man-overboard scenarios.

Useless, Landa grumbled. It'd be stupid to engage the beacon now. Its signal would never breach the *Naumtsev's* titanium hull and they were thousands of miles from civilization. He dropped it on the desk. *So, what now?*

There was a sound. Something had moved.

Landa remained still. His workbench was out of view of the security camera closer to the *Cyclops.* The door to his right was still closed. He slowly turned his head to the left to confirm the well was sealed. *Did the ship have rats? Could something have slithered in?*

He chuckled at his paranoia. Any sound, even from himself, would certainly be amplified within the sealed chamber.

∾

Landa was unaware of the four dark eyes watching him from five yards away.

Pilar whispered, "*Silencio! Landa está aquí!*" In a state of undress, her eyes bugged from inside the *Cyclops* hanging in the moon well.

Chandler looked up from their intimate embrace. He tried to peer down through the minisub's dome. "*Now* Landa decides to repair stuff?"

Chapter Forty-Five
A Douse of Cold Water

Straddling his body, Pilar's bare skin was warm and had a spicy citrus scent. Her hair framed her delicate face, with ringlets obscuring her breasts.

Chandler was conflicted, enamored but frustrated with Mr. Landa just yards away.

When he gazed into her eyes, her lashes fluttered. But rather than seeming alarmed, he saw a grin uncurling from a corner of her lips.

"What do we do?" Chandler stammered.

Moments earlier, when Pilar had proposed "somewhere warmer," Chandler had noticed a certain glint in her eye. He allowed her to pull him by the hand.

He'd presumed she meant her quarters. "Not my cabin," he had panted, "Not with my mom next door."

"And I cannot be next to Nikto," she'd grinned. "I know somewhere far from others, private, very intimate."

Chandler had swallowed as she'd tugged him towards a companionway. The few glasses of wine had been the only vaccination against having a full panic attack.

He'd been puzzled when they'd climbed down towards the moon

well. "This won't be any warmer…"

Pilar stroked his lips with a finger, "*Tranquilo.* We will make our own heat."

His eyes went the size of saucers. When they'd entered the moon well, Chandler watched her climb up a ladder to the *Cyclops.* When she'd used the word "intimate," he figured she meant romantic, not so confining.

Pilar opened the hatch on top of the *Cyclops.* She paused with a knowing grin, "This is it. Are you ready?"

His eye twitched at the prophetic words, "Yes." He would follow her into a lava pit.

Suspended by four cables, the *Cyclops* swayed as they climbed into the sub. They made gentle movements and remained quiet. The cockpit was only ten feet long and five feet in diameter. Chandler twitched like a squirrel to look out the dome to assure they were alone.

With the low ceiling, they had to stand on their knees. He looked down at the metal floor. The space had not been designed for comfort. Then he saw her; their eyes connected like magnets.

In a single move, Pilar lifted and removed her sweater. "I'll place my clothes on the deck." With her top fully exposed, she grinned. She almost seemed to enjoy watching his discomfort. "Is this okay?"

His breaths quickened. He stammered, "You're…beautiful."

Pilar's entire face glowed. Her eyes became glossy with joy. She reached down to grasp the top of her pants. With a side-to-side wiggle of her hips, she slid them off.

Chandler had to wipe his brow. It was indeed warmer, just as she'd promised. He felt lightheaded just from gazing at her. He wondered if the oxygen was growing thinner in the small space.

During untold sleepless nights, Chandler had rehearsed this precise moment in his mind. As with any past challenge, he knew he could handle such a glorious predicament. This was really happening, and he'd been blessed to have her affection. *Good things come to those who wait.*

He inhaled and flexed when he removed his shirt. He dropped it on the deck and looked at her, drinking in the stunning woman just two feet away. The gorgeous, intelligent, bold, and funny lady who truly liked him for who he was.

Pilar shook her head to brush hair from her shoulders. She put her arms around Chandler to pull him in for a deep, swirling kiss.

All his senses were heightened. Her mouth tasted like the honey they'd enjoyed on brie. He could hear the clinking from bracelets on her wrists. Her breasts were warm against his chest. They began to breathe in unison. This exceeded anything he had envisioned.

Pilar pulled him down onto the deck. Her hands explored his back. She cooed in Spanish. Her skin was hot, and her curves were like satin.

Chandler had been nervous about his inexperience. He'd always wondered if some innate instinct would take over, as it does with animals. No one taught animals how to make love; they just figured it out. Easing his dilemma, Pilar was taking the lead, which was precisely what he needed. And he loved every prolonged second of it.

The *Cyclops* began to sway when Pilar wriggled to climb on top of him. The weight of her body was comforting and made him feel safe. The air was filled with her fragrance. When she bent to kiss him, their bare stomachs touched, and her hair covered his eyes. With just his sense of touch, he reached down her long back, their skin now sprinkled with perspiration.

Then blinding lights came on.

They froze like undressed mannequins, realizing someone had entered the moon well.

Chandler watched Ned Landa step to his tools, no longer facing the *Cyclops*.

Lying on top of him, Pilar whispered in his ear, "He did not see us."

"What do we do?" Chandler stammered, "We can't leave."

Pilar bit her lower lip with a devilish grin. "Let us see how quiet we can be."

ℰⅅ

"Kapitan, as we had feared, there is a short circuit," Pavlo uttered with weary eyes. Beside him stood Aleksei, their new chief engineer since the death of Ivan Popov.

Seated at his desk, Nikto rubbed his temples. He wondered how much more he could endure. "How? Which circuits?"

Aleksei brushed oily bangs from his face, "Water leaked through ventilation to the battery compartment. Errors in several circuits."

"Which circuits?" Nikto barked, losing patience.

"Mostly nonessential," Aleksei spoke fast. "Sonar circuits, radar, communication, thermostat."

Nikto slapped his desk, "You consider sonar, radar, and our temperature unimportant?"

The men stood mute with hands behind their backs.

Aleksei responded, "They are not vital, as we can make the repairs within two or three hours."

Nikto paused, "It is repairable?"

"*Da, Kapitan,*" Aleksei nodded. "We have isolated the battery. We have a spare, but in the forward battery room. It has to be transferred to the lower level."

"How cold is it now in the lower levels?"

Pavlo replied, "Fifteen degrees Celsius."

The captain gritted his teeth as if they were imbeciles, "Do you think our crew and guests can survive at fifteen degrees for three hours?"

Nikto's concerns were twofold. With his original engineer gone, the remaining men's collective electrical skills were subpar at best. More frightening, the very thought of a short circuit in the battery compartment sent a cold shiver down his spine.

His job was to lead his men. Their job was to operate the vessel. His knowledge of the electrical systems was rudimentary, so he had to recollect everything he knew.

All submarines required electric power to operate. They were equipped with diesel engines when the reactor wasn't in use, and batteries for backup.

The battery rooms were in the lower levels to stabilize the vessel. Each battery was five feet tall and over 1,500 pounds. The combined weight of the batteries helped provide ballast to keep the bottom of the vessel pointed down.

The *Naumtsev* had two battery rooms: one smaller room beneath the officer's quarters and an aft room on the lowest level near the center of gravity. In an emergency, the batteries could power systems needed for lights, life support and propulsion.

But a short circuit... Nikto squirmed with a gnawing migraine. He knew the fate of the ARA *San Juan*. When Argentina's submarine vanished in 2017, it had suffered a similar failure.

The *San Juan* had been returning to base from a routine mission. In its last transmission, the captain reported a leak had caused a battery to short circuit, and the crew had been working feverishly to isolate and repair the battery.

On the day the submarine vanished, they had a maximum oxygen supply for seven days. Over a year later, it was found resting 3,000 feet beneath the surface of the South Atlantic, with all its crew dead. The *San Juan* was too deep to recover.

With his head throbbing, Nikto looked at Aleksei. "What systems are down until the repairs are done?"

"Circuits to the lower levels," he replied. "Heating, machines, doors may not function."

"Kapitan," Pavlo raised a hand. "The winch for the anchor is on the lower level. The anchor cannot be raised."

Nikto folded his arms. The vessel would have to remain shackled thousands of feet below ice for hours. He wondered if there was another way to sever the chain.

"No one is in the moon well or lower levels, correct?"

"Thankfully no," Pavlo assured. "Otherwise, they would be trapped in there."

☙

Cynthia Engel's cellphone roused her from a deep sleep at 5:00 am. Her husband Chuck kept snoring like a bear, impervious to random calls that were commonplace with his wife's profession.

The caller-ID displayed it was her commander, Gregory Law. She cleared her throat and mumbled, "Hello, Officer Engel."

Without any pleasantries, he asked, "Do you know the PNA in Argentina?"

"PNA?" She stood and put on her glasses, "No sir?"

"It stands for Prefectura Naval Argentina. It's their coast guard, bigger than their navy."

Engel proceeded to the kitchen; this didn't seem like a short conversation. "Why are you waking me about Argentina's coast guard?"

"Because they woke me about something they found," Law retorted. "They saw your alert about anything unidentified or possibly hostile."

"What'd they find?" Engel dug through a drawer to grab a pen. The only paper she could find was the back of a take-out menu.

"Do you know what a communication buoy is?"

"Of course." She spat her words, excited, "Lockheed Martin designed a few. Submarines use them to communicate or connect to satellites. Tethered with a cable and disposable."

"Well, a fishing boat in Argentina found one," Law replied. "They had no idea what they caught. And Ushuaia has very limited forensics."

Engel pruned her face, "How does this connect to us?"

"When they examined the buoy, the circuits had digits identifying the manufacturer." Law paused, "It's Russian."

Engel scribbled the information. She repeated aloud, "A device used by submarines to communicate was found off Argentina and it's Russian." She stopped writing, "But what if—"

"We already asked Russia," Law interrupted. "Their Defense Ministry insists they have no vessels anywhere in that vicinity."

Engel chuckled, "I want to get my hands on that buoy."

"That's not all," Law added with a grim pause. "They found signs of tampering so the buoy couldn't self-destruct. One could deduce that means someone onboard—"

"Wants to be found," Engel exclaimed with a glint in her eyes. "Gregory," Her voice became coy, "Would it be a complete waste of time to ask for permission to go to Argentina?"

"Yes," he snapped. "Impossible."

She withdrew, insulted. "Why impossible?"

"Because I need you in London." His voice warmed, "NATO Maritime Command. You're the best person to explain this to thirty international naval officers. So, find that passport again."

Chapter Forty-Six
The Face of Jupiter

Captain Nikto entered the parlor to find Professor Arrison writing in her journal. Just seeing her, so engrossed by their environment, made him feel better.

Nikto wore a black wool trench coat that would've been stylish if he was in New York or Paris, versus a former-Soviet submarine. He carried an identical coat for his guest.

"I brought you this," he announced. "The lower levels may grow colder."

Arrison looked up and smiled, "I would love a coat." She stood to greet him. "Is it supposed to be this cold?"

"Consider our location," Nikto shrugged, choosing not to elaborate. "I remember my first submarine as a recruit. Greenland. It was this cold, except in engineering with all the steam pipes. I made a bed out of towels under the pipes to stay warm."

"I take it you've been to Antarctica before?"

"Of course." Nikto helped with her coat, "The only continent with no government or political activity, and no *permanent* human residents. A paradise."

Arrison paused to consider his perspective. "The world community's treaties do protect Antarctica as a scientific preserve."

"As they should." They walked towards an Iris window. Nikto shouted at an intercom, "Pavlo, spotlights."

Their vista of pure black illuminated to reveal a haunting landscape. The *Naumtsev* was anchored just ten feet above the ocean floor. The ground was gray silt. Above it, nothing but black. It looked like the surface of another planet, but without any stars.

"Remarkable," Arrison inched closer to the window.

"Hidden from the sun for over 100,000 years," Nikto stated as they faced out. "Biodiversity thrives under the ice."

As her eyes adjusted to the contrast of the seafloor, she could see purple and blue flower-like plants. They were alive, moving slowly. Rows of white, crystalline sea squirts stood two feet tall that looked like sculptures of blown glass. It was like an alien planet.

"A luxuriant garden," Nikto smiled, "A lost world of unknown species."

"Icefish," Arrison exclaimed. Two ghostly, almost translucent fish slithered by. They were a meter long with heads shaped like crocodiles. "They have no red blood cells. Glycerol in their blood acts as antifreeze."

Nikto smiled at her palpable wonder. "Kana used to say the water under Antarctica is like Mount Everest. Magical, yet so hostile few have ever experienced it."

❧

Patrice Arrison felt like she was watching a computer-simulated world at the Smithsonian. Goosebumps tingled across her scalp, from either the realization of her environment, or the room's plunging temperature.

Before her was a pristine world, unaffected by human activities. It'd be an invaluable resource for biodiversity research.

An elegant feather star waved its frond-like arms, probing for food particles. Its appendages were like vibrant peacock feathers, but they were alive. Few knew it was an animal that could swim. The bizarre scene was similar to what Mars looked like in 1950s science fiction.

To the side she identified hypothermal vents. The waist-high mounds were essentially mini volcanoes. They emitted minerals that looked like dark smoke, a process from the interaction of seawater and hot magma from deep underground.

Arrison squinted; she thought the vents were crusted with fossilized shells, but they were stirring. She realized they were covered with tiny yeti crabs, heaped on top of each other, thriving near the plumes of mineral-rich hot water.

She shrank, "Those arctic sea spiders are enormous." Three giant sea spiders appeared in the foreground. Arrison reviled anything that looked like spiders. The bright orange arthropods had eight spindly legs that could span the width of someone's face. The lanky creatures looked like an arachnophobic's nightmare.

"But look there," Captain Nikto's offered. He pointed to a small octopus slinking on the seafloor. It was eerily white with black eyes.

"A ghost octopus," Arrison's face softened. The octopus was the size of a kitten. It had only been discovered in 2016. It was entirely white due to no need for camouflage in complete darkness. The small octopus indeed looked like *Casper the Ghost.*

Nikto smiled, "I believe it's drawn to our lights."

They were amazed to watch the octopus pounce on a sea spider. Its tentacles crushed the twitching insect-like creature.

When Arrison released an astonished huff, her breath was like smoke in the frigid room.

Nikto spun to the intercom. "Pavlo, update? It is growing colder."

Pavlo replied through static, "At least two hours. Considering the battery's weight—"

Nikto turned off the speaker before he could say more.

ᔕ

Ned Landa tried the controls for the moon well's doors a third time. Nothing. It wouldn't open. He stepped back to study the doorway. No sign of any mechanical breakdown, at least on the surface.

Landa crossed his arms. His thin short sleeves weren't enough to combat the falling temperature. He looked up at the security camera and stepped closer to the *Cyclops* to be within view. He waved at the camera, "Hey! Anyone there? I'm trapped in here!"

No response. He searched the room to find a large crowbar. He attempted to wedge it in the seal between the doors. The bar slipped off the polished steel and he screamed profanities.

&

"What's he doing now?" Chandler whispered. He and Pilar were lying side by side to peek out of the *Cyclops*.

"He said we are trapped," Pilar cooed. "The door is broken?"

Great, Chandler sighed. Though nothing was more breathtaking than seeing Pilar's body, he reached for their sweaters and placed them over her like a blanket.

She cuddled closer. "We could be trapped in worse places."

He grinned. If he had to be stuck in a locked chamber, it was in the warm, sensual arms of a spectacular woman.

But it was a fact it was growing colder. He guessed the *Cyclops* had a heating system. Pilar said she could operate the sub, but they couldn't risk starting its engines. He pulled more clothes onto her shoulders.

Chandler wondered how long they could hide. The air felt forty- or fifty-degrees Fahrenheit. He recalled reading about hypothermia. At forty-one degrees, a person had only fifteen or twenty minutes before a loss of coordination and strength. They couldn't put their clothes on without rocking the sub. There was only one conclusion: they'd have to inevitably announce their presence. *Maybe Mr. Landa would be cool—*

They jolted at a voice. It was Captain Nikto's grim voice over the speakers. *Have we been discovered?* Chandler's mind spun, *like an angry father finding a boy in his daughter's bed?*

&

"Mr. Landa," Nikto's voice boomed. "You are in the moon well?"

"Is that rhetorical?" Landa looked at the camera with a warped grin, "You're probably looking at me. The door's locked. I think it's jammed—"

"Repairs are underway," Nikto cut him off. "However, the pipes on the lower levels could freeze—we will freeze—unless we pull anchor as soon as possible."

"Then pull anchor," Landa raised his arms. "What do you want from me?"

"The well doors to the water are hydraulic," Nikto replied. "You should be able to operate them from inside."

"Okay, Landa lifted a brow, "Why would I want to see water?"

"You boasted you've repaired hulls using underwater torches."

"Yes…" Landa stood erect, alarmed where he was going with this.

"The windlass is inoperable. We cannot raise the anchor. We are stuck." Nikto paused, "Unless…"

"I get it…" Landa pinched the bridge of his nose. "Unless you cut the anchor's chain."

"Precisely," Nikto replied. "A diver with an acetylene torch could easily sever the chain. It seems you are the only person in the lower level with access to the ADS suits."

Are you kidding? Landa wanted to shout. He flashed a mocking smile, "Let me guess, you have an acetylene torch in the same room I'm trapped in?"

"Indeed, we do. We are all grateful that you understand. The anchor is just below the bow."

Landa muttered, *and thousands of feet under ice, in complete dark.*

Chapter Forty-Seven
One Small Step

Professor Arrison hovered behind Captain Nikto in the control room. The entire crew wore thick coats. They stood, glued to their monitors.

The fuzzy video feed showed the dive platform lowering from the moon well. Landa was standing on it, geared in his ADS suit. Night vision gave the image a grainy, green tint.

"The hawsepipe is thirty meters forward," Nikto spoke into a mic. "That's the hole for the anchor at the base of the bow."

Landa didn't respond. The room could hear the echo of his breathing within his helmet. He held the rails of the platform as it touched down on the seafloor.

"Copy," he finally exhaled. "Please aim every light you got."

When the spotlights came on, the view onscreen was filled with flurrying lifeforms that looks like mosquitos or moths. The crew exchanged unsettling glances.

☙

Without anyone to assist, Ned Landa had required extra time to install his ADS. He'd stepped into a suit and had to push against a wall for the back to clasp onto the breastplate. He installed his dome helmet, adjusted the neck ring, and locked the collar. With the icy water and lethal pressure, there was zero margin for error.

After securing his gloves, he plodded like Frankenstein onto the platform. Behind him, he rolled a small cart holding the acetylene torch and two tanks the size of fire extinguishers. He could feel every ounce of the suit's weight. Inside the helmet smelled like sweat from its previous user.

Ned Landa wasn't inherently religious, but he did consider himself spiritual. And the Marines had given him a strong sense of service. As such, he recited a brief prayer. Despite the motives of the captain and crew, he wanted everyone to survive. And, perhaps, he could see dry land and his daughter again someday, miles from any body of water.

Once submerged, he felt more agile. Though the ADS had a heating element, he still felt a chill through the metal. There was a bleak silence underwater, aside from a murmur like an underwater faucet. *Let's get this done*, he groaned as the platform landed on the seabed.

LED lights illuminated around his visor. When he saw the underwater landscape, he halted before stepping off the platform. All he saw was stark gray and black. The ground looked like a moonscape. He saw a few flower-like blooms and fissures that looked like large anthills. In the beams of light, plankton drifted like snow flurries.

"Gain your bearings," Nikto's voice crackled.

"I heard you before," Landa replied. "Thirty meters towards the bow."

Knowing he was being watched, he didn't want to appear hesitant. When he stepped off the platform, he felt like Neil Armstrong. The surface was soft like wet clay, probably millions of years of sediment. He was relieved he didn't feel any signs of claustrophobia. Above him looked like a starless night sky. The view ahead vanished into the shadows. A few crystalline fish at his knees reminded him he wasn't on a midnight walk on the surface of Antarctica.

Even with lights, he couldn't see the anchor chain through the gloom. Nikto had said it was less than a hundred feet. He tried to envision a straight line towards the bow. He would walk to the chain, cut a link with the torch, and then follow his path back to the platform.

I can bust this out in twenty minutes, he estimated.

When he pulled the torch cart, its wheels got stuck in the muck. *Great,* he growled as he dragged it like a plow.

The floodlights flickered off. In the blackness, bioluminescent lifeforms flurried around his helmet like glowing insects.

"Christ!" Landa swooshed his arms. Some organisms looked like electric dragonflies. When the ship's lights resumed, he scolded, "Steady those lights!"

"Our apologies," Dmitri's voice replied. "Circuits are unstable."

Landa looked around, wondering what else was out there. He could hear his own hurried breaths. When he turned towards the bow, he smiled. "I see the chain, about fifty feet." In the unnerving darkness, he finally saw the *Naumtsev's* anchor planted in the silt.

Before the Marines, he didn't know submarines used anchors. They were not the fluked design used by surface ships. Larger submarines used "mushroom" anchors, called that because of their shape. The *Naumtsev's* six-foot-wide anchor looked like a giant inverted mushroom. It had been dropped straight down from its slot in the hull. It was connected by a heavy-duty chain, with links almost a foot in diameter and an inch and a half thick.

The lights sputtered off and he stopped again. "Can you manage your damn lights?" Landa barked. When the lights resumed, he walked faster before it could happen again.

He approached the anchor. Its chain stretched up into the vessel. If the winch didn't work, it'd be impossible to move the enormous weight. Cutting the chain was the only option. As he'd done with salvage operations, he primed the torch by opening the valves to the tanks of acetylene and pure oxygen. Flexible tubes led from the tanks to the handle.

Landa held the torch like a pistol. He aimed it at one link, just below eye-level. When he pressed the trigger, it ignited a spark over 10,000 degrees. The pressured flame was too hot to be extinguished by water. It could cut through anything manmade.

"Steady," Nikto's voice hissed in his headset, "Focus on that single link."

Landa shook his head, ignoring the captain's babble. The torch's tip spewed bubbles with a blinding arc. The link was as thick as a stick of butter, and cutting it was just as easy.

ဢ

With clouded breaths, everyone in the control room leaned towards the monitors. They knew the ship's safety depended on Landa's quick work, as the inside repairs continued.

"Have you begun to cut the link's other side?" Nikto asked into the mic.

Landa turned off the torch and looked at the camera, "Never micromanage your only volunteer!"

Nikto pursed his lips and said nothing.

"What is that?" Arrison stepped closer to a screen and squinted, "By his foot?"

Dmitri zoomed the image towards Landa's legs. There was a small object that looked like an orange asterisk.

"Is that a sea spider?" Arrison exclaimed. The spindly creature was the size of a man's hand. "It's climbing his leg."

Landa shut off his torch. He shouted, "What are you saying?"

"Your leg," Nikto replied. "Mind your leg."

They saw Landa look down. One sea spider was scaling his leg, another climbing his boot.

The captain shrugged, "Perhaps you stepped into a nest."

"A nest?!" Landa yelped. He dropped his torch when he looked down. The skeletal creatures appeared to be all legs. Two were crawling up his dive suit, with two more approaching his feet. His reflexes made him hop and swoosh his hands towards his legs.

"Try not to panic, Ned," Arrison pled. "Your vitals will escalate."

Landa paused; she was right. He needed to remain cool. It was obvious these "spiders" couldn't harm him. But when he looked down, he saw a single-file trail of sea spiders scurrying towards him. Dozens, like gigantic ants at a picnic. "What the—"

"Ignore them," Nikto commanded. "They should be harmless."

"Wanna' trade chores?" Landa roared. He turned away from the chain.

"Mr. Landa," the captain spoke with his imperious brogue, "Your suit is forged aluminum. Ignore those parasites. You must focus on your task!"

Landa squeezed his eyes closed. He hated when the captain was right. When he looked down, there were now a dozen spiders crawling on his suit. He tried to slow his breathing, *the greater the conflict, the greater the triumph.* He turned to walk back to the anchor. He lifted the torch and reignited the flame.

For this job, Landa wanted tunnel vision to focus on one link. He'd already severed one side; now he had to cut the other. *Eyes on the chain!* In his peripheral vision, he could see twig-like legs of the spiders tapping on his visor. He just stared at the link.

Every time the ship's lights flickered; tiny curious eyes gleamed in the blackness around him.

No one uttered a word in the control room. Arrison shuddered seeing the creatures crawling on Landa's suit. With a final spark, they saw the thick chain fall to the ground.

"It's released," Landa announced through static. "I am outta' here."

A few of the men clapped as they returned to their consoles.

"Initiate auxiliary." Nikto looked at Pavlo, "Get status on the repairs. We cannot ascend until the moon well is secure."

Onscreen, they saw Landa turn back towards the platform. His breathing sounded labored through the speakers. He left the torch behind and trudged in a straight line, ignoring the neon spiders. "I'm headin' back," He panted, "As long as I can see."

In the video image, a white blur dropped into frame from above Landa.

Arrison squinted at the image, "Is that a ghost octopus?"

Something blocked Ned Landa's view. It was like a mop had been dropped on his visor. Inside his humid helmet, he saw a slither of suction cups. A small white octopus had landed on his dome.

"A ghost? Landa shouted. "What the hell?" He swooshed his head from side to side to try to sling it off.

"Ned, we're monitoring," Arrison had a calming voice, "It's a juvenile octopus. Completely harmless."

Landa reached to pull it off, but his arms didn't have enough range. "Get this goddamn thing off!" He swirled his helmet in a figure-eight. The octopus held on tighter.

A second and third octopus dropped from above like tiny parachutes. They attached themselves to his helmet, leaving almost no visible glass. Their legs squirmed to get a grip.

Just inches from his eyes, Landa could see their white suckers becoming bioluminescent. Then their tiny beaks began to tap the glass. He released a primal roar, "Get them off!"

"They're probably trying to eat the spiders," Arrison guessed, "Or attracted to your light."

With the interlocking tentacles, he had no view through the glass. Landa thrashed his arms and ran like a man on fire. He felt a tightness in his chest with an onset of claustrophobia. The final straw was the creatures' bird-like beaks scraping the glass.

He had a flashback to when he worked in a bakery when he was twelve. Elderly ladies would wait outside for the store to open. If the shop were a minute late, the angry ladies would knock pennies on the glass. *Tap, tap, tap.*

It was the same sound as the beaks hammering his helmet. With no remaining ego, Landa screamed.

Blind and disoriented, he ran away from the *Naumtsev*, into the pitch-black void.

Chapter Forty-Eight
Clash of the Titans

"He's running the wrong way!" Pilar exclaimed, watching the small monitor.

With Landa gone, Chandler and Pilar had activated the *Cyclops'* auxiliary power to provide heat and to hear any broadcasts. They hadn't announced their whereabouts, and they couldn't believe what they were seeing.

The video was the same stream as in the control room. On the gritty feed, Ned Landa was staggering away from the vessel into darkness.

With both of them fully dressed, Chandler remained close to the screen. "He doesn't know he's going the wrong way."

Captain Nikto's voice crackled through the speakers, "He's suffering narcosis or panicking."

Onscreen, the ship's spotlights flickered again. Landa was lost in the murk.

Chandler looked at the control panel, "You said you can operate this sub?"

"Nikto taught me." Pilar bobbed her head, "I would practice by collecting conch shells."

Chandler paused to summon every ounce of courage. He reached for the mic, "Captain Nikto, this is Chandler," He stammered, "I'm in the moon well with Pilar."

Her eyes went round at his disclosure.

In the control room, Arrison did a double-take hearing her son's voice.

Chandler continued. "We can take the *Cyclops* to help Mr. Landa."

"How are you there?" Nikto barked with a narrowed eye. "The doors are not repaired."

"Does it matter?" Arrison scowled at him. She was proud—and shocked—of her son's offer.

"Time's running out." Chandler spoke fast, "With the anchor cut, the sub will begin to drift."

Inspired by her son's bravado, Arrison looked at Nikto, "Pilar can operate the *Cyclops*?"

"Yes." His eyes shot between her and the monitor. "She is proficient."

Arrison shoved him aside and shouted into the mic, "Then go, hurry!"

"Seat belts!" Pilar wriggled into the pilot's seat. "It's an eight-foot drop."

Chandler sat beside her and fastened his harness.

"We lost Landa's signal," Dmitri's voice stated. "Forty meters off the bow, portside."

Pilar sat behind two joysticks to propel the vessel forward, reverse, left and right. Secondary levers controlled the outside grappling arms. She looked at a large red switch labeled "drop."

She turned to Chandler with flared eyes. "You secure?"

He gripped his harness and nodded.

She hit "drop" and cables released the *Cyclops*. The 18,000-pound vessel dropped eight feet into the well with a brutal splash.

Chandler's head jarred. Black water covered the large dome in front of them. In seconds, gravity pulled the *Cyclops* towards the ocean floor.

Pilar throttled the controls. The propellers engaged and the sub halted three feet above the sand. Their spotlights revealed nothing but particles floating against a vacuum of black.

"Towards the bow," Pilar shouted. "I think he went west."

Chandler snapped, "How do you know west?"

The control room was as quiet as a crypt. Cameras on the hull followed the *Cyclops* as it zoomed towards the bow. Bioluminescent life forms swarmed the sub, curious.

The video feed from the *Cyclops* revealed the anchor embedded in the sand. The severed chain was curled beside it like a lifeless python. With the currents, the *Naumtsev* had already drifted several feet above its original position.

Pavlo frowned, "If we keep moving, the platform will be useless."

Nikto sneered at his pessimism but didn't disagree.

Pilar hoped she hadn't oversold her piloting skills. Her steering jerked the craft left and right. Chandler clutched his seat like a nervous driving instructor.

She halted five feet above Landa's last known position. "Where did he go from here?" Nothing was visible in front of them except radiant lifeforms darting like gnats.

Chandler pointed downward. "Aim the lights at the ground."

She tilted the sub like a one-eyed orca to look down. Chandler heaved like he might puke. Outside the dome they saw Landa's footprints in the silt as clear as day.

"We got his trail," Chandler announced.

Pilar followed his prints. Landa had trekked in a straight line away from the *Naumtsev*. When she reached fifty meters, she slowed the sub. Lights revealed the footprints had begun to swerve, erratic. It was evident Landa had become disoriented. Pilar prayed he hadn't lost consciousness.

"Mr. Landa, do you read?" She raised her voice, "We are on the way." Nothing but static.

They both gasped when the tracks stopped. Lying face down in the sand was Landa. His suit was crawling with skeletal sea spiders, and his helmet was shrouded by small white octopuses.

"Mr. Landa!" Pilar shouted. The man didn't move.

Tap, tap, tap, the old ladies' pennies kept hitting the glass. They tapped harder, from all sides like stereo. Relentless and deafening. *Just stop!*

Landa was blind. With his visor face-down in the muck, there wasn't even the unsettling glow of tentacles. When he tried to breathe in, his chest was restricted by the suit. His air was becoming shallow and muggy. Unable to get up, Landa was entombed.

His brain began to wander. When the tapping slowed, he heard twigs brushing against a window. *Maybe it's an autumn night with a gentle breeze.* A cabin in the mountains perhaps, with a fireplace, the kind of home he always wanted. A place his daughter would actually visit instead of a Miami apartment.

The brushing twigs made a gentle ticking sound. *Raindrops on a tin roof.*

With a blast of static in his headset, Landa's eyes sprung open. Thrust back to reality, he was no longer in a cabin on a fall night. *Because I'm imprisoned hundreds of meters below ice.*

With a surge of dread, he recognized the sound of the twigs. It was the spindly legs of the spiders crawling on his suit. Like fingernails skimming the hood of a car.

He couldn't move his arms backwards or stand. He was a paralyzed prisoner being steadily tortured. He decided it'd be better to dream than scream. It was time to check out.

"Gotcha!" A female voice made him flinch. Before he could decide if she was real or not, the scrape of metal under him felt like a bulldozer trying to pry him off the ground.

The *Cyclops'* two robotic arms tried to slide under Landa's suit like spatulas.

"I think I got him!" Pilar focused, tense. When she steered forward, the motion rolled the man like a log. Sea spiders scurried away from the commotion.

Landa looked up from the sand. They could hear his breathing through static. Though still blindfolded by two octopuses, he faced the *Cyclops.* Ned Landa was alive.

"Mr. Landa, I am here." She extended a mechanical arm with an open claw. Even with partial vision, he understood. He reached for the claw and Pilar bumped the speed to inch forward.

He stretched his arm as far as his suit would allow. The *Cyclops* crept closer. When his glove finally touched the claw, Pilar didn't shut it to avoid crushing his hand.

Landa clung to the tip and pulled himself towards the craft. With a labored crawl, he was able to grasp the mechanical arm with his other hand. Using both arms, he secured a grip.

"I'm on…" Landa's voice was hoarse.

"We got him!" Chandler exclaimed. "Full reverse!"

The propellers forced the vessel backwards. With an audible grunt, Landa heaved himself into the arms of the *Cyclops*. As the craft turned, more sea spiders wafted off.

Pilar and Chandler smiled at each other. The *Naumtsev*'s lights were just fifty yards ahead. Outside the vessel, they could see Landa cradled in the *Cyclops*' arms like a child. The last two octopuses pulsated off his helmet, back into the shadows. They could see the man's smile.

"We have him." Chandler nodded to the monitor, "We're coming—" He shuddered at Pilar's petrified shriek.

A monstrous purple head soared by the window. Like the shimmer of a gothic phantom, the beast made a fast pass. The colossal squid had returned.

It's back? Chandler blinked. If they hadn't both seen it, it could've been a vision conceived by anxiety and exhaustion.

Her voice cracked, "It was the big one?" They leaned forward to look out the dome.

With hollow thumps, their fear was confirmed. Tentacles latched onto the side portholes. Suction cups the size of donuts pulsated on the glass. When Pilar turned back to the dome, she screamed to see a large golden eye watching them.

Chandler lunged for the controls. He pushed forward and the *Cyclops* dropped into a nosedive. She grasped the sticks and pulled back, spinning the sub skyward.

"Whoa!" a voice boomed. Their knee-jerk reaction hadn't considered Landa. "I'm out here!"

"He's still holding on!" Pilar looked down to see Landa hanging from the minisub with one arm.

With a loud thud, their view was blocked. The huge squid had covered the dome. They were horrified to see into the squid's mouth. A parrot-like beak appeared, the size of two shovel heads.

Like a knife scratching a plate, the slobbering beak tried to bite the glass.

Professor Arrison couldn't believe what they were witnessing. The cameras showed a fifty-foot colossal squid attached to the *Cyclops*. The critical difference from earlier was the squid was larger than the minisub. *A mythical kraken versus a Cyclops.*

"It might think you're another squid," she speculated. "Follow our lights!"

The squid's tubular mantle spanned the length of the minisub. More worrisome were its eight arms and two longer tentacles. They fondled the vessel, probing for a way in.

Nikto gripped the mic, "Pilar: follow my signal, forty-five meters."

Two tentacles slithered onto the minisub's rudder, causing it to buck and zigzag. Its remaining eight legs gripped the vessel, blocking their visibility.

"Landa, hang on!" Chandler felt queasy with the swaying motion. The cabin smelled like ammonia. He knew squids secreted the chemical but how were they smelling it? *Has it pierced the vents?* The engine made a whirring sound with whatever the squid was doing outside.

"I see lights," Pilar panted. Through tentacles, she saw a glimpse of the *Naumtsev's* lights.

Landa's voice shouted, "Keep going. Thirty yards."

At the base of the dome, they could see his helmet. He was still hanging on. They both cringed as the beak made a visible scratch on the glass.

Onscreen, the crew watched Landa dangle from the *Cyclops* by one arm. The squid shifted its legs as if seeking a better grip. *Or trying to open it like a tin can,* Arrison shaded her eyes.

"Open astern valves," Nikto commanded. "Full reverse slow."

"Full reverse," Pavlo confirmed. "Two knots."

Arrison nodded, "Closing the gap..." Backing up towards the *Cyclops* was a smart move.

"Two-zero meters and closing," Pavlo focused on his screen.

"When the *Cyclops* is under the well, raise the platform." Nikto gestured, "We'll pull them into the ship."

Ned Landa bent his right arm at a forty-five-degree angle to hang onto the sub's claw. He locked the ADS joint at the elbow and prayed again. Suspended below the squid, he looked away so his lights wouldn't draw attention. Hopefully his suit would conceal his scent.

The massive squid kept writhing. It twisted and pumped like a hand trying to open a jar. Landa heard grinding sounds that were either its hooks scraping the hull or its beak snapping.

Despite swerving, they were moving closer to the *Naumtsev*. "Ten more meters."

"Stay on your course," Nikto's voice crackled. "We will catch you."

Landa shouted back, "Can you electrocute this thing like the pirates?"

"Of course," Nikto replied. "And your conductive metal suit will cook you alive."

Landa didn't reply. The *Naumtsev* was now five meters away and closing. The dive platform was still hanging below it. The larger sub maneuvered to catch them under the well.

Landa looked below his feet to wait for the platform. Timing was crucial; when it appeared, he had to drop. *This is it.* He took a deep breath, unlocked his arm and let go. Despite the suit's weight, he fell in slow motion to the platform. He lunged for the controls on the rail.

The winch's motors came to life; the platform began to rise. It lifted the *Cyclops*—with the squid—towards the *Naumtsev*.

"The door to the moon well has been repaired," Aleksei proclaimed, standing with two engineers. The door slid open.

"Outstanding," Nikto replied. "We are on the way."

When the men entered, they stopped in their tracks. In the center of the floor, tentacles the size of fire hoses reached out of the well. The winch's gears screeched to lift the *Cyclops*. When the top of the sub appeared, it was covered with arms that slithered like giant cobras.

"Get the prod," Aleksei pointed to a wall. A man grabbed a ten-foot pole.

Latched to the *Cyclops*, the squid's twelve-foot head raised out of the water, nearly touching the ceiling. Its dilated eyes appeared angry at being forced to enter the bright room. Tentacles unfurled to clutch the rails.

As the platform ascended, there was a man standing on the corner wearing full ADS gear. It was Ned Landa.

Captain Nikto, Dr. Arrison and two men jogged into the chamber. They halted, horrified. They covered their eyes with the burn of ammonia. An ink-like fluid pooled on the floor. As cables raised the sub out of the water, the colossal squid uncoiled, gripping anything in its way.

A crewman tried to thrust a prod into the beast but slipped in the ink. Tentacles wrapped around his neck. Another man was blocked as the squid overturned gas tanks and equipment. The squid's skin turned a shade of crimson. It began to crawl into the room.

Like an automated cyborg, Ned Landa lifted a gaff from the wall. Invincible in his suit, he plodded towards the beast and plunged the harpoon into the center of its eye. Black fluid spewed. Landa pushed the spear deeper and twisted with a wet crunch. The squid's legs convulsed.

With a squeak like bare feet in a bathtub, the squid slid off the *Cyclops*. The 1,500-pound beast fell straight down and splashed into the well below.

"Seal the doors!" Nikto bellowed.

Aleksei hit a lever. The well doors closed like a guillotine, severing two tentacles that had tried to hold on. The eight-foot-long legs thrashed on the deck like beheaded serpents.

Arrison scaled the *Cyclops* to help open the top hatch. It swung open with a clang, and a sweaty Chandler and Pilar peeked out. Arrison grasped her son with an impassioned hug.

He looked at his mother with misty eyes that conceded her affection.

Before they could exit the sub, Pilar gazed down at the severed tentacles curling on the deck.

Chandler looked at her with a bitter expression, "Please don't say calamari tonight."

PART VII
CASTING THE NET

"The problem when you cast your net that wide
is you inevitably catch something you do not want to catch."

—Edward Felton, Professor and
Deputy US Chief Technology Officer

Chapter Forty-Nine
The Transpondian

Middlesex, England, UK

The flags of NATO's thirty nations stood before the inspiring three-story brick building. Located at the Northwood Headquarters in Middlesex, the Allied Maritime Command (MARCOM) was NATO's central hub for all naval matters in the North Atlantic Alliance.

Already exhausted at 9:45 am, she waited in the lobby until her name was called.

"Officer Cynthia Engel?" The handsome man had a fitted uniform and salt-and-pepper hair. "I'm Webster, Commander of NATO Subs."

"H-hello," Engel stammered, "I'm Navy Officer Engel but you already know that." She blushed with a grin. As predicted, she was awed by his charming English accent.

"Thank you so much for coming." Webster used both hands to shake hers. "We are astounded with your discovery. May I get you tea? Biscuits?"

Engel blinked, incredulous. They were actually happy to see her? She wasn't used to being treated with such respect. *Maybe it's a British thing?*

෨

Engel loved the jaunt so far, though she'd been in the country for only four hours. It was her first trip to Europe. She and Chuck had been saving to go for their fifteenth anniversary. When this sudden opportunity came about, he'd understood the gravity of the situation. With all the excitement —combined with a six-hour time change— her morning was a blur.

Most transatlantic flights were scheduled late in the day so, in theory, one could sleep during the trip and wake up refreshed in London. Of course, it hadn't worked out like that. The coach seats weren't comfortable, and her slumber was never deeper than a twilight where she could still hear babies crying around her.

When the pilot had announced their approach to Gatwick, her adrenalin kicked in though it was still dark out.

I'm actually in England. Her eyes smiled as she gazed out the window. Engel's favorite holiday movie was the British classic *Love Actually.* So, she imagined exactly what Londoners would be like: warm, attractive, funny, with better manners than in the states.

It wasn't even 6:00 am when she'd exited the concourse. She'd tried to shove out of her mind it was only midnight in the US. Figuring a giant coffee would clear the fog, she'd found a European version of Starbucks called Café Nero, only to learn there was no such thing as a "large coffee." It was all espresso and tea. She didn't want to attract attention as a Yank, but had to request a "café Americano," which was espresso and hot water.

She couldn't wait to enjoy her coffee during her train ride to King's Cross. She'd quickly learned Londoners weren't like the ones in *Love Actually.* They were the same impatient, fast-talking sorts found in any large city such as DC or Manhattan. Within minutes she had a train seat to herself as dawn flickered through slate-gray clouds.

It provided perfect time to review her files. She'd been invited to present at the Maritime Operational Conference at MARCOM Headquarters in Northwood. The audience included thirty-nine Fleet Commanders and NATO reps from allied nations.

The conference had been planned to discuss maritime topics to enhance international cooperation and to update leadership about any threats affecting member nations.

But then came an ambitious US Navy report authored by Intel Analyst Cynthia Engel. The meeting's agenda had to be quickly amended.

Engel opened her laptop to review her presentation. From her past experiences, she figured a roomful of officers would be more receptive to color pictures than complex dialogue.

She'd researched her host, Admiral Carl Webster, Commander of NATO Submarines. The handsome, fifty-nine-year-old Royal Navy admiral was responsible for mission assignments to all submarines in the alliance, including execution of any security exercises.

Basically, as leader of all NATO submarines, Webster would be the person to convince.

Webster led Engel to MARCOM's large conference room. Long tables had been placed in a U-shape, facing a podium with a seventy-inch screen behind it.

When Engel entered, the fifty attendees sat upright with courteous smiles. From the smoky rooms of Key West to the impolite rooms of Colombia, and now on to London, it felt like the rooms were growing larger and more professional.

"This is my first time across the pond, as they say…" Engel's voice trailed, wishing she hadn't used the cliché. "And I wish it were under better circumstances."

From behind the podium, she projected an image of a recovered C-Buoy on the large screen.

"This is the first communication buoy we recovered. According to Lockheed Martin, it isn't one of theirs. It appears to be a prototype, never put into use, constructed with Russian components." Engel looked at her audience. "It was found off the southern coast of Argentina."

She momentarily locked, realizing the room of high-ranking faces. They included the white-haired Captain Berryhill from Connecticut representing the US. She took a breath and resumed.

"The beacon transmitted at an extremely low frequency to avoid detection. Our forensics were then able to identify its signature." She paused with a grin, "We've now identified six other transmissions from other buoys. We found three more, confirming our projections."

The image changed to a color graphic of the South Atlantic. Six red dots on the map formed a sweeping curve, traveling south of Argentina, then looping northwest of Antarctica.

"This is its track." She traced the path with a laser pointer. "It coincides with a heat stain we picked up off Patagonia." The beam coiled north into the Pacific.

"What does Russia say?" Captain Berryhill bellowed without raising his hand.

"Their Ministry of Defense denies having any subs in the area. Nor do they admit to losing any. That wasn't a shocker; it would make them appear incompetent." Engel paused at a few chuckles. "No country would want to admit they can't guard their own equipment."

"However," She flashed an ironic smile, "They did say if we find one of their subs, they demand we return it."

There was a mix of scoffs and chuckles.

Her expression tensed, "Russia can't afford any more humiliation after '*Operation Odessa.*'" Seeing a few blank stares, she knew it'd be wise to recap the project.

Engel paced the stage, "A Miami FBI taskforce called themselves 'Operation Odessa,' named after the port in the Ukraine. They were investigating a rise in Russian crime in Miami. But what they uncovered was startling." She looked up, "The $35 million sale of a Soviet submarine to the Cali cartel."

The room shifted in their seats, curious.

"It's no longer classified; Netflix even has a documentary about it. A Russian mob enforcer joined a Cuban businessman who had ties to the Cali cartel. They'd heard about equipment left behind in the former Soviet Union. Everything —literally everything— was for sale. It was the Wild West. Their first deal was buying two Russian Kamov helicopters for a million dollars each to sell to the cartel.

"The men were then heroes with the Colombian narcos. Their next plan escalated: to purchase a submarine from the Russians."

A few officers in the front frowned at each other, dubious.

"To prove to the cartel their plan could work, the men were able to gain access to a Russian base littered with Cold War equipment. The men made a deal with the cartel to sell them a Russian submarine for $35 million. Cartels were already using homemade narco-subs, so a real submarine would be a game changer in the smuggling world.

"One of the men convinced the cartel to give him $10 million cash as a down payment. Unknown to his partners, he'd been planning to steal the money all long. The submarine deal fell apart when he vanished with the $10 million." Engel lifted her shoulders, "For all we know, he or someone else could've pursued a similar deal."

The entire room murmured with overlapping, "Can this happen again? Could terrorists do that?"

Commander Webster raised a hand, "The GCC reports an Iranian Fateh-class submarine heading southeast from the Gulf of Oman. Any connection?"

Engel's gears locked at the question. They were now concerned about a Mid-East terrorism aspect? She knew the Gulf Cooperation Council was a union of Arab states. She'd been so focused on her corner of the globe, she had no updates on that region.

"I don't see a connection unless they're following the same intel we are. Iran has no duty to report their patrols." Eyeing the room, she knew Iran was not a member of NATO, but they were the only Gulf nation that had submarines. Could Iran know about the same rogue?

Iran was still a State Sponsor of Terrorism, with ongoing support for terrorist groups in Syria, Iraq and throughout the Mid-East.

If there was any way for the room to get quieter, it did.

Engel snapped out of her daze and clicked back to the map, "Using the rogue's prior path, we can project a future trajectory into the South Pacific."

Commander Webster stood. "A rogue nuclear-armed vessel — by definition— is a global terror threat." He remained austere as he turned to his peers. "Our partner nations can deploy subs and ships immediately. It needs to be located and then stopped."

"Commander," Engel interjected, brazen, "Before any sort of attack, I have reason to believe the rogue's holding hostages who may be responsible for the signals."

The room seemed to frown in unison. *Signals?*

Engel projected a magnified image of a copper wire in a red casing. "The buoys are designed to self-destruct. Our forensics examined this wire in the buoy. The wire had been *manually* cut with a sharp instrument, versus some other failure." She looked at the crowd, "I believe a saboteur made it so it would not self-destruct."

A wave of dissent passed through the room.

A Japanese captain raised his hand. Engel knew Japan was not a NATO member but were long-standing partners.

"Do we know the captain's motives?" Captain Yamato asked. "Possible radicalism?"

Engel hadn't meant to shift the focus. She'd been immersed in where the rogue was and how it got there. The room now feared a terror threat.

"Not yet," she pursed her lips. "I can disclose we have a witness in protective custody in DC. I believe she has insight into the captain's motives. She says he's not a terrorist, and it has nothing to do with narcotics. If you can just wait, she's ready to talk."

Webster turned to her, "Officer Engel, you brought this matter to us." For the first time, his tone seemed combative, "Do you expect us to sit idle?"

Chapter Fifty
Ears Everywhere

The mighty Poseidon ascended over the Southern Ocean, restless and on the pursuit.

The P8-A Poseidon cruised north as the sea below merged into the South Pacific. It had been dispatched by the Royal New Zealand Air Force. It was their first P8-A, procured from the US as part of a 2019 agreement. Like its American counterpart, it was a sophisticated anti-submarine and surveillance aircraft.

It was not a solo mission. Joining the aircraft would be two additional Poseidons from the Royal Australian Air Force in Edinburgh.

The plane began to drop an array of sonobuoys from its fuselage. Each one looked like a tube of PVC, about three feet long and five inches in diameter.

Sonobuoys were acoustic transmitters that listened for sounds to detect submarines. The canisters were designed to deploy upon impact. An inflatable float with a transmitter would remain on the surface.

To avoid detection, the Poseidon dropped passive sonobuoys that would emit no sounds underwater. They would simply listen, waiting for sound waves, no matter how small, from any engine, propeller or even doors closing. The results would be transmitted via radio to authorities.

Small parachutes ejected from the buoys to slow their plummet to the sea. In the plane's trail, a broad pattern of devices dotted the skies. The planes from Australia would add hundreds more.

If any submerged vessel attempted to travel into the South Pacific from any point between New Zealand and the northern tip of Antarctica, the ears of multiple nations would know.

∽

Seated in the parlor, Captain Nikto and Dr. Arrison focused on their chess pieces as if trying to move them through telepathy. The Soviet-era *Averbakh* chess set had been handcrafted in 1945.

"No," Arrison shook her head. "Knight takes queen, see?" She made her move.

Nikto knitted his brows. "Touché. Again," he grunted. He pushed back from the table and tapped his glass over his mouth for the last few drops. He plopped his glass down and gave a lopsided grin.

"Who could have predicted I'd meet another scientist," his words were slow, "who is also the perfect…" He rolled his hand to place the word, "*Supruga.*"

"Su…pruga?" she attempted, curious.

He replied with flair, "*Supruga* is like a…partner. A spouse."

Arrison recoiled at his words, "Let's not overestimate our acquaintanceship."

Nikto's eyes darkened, "Patrice, you would agree there are no accidents in nature. I lose Kana, a scientist most dear to me. Then fate delivers you —quite literally— onto my vessel."

She matched his posture and leaned in. "I was delivered on your vessel with my son and a soldier because you nearly murdered us."

Nikto leaped upright to stand over her. "You call me a killer after what I've shown you? I have provided you astonishing opportunities of a lifetime."

"Archeology and rare species I can never tell anyone about?" She stood, voices clashing, "Discoveries I can never share with another human?" Her eyes hardened, "And you're encouraging Pilar and Chandler, so he'll want to stay."

"That is not true, Patrice!" Nikto roared.

"That's *Doctor* Arrison," she corrected. "You and your infinite promises: the Lost City of Heracleion. Loki's Castle in the Arctic Sea. You want me perched at your side as we crisscross the seven seas for the rest of our lives."

He snarled, "There is a reason I keep moving."

"Sins catching up to you?" She cocked her head for a response.

The palpable tension was axed by the intercom.

"Kapitan, I need you in control immediately," Dmitri's voice exclaimed.

"I am on the way." Nikto turned to exit, enraged.

"You don't get off that easy!" Arrison balled her fists and stomped in his path.

The captain charged into the control room like a locomotive. Arrison shadowed him, refusing to let him out of her sight.

"What is the calamity?" Nikto bellowed.

Wearing his headset, Dmitri turned. "I detected a plane making a regular pattern of drops. I believe it was dropping sonobuoys."

"What are sonobuoys?" Arrison wedged herself between the men.

"They are hydrophones. Listening devices," Nikto retorted.

Pavlo interjected, "Even if we go deeper, it will be impossible to escape their sonar. We can't just turn around—"

"Mind your radar!" Nikto glowered at the man's spinelessness. "Radar," he muttered as if a memory was surfacing. "Dmitri: last week you reported a tropical depression on the other side of the globe."

"*Da, Kapitan,*" Dmitri accessed a different screen. "A tropical storm in the Northwest Pacific. 2,000 miles east of Papua New Guinea. It meant nothing to us."

"It means something now," Nikto barked. "What is its status?"

Dmitri ran his finger across the screen, "It reached 119 kilometers per hour. It is now named Typhoon Dakkar."

Arrison was silenced by the shifting priorities.

"Location?" The captain pivoted to Pavlo.

He trembled to study his radar. "The cyclone is now in the South Pacific. It has shifted towards French Polynesia."

Nikto stroked his beard. "At our current speed and direction, where would we intersect the cyclone?"

"The storm is 1,400 miles northwest of Tahiti," Pavlo stammered. "Moving at twenty knots."

"We can travel twice that speed." Dmitri added, "We are now 2,700 miles south of Polynesia."

Nikto mumbled the math, "At forty knots we will intersect in less than two and half days."

"Intersect?" Arrison exclaimed, "The storm?"

The captain ignored her. "Plot a course to Tahiti, four-zero knots." He folded his arms, resolute.

Arrison scowled at the men, "We're steering *towards* a typhoon?"

"We will be under the storm. The churn will obscure any sonar." When Nikto turned to her, his eyes were like daggers. "Only the insane would travel into a cyclone, yes?"

Chapter Fifty-One
Revelations at Chalet El Palomar

Nikto tossed and kicked the sheets in bed. His cabin was almost eighty degrees due to a faulty condenser. He'd taken a shot of vodka before bed in some archaic belief it would help him sleep.

He draped an arm over his eyes and chanted her name, *Kana*. The room was quiet, aside from the lulling hum of the engines. He tried to calm his breathing. Using what little he could recall of Kana's meditation techniques, he wanted to experience another lucid dream. He needed a break from reality. *Kana... I want to be back... Kana...*

Nikto sprawled on top of his sheets. His pulse began to slow, as did the chants.

"Which do you like?" Kana smiled at a basket beside their bed in the private chalet. "Today we have chocolate *santafereño* and *carimañolas* pasties."

"Your Spanish is getting better." Nikto sat up in bed. "I have gained ten pounds with these breakfasts."

Kana stood, nude from their slumber. She put on a gown, "I will prepare some café."

Nikto smiled at how the window's exposure allowed the dawn

to cast a perfect golden aura on her porcelain skin. It was their first morning as husband and wife. They'd been secretly married by a *notaria* in a private ceremony in El Palomar.

But as she walked away, his joy faded. A disquieting intuition knew this was a fleeting affair. A perfect moment in paradise that was not destined to last forever.

Nikto looked down at their bed. For as much love as it had supported, it also held its secrets. It was in bed where Nikto had explained how he had stolen the *Naumtsev* from Russia. In the very same bed, Kana had terrified him with her health condition. Severe asthma made her more fragile than her design team would ever guess.

He couldn't shake the memory of the first time he'd witnessed her bronchial attack. Her eruption of coughs; her struggle to inhale. He had been petrified until she used her medication.

Kana had explained how Colombia's tropical climate had worsened her asthma. The humid air was harder to breathe. The lush flora was full of pollen and other triggers. The polluted air over Buenaventura was even worse.

Holding her, Nikto had promised, "Soon, you'll be in the cool, filtered air of the *Naumtsev*. Safe forever, experiencing the world like you have never seen it."

He lit a cigarette in their chalet's bed to expel the memory. As fragile as Kana could seem in some matters, she was bold in others.

"How could one man steal an Akula?" Kana had once asked with a blunt smirk.

Nikto had laughed at her candor. "It was not one man," he'd chuckled, "It required many."

He'd proceeded to demystify the details. He was concise, yet thorough. Kana's intellectual and scientific mind had absorbed the technicalities with few questions.

"There is one element that makes everything I'm about to tell you possible," Nikto had explained. "Russian soldiers, specifically the lowest rank, are paid 23,000 rubles a month. That's less than $300 per month." His eyes glinted, "Cash is king, and the cartel had plenty."

"Russia was on the eve of a ten-year lease of an Akula to India.

A $4 billion contract for the government. The vessel I now call the *Naumtsev* was docked at Kronstadt Naval Base, one of several Akulas being considered for the lease."

Nikto had flashed a sly grin, "I had a radiation expert on my payroll. An authority on emergency nuclear response who was eager to retire. For $10,000, he falsified a report the sub had experienced a nuclear incident while docked, triggered by a design flaw. It had allegedly caused a fire killing a dozen sailors; men who would later be part of my crew."

Kana had frowned to consider the scenario. "Wouldn't the Russian government want more experts and time to investigate?"

"Quite the opposite," Nikto shrugged, "If news of the design flaw leaked, it would jeopardize a $4 billion lease. The government was still reeling from a similar real incident in July 2019. A nuclear sub, the *Losharik*, had an accident in the Barents Sea. A combustion explosion killed fourteen men. Putin staunchly denied the event, but the news leaked. He was forced to acknowledge the accident.

"For my bogus accident, we claimed it occurred in engineering, so no evidence had to be visible outside. Nothing any exterior sensors could detect. When officials received the report with the forged radioactive readings, they knew it'd be too costly and time consuming to decontaminate. They wanted the sub gone immediately," he accentuated the word. "Before India —or the entire world— learns of another humiliating accident.

"They needed a captain to make the sub vanish. It couldn't just be towed." Nikto grinned, "My expert suggested me. I was a retired, decorated captain, living in Baltiysk, in a trailer, on a shitty pension." He lifted a brow, "He told them I had pancreatic cancer, with just months to live." He leaned closer, "I was hired for a suicide mission."

Kana's jaw fell open, but she said nothing.

"Russia offered me $100,000 to bestow to my relatives if I would take the contaminated vessel faraway and sink her. Deep.

"I had already gathered two dozen former sailors, all destitute or without families or both. I paid them $5,000 each —nearly a year-and-a-half's pay— to sail the world, without federation rule, with a promise

303

of more money in exotic, tropical Colombia." Nikto smiled, smug.

"To limit witnesses, we chose 4:00 am on Easter Sunday." Nikto squinted out the window to recall, "There was just a skeleton crew of guards at the port. Most still drunk from Saturday night. Hours before dawn, a tug pulled the *Naumtsev* to cruising depth." He snapped his fingers at the simplicity, "We were gone."

Kana's eyes danced to process. "I find it hard to believe the government would be so quick to discard a vessel that cost over $2 billion."

He rolled his shoulders, "The sub was over twenty-five years old. Suffering its age, obsolete systems, requiring exorbitant repairs. But the lease of a similar Akula would yield $4 billion." He touched her cheek, "With your help, we are now making those repairs and upgrades."

"Where did the authorities think you were taking it? Wouldn't they want to confirm?"

He shook his head, "They didn't want to know anything about it. Complete deniability. Russia already has seven sunken nuclear subs. They were also abandoned as too costly to retrieve or cleanse. The deep water is considered sufficient to contain radiation."

Kana's face softened with a dimpled grin, "So not only did you steal the sub, they also unwittingly paid you $100,000 to do so?"

"That is true." He smiled with a broad shrug, "I had no relatives to inherit it."

Nikto blinked from his daze to see Kana return with their coffee. She climbed into bed and cuddled close. After her first sip, she expelled a gentle cough.

"Are you okay?" Nikto tensed, fearing another attack.

She cleared her throat with a hand to her chest, "I am okay."

"You have your meds?"

"I do," she motioned to a bottle of Albuterol by the bed.

"It just frightens me that—"

They jolted at three abrupt knocks. Nikto and Kana turned to the chalet's front door.

Who is it? Kana mouthed with wide eyes.

Nikto didn't reply. No one was supposed to know they were together in this place. With three harder blows, he knew the sound: it was the stock of a rifle pounding the door.

Before he could react, the door crashed inwards. Two men with assault rifles stormed into the room. Behind them, Don Ricardo Salazar entered the chalet with an unhurried stroll. The narco boss appeared elegant, with coiffed hair and wearing a red dress shirt.

Salazar gaped at the couple as if shocked, "Captain No One and his lead engineer..." He rasped like a snake, "I am interrupting your private honeymoon?"

Nikto shouted, "What do you want?" He stood, firm.

"You know what I want," Salazar adjusted his cufflinks. "What you were paid to do."

The armed men spread out, one towards Nikto, the other to Kana's side of the bed.

Nikto didn't budge, "The *Naumtsev* will be ready to sail in seven days."

"I grant you five," Salazar leaned to stroke Kana's polished toes. "But without your scientist. You need to focus on your job without any distractions." He barked Spanish to his men, "*Llévate al Dr. Kana, ahora!*"

One man pushed the barrel of his gun to Nikto's temple. The other grabbed Kana by her ankles. When he tugged her off the bed, her body slammed onto the floor.

"Kana!" Nikto bellowed, "Savages!" The man pushed the gun harder to his eye.

Nikto fumed to hear his beloved's ghastly screams. The man dragged her out the door as her fingernails scraped the wood floor.

Salazar turned to Nikto with searing eyes. "The sooner you complete your run, the sooner you will see your bride." He walked backwards out the door. The man at Nikto's side withdrew, keeping his rifle aimed. They vanished within Kana's fading cries.

Nikto felt powerless, gasping with fury. She wasn't a mere scientist. *They've taken my wife!*

Then he saw it. On the bedside table was Kana's medication. The albuterol and her inhaler. *She doesn't have her meds!* His chest tightened, horrified.

Nikto quaked at another deafening bang on a door.

ᴄᴑ

Nikto sat upright, gasping, and profusely sweating. He darted his head to realize he was in his quarters on the *Naumtsev*. There was another knock on his door.

"Kapitan, it is me, Aleksei," the voice shouted.

"*Voyti!*" He wiped his face with a sheet. "Come!"

He saw the silhouette of Aleksei enter. "You need to come with me to the moon well. Now."

"What's going on?" Dr. Arrison stood at her door, squinting from the light. "What time is it?"

Still disheveled, Captain Nikto glared into her eyes. At his side were Aleksei and a guard aiming a Makarov.

Nikto turned to the guard, "Force her to come with us or shoot her in the knee."

Arrison was petrified with confusion. The guard shoved her by the shoulder. None of her pleas were answered as the four stomped down two flights of steps.

They approached the moon well. Nikto smacked the controls and the door opened.

Ned Landa was at the workbench. He flinched and turned, surprised by the door. On his bench was a disassembled C-Buoy.

"Mr. Landa," Nikto proclaimed in a rigid voice. "You are a traitor and a saboteur." He cocked his head, "Why am I not shocked?"

Landa flexed his biceps and stood but didn't respond.

Arrison's voice trembled, "What's happening?"

Nikto snapped his head to her, "Your colleague altered my buoys so they can be tracked." He became louder, "He has created a virtual path to our vessel!" Nikto leaned within inches of her face, "Are you his accomplice?"

Chapter Fifty-Two
Between the Columns

Washington, DC

Officer Cynthia Engel entered the building's twenty-foot-high doors. She was still exhausted, blaming jet lag, though it had been three days since her trip to England. She thought it sounded high society to complain of jet lag.

It was the morning crowd, everyone rushing while juggling their phones, coffees, and briefcases.

I know he's here, Engel mumbled. She was searching for one man within the herd. She knew his morning routine like a stalker. He was tall, lanky, and bald and knew how to wear a nice suit. Engel scanned the crowd, *where is he?*

It was a clear, sunny morning at 950 Pennsylvania Avenue, NW. The United States Department of Justice building housed the DOJ offices, including that of the US Attorney General.

Engel was on the hunt for attorney Donald Bronstein. He'd been a US Attorney for the Southern District for twenty years, renowned for drafting unique immunity agreements for key witnesses. He had been hand selected to compose Mirta Salazar's agreements to be protected by the US's Federal Witness Protection Program.

There he is! She saw Bronstein's bald head above the masses. He had his shoe up on a pedestal, telling a story to a woefully bored employee. Engel moved in for the kill, recalling everything she knew about the man. Though he appeared cerebral, he was a family man who enjoyed useless movie trivia and loved to boast how he'd gone to school with actor Matt Dillon.

Bronstein locked eyes with her and began to walk the other direction.

"Wait up… Donny!" Engel shouted in his trail until she caught up.

Bronstein did an exaggerated glance at his watch, "I just hung up with the Attorney General —who's a dear friend— and she signed off on Salazar's agreement." He didn't slow his stride, "But no one cares about the captain's motive four years ago."

Engel huffed, "How could they not care why this Nikto captain did it?"

"Because it had to be money. They're drug dealers." He spoke with a quick, dramatic flair, "And because —as we speak— they are 99.999 percent sure they've found it."

"Found it?" Engel stopped in her tracks. "The rogue sub?"

"Obviously the rogue." Bronstein groaned, having to elaborate. "Hydrophones picked up its sound. Heading north in the South Pacific, somewhere between Chile and New Zealand."

Engel's eyes ricocheted, unsure where to start. Part of her wanted to gloat how her predictive models had been correct.

Bronstein lectured, "Their focus has to be the rogue nuclear submarine." He paused for weight. "So why this Captain 'No-One' stole it years ago isn't the priority."

"Wouldn't you want to know, Donald?" she mocked his name. "Mirta implied he was fleeing something, maybe something even more dangerous."

"Because, *Cindy*," Bronstein looked around as if spies were hovering, "You'll hear the news eventually, but NATO has convinced the Navy to create an operation. They're going to annihilate this thing either way."

She went deadpan at the inference. "How can they? They can't make this public." She stammered, "What about the Senate Intelligence—"

"They're labeling it an exercise," Bronstein cut her off with a clever grin. "An impromptu RIMPAC exercise, like the ones NATO does every year."

Engel's eyes twitched at the concept, *an exercise*. It was genius. Navy exercises were so commonplace, their press releases rarely made the mainstream news.

Unlike computer-simulated war games, the Navy and NATO conducted exercises using real troops, aircraft and ships, practicing what they'd do in real emergencies. They were given a fictitious scenario to respond to that could hypothetically occur in the real world. *Like a rogue nuclear submarine,* Engel nodded into space.

NATO didn't usually train in the Pacific, but RIMPAC exercises were specifically for that region. RIMPAC, or "Rim of the Pacific exercises," were overseen by the Navy's Pacific Command at Pearl Harbor. Other countries are invited to participate such as Australia, Japan, New Zealand and the Republic of Korea.

So, Engel surmised, *the sudden presence of warships, aircraft and submarines wouldn't be considered out of the ordinary.* If the rogue turned out to be some explainable anomaly, no harm no foul. But if they stopped a real threat, the Navy and all participating nations would be heroes.

"Cindy, I gotta' run," Bronstein pointed at his watch.

"This is for me," Engel implored. "I know everyone's goal is to stop it." She stepped closer, "I want to know the captain's motives. Even if it was years ago."

"What are you asking?" Bronstein shrugged, abrupt. "Mirta Salazar has already testified. They already found the vessel. She's now being prepped for a new life 800 miles away."

"Give me twenty minutes with her," Engel pled in a high whisper. "I have questions about Nikto and his reasons."

"I don't have the authority," Bronstein quivered his head, staunch.

Engel startled him with a punch to his shoulder. "Come on, Donald! Of course, you have authority." She moved into his space, "I wrote Kayla a sorority reference letter and gave her like a thousand service hours; I've never even met her! I did that for you! Give me just fifteen minutes with Salazar. Before she's whisked off to work in some Whole Foods in Paducah."

Bronstein released a weary groan and buckled his knees in resignation.

Engel's stance eased with an imperceptible smile. She'd get her favor.

Chapter Fifty-Three
Squaring the Circle

"Once is happenstance. Twice is coincidence.
The third time it's enemy action."

—Ian Fleming, *Goldfinger*

The *Naumtsev* was discovered by the Allied forces at 4:55 pm Tahiti Time.

Sonobuoys picked up an unidentified submerged vessel 2,004 nautical miles south of Polynesia. It was traveling due north, at an unprecedented forty knots.

The plan was to have an array of sonobuoys so tight it'd be impossible for a submarine to pass through them without detection. A perfect starting point with location, velocity, and direction. A Poseidon could then fly over the area using magnetic anomaly detectors. If they could pinpoint the correct area, the vessel would be found. But since it was a moving object, locating it in one spot did not promise continuous tracking.

No plane could remain above the submarine indefinitely. The Poseidon's fuel range was 2,300 miles, and the unidentified sub was 1,100 miles east of the closest base in New Zealand. The plane could drop a buoy to mark the position and then signal all planes and ships in pursuit. But the marker would have to be adjusted for currents and wave action. In other words, nothing was infallible.

In prior wars, a pursuer could force an enemy sub to stay submerged to the point of battery or air exhaustion, forcing it to surface. However, a nuclear sub couldn't be made to stay down until air or power depletion since those necessities were virtually unlimited.

The Allies had a good starting point. More sonobuoys would be dropped in the rogue's projected path for ongoing monitoring. And, unknown to the rogue, many more forces were on the way.

❧

Dr. Arrison sat on a corner of her bed with a gray look of dread. Ned Landa stewed on the other side of her cabin with his arms crossed. They turned as the door swung open.

A tall guard heaved Chandler into the room. As he objected, "Why are you taking me—" the guard slammed the door with an audible clink of the lock.

Chandler tugged the doorknob. "They locked it?"

"Yep," Landa grunted. "Just another jail."

"Are you okay?" Arrison smoothed her son's hair.

Chandler looked at them, trying to compute their predicament. "Why are we locked in here?"

"Hoping the inmates talk." Landa pointed to the intercom, "So he can listen."

"How do you know we're not here for our safety?" Arrison frowned, "He said we're heading towards a Category 4 typhoon."

"Wait, what?" Chandler's mouth dropped. "Into a typhoon?"

Landa raised his hands for them to settle. "Subs don't feel cyclones at a hundred meters. My guess, he's moving towards the storm to muddle any sonar. He figures no one would follow."

Arrison and Chandler flinched when Landa roared, "I hope he is listening!" He put his face to the intercom, "You reject the laws of society? So, we're supposed to follow yours?"

After a second, Chandler looked at him, "Is it true? You sent signals?"

"How are my actions any different than his?" Landa was still raucous, "He retaliates against his enemies." He thumbed to himself, "Nikto is my enemy!"

☙

The captain's presence in the control room made everyone tense. The crew didn't smoke or chitchat as they remained fixed on their stations.

Nikto stepped behind Dmitri. "Have you decrypted the data?"

"Partially." Dmitri adjusted his glasses to buy a few seconds. "Keep in mind data from the satellite is already two days old—"

"What do you have?" Nikto interrupted with a growl.

"The term 'NATO' is used heavily. As well as sudden chatter between the US and the navies of five Pacific nations. I don't have the content, but the term 'rogue' is repeated."

Nikto's bloodshot eyes didn't blink. "And more sonobuoys?"

"An ongoing pattern of drops. Hydrophones can hear 1,800 meters. We cannot dive below their abilities," Dmitri's voice trailed with nothing positive to add.

The captain's silence was unusual, as if his gears were being overworked. He turned to Pavlo. "If any western forces were to," he rolled his hand, "be in pursuit, when would they arrive at the storm?"

"At the typhoon?" Pavlo's tone marveled why anyone would go to a storm. "Hawaii and New Zealand are approximately 2,000 miles from the eye. With an average speed of thirty knots, it would take sixty hours each. Two and a half days. Same as us."

Nikto leaned over his shoulder to study the map. "Australia and Asia are even farther."

Pavlo looked up. "We cannot accurately predict. Their vessels could have already been out to sea."

"So there we have it," Nikto stretched his neck with a crack. "It will be a race to the cyclone. Maintain four-zero knots at a depth of one-zero-zero meters."

There was a mix of nods and weary eyes from the crew.

Nikto spread his arms with a delirious smile. "All ships can submerge. But only submarines can come back up."

Chapter Fifty-Four
The Black Cauldron

Typhoon Dakkar was becoming one of the most intense storms ever recorded in the Southern Hemisphere. It had been reclassified Tropical Cyclone Dakkar, as its designation changed when it entered the South Pacific.

The system had begun as a tropical depression, 2,000 miles east of Papua New Guinea. The storm developed as it moved southeast, acquiring gale-force winds. With escalated strengthening, it reached Category 5 status.

In advance of the storm's projected arrival in Tahiti, including all islands of French Polynesia, shelters were opened with a nationwide curfew. The last storm in the vicinity with the same magnitude was Tropical Cyclone Winston in 2016. It had inflicted severe damage, with 40,000 homes damaged or destroyed, and had killed forty-four people.

ം

"This is not ideal," groaned Admiral James Farragut. He was commander of the US Pacific Fleet, and responsible for crafting the naval exercise. His excuse to the nations about the short notice was that

314

real emergencies happen without notice.

"We can skirt the storm, easy enough," replied Torrance, his Fleet Master Chief. "Our storm exercises are for situations just like this."

"Not exactly like this," the elder Farragut scoffed as he sipped his Earl Grey.

From their Pacific Command headquarters in Pearl Harbor, the men watched satellite images of Dakkar. The irony of being in sunny, beautiful Hawaii, with just a mild breeze rustling the coconut palms, as they stared into the eye of a Category 5 monster.

Their dilemma: five allied nations had already set sail to pursue the rogue submarine, just as a tropical cyclone was swirling into their Pacific stage.

"Our ships weather storms all the time," Torrance shrugged. "Our carrier can withstand at least a Cat-4. Hell, they're built to withstand a nuclear shockwave."

Farragut glowered, "Let's hope it doesn't get to that."

"That's my point, sir. The threat of a nuclear-armed vessel under the control of an adversary is more critical than a storm. We have their projected course. We cannot pass this opportunity."

Farragut gnashed his teeth. He knew his ships had the ability to avoid storms. At thirty knots, a ship can move to any point within a 700-square-mile radius within thirty minutes. At ninety minutes, that area grows to over 6,000 square miles.

"Agreed," the admiral stood. "We can issue a 'sortie code alpha' if needed," the command to immediately move vessels for storm avoidance.

"I'll order all surface vessels to remain a hundred miles from any storm bands." Torrance raised his brows, "Let's hope the rogue and the storm do not intersect."

"That's why we got non-surface vessels," Farragut finally grinned. "Our subs won't have to stop."

⁋

Dmitri squeezed his eyes closed. He did not like what his monitor was showing.

His fingers trembled from not having a cigarette. In fact, the entire crew had heightened anxiety after running out of anything with nicotine. The *Naumtsev* had not replenished any cigarettes or tobacco during their last stop in Africa.

"The captain only cares about the woman and the boarders," crewmen had rumbled, "His mind has been absent. His anger."

The data Dmitri had decrypted would certainly not help the captain's temper. Broadcasts revealed the US Navy's plans in the Pacific and which navies were participating. Vessels would be converging from all corners of the ocean with a cyclone for a bullseye.

"Kapitan," he spoke into the mic with an uneasy pause, "I have vital information I need to share."

PART VIII
OPERATION ARGONAUT

"Fate whispers to the warrior, 'You cannot withstand the storm.'
The warrior whispers back, 'I am the storm.'"

—Unknown

Chapter Fifty-Five
Roll Call

New York

"In the spirit of transparency, the Navy has initiated Operation Argonaut," Secretary-General Jaime Aquilino announced to the fifteen members of the UN Security Council.

The members had arrived at the United Nations Headquarters in Manhattan, with the flags of the 193 UN members lashing in the breeze.

The headquarters was home to the principal organs of the United Nations, including the General Assembly and the Security Council, which had the duty to uphold international security.

The Council Chamber was identified by its large horseshoe-shaped table. The fifteen members sat at attention under a mural dominating the east wall depicting a phoenix rising amidst images of war.

Meetings of the council were not open to the public, and no verbatim record of any statements were kept. Following rules, a brief communique would eventually be published. In this case, it would be well after the conclusion of the operation. So no meddling press.

Secretary-General Aquilino continued into his mic, "Operation

319

Argonaut is being monitored by the US Bureau of Counterterrorism."
He lifted a report that had been printed minutes earlier.

"Leading the Pacific Fleet —the world's largest covering 100
million square miles— from Pearl Harbor, will be the USS *Wasp*, an
amphibious assault carrier. Also the USS *Missouri*, a Virginia-class
nuclear attack submarine.

Cruising from idyllic Oahu, Hawaii, Admiral Farragut led
Operation Argonaut from aboard the *Wasp*.

The advanced carrier was over 843 feet long, with a landing deck
and a displacement of over 40,000 tons. On its deck were two MH-60
Seahawk helicopters, equipped for anti-submarine warfare, search and
rescue, and medivac.

"To pursue the rogue from the northwest," Aquilino's voice
continued in the member's headsets to be translated, "Japan has offered
an attack submarine and a Kongo-class destroyer."

It had been a tranquil morning in the shadow of Japan's Mount
Fuji. Traveling in calm seas from the Port of Schimizu was a guided-
missile destroyer and an attack submarine, the JS *Ōryū*.

The 528-foot destroyer was equipped with guided missiles with an
Aegis Combat System, one of the few ships outside the US to have the
capability. It was also equipped with two varieties of anti-submarine
torpedoes.

Japan's JS *Ōryū* attack submarine had been commissioned in 2020.
The 275-foot Sōryū-class vessel had the largest displacement of any sub
used by post-war Japan. The *Ōryū* had six torpedo tubes and was armed
with Harpoon missiles.

Aquilino's voice continued, "Also on the hunt from the northwest,
the Republic of Korea Navy has deployed a *Gang Gam-Chan* destroyer."

Through dense rain from a heavy monsoon season, the ROKS *Gang
Gam-Chan* destroyer departed the Republic of Korea fleet at Busan
Naval Base. The 4,400-ton ship was equipped with eight harpoon
missiles and two triple "Blue Shark" anti-submarine torpedoes.

"From the southwest, we are fortunate enough to have a Hobart-class destroyer, courtesy of the Royal Australian Navy."

The paradox of departing a serene morning in Trinity Bay to head towards a hurricane to search for an enemy sub had not been lost on the crew of the HMAS *Hobart*.

It was the lead destroyer used by the Royal Australian Navy. The vessel cruised northeast at thirty knots from Cairns Naval Base on the east coast of Queensland, Australia. It had a range of over 5,000 nautical miles, with an array of arms including anti-submarine torpedoes, and an MH-60 Seahawk helicopter for any search-rescue.

"Rounding out the south, in the event the rogue sub were to retreat, New Zealand has offered a Protector-class patrol vessel."

Representing the Royal New Zealand Navy, the P55 *Wellington* patrol ship headed north-northeast from Devonport Naval Base on Auckland's north shore.

The 278-foot Protector-class vessel had an ample range of over 6,000 nautical miles. In addition to a complete arsenal of weapons, the ship carried one SH-2G Seasprite helicopter that was equipped with sensors to detect submarines of all varieties.

Aquilino put down his notes and gazed at each council member, "If there is indeed a rogue nuclear vessel, belonging to *No One* anywhere between Antarctica and the Arctic Circle, I assure you it will be tracked. Surrounded. Neutralized."

Chapter Fifty-Six
The Devil and the Deep Blue Sea

Hunched behind his desk, Captain Nikto looked like sallow leather. He gripped a framed portrait of Kana in one hand and a glass of Beluga vodka in the other.

When he squeezed his eyes closed, a tear escaped to slide down his cheek. Nikto touched her face in the photograph. "I am sorry. I am so very sorry." He sloshed more vodka into his glass.

Nikto flinched as his door swung open and Pilar barged into the room. With hair flailing, she roared, "What did you do to them?"

He rolled his eyes to her, "They cannot be trusted."

"To conceal your existence?" Pilar taunted, not allowing a second for him to preach. "The world needs to know!"

She looked down to see Kana's portrait in his hand. "Poor Nikto," she mocked. "They took your wife, so you kidnap me." She motioned around her, "Steal their vessel." Pilar leaned forward on his desk, "You just know how to react and imprison."

Nikto stood, rekindled by fury. "You think they simply took Kana?" His voice became louder, "Your father killed her!"

Silence. Pilar didn't move. Nikto seemed to swell over her.

"She had asthma!" Nikto bellowed. "Your father's savages did not know she needed medication!" He stepped around the desk to further rebuke, "When she had her next attack, his men watched her suffocate! Can you imagine the panic? The horror? To die alone, gasping, in a soiled cell!" His voice echoed in the small space.

A flash in his psyche made his knees lock. He could see Kana, shrieking as she gulped for air. Clawing at the walls of a gritty cell. Depleted by the vision, Nikto dropped into his chair.

He cocked his head at Pilar, "All so I would transport your father's precious narcotics."

Her eyes flickered, speechless.

"I did take you." He smiled with pathos, "To protect you from that life. Surrounded by the very same savages."

She blinked with thick tears. "But my father was arrested. His entire operation is gone. Who is left to escape?"

"Who am I fleeing?" Nikto reached across the desk for his bottle, "The beasts who tried to buy this vessel in Russia." He looked at Pilar, "The same men your father was going to sell it to."

When he realized her blank expression, he leered, "Your *padre* did not tell you about them?"

⌘

845 nautical miles north of Tahiti, the USS *Wasp* sliced through fifteen-foot swells. The ship was still a day away from the projected intersection of Tropical Cyclone Dakkar and French Polynesia.

The bridge of the *Wasp* was alive with officers. Though Admiral Farragut was aboard to lead the effort, Captain Paul Ross was on the bridge to command the ship.

"Captain, I have something," Petty Officer Lucía, the Aerographer's Mate, approached. Her job was to monitor meteorological data.

"What do you got?" The fiftyish Captain Ross peered through bifocals to see Lucía's tablet.

"Here," she pointed. "Have you ever heard of the Fujiwhara Effect?"

"I have not."

"There's a small tropical depression moving north from the

323

Cook Islands."

"Another storm?" Ross barked.

"It's very small," Lucía bit her lip, "But it's threatening a phenomenon known as the Fujiwhara Effect, an event when two storms come together to rotate around a common point." She touched the screen. "If two cyclones pass within 900 miles of each other, they can orbit one another like water circling a drain. When they reach 190 miles of each other, they can merge into a superstorm."

Ross shook his head at their hapless luck, "What's the likelihood of it affecting our mission?"

"It's rare," Lucía's tone tried to pacify the man. "The effect is more common in the Pacific because there's more open water for storms to converge. It's an ominous visual for us meteorologists but disturbing to anyone in its wake."

Ross kneaded his brows and muttered, "From bad to worse."

"Any update with the rogue we're tracking?" Lucía enquired.

"It's still advancing in a straight line." Ross nodded to his display, "Confirms the sonobuoys' track. The rogue's heading north-northeast."

The young officer frowned, "Do you think it plans to get lost under the storm?"

"It'd be a good plan," Ross shrugged. "Sonar will become useless. And we will have to halt due to the storm." He turned to her with a sly smile, "Fortunately, our subs don't have the same restrictions."

೮೨

Captain Nikto's monitor flashed to life. The screen filled with the face of Pavlo from control.

"Kapitan, we have coordinates for the navy vessels." He paused for a response. There was none.

Nikto was slumped in a chair beside his desk. His face was propped on an elbow with an empty glass in his other hand. With deep, guttural snores, he was out cold.

"Kapitan?" Pavlo tried again.

Pilar watched from behind Nikto's desk. She was crouched, unseen by the monitor's camera. The captain, in his inebriated stupor, had

324

divulged grave information the guests needed right away. She crept towards his desk drawers.

"Kapitan Nikto?" Pavlo made one last attempt before switching off the feed.

With nimble fingers, Pilar slid a brass ring of keys from a drawer without making a sound. As Nikto snorted and wheezed, she slinked out of the room like a cat.

Chapter Fifty-Seven
Blood on the Mermaid

"Escape?" Arrison's face contorted, irritated with Landa. "How do you propose we do that? We're sealed 300 feet underwater in the middle of the largest ocean!"

Landa stuffed his hands in his pockets, stewing like a boiler.

The three were still confined in Arrison's cabin. She and Chandler sat on opposite corners of the bed. Landa stared at the door as if willing it to open.

Arrison covered her eyes. *How has it come to this?* Emotionally depleted, she wanted to cry but wouldn't in front of the others.

Things had been so enchanting until just forty-eight hours earlier. *What happened?*

Aside from the battery emergency—and narrow escapes from various sea creatures—Antarctica had been exhilarating. She'd witnessed marine life firsthand like she'd never imagined. When they'd briefly surfaced after anchoring, Nikto kept his promise to prove the phenomenon of "bleeding ice" was true.

She'd read about bright red "blood" flowing from a glacier in Antarctica. The *Naumtsev* had surfaced, hidden off the coast of

Antarctica's northernmost peninsula. Bundled in coats, Nikto had taken her to the upper deck to see the bloody ice with her own eyes.

Arrison had expected the red to be like ribbons of raspberry through vanilla ice cream. The reality was more unsettling. Streaked and puddled on the frosted plains were splashes of crimson that looked like a murder scene. If it had been the North Pole, she would've feared it was a slaughter of polar bears on pristine snow.

But the glacial melts were revealing red algae called *Chlamydomonas nivalis,* which had been hidden in the ice. The algae thrived in freezing water and remained dormant in snow and ice. If the snow melted, the vivid red blooms of algae spread their spores.

In the third century BC, Aristotle called it "blood snow." Though intriguing, the visceral image was foreboding. It seemed to symbolize the death—or murder—of a continent. The world had thrust a rusted dagger into her side.

Upon reflection, Arrison frowned to realize every discovery they'd experienced had come with a deadly price. Islands in paradise were swarming with ruthless pirates. Atlantis guarded by zombie sharks. A torpedo nearly destroyed them after witnessing a secret undersea Eden. An alluring African coast had been toxic and dying.

Can natural beauty and adventure still exist in the modern world?

Arrison chuckled at the irony how Nikto had promised to show her so much more. When he'd announced they were going to the South Seas, it had been one of her bucket-list destinations. Another half of the globe of discoveries.

There was *Zealandia,* a theorized new continent north of Australia. The nearly two-million square-mile landmass, which had once been crawling with dinosaurs, had recently been confirmed by scientists. It was estimated the lost continent had submerged 85 million years ago.

And there were glowing sharks discovered off the northern Hawaiian Islands. A new species of lantern shark, with bioluminescent abdomens, had been witnessed over a thousand feet below the Pacific.

On a humbler level, Arrison had dreamed of seeing the islands of the South Pacific. Nikto had promised to take her ashore at Monuriki Island off Fiji, an uninhabited island where the movie *Cast Away* had been filmed. And Turtle Island, which had served as the setting for the movie *Blue Lagoon*.

But like most fantasies, none of it was going to happen.

Nikto had become Dr. Jekyll, transforming into a reclusive madman, hell-bent on hurtling, full speed, into a tropical cyclone. She shrank, *he threatened to have me shot in the knee!*

Arrison felt like a child, with only a desire to feed her passions. She'd ignored the wellbeing of others, with only a concern for her lifework. As Landa had warned, they'd been inmates all along.

Her emotional dam finally cracked, releasing a deluge of tears.

"Are you okay?" Chandler approached his mother. He could read her face and he understood her sorrow. When he put his arm around her, he realized he'd never been the one to comfort her.

The clank of the door's lock made all three turn. When the hatch opened, it wasn't Nikto or an armed guard. Standing at the threshold was Pilar.

Chandler was unnerved by her appearance. She wasn't the radiant, lively siren he knew. Pilar's eyes were stained with wet mascara.

"Nikto doesn't know I am here," Pilar was hyperventilating as if she'd been crying. "He won't be out for long."

Landa and Chandler helped her to a chair.

Arrison asked with maternal empathy, "What's wrong?"

"We are all in trouble." Pilar looked at the three, "And not just from Nikto."

❧

Tropical Cyclone Dakkar surged to over 500 miles wide. From its clockwise rotation, storm bands stretched from its eye like 200-mile-long tentacles, pulling its devastation across the sea, grappling any landmass or vessel in its path.

Forty-foot waves surged, choreographed to pulses of thunder and lightning like a foreboding opera. To observers above, Dakkar's path appeared evident: straight through the islands of French Polynesia.

To better study the beast, a Lockheed WC-130J Super Hercules aircraft, also known as a "Hurricane Hunter," penetrated the storm's eye at 10,000 feet. The plane sent back images to be further analyzed by observers below.

∽

Japanese Captain Sato studied the storm images from aboard his sub, the JS *Ōryū*.

"Maintain one-zero-zero meters to remain below the churn," Sato directed his helmsman.

A young sonar tech approached, "I've picked up something. Unexpected."

The stoic Japanese captain approached the woman's monitor.

"It's a submarine but not the rogue," the officer pointed to her screen. "The buoys picked it up arriving through the Coral Sea. It is thirty miles west of our position." She paused to look at her captain. "I believe it is a Fateh-class sub."

"Fateh?" Sato scoffed, incredulous. "Nobody invited Iran."

"From the sound signature, I am not uncertain."

This development troubled the veteran captain for two reasons. One: Iran was a state sponsor of terrorism. A US State Department report affirmed Iran was still funding international terror groups, labeling Iran, "the world's worst state sponsor of terrorism." More troubling, they had attack subs. Though they weren't nuclear —which Iran desperately craved— the Fateh was a 527-ton armed submarine.

Sato's second concern was why an Iranian sub was heading their same direction. Iran was not invited by the US Navy, nor were they a member of NATO.

An Iranian sub racing towards the same target was too big a coincidence. Had Iran been following the same intelligence about the rogue which was a possible nuclear vessel?

Sato turned to his communications officer, "Alert Admiral Farragut about Iran right away."

∽

Landa was spellbound by Pilar's account as he sat with Arrison and Chandler.

"Nikto is completely despondent." Pilar's voice was frayed, "He believes at least six warships are on our trail."

Landa's eyes flared, *because of my buoys?* He maintained a poker face, "Whose vessels? How sure is he?"

"Nikto is certain." Pilar fidgeted with a tissue, tearing it to shreds. "Military vessels from multiple nations."

The three exchanged somber glances. Landa's plan with the C-Buoys had been to get the attention of the outside world, not to get destroyed by a fleet of warships.

"Nikto told me he'd rather go down with his ship." Pilar wiped her nose.

"We need to get *out*," Landa's baritone echoed.

"He removed all escape capsules," Pilar shrugged. "No other way off."

Chandler asked, "What about the *Cyclops*?"

Landa turned to him, intrigued. "Pilar knows how to pilot it."

"It can't be launched at forty knots," she replied. "The well doors cannot open at that speed."

Arrison stood with an anguished smile. "Do we have to leave Nikto?" She labored to appear hopeful, "Maybe we can convince him to do the right thing. He's a man of science—"

"We can't," Landa interrupted, firm. "He's smart enough to know he's a global criminal."

"You're wrong." Pilar captured his eyes, "Nikto believes he is a savior. He told me he's been protecting the *Naumtsev* from others much worse."

Landa's face warped, "Who?"

Chapter Fifty-Eight
Turbulent Truths

Officer Engel sat in a witness room that didn't exist on any DOJ floor plan. She'd had to walk through a labyrinth of humming fluorescent halls until she came upon a room used to create new passports and identifications. A guard then led her to the small glass room.

Mirta Salazar was seated at the table. Unlike in Colombia, Mirta appeared unruffled and content. Her hair was styled, and she was dressed chic, as if ready for a trip.

"Ms. Salazar, this is the last time we'll meet." Engel sat across from her, much more relaxed than during their first meeting. "You're off to a new life."

Mirta nodded but her eyes darkened with an unceasing fear.

"So tell me, what are you still so frightened of?"

Mirta stalled by adjusting an earring. She looked at the walls to confirm they were alone.

"You have no reason not to tell me," Engel implored.

"The reason Nikto stole the sub…" Mirta replied in a loud whisper, "was the precise reason why I chose to testify against my husband."

Engel frowned, "Why?"

"Ricardo had been approached by *very* dangerous people."

"Dangerous?" Engel tried not to smirk, "No disrespect Ms. Salazar, but your husband was a top-ten narco."

Mirta frowned, insulted. She asked as if it were a test, "What people are worse than narcos?"

ఴ

Landa, Arrison and Chandler remained seated as Pilar explained her account.

"They originally tried to buy this sub through the Russian black market."

"They *who?*" Landa asked, frustrated.

Pilar took a deep breath. "*Terroristas.* They were Iranian terrorists."

Landa frowned to process, "Iranians were trying to purchase old Soviet equipment?"

ఴ

"Yes," Mirta Salazar replied to Officer Engel. "Bought through corrupt Russian officials which are in no short reply."

Engel felt a chill. The concept was eerily reminiscent of Operation Odessa when criminals had obtained Soviet military vehicles with almost no difficulty.

"My husband used to joke," Mirta gave a poignant smile, "Potatoes were guarded better in Russia than their weapons."

Her smile vanished, "This was well after 9/11, so when the Russian captain, Nikto, learned terrorists were on the verge of buying the submarine —with all its weapons— he stole it first."

Engel blinked, entranced. "That's when he took it from Russia?"

Mirta nodded, "Nikto finally accepted my husband's offer to buy it for the cartel. I guess he considered drug dealers preferable to terrorists." She chuckled at the absurdity.

She crossed her arms as if chilled. "The same terrorists then approached my husband in Colombia. They were insistent. They offered him triple his price. Cash was supreme to Ricardo, more than any of his product. When he agreed to sell it to them, I decided to run."

She swiped her hands together, "So did Nikto. It was too much."

✿

Pilar had a detached gaze to recount Nikto's words, "The world's greatest threat is not underpaid Russian scientists selling their skills to enemies. More deadly is the nuclear black market. They have no accounting of their own assets. Some sites are guarded by little more than a chain fence and a watchman earning a slave's wage."

Chandler slid closer, "Nikto stole the *Naumtsev* from Russia to keep it from terrorists. Then took it from the cartel to avoid the same people?"

Pilar nodded, "The radicals who are still out there." Her face hardened, "They are unrelenting."

✿

"It's called narco-terrorism," Officer Engel exclaimed. "Smuggling to finance extremist activities."

"No," Mirta Salazar shook her head. "It was not for funding. It was the ship. The Iranians wanted what they couldn't have: a nuclear submarine. Complete with its arsenal."

Engel wasn't a terrorism expert, but she knew about enemy navies. The Islamic Republic of Iran had submarines, but none were nuclear.

The country was forbidden to produce certain nuclear materials, and it desperately wanted to modernize with nuclear submarines. Iran resented not being part of the "nuclear submarine club" which only allowed certain nations to have nuclear subs: the US, Russia, China, France, Britain, and India.

The crucial obstacle for Iran was the ability to obtain HEU, Highly Enriched Uranium.

Engel was flushed by the realization: Iranian extremists had almost obtained a nuclear vessel through underworld means. *But this Nikto stole it first.*

✿

"But the captain said he discarded all the weapons," Chandler interrupted Pilar.

"Do you realize what fuels this vessel?" She motioned around her, "Enough weapons-grade uranium to arm a dozen nuclear warheads."

"Completely untraceable," Landa mused, "From a forgotten sub."

Arrison blinked to amass the pieces, "Nikto is still running from terrorists."

"That's why we keep moving," Chandler added under his breath.

☙

A tear rolled down Mirta Salazar's cheek. "Nikto then took my daughter."

Engel said nothing, allowing her the intimate moment.

"So my husband would never try to destroy the sub or help anyone else find it." Mirta dabbed her eye, "Pilar is probably in a better world."

Mirta sat up to regain her poise. She turned to Engel with hopeful eyes, "The Navy has a mission to find them?"

Engel didn't know how to respond. Seeing Mirta's face, she recognized a maternal spark they shared as mothers.

"They're tracking it now," she replied. "But I don't know of a plan to take survivors."

Any color drained from Mirta's face. "They plan to destroy—"

"No. I don't know," Engel stammered. "I believe there are others like your daughter onboard."

"Who?"

"When I was given this case, there were three people missing off Key West." Engel spoke faster, "Nothing was ever found which is unusual for three people. They vanished during a report of the anomaly they're now pursuing." She leaned closer, "If the captain has any conscience, maybe he has them. Along with your daughter."

"What can we do?"

"The hunt is like a runaway train. I have zero authority," Engel touched her hand. "But I now have contacts at NATO, and I'll be talking with my commander. You're meeting again with Bronstein. He always brags of all his friends at the DOJ. My hope is the Navy attempts to communicate, to seek answers, before anything so…final."

334

༺༻

"Which is exactly why I'm not going down with him," Ned Landa bellowed. "Despite all his noble intents."

The four scowled at their dilemma. They rolled their eyes to the four corners of the room with the groaning bulkheads.

"Can we slow the ship enough to launch the *Cyclops*?" Arrison asked.

Pilar shook her head, "I have no access to navigation."

"You have access to engineering," Chandler raised a brow. "What about a radiation warning alarm?"

Landa's eyes ignited. "The reactor's SCRAM switch!"

"What's that?" Arrison asked.

"An emergency power-off switch," Landa replied. "All reactors have a SCRAM switch. If it's like American vessels, it's a switch located near the reactor in a place easy to hit as the crew evacuates."

"What happens if we hit it?" Chandler asked.

"Reactors have rods held in place with a claw. When the SCRAM's hit, the rods are dropped into the core, stopping any reactivity." He looked at the three, "The sub will automatically have to slow."

"Wouldn't they investigate and see there's no emergency?" Arrison asked.

"Doesn't matter," Landa leered. "We'll be waiting in the moon well—"

Chandler finished his sentence, "Ready to launch the *Cyclops* when we're slow enough."

All four were thrown to the side like bowling pins. Arrison gasped as they toppled onto each other and the lights flickered.

"The ship's listing to the side!" Landa shouted. The room swayed twenty degrees before swinging upright.

Arrison held onto Chandler, "You said we can't feel a typhoon."

"We can feel a tsunami swell." Landa looked up, "We're too shallow. What are they doing up there?"

"Nikto's not in control," Pilar replied. "He's passed out."

Landa balled his fists, "Then we need to move. Now!"

Chapter Fifty-Nine
Marching Orders

Rain lashed at the windshield of the USS *Wasp*. Wind gusts of fifty-knots shrieked like banshees, though the ship was still a thousand miles from the eye of Tropical Cyclone Dakkar.

Captain Ross held onto a console with one hand and gripped a radio in the other. "RIMPAC: this is Ross with the USS *Wasp*." He paused as the crew staggered around him. "We're already encountering thirty-foot seas. Over."

"Copy *Wasp*," an Australian accent replied through static. "This is Captain Steven Capell with the HMAS *Hobart*. We are 1,400 nautical miles southwest of Dakkar. What is your position? Over."

Ross shuffled behind his radar tech, "Current whiskey nine-eight-zero nautical miles, bearing zero-one-zero north of Tahiti the projected intersection with the rogue." He adjusted his specs to add less formally, "Problem is, Dakkar is now 600 miles in diameter. Its bands reach 200 miles beyond that. Over."

"Fair winds, Captain," Capell replied. "We'll have eyes south if the rogue retreats. God speed. Over."

The bridge's view swung skyward as the *Wasp* crested a thirty-foot swell, and then plunged into a trough of black water. The crew swayed into each other in the tight space.

Ross lifted the radio, "All Argonaut vessels: the *Wasp* is holding position. You must do the same if you are within one-zero-zero miles of the outer bands." He paused with another floor-dropping roll. "However, our subs can proceed: the JS *Ōryū* and the USS *Missouri*. Exercise caution. Over."

The speakers crackled with acknowledgments from the Allies.

"Captain Ross," a coarse voice entered the bridge. He turned to see Admiral Farragut. Tall and lean, the man had to grip the back of a seat for balance.

"Yes, Admiral." Ross tried to read the elder man's eyes.

Farragut spoke close so only he could hear. "Pacific Command is tracking a sub heading east from the Coral Sea. It has been identified as Fateh-class." He paused, grim. "Seems Iran now has an interest."

"Iran?" Ross frowned to recall what little he knew of their sub. *Fateh*, which meant "Conqueror," was Iran's home-grown submarine. It lacked modern features such as anti-ship missiles or a quiet propulsion system, but it was not to be ignored as Tehran was determined to become a formidable power.

Tehran, Ross tightened his jaw at the word. *The capital of a terrorist state.*

He looked at the admiral, "Should we confront?"

"No time for diplomacy," Farragut replied. "We have to be the first to catch the rogue."

 C/D

Pilar led Landa, Arrison and Chandler through the passage outside their quarters. Arrison paused at the companionway to the lower levels.

"Engineering's this way," Pilar pointed, quaking with nerves.

"You and I will go," Landa looked at her. "It doesn't take more than two people to hit a switch." He looked at Arrison and Chandler, "You go to the moon well. We'll meet you there."

They staggered against the wall as the vessel swayed again. The steel structure gave a hollow groan.

Chandler's lips twitched into a smile for Pilar. Her eyes returned the emotion. He and his mother turned and rushed down the stairs.

Landa and Pilar continued towards the stern.

With the wavering deck, Landa and Pilar had to use handrails to move towards engineering. As they jogged the narrow path, the passage became darker and more industrial.

When they reached a sealed door, Landa tried to recall the night he had helped in the reactor room. "The SCRAM switch should be in there."

Pilar lifted a badge from her hip. When she swiped it on the controls, she lost her balance when the vessel swayed. The door didn't open. Struggling to remain steady —gripping Landa's forearm as an anchor— she tried again. The hatch opened.

"Look for the switch," Landa huffed as they entered the sweltering room.

Their jaws fell to realize the walls were covered with hundreds of indecipherable buttons and switches. They all looked the same, on all four walls. It was futile.

"We can't press them all?" Pilar asked.

"Too dangerous," Landa darted his head, "It could give away our presence or accidentally unshield the reactor."

As they scanned the walls, they realized all signs were in a Slavic script.

"Can you read Russian?" Landa groaned,

They flinched at a clang of the hatch. When Landa turned, he saw two large, uniformed men. The two engineers frowned at them.

Landa sized them up in seconds. The men were Colombian; one stocky, the other wiry and muscular. They weren't armed but might warn others with their radios.

The taller man sneered at Pilar, "*Qué haces aquí, princesa?*"

Landa was ready to slug the man. He understood Spanish, and the thug had asked why they were there, and he'd called Pilar "princess."

Before he could speak, Pilar roared like a lioness.

"The captain ordered radio silence!" She spat rapid Spanish with a scowl like Medusa, "Where have you been?"

The two men froze and glanced at each other.

"Off on another smoke break?" She stepped into their space. "Can't you feel we've entered the cyclone? I had to come find you!"

The shorter man stammered, "We were gone for a moment—"

"If you heard the message," Pilar didn't lower her voice, "Nikto ordered everyone to the mess hall so we can center our ballast!" She shrieked, "Now!"

The men turned to sprint out the room.

Landa turned to her in awe. "Is centering ballast even a thing?"

"I don't think so." She smirked, "And I can read some Russian."

૨૭

Arrison and Chandler landed on the third deck. They turned the corner and stopped, realizing where they were.

"Nikto's office?" Chandler asked in a low voice. He looked at the door to the captain's study. There were no sounds emanating from the room. No shouts, commands, or snoring.

"You think he's still in there?" Arrison whispered.

"I don't know," Chandler stammered, "but we need to get to the well!"

Arrison drifted towards the door as if to smell or feel Nikto's presence one last time. She turned to Chandler with rueful eyes.

"What if we can change his mind?" Her forehead creased.

The door swung open. A disheveled Nikto appeared with hair hanging in his face.

"Change my mind?" His eyes blazed.

Chapter Sixty

Farewell to the Mad King

The USS *Wasp's* bridge swung like a pendulum in the turbulent sea. The crew was clammy and the bridge was dim, brightened by pulses of lightning.

Captain Ross stood over a sonar monitor with Coyne, his spirited young deck officer. "Our subs are still closing in."

"Yes, Captain," the wide-eyed Coyne replied. He tapped the screen, "Dakkar is here, 573 miles west of Polynesia." He pointed at a blip north of the storm, "We're here, stopped 700 miles north." He tapped four spots encircling the entire scene, "Our ships from Japan, North Korea, Australia and New Zealand are holding position."

Ross pointed to two pulses that continued to move. "These two are still advancing."

"Yes," Coyne nodded. "Our subs are proceeding towards the rogue's projected position." He paused before pointing to a third blip west of the storm, "This is the unidentified sub from Iran. There is a chance it's closer to the rogue. We've lost its trail."

Ross wiped his face with his hand.

"I do have one question, sir." Coyne lowered his voice, "Is there a plan for any hostages?"

Ross squinted at the unsteady horizon. "Anti-sub warfare does not produce survivors."

☙

Like a toddler who'd been spinning in circles, Captain Nikto plopped into his chair. "It is true!" He barked with a slur, "I was guarding the world from devastation, but you were never content with the wonders I offered you."

Wary of the belligerent man, Arrison remained at the threshold with Chandler. The man's heavy breathing made the room smell like alcohol. They watched him swirl a crystal decanter to realize it was empty.

"Captain," Chandler pled, "You can still surrender. I'm sure you could negotiate, maybe get amnesty for the safe return of the uranium?"

"So they can create more weapons?" Nikto scoffed. "They can make more, more, *bol'she, bol'she!*" He rolled his hand.

Arrison stepped towards his desk like approaching an unhinged tyrant. "You're a man of science." She kept her voice calm, "All your discoveries. Atlantis. Reefs never touched by man. New species. I believe you'd be celebrated as an academic hero."

"I discovered nothing," Nikto shook his head. "All of it has been there. No one has cared to look."

Chandler and Arrison ducked as Nikto hurled the empty decanter across the room, shattering on a bulkhead.

Nikto half-stood, his eyes honed on Arrison, "You could have been my queen. Amphitrite, the goddess of the seas! The personification of the oceans. Who would turn their back on such a privileged opportunity?"

Arrison was staggered by his arrogance. Before she could argue, the room lunged to the side. Antiques and frames tumbled off the shelves.

Nikto turned to his monitor, enraged rather than alarmed, "Control! What is happening?"

After a flicker of static, Pavlo's perspiring face appeared, "*Izvinite Kapitan.* Pilar said you were not to be disturbed under any circum—"

"You take orders from a child?" Nikto roared, "Update?"

"We are at a hundred meters. It is not deep enough. The storm is too strong. However, the destroyers can no longer approach. But their subs are closer. Forty nautical miles." Dmitri paused as if to gather his wits. "Kapitan, there is a third sub, from Iran."

Nikto dropped into his seat like a stone. "Of course they are." He threw out his hands, "Sent by the radicals I've been fleeing every day!"

Arrison watched the man's pained expression of absolute defeat. Once bold and extravagant, he'd been reduced to an eroding heap. She didn't know if she should fear him, or weep for him.

Nikto turned to his monitor, "I am on my way." He stood, requiring both hands on his desk.

Arrison retreated to Chandler's side. "You won't surrender?"

Nikto squinted one eye, "I will plunge this vessel to the seafloor myself before I resign it to another nation."

Arrison and Chandler tensed at the notion. She could tell from the coal in his eyes he meant every word he was spewing. She clutched Chandler's hand and stepped back into the hall as the captain staggered towards the door.

Arrison now understood he was a lost soul, with no desire for redemption. *Does he insist we die with him?* Her eyes welled; it was time to get to the *Cyclops*. But how?

She reached for Nikto with a sly smile, "Captain, would it be safer if we remain in our quarters?"

Nikto's brows snapped together. "Yes." He squared his shoulders to seem in control, "Remain in your quarters until further notice."

Arrison nodded, demure. She had hoped he'd take the bait.

They watched the man who called himself Captain Nikto march up the companionway to disappear into the shadows. It was the last time she'd see the man.

Arrison grasped her son's hand to hike down to their terminus.

ᜒ

Pilar and Landa examined each wall of engineering as if it were a rare stamp exhibit.

"Look for a red trefoil symbol…" he muttered a fourth time. "It should be universal."

Pilar squinted one foot from a panel, "I can speak more Russian than I can read."

"The SCRAM switch should be in a clear place. Maybe red." Landa's forehead furrowed, "I think it's also called an AZ-5?"

"This one says A3-5!" Pilar exclaimed. She pointed to a red switch.

Landa studied the button. It did make sense; the switch was eye level, four feet from the reactor door.

The entire room lunged like a plane in severe turbulence. Pilar and Landa fell into each other.

"We have no choice," he exclaimed. "Let's do it."

She appeared clear and decisive, "Okay."

He placed a thumb on the button and looked at her for any last-minute retraction. She nodded. Landa closed his eyes with a silent, *three, two, one* countdown. He pressed the button.

A shrill alarm wailed and red strobes flashed above the doors.

There was no turning back. Time to run.

Chapter Sixty-One
An Unsheathed Sabre

Iranian Captain Soltani had a demonic glow from the red lights of the Fateh's control room. The fifty-year-old officer loomed over his men in the tight, humid space.

"Is it our target?" The perspiring Soltani barked in Farsi to his sonar tech, "Yes or no?"

Soltani was proud to lead the Republic of Iran's premier submarine, one of the few vessels to evade global intelligence.

The Fateh could operate 200 meters underwater for five weeks. Though it was non-nuclear, the sub was equipped with sonar, guided missiles, and torpedo guidance.

The world knew little about the weapons of the Iranian vessel. One was the *Hoot* "Whale" supercavitating torpedo, which could attain speeds of over two hundred miles per hour, four times faster than a standard torpedo. It used rocket exhaust to vaporize water in its path, allowing it to travel in a gas bubble with minimal drag.

But Soltani's goal was not to sink the Russian Akula. Yet.

"I confirm," the Iranian officer replied. "It is an Akula-class vessel. Approximately five nautical miles. Depth: nine-zero meters."

"It is the trophy…" Soltani unfurled a yellowed grin, "Our torpedo has a range of six miles, correct?"

"Affirmative."

"Attempt communication and standby launch tube one."

"Captain," the man frowned with his headset. "I hear something else."

Soltani bent towards the man, curious.

"Repeating cycles. Sounds like an…emergency alarm."

"From the Akula?"

"Yes. And the sound helps confirm their position."

✑

The *Naumtsev's* control crew remained planted at their stations through cringing blasts from the reactor alarm. They reached for the rails with another powerful sway of the vessel. A younger crewman hunched over to vomit into a pail.

"*Obnovit'?*" Nikto yelled as he plodded into the room.

Dmitri ignored the captain's feral appearance. "The Iranian sub is west. Four miles. They are making no effort to conceal their presence."

Nikto fell into his seat. "Looming like a vulture. Waiting on the fringe to harvest my uranium from the sea floor." He pointed up with flaying arms, "What is the alarm!"

"The reactor emergency system," Pavlo stammered. "No one's responding in engineering."

Nikto shifted his jaw, "Perhaps an aftereffect of the short circuits?"

"Negative. It's a manual SCRAM. Triggered in engineering."

Nikto gritted his teeth, overwhelmed. "Slow to one-zero knots. Maintain depth."

"But Kapitan," Pavlo's eyes bugged, "If it's the reactor, we should surface!"

"Are you a coward or a fool?" Nikto snarled. "Your plan is to surface? In a typhoon?"

Chandler pulled his mother by the hand towards the moon well. With threadbare nerves, they quaked as the alarm repeated. It echoed throughout the passageway and strobes flashed every thirty feet.

"They did it!" Arrison respired, happy but petrified. "Will they slow the ship?"

"They have to. We don't have a plan B," Chandler panted. When he tugged her arm, she stopped by the doors to the grand parlor.

"The stairs are this way," Chandler contested. But he understood his mother's mournful eyes as she gazed into the parlor.

"Please…" There was a choke in her voice, "Just one last look."

Chandler knew he had no choice. Pilar and Landa would still need several minutes to get to the moon well. Before he could argue, his mother proceeded into the room.

They halted at the disheartening reality. Chandeliers were swinging. Teardrop crystals had shattered from fixtures. An antique mirror had fallen, its jagged shards on the rug. Scattered across the floor were artifacts and books that had tumbled from the shelves. As the vessel swayed, they looked up to hear creaks from the oak paneling.

It was a jarring reminder of the exhilaration they'd felt the first time seeing the room. Unless it was his imagination, the air now smelled musty as if water had somehow seeped into the rugs. A grief similar to seeing a beautiful manor fall into decay.

Chandler attempted, "Mom, we need to get to the well."

Lost in her dread, Arrison continued to a window. Considering her yearning gaze, Chandler knew she deserved one last look. But the view outside was an indigo churn. No vibrant reefs, no glistening sea life.

She looked at the deck to see her journal lying in a heap. It had been on a table they'd used for games, now cast aside like rubbish. She lifted it and thumbed through the pages, pausing at a few sketches.

Her lips quivered, "Do you really believe he's beyond saving?"

"Kapitan," Dmitri exclaimed, "The Fateh has locked torpedoes." He turned to the captain and paused, "Perhaps it is time? *Sluchaynost?*"

Nikto stood upright. He puffed out his chest, but his eyes swam at the notion. He realized his men's eyes were on him, waiting.

"*Da,*" In Russian, he nodded, "Arm the fallback."

The *sluchaynost* order was received in the torpedo room within seconds. A team of six men reported to their station as they'd done in countless drills. This time, they knew it wasn't a drill.

The men reached up to grasp one of the ducts that ran along the ceiling. The gray pipe was fifteen feet long and fifteen inches in diameter. It was identical to ducts that ran throughout the entire vessel. The men used a winch system to move the enormous pipe from the ceiling and lower it to shoulder-level.

The men took a breath to proceed to the next step: they ripped the paper sheath off the pipe. As they tore the covering like unwrapping a package, a bright green cylinder became visible underneath. One end of the pipe was cone-shaped with red and white stripes. Once fully unsheathed, the men stepped back to study their handiwork.

Before them was a pristine torpedo, a Russian SET-40 that had been hidden in plain sight. Though an older soviet weapon, it could travel at twenty-nine knots, delivering eighty kilograms of explosives.

The six men pivoted the weapon so it could be loaded into a torpedo tube. Four men helped guide it as the other two monitored the controls. When it was secure, the hatch was closed and sealed.

On the controls, a button with a water symbol was used to flood the tube with seawater to equalize the pressure. If —or when— the captain gives the order, the tube's outside muzzle door to the hull would open, allowing the weapon to be launched. Due to the sparse crew, a timer had been added to the controls to program a launch if hands were needed on multiple tubes.

A man hit the water symbol to flood the tube. After everyone gave a nod with a thumbs-up, he radioed the control room.

The weapon was ready to fire.

Chapter Sixty-Two
Drifting Ashes

Chandler placed an arm around his mother to usher her out of the parlor. With a sloping roll of the *Naumtsev*, he knew they needed to get to the moon well right away.

"Let's move!" a voice boomed from the hall. It was Ned Landa. He and Pilar stood outside the door. "Time to go, clock's ticking."

"Do you think the ship's slowing?" Arrison asked, hopeful.

Before anyone could reply, the vessel pitched forward almost twenty degrees. The four tumbled onto the floor.

"Something's happening!" Landa looked up. "That wasn't the storm."

∽

The Iranian captain commanded his helmsman to proceed towards the Akula, "Full speed!"

His sonar tech shouted, "The Russian captain is not responding to our demands!"

Captain Soltani pumped his fist in the air and cursed, "*Kos Nagu!*"

Soltani had a dilemma. His mission was to capture the Akula for his glorious Republic. There were *parties* in control above his pay grade.

Whether they wanted the vessel for national use or for its uranium, was not his concern. He'd been given a job and Soltani had never failed.

In the event of a botched seizure, his order was to sink the Akula with extreme caution. Its nuclear reactor and weapons had to be preserved. That would require a very specific torpedo blast.

A torpedo strike would need to be below the hull versus a direct hit. The blast would create a gas bubble that would expand so quickly, its shockwave would rupture the hull, bursting seams, bulkheads, and hatches. Once the bubble collapsed, water would rush in to fill the void. The vessel would sink to the ocean floor.

Soltani knew his Hoot torpedo would annihilate the Akula. He needed to launch a lower-grade weapon.

"The Akula is approaching 400 meters," exclaimed the helmsman.

"Prepare a Valfajr torpedo," Soltani shouted. "Target the stern to preserve the reactor."

"Valfajr ready, Capitan," a voice replied from the torpedo room.

Soltani narrowed his eyes to consider any contingencies. "Fire!"

∾

The *Naumtsev* pitched forward as it launched its countermeasures.

When Nikto had discovered the Fateh's sonar locked on them, he needed an instantaneous defense. He'd hoped an Iranian vessel would have archaic weapons so his countermeasures would create a sufficient deception.

Amidst the piercing alarms, Dmitri roared, "The Fateh has fired!"

"Emergency deep!" Nikto shouted. "Flood forward ballast!"

The crew gripped the rails and ashtrays tumbled as the *Naumtsev* dove forty-degrees.

∾

In the parlor, Landa, Pilar and the Arrisons struggled to stand. Considering the sub's maneuvers, Landa rushed to look out a window.

"My god..." He angled his neck to look up. "He launched countermeasures."

Shimmering against the surface was a curtain of bubbles. Small drums dotted a perfect line stretching into the gloom, all spewing effervescent bubbles.

Chandler gasped, "Does that mean someone fired—"

There was a muffled *whump* overhead. A jolting thrum rattled Landa's entire skeleton. The lights went out and the bulkheads shuddered like amplified bass.

When the boom faded, Landa felt like he was wearing earplugs. Then a shrill ringing.

Were we hit? Landa wondered. Everything was pitch black. *Are we sinking?* Feeling his own torso, he knew he was dry and breathing. The reactor alarm resumed, and he heard the gasps of the others.

Landa realized they had narrowly dodged a torpedo.

With a mechanical *clack*, the lights came back on. Pilar was in Chandler's arms, Arrison at his side. Their eyes were round with horror.

"Look!" Arrison pointed out the window.

Two hundred yards away, a pulsing blast created a sphere of light. Landa could see a white trail emanating from the *Naumtsev.*

"We just fired a torpedo," Landa shouted, incredulous.

"He lied about having weapons?" Chandler turned to Pilar, who appeared equally mystified.

It was surreal seeing a blast with no sound. In that instant, Landa realized what was coming: a shockwave. He roared, "Hold on!"

The entire *Naumtsev* jarred like hitting a wall. There were deafening groans of buckling steel. Landa prayed that Nikto's speeches about high-tensile plating would keep the sub in one piece. The lights sputtered but the alarm never stopped, *wah…wah…wah…*

As the vessel leveled, the four remained transfixed to the window. Pulses outside illuminated an immense object, the silhouette of another submarine. The smaller vessel had been fractured in half. The *Naumtsev's* torpedo had been a direct hit.

They drifted closer with a more daunting view. The flickers of light in the other sub were electrical fires or fuels burning. They looked like flashbulbs.

The *Naumtsev* loomed perilously close as if Nikto wanted to savor his conquest. Arrison's jaw dropped at something out the window.

Within the glare of the sinking sub, dark specks appeared. The particles floated like ants from a log. That's when Landa realized what they were witnessing: the flecks were people. The other vessel's crew. Drifting from the shattered hull. All dead.

He understood Arrison's tears. She was crestfallen about her oceanic hero. This Captain Nikto was responsible for all of it. There was no saving him.

Patrice Arrison stood and took a decisive breath. "Let's go."

Nikto sat in his command chair like a brooding King Lear. His crew remained silent amidst the alarms, fixed to their monitors with eyes that didn't move.

"Now stop the alarm," Nikto threw a hand towards the ceiling.

Pavlo stammered, "It cannot be turned off. The reactor requires a diagnostic. We are still beneath the storm..." His words trailed, realizing Nikto's eyes were dilated and vacant.

Dmitri attempted, "The two navy subs have stopped."

Nikto was perspiring and his breaths seemed labored. His eyes remained fixed on the video of the sinking Fateh.

"Kapitan," Dmitri gave a weak smile, "At least the Iranians are gone."

"They will never be gone." Nikto retorted under his breath, "That was one sub. They are not the only savages in that world. The nightmare will never end."

The room was mute aside from the grating alarm.

"We have slowed to ten knots," Pavlo uttered. "We must address the reactor."

Nikto struggled to stand. His eyes spun around the room, devoid of emotion. He wiped his brow and mumbled in Russian, "Dmitri, you have the conn," He turned to exit, "I will be in the parlor. Alone."

When Nikto was gone, the entire crew turned their heads to Dmitri. With the room spinning, their nauseous faces pled for any rational command.

Chapter Sixty-Three
The Bronze Warrior

"A confirmed torpedo blast," the USS *Wasp's* sonar tech shouted. "It wasn't one of ours."

Captain Ross needed to alert his submarines. He lifted his radio, "USS *Missouri* and JS *Ōryū*: this is Ross. Stand-down, repeat stand-down until we clarify. Over."

"Who fired at who?" Officer Coyne asked, "Was it the rogue?"

Ross didn't know. He turned to his sonar tech, "Broadcast our demand for surrender. All channels. All languages: English, Spanish, Russian," he paused, "and Farsi."

He had received orders to solicit a surrender before attacking any potentially hostile vessel. Ross would wait for a response, but not too long. Something might be preparing to fire again.

ભ

The reactor alarm was amplified within the moon well. Chandler wanted to cover his ears.

They had entered the chamber to see the *Cyclops* swaying from its cables. The *Naumtsev's* sloshing motion was increasing. Pilar led Arrison and Chandler to a ladder leading to the *Cyclops'* top hatch.

Chandler helped Pilar and his mother up the steps.

Landa approached a panel beside the well door in the center of the deck. "Get in the sub!" He shouted over the alarm, "I'll get the door open."

Pilar opened the *Cyclops'* hatch. Arrison climbed into the sub, cautious of the swinging motion. Pilar gripped Chandler's hand to help him up the ladder and into the entry.

"Damnit!" Landa growled from the controls, "We're still going ten knots. It's not slow enough." He pounded the panel with a fist. "I have to manually override."

"From out there?" Chandler peered down from the hatch, "We need you inside."

"Get in!" Landa snapped. "And seal the hatch!"

Chandler was dumbstruck. Pilar looked at him with a nod. They needed to be buckled and ready in the *Cyclops*.

The *Naumtsev's* crew was terrified, but their backgrounds dictated they show no fear.

The men had survived innumerable challenges. Half the crew had fled the Russian navy. The others had escaped a brutal cartel. Together, they'd survived pirates, attacks from nations, nuclear emergencies, and ferocious beasts.

But they had never been surrounded by a half-dozen warships, beneath a Category 5 cyclone, with a possible reactor meltdown. And now, without a leader.

The room rolled to the side, pummeled by waves. Two more men turned to vomit.

"Do we slow?" Pavlo shouted over the relentless alarm, "Or do we dive?"

Dmitri fidgeted with his glasses. After swift deliberation, he decided a radiation concern was more critical than seasick crewmen.

"All engineers to the reactor! Commence diagnostic." Dmitri turned to Pavlo, "Periscope depth in case we must vent."

Landa glared at Chandler until he entered the *Cyclops* and secured the hatch behind him. With the three safe inside the minisub, Landa

353

could focus on the control panel. The switch for the well door wouldn't operate. He tore a panel off to study the wiring.

He confirmed what he'd hoped: the homegrown system was basic, not reliant on advanced computer chips.

The circuit for the well door received a current only when a switch was pressed. This circuit was broken —not allowing the door to open— due to the *Naumtsev's* speed. Like hot-wiring his '67 Impala when he was a teen, he knew if he provided electricity to the circuit, it'd react the same as the switch being pressed.

Landa would need to locate any wire that had power. Applying that "hot" wire to the circuit might open the well door.

There was at least one hot wire since the electronic pitometer was displaying the *Naumtsev's* speed. He located the wire and yanked it out. Landa glanced at the well door. The platform had been folded aside so the *Cyclops* could drop straight into the water.

He looked up at the minisub's dome to see Pilar seated at the controls. At her side were Arrison and Chandler.

"Lower the sub!" He shouted into a mic. "All the way to the door."

"Okay," Pilar's voice crackled from a speaker. The gears groaned to lower the *Cyclops*. With the ship's motion, the sub clanged against the rails. It stopped a foot over the well door. With the dome now eye-level with Landa, Pilar looked at him, waiting for the next step.

Landa put on rubber gloves. He held the exposed wire for the door in one hand, and the hot wire from the pitometer in the other. After a sharp breath, he touched them together.

With an instant roar of water, the well door opened. The churn was like foam at the base of a waterfall.

"Drop!" Landa looked at Pilar, "Now!" The room's pressure was preventing an immediate flood, but water was rising.

"No," Pilar's voice echoed. "Not without you."

He looked into the dome to see Pilar shaking her head, emphatic.

The wires in his hand were sparking. He knew if he let go, the doors might close. He couldn't take that chance. When he looked at the *Cyclops*, their three faces appeared petrified, motioning for him to join them.

Landa bellowed, "Disengage!"

The deafening gush of water was now entering the chamber, a foot deep. He didn't know how much longer he could hold the wires.

"We need you!" a chorus of voices cried from the *Cyclops*.

Landa squeezed his eyes shut; he needed to compartmentalize. He ignored the irony how he had wanted off the vessel more than anyone. But if the three didn't escape, they would all die. The *Naumtsev* would either sink from its own failings or be annihilated by its enemies.

With clashing emotions, part of him wanted to take the gamble. He could toss the wires aside and scramble up to the sub's hatch. Maybe a fifty-fifty chance the door would stay open.

But taking a chance with their lives would be wrong. A young girl, a mother, and her son. Their odds were better if they escaped now. Maybe a navy vessel would catch them on radar and save them. *Arrison would finally have her big story,* his mouth twitched with a smile.

Marine or not, his duties of valor were etched onto his ego. Despite their pleas, they did not need him. Pilar could operate the *Cyclops*. They were brave and intelligent.

Landa opened his eyes; only seconds had passed. He studied each of their faces behind the glass. With a wistful smile, he shook his head, "See you above the waterline."

He lunged to kick an emergency release. The cables detached and the minisub dropped into the froth like a brick.

The *Cyclops* was gone.

Chapter Sixty-Four
Breach Delivery

The *Cyclops* tumbled like a barrel plummeting over Niagara Falls.

Though Chandler was strapped in, he grabbed anything he could hold onto. The vessel spun like a sickening carnival ride. The screams of his mother and Pilar resonated in the dark cockpit. He didn't know which was up.

In one of the rolls, he saw the belly of the *Naumtsev* over them. Then it was gone. Just a view of indigo.

"Engage fins," Pilar cried, gripping the levers. "Trying to balance rudders."

Though there was no concept of up, the *Cyclops* seemed to level. Chandler's stomach remained in his throat as if nothing had slowed.

He turned to his mother. Her bloodshot eyes locked onto his and she smiled. Though they were clammy and scared in the tight space, they were alive.

"What about Landa?" Arrison rasped, breathless.

There was a moment of silence. No words were needed to recognize his sacrifice.

Pilar studied the radar. "Storm's going northeast; I'll try southwest."

She turned to the Arrisons with an ashen face. "I'm not sure how much oxygen we have."

"Flooding in the well!" Pavlo shouted in Russian, frantic.

A man checked the Hull Opening Indicator Panel to see a red light. "The well door is open!"

"Impossible!" Dmitri shouted over the alarms.

"It's not impossible if it's flooding!" Pavlo spewed, ready to fight.

Dmitri's jaw tightened; he couldn't spare any engineers. They were busy inspecting the reactor.

The room was thrust sideways almost forty degrees. Men tumbled. One man smashed his face into a steel column.

Dmitri looked up, "A tsunami swell; we're too shallow you idiot!"

"You ordered periscope depth to vent!"

Dmitri turned to his mic, "Engineering, status of the reactor?"

A voice crackled, "We've just begun diagnostics."

Thirty feet above the control room, spears of lightning revealed forty-foot swells. Eighty mile-per-hour gusts wailed. The skies were gray with sweeping rain.

The new tropical depression that had originated in the Cook Islands was now a Category 1 cyclone, 180 miles from the eye of Dakkar. Opposing currents were drawn into a spiraling dance between the eyes creating a Fujiwhara Effect. Rival waves clashed like cymbals.

The *Naumtsev*'s sail and rudder emerged from the waves. The 375-foot prehistoric monster was recovering from a fifty-foot wave that had thrust it to the surface. The entire submarine wallowed for several minutes before arcing back under the sea like a whale surfacing for air.

&

"The target has breached!" The USS *Wasp*'s deck officer proclaimed. "Repeat, the rogue has surfaced. Seven-one nautical miles due south."

Admiral Farragut approached as Ross navigated the whitecaps. Farragut knew the *Wasp* was the closest ship to the sighting, but they couldn't approach due to the storm. Their submarine, the USS *Missouri*, would be closer.

The rogue surfaced in a storm? Farragut needed to understand why. His primary concern —and the reason for the operation—was to avoid a nuclear attack from a hostile vessel. But a submarine would not surface if it intended to fire a torpedo or a missile. The weapons' accuracy would be defeated by the enormous swells. It'd be like aiming a rifle from a bucking bronco.

The *Wasp* had been broadcasting a demand for surrender for hours. Barring a nuclear incident, there was only one feasible reason the sub would surface.

He lifted his radio, "Attention *Missouri* and *Ōryū*: halt all torpedoes. Do not fire. The rogue may be surrendering."

❧

Water was touching Landa's shins, and the room smelled like brine. Before exiting the moon well, he gave the workshop one last glance.

His heart pounded, realizing he had no plan. He'd been so focused on getting the three off the sub, he hadn't considered his own fate. They were being hunted by warships. The captain was losing his mind. He knew the bleak reality; his options weren't just limited, they were nonexistent.

With no weapons, he couldn't seize the control room. Even if he forced them to surface, he couldn't survive in a cyclone. He would never take his own life, and he shuddered at the thought of drowning. His only option was to beat Nikto to death before going down with the ship.

Landa paused to see the emergency kit on the wall. It had once contained a life vest and a locator beacon. Now it was empty. For an instant he wondered if there were more vests elsewhere. He shrunk, realizing they'd be useless in the middle of the raging Pacific.

Seeing the box's warning emblem —with a water symbol— gave him a sense of déjà vu. Where had he seen that sign? His blood pressure spiked with an epiphany. *The water symbol!*

Landa knew what he had to do. Considering the sub's motion, they had to be near the surface.

He would have to wrangle and restrain one of his most petrifying fears.

Sergei Rachmaninoff's *The Isle of the Dead* played from the parlor's Steinway.

With his eyes closed, Nikto's fingers struck the piano keys with the same ache as the symphony itself. The heaving and sinking chords suggested oars struggling against nature.

He opened his eyes to look up at a painting of Kana. Rather than weeping or muttering rambling apologies, Nikto smiled at her.

He kept playing, lost in his music. His fingers pounded harder to muffle the faraway alarms. Nothing else in the room mattered; none of the sliding furniture, none of the tumbling fixtures.

Nikto saw the intercom switch beside the piano. He smiled at the opportunity to share his reverie with his loyal, fearless crew.

Landa climbed the second-level passageway. With the extreme angle, he felt like he was hiking uphill. His arms ached from pulling the handrails. Blinding strobes flashed and the alarm grew louder the farther he progressed. But he knew he was getting closer.

After every fifth blast of the alarm, a garbled recording warned in unintelligible Russian, "*Preduprezhdeniye reaktora,*" He had to ignore all of it. *Tunnel vision!*

Landa tilted his head at a new sound: a piano began to play a somber melody over the P.A. Was the captain performing one of his concertos during a catastrophe? It was further proof of the man's dementia.

He tensed to see a crewman heading his way. The man was running along the narrow path. His face was sweaty, petrified with panic. Before Landa could react, the man bumped him aside. He mumbled something in Russian and kept running.

Landa located the torpedo room and entered. In a frenzy, he began to open and slam a half-dozen compartments. *Where'd I see that damn sign?* Landa growled.

He smirked when he opened a stainless locker. He pulled out a canvass bundle the size of a large duffle with a rope attached. Carrying it with both arms, he progressed to a torpedo tube. He dropped the bundle at his feet so he could study a control panel.

Landa squinted, trying to focus with the incongruous piano playing amidst the alarms, strobes, and the Russian warnings. It was too much stimuli and he had only minutes.

There! It was the switch with a water symbol. Beside it was a digital timer.

His eyes blinked at the pace of his heart. He opened a hatch to a torpedo tube and shoved the bundle inside. Without a second to reassess, he entered 00:20 on the timer. His thumb hovered over the water symbol. *Three, two, one...* Landa pushed the button. It was now or never.

Holding the bundle's rope, Landa did something straight out of his nightmares: he crawled into the torpedo tube.

Nineteen...eighteen...seventeen... He muttered a countdown as he entered feet-first. It was a tight fit, but he knew Navy SEALS have exited through torpedo tubes. With his wide shoulders, he contorted with one arm at his side, and one stretched before him to close the hatch. He squirmed like a burrowing insect, deeper into the tube. He pulled the hatch closed. With a metallic click, it was sealed.

Landa did not suffer from claustrophobia. In the Marines, he was diagnosed with cleithrophobia, the fear of being trapped. Nightmares of falling through ice or being buried alive. It could be triggered by confinement in a small place. Like a torpedo tube.

It was pitch black and he could hear his own gasps. *Fifteen... fourteen...thirteen...* His shoulders felt crushed. When he tried to breathe in, his chest was confined by the walls. He feared a panic attack. Screaming would only deplete his oxygen. *Eleven...ten...nine...*

If his plan failed, he'd suffocate with a slow death. No one would know he was in a tube. If the plan succeeded, he estimated a five percent chance for survival. *Seven...six...*

His thoughts were disrupted by a thunderous gush. Cold water soaked his spine like needles. The tube was filling with seawater to balance the pressure. Landa knew it would only take seconds for the water to cover his face.

In an attempt to slow his breathing, he tried to envision his twelve-year-old daughter Erica. She was tall, strong, and loved to read. But that was a year ago. Landa hadn't seen her since. He had written her a birthday card before he'd traveled to Key West, but it was never mailed. Erica would never know what happened to her daddy. *The people I've met. The things I've seen.* He choked on a tear as icy water reached his lips.

Landa drew in a final breath for the inevitable. *Three...two...*

His submerged ears could hear the hum of the tube's exterior door opening. The bundle was still at his feet. He kicked the bale with all of his might and gripped the rope.

Fifty feet beneath the ocean's surface, the muzzle door opened on the *Naumtsev's* forward hull. Landa's bundle emerged from the sub as if it were a slow-motion cannonball. CO-2 cartridges instantly inflated the life raft. As it expanded, it raced towards the sky.

Chapter Sixty-Five
The Farewell Pirouette

Landa let the principal of buoyancy do all the work. He held onto the rope as if it were a runaway hot air balloon.

In the murk, fifty feet felt like an eternity. He ignored a searing pain in his ears from the pressure. Unable to take a deep breath, his lungs were on fire.

The orange life raft splashed to the surface; Landa arrived seconds later. He inhaled like a vacuum before a ten-foot breaker washed over him. Using both arms, he followed the rope until he reached the raft and heaved himself aboard.

Landa sprawled on his back to catch his breath. He held handgrips as the raft climbed and dropped over swells. Distant rumbles of thunder made him smile because they were terrestrial sounds. He was back in the world of real oxygen, out of the abhorrent *Naumtsev*.

He sat upright to study his predicament. The raft was PVC vinyl, five-by-five feet, covered with a small tent to shield against exposure. He had no water or rations.

Peering out the tent's flap, his brain shifted to logistics. He was in the center of the Pacific, on the fringe of a Cat-5. Rain pelted his raft with almost zero visibility. His situation would be hopeless if it hadn't been for what he'd stolen from the moon well. He reached into his pocket to pull out the PLB, the Personal Locator Beacon.

He held the small device closer to his eyes. It was supposed to be water-activated. A tiny red light confirmed it was emitting a signal at the rescue frequency of 406 megahertz.

Landa gave a wide smile —until he leaned over the side to puke.

೮೨

"An emergency beacon!" Officer Coyne shouted. "Picked up by SARSAT. One-nine miles south." He turned to Farragut, "Sir, it's in the vicinity of the rogue."

Farragut frowned, staggered by the news. SARSAT was short for the Cospas-Sarsat Program, an international satellite search-rescue initiative. Was the submarine's crew evacuating?

"How accurate is the signal?"

"The GPS is usually accurate to within a hundred meters."

Farragut studied the purple horizon. *Nineteen miles.* He couldn't jeopardize the *Wasp* by traveling almost twenty miles closer to the eye.

He turned to Coyne, "Prepare an MH-60 to check it out."

"Aye, Sir." Coyne smiled at the idea. MH-60 Seahawks were helicopters specifically designed for search-rescue and anti-sub warfare. With an airspeed of 180 knots, it'd be eight times faster than the *Wasp*.

The ship carried two Sikorski MH-60R Seahawk helicopters. Using a shuttle and track system, one was pulled out of the ship's hangar, onto the aft deck.

Through gusts of rain, a rainbow of officers spread out on the flight deck. The Navy used colored jackets to identify each person's duties. The aircraft handler, responsible for the movement of aircraft, wore yellow. Blue jackets pulled aircraft out of the hangar. Green for maintenance and landing personnel. Bright red remained on the sidelines as firefighters.

With the thirty-foot rollers, the Seahawk was locked to the deck using an umbilical system. Upon the chopper's successful return —

God-willing— the same cable system would be used to winch the craft safely back to the deck.

Dakkar was creating an unforgiving flight environment. Flying a Seahawk in good weather was demanding; in a cyclone it would be terrifying. The ultimate test of hand-eye coordination and technology.

The naval aviator, Lieutenant Commander Lee Malone, along with his copilot and two aircrewmen, huddled in the wind to jog out to the chopper. Within minutes, the Seahawk rose unsteadily from the *Wasp's* deck and into the gray unknown.

෧

Captain Nikto continued to play his piano through the alarms and groans of warped paneling. After each page of music, he'd glance up at Kana's portrait. He grinned, almost tongue-in-cheek, is if sharing a secret only they knew.

"It will be deep," Nikto beamed at the painting, "And magnificent."

He closed his eyes, lost in his dream. As the melody became more impassioned, furniture and fixtures slid across the floor.

With an abrupt thrust, the room rolled to the side. Nikto's eyes sprung open to see armchairs and debris shoved to the wall with centrifugal force. His piano began to slide, its legs grating on the wood floor.

His pupils flared, snapped out of his fantasy. He looked up to see the chandelier hanging parallel to the ceiling. With a jarring crash, the framed portrait of Kana fell, impaled by the bill of a swordfish mount that had fallen. Nikto's face became red with rage.

When he tried to stand, he was pulled to the wall like a magnet, unable to resist the force. The entire vessel was revolving.

Waves heaved the 48,000-ton *Naumtsev* to the surface. Tides began to rotate the sub clockwise within a yawning 300-foot whirlpool.

The Fujiwhara Effect was forcing two opposite currents to clash. Warm water from the west was merging with colder from the south. Boosted by the winds, the circling body of water had created a massive vortex.

The *Naumtsev's* fin and tail soared above the waves. With the upper deck exposed, it revolved within the vortex like a fan blade.

 e/o

"Sweet Mother..." Commander Malone uttered from the Seahawk. "That's the biggest whirlpool I've ever seen."

Despite the Seahawk's cruising speed of 105 miles per hour, it had taken nearly twenty minutes to arrive due to the shear. Malone and his crew had been tracking the beacon, but the spectacle of a long black object in a whirlpool dominated their focus.

When they recognized the Akula-class Russian submarine with some sort of modified sail, they radioed the *Wasp*. The fabled rogue was real.

"You don't see that every day," Malone marveled. The large sub was listing to its side, struggling within the vortex.

He'd heard stories about massive whirlpools in the North Atlantic called maelstroms. Sailors had described some over 160 feet in diameter. Tsunamis had created immense whirlpools off Japan.

"Look, a life raft," his copilot pointed. "Two o'clock." Near the fringe of the spiral, they saw a tiny orange square bobbing on the waves.

e/o

Landa found it easier to vomit by lying on his stomach with his head out the tent. He was now oblivious to the motion. His entire body convulsed with dry heaves.

There was a hum in his ears, probably hearing damage from the blaring alarms. As the drone became louder, he looked up. With eyes stinging from salt, he saw a speck in the sky. He instantly recognized the shape; it was a hovering Seahawk. Grinning in his wretched condition, it was the most beautiful piece of machinery he'd ever seen.

The chopper hovered sixty feet above him. Landa waved to let them know he was alive. The Seahawk began to lower a rescue basket using its hoist. To add insult to injury, the gusts from the rotors were adding hurricane-force winds. Getting the basket to him would be tough, like landing a swinging yoyo on a golf tee.

Landa turned to see the massive *Naumtsev* a hundred yards away. It was daunting to see it floating at a forty-five-degree angle with its stern under water like a giant sundial. He tensed to realize he was drifting closer to it. He had to keep one eye on the whirlpool and one on the basket. The currents were beginning to pull his raft. *Now eighty yards.*

The basket was swinging towards him. He reached for it, but it was beyond his grasp. When it swayed back, the raft fell into a trough between swells. The basket sailed over his head.

Landa saw the whirlpool's tendrils reaching for him. The currents gurgled and splashed against his raft.

He looked up to see two airmen peering from the chopper's side door. The basket was coming towards him again. This time, they swung it lower, perhaps to slow it in the water.

Landa gripped the raft's tent with one hand so he could lean farther out with the other. The basket was headed straight for him. He needed to grab it or the steel basket might pummel him.

He crouched and sprung from the raft. He knew if he missed, he'd land in the water to be drawn into the whirlpool. When he felt the basket, he clasped his fingers like claws. With a sturdy grip, the raft sailed out from under his feet, into the vortex.

Using his last surge of strength, Landa pulled himself into the basket. The cable began to lift him towards the Seahawk. After all he'd endured, he was unaffected by swinging through fifty-knot gusts. The fresh air felt good on his scalp.

As he approached the aircraft, he realized his saviors were soldiers. They would assume he was Russian or maybe a terrorist. His odd black uniform wouldn't help. When the basket arrived at the chopper's door, two crewmen pulled him hard into the cabin.

One man barked, "Sir, are you armed?"

Without pause, Landa exclaimed, "My name is Landa, Benedict. Former engineer-mechanic, United States Marine Corp." His red eyes looked like he might cry, but his entire face beamed.

"Benedict," A crewman checked a digital clipboard, "Is that Ned Landa?"

"That's me." Landa saw him check a box. Beside it, he saw the names of Chandler and Patrice Arrison. He felt like someone who'd been found after missing for decades in the Bermuda Triangle.

"Whoa!" the copilot shouted. Their attention was drawn outside. Through sheets of rain, they could see the rotating submarine. Its stern sank deeper, which raised its bow into the sky.

Landa's mouth dropped to see his first aerial view of the massive Akula. The vessel was rising upright, reaching higher than the Seahawk. The portion above the water was the height of a ten-story building. Its bayonet nose pointed skyward like an enormous, vertical swordfish.

℘

Captain Nikto plummeted to a bulkhead among shattered fixtures. He hissed in pain. As the lights blinked, he tried to understand his view. He was mid-parlor, near the entrance. Nikto rolled to his side to see an intercom switch by the door. He pounded it.

"Control, status," he wheezed in Russian.

After an unnerving pause, "Kapitan," Dmitri's voice huffed, "All stations are abandoned. The stern is flooded. The uneven weight might—"

With a whale-like roar, the *Naumtsev* turned vertical. Nikto gripped a bookshelf to hang on.

"Emergency deep," he bellowed. "Flood forward ballast tanks! *Privet? Zatopit' tanki!*"

℘

Ned Landa estimated half of the *Naumtsev* was above the water.

The officers tilted their heads at the pirouetting steel ballerina. With its spear and fin, the submarine was a remarkable sculpture. The parlor windows were its vacant eyes.

With simultaneous gasps, the men watched the submarine surge and then sink, straight down, sucked into the vortex. Only fifty feet visible; then forty, then twenty.

Landa's emotions collided. Astonishment twisted into sorrow to see the *Naumtsev* disappear. It had been his prison, but also an instrument to learn so much about a world invisible to most.

The bow was gone. Like Excalibur, its steel lance was the last to vanish beneath the waves.

∾

Eleven hours later—and sixty-six miles south—the *Cyclops* splashed to the surface.

Within a churn of foam, it jostled to a stop. It didn't move, no engines or lights to assure the coast was clear.

Though the storm was far from gone, Pilar had watched it on her radar, shifting north of French Polynesia to just graze the islands. Through the dome, she could see the seas had calmed. The skies were overcast with no rain.

With a turn of the wheel, she opened the *Cyclops'* top hatch. After it fell back with a clank, she peered out with Dr. Arrison and Chandler. Their three heads looked like prairie dogs.

They inhaled the ocean air. Pilar could feel the wind drying her clammy skin. Color was returning to Chandler's face.

But when Pilar looked up, her eyes bulged. She jabbed Chandler to look up.

Fifteen feet above them, four uniformed men aimed M4 rifles at their heads. The *Cyclops* had surfaced beside the stern of a large, gray ship.

When the four sailors realized the condition of the occupants, they lowered their weapons.

Pilar read the ship's stern. It proclaimed, "HMAS *Hobart.*" Above it was a blue flag containing the Union Jack, the Southern Cross and commonwealth star. The national flag of Australia.

Without words, their eyes glistened at their good fortune. With the *Cyclops'* dwindling oxygen, Pilar had surfaced beside a ship, calculating high odds it'd be a friendly vessel. The risk had paid off.

Pilar's lip quivered as she tried to harness her emotions. As she accepted they were alive and safe, she looked heavenward with a smile that sparkled like a sunrise.

Chapter Sixty-Six
Return to Terra Firma

Four Months Later

On the humid southern grounds of Tallahassee, cherry trees blossomed with bursts of pink. Spanish moss hung like garland from the limbs of majestic hundred-year-old oaks.

The Westcott Memorial Building served as the architectural centerpiece of Florida State University since its construction in 1910. In the center of its plaza was the historic Westcott Fountain, reflecting the building's sculpted brick towers.

An immense banner over the bronze doors proclaimed, "Welcome back to life Professor Patrice Arrison and Chandler!"

A half mile across campus was the building for the Department of Earth, Ocean & Atmospheric Science. The state-of-the-art building contained over thirty labs, a broadcast studio, and a 280-seat auditorium.

Displayed outside its doors was a framed poster of Professor Patrice Arrison. The portrait looked like a celebrity headshot. She was beautiful, with a smile of shrewd confidence.

Students hovered around the poster that read, HIDDEN WONDERS

369

OF THE SEVEN SEAS BY DR. PATRICE ARRISON. MON. – SAT., 7:00 PM.

എ

Six hundred miles away, Paducah, Kentucky was five hundred miles from the closest coast. That distance had been a special request from its new resident.

The locals preferred their coffee from mom-and-pop shops versus the corporate chains. On the outskirts of town, the Cuppa Coffee House was in a former barn off Highway 62.

Navy Intel Officer Cynthia Engel opened the door to inhale the warm aroma of ground beans. Her eyes had to adjust to the dim light to look for her appointment. A few locals smiled, curious about the stranger in slacks and navy blazer. She wasn't wearing her uniform due to the clandestine nature of her rendezvous.

She nodded along to the soft bluegrass as she scanned the room. Then she smiled to see Mirta Salazar seated in the rear corner. Mirta waved her over with a grin. She was dressed in a white tank with a chic cardigan. She appeared fit and happy.

Mirta stood to greet her, "I remember you enjoy latte with two Splenda." She and Engel shared a brief, spontaneous hug.

"I love your Louboutin heels." Engel sat and whispered, "But you shouldn't be the swankiest lady in town when you're in witness protection." There was an awkward silence as they sipped their coffees.

"I apologize it took this long." Engel fidgeted with her cup, "But the logistics to visit you here required a lot of signatures."

Mirta forged a smile. "So, is your Navy pleased? Your country captured a nuclear submarine? The Russian captain dead?"

"You know I can't comment." Engel leaned closer, "But anything that was achieved was thanks to you."

As they spoke, Engel glanced over Mirta's shoulder every time the door jingled.

"CNN says Russia demands their submarine back," Mirta tried again. "But your Navy insists it was just a storm exercise?"

With a grin, Engel shifted the subject, "Do you like it here? Gorgeous countryside." She checked the door again, needing to buy a few more minutes.

Mirta lifted a shoulder, "The Spanish population is small, but the green hills remind me of home. The only watercraft here are on Kentucky Lake." She paused, noticing Engel glancing behind her.

Engel's lips trembled with a grin. She fought to contain her joy.

Mirta glowered at her odd demeanor. She asked, "How is Pilar?"

"Why don't you ask her yourself?" Engel lifted her chin to motion behind her.

Puzzled, Mirta turned. Standing behind her was Pilar as if standing in a spotlight. She was beautiful, with a radiant smile and a braid over a shoulder.

Mirta's eyes flooded. The last time she had seen her daughter she was a lanky teen. Scraped knees from skateboarding. She now looked like a young woman, elegant and poised.

Mirta shoved the table back to stand. She clutched Pilar with an unyielding hug. They gripped each other; noses buried in each other's hair. They sniffed back tears with whispers of love.

"*Mamá*," Pilar pulled back with a smile, "I want you to meet someone."

A young man, handsome but casual in flannel, stood beside her.

"This is Chandler," Pilar put her arm around him.

With blushing dimples, Chandler offered his hand, "I've heard so much about you. You're as beautiful as your daughter."

Rather than shake his hand, Mirta pulled him in for a powerful embrace.

Engel sat back with the widest smile since Christmas. In her profession—without ever knowing the outcome of her efforts—it wasn't every day she was confident of a job well done.

の

Patrice Arrison sat across from Dr. Loretta Graen, FSU's Vice President of Research. Arrison felt a wave of melancholy as she studied the room. The office's antique fixtures and Persian rug reminded her of the *Naumtsev*'s parlor.

"This is an uncomfortable request," Dr. Graen stirred in her seat with unease. "The university has asked that you conduct any future presentations off campus."

Arrison winced, confused, "Like the school doesn't want to endorse my findings?"

"Your speeches are fascinating," Graen installed a smile. "The students love it, but—"

"But FSU doesn't approve its content?" Arrison interrupted. "Like it's all a lie?"

"Patrice," Graen tightened her lips. "When you tell your students how you strolled through Atlantis, it's like a professor lecturing how he found Bigfoot without any evidence."

"I've given you the coordinates," Arrison stammered, defensive. "Approximate anyway."

Dr. Graen cocked her head, "Do you think Cuba would allow the US to drag sonar equipment in their waters? At whose expense? And the swirling symbol you drew has no proven connection to myths about Atlantis." She threw out her palms. "And how did you get there?"

Arrison bit her tongue to avoid answering. After she'd signed a stack of government nondisclosures, she was not permitted to mention anything about a Russian submarine. She'd crafted a vague story about being held hostage on a cartel's homemade narco-sub.

She gave a bitter chuckle realizing the government had allowed her to tell the other tales because no one would ever believe them.

Dr. Graen motioned towards the door, "I spoke to Professor Cox in Geography. Kevin said he's never heard of any village near the Ghana border called Mohamé."

"It's tiny…" Arrison stuttered, "and vanishing as we speak."

Graen thumbed over her shoulder, "Alvin Cash in your own department said it'd be impossible to visit the seafloor under Antarctica in a homegrown narco-sub."

"So I was hallucinating?" Arrison's brows snapped together, "I know, maybe I was hit on the head from the boat accident and I dreamed everything else?"

Graen shrugged, "We're just delighted you and your son are physically okay."

The Challenger Learning Center—named after the fated space shuttle— was away from FSU property, closer to the state's capital. It offered lecture rooms and a 128-person theater.

Professor Arrison stood behind a lectern before a mix of students and locals. Behind her, the theater's enormous LCD screen provided vivid images of her sketches and charts.

"Everything I have described," Arrison smiled to conclude her presentation, "The encounters, the colors, the brilliance, the threats, the grandeur; we did not discover these things. As a brilliant man once said, 'All of it has been there. No one has cared to look.'" She paused, earnest, "We just need to care to look."

The audience applauded. A student in the third row raised her hand.

"Professor Arrison," the young woman stood. "Is there any tangible or physical evidence you can share?"

Arrison's smile faded. "Regrettably no." She withdrew to the safety of her lectern. "Any evidence or proof was unfortunately lost with the sub."

The student said nothing and there were no more questions.

♡

Arrison arrived home at her two-story condominium complex near the ramp to I-10. She parked in her space between a dumpster and a phone booth no one used anymore.

The day had crushed her spirit. Pencil-drawn sketches, ambiguous coordinates and colorful stories weren't cutting it. Her audiences were dwindling, and she was losing credibility with her scientific peers.

Arrison was happy Chandler was traveling with Pilar but being alone wasn't helping her disposition. She found herself playing mental games of reminiscing. *136 days ago today, I was crossing the equator off the coast of Africa.*

Arrison stepped over a forgotten litterbox to gather her mail. Within a stack of bills was a box the size of a large brick. She guessed it was another textbook but was stumped to see a return address belonging to Ned Landa. Her eyes fluttered to imagine the possibilities. A corner of

373

her mouth lifted into something resembling a smile.

She entered her small but pretty condo. Everything was so perfect—from the ocean art to the marine throw pillows—but she realized it was like her grandparent's house. Perfect because no one was allowed to touch or move anything. The silence was deafening.

She rifled through bills at the kitchen counter. Due to her unplanned absence, she hadn't caught up on all her debts.

Arrison saved Landa's package for last. The box was heavy and made an odd clunk when it shifted. She opened one side to find a handwritten card. When she read Ned's scrawl, she could hear his coarse voice.

> *Patrice,*
> *Looking forward to seeing you on Christmas Break. Your agenda sounds great. Can't wait for you to meet Erica. I told her all about you, most of it's true. It'll be fun to reminisce.*
> *See you soon,*
> *Ned*

Arrison smiled with a joy so profound the emotion felt alien. When she turned the box, a large ADS dive glove plopped out. It landed on the counter with a metallic thud. The burgundy and silver glove was the size of an oven mitt.

With her mouth agape, she lifted the glove as if it were the Holy Grail. *Landa kept it?* It was proof her tales weren't some delusion.

She noticed the glove made a jingling sound. When she flipped it over, six gold coins fell out, bouncing and spinning on the counter. As fast as a wink, she lifted a coin to her eye. It was the size of a cookie and shimmered with a swirling symbol. The symbol of Atlantis.

Her eyes went as round as 24-karat doubloons.

Epilogue
Ghosts of Oceans Past

"Is this the fourth or fifth time I've had to talk to you people?" Ned Landa taunted with fists on the table in the small room.

His two hosts, a female officer and a decorated Navy admiral, crossed their arms to wait for him to calm his theatrics so they could proceed.

When Landa had been escorted to the room, he'd noticed there weren't any cliché two-way mirrors. When he'd looked up, there were no cameras. The chairs were comfortable, and they'd offered him a bottled water. It wasn't an interrogation room, and he wasn't in any trouble.

However, he had been forced to travel, again, from Miami to the National Maritime Intelligence Center in Suitland, Maryland. The Navy promised to reimburse him for his expenses, but he had to save all receipts, and the tedious forms weren't worth the trouble. He'd already told them their fifteen-dollar food per diem was laughable.

All Landa was sure of, was he was seated within the Office of Naval Intelligence, and they claimed this would be the last time.

His female host was pleasant but bookish. She'd introduced herself as Naval Intelligence Officer Cynthia Engel.

Seated beside her was a thin, tanned man wearing dress blues. He had introduced himself as Admiral James Farragut, Commander of the Pacific Fleet.

In a previous life, Landa would've been intimidated. But with everything he'd survived—much of it hundreds of meters underwater—nothing unnerved him anymore. He just wanted these people to get their queries over with.

Officer Engel smiled like a schoolteacher, "Mr. Landa, you need to appreciate how you're among very few witnesses."

The more somber Farragut chimed in, "We need to know if you are one hundred percent confident you saw the rogue, Typhoon-class submarine sink and how?"

Landa rubbed his face with both hands and groaned, "Again... the sub was taking on water. I opened a well door on the lower hull. When the vessel slowed, water entered the chamber. When I opened the doors leading into the hall, water would've risen beyond sealed compartments."

Engel and Farragut scribbled notes, referencing a paper diagram of an Akula-class submarine.

Landa frowned, "Didn't you interrogate your own chopper pilots? The sub was disabled. It was caught in the vortex." He paused to capture each of their eyes. "That's when it sank. Straight down. Like a cinderblock." He threw his hands out, *that's it.*

Engel nodded to Farragut, "Our sonar lost track of the vessel at 1,400 feet and falling. Just as he's describing."

"Don't your choppers have video?" Landa exclaimed. "Watch it yourself."

Farragut narrowed his eyes at Landa, "The cameras were disabled, probably a lightning surge. Regardless, the rain and shear made visibility almost zero."

Landa suddenly understood. This wasn't about gathering facts. It was about them confirming which story he planned to go with. He cleared his throat and smiled to seem more obliging.

"Is there a plan to recover it?" Landa asked, eager. "At least for the uranium, right? You can't just leave it there. I want to offer my services to help with any operation."

"This matter is concluded," Farragut closed his file. "The sea provides infinite reactor cooling. Any escaping radioactive material would have a near-unlimited dilution. It's the safest place it could be."

"Leaving the sub in place is preferable to retrieving it." Engel bobbed her head, "Deep in the center of the Pacific."

As her words rolled off her tongue, Landa felt the hairs on the back of his neck stand. He had heard those precise words. Like a jolt to his brain, he could hear Captain Nikto's voice.

"Deep in the center of the Pacific they planned to create an undersea sub station."

Landa sat upright, rigid. His eyes danced to reconcile the memory.

"Sunken cargo containers. Hundreds of them," Nikto had flashed a wily grin, "All of it connected, sunken and pressurized."

In his mind's eye, Landa could see a ghostly *Naumtsev*, restored and cruising like a phantom beast over a collection of structures on the seafloor.

"Like an entire city," Captain Nikto had shrugged. "A place to hide."

Afterword

When I visited Disney's Magic Kingdom as a child, my favorite ride was *20,000 Leagues Under the Sea*. I could sit in a "real" submarine, my nose just inches from my own window. With Captain Nemo's recorded narration, I witnessed the gaping jaws of giant clams, sharks circling a reef, and divers harvesting the seafloor. We traveled beneath blue and green shimmering icebergs. Volcanic activity revealed a sunken Atlantis, only to be attacked by a giant squid. Then back safely to the dock. It was pure magic yet rooted in the real world.

I wondered if I could capture that same sense of magic and adventure. I knew mysteries still existed under the sea. To quote NASA oceanographer Dr. Gene Feldman, "We have better maps of the surface of Mars and the moon than we do of the bottom of the ocean." There are still things human eyes have never seen.

Every living thing in this story is real, including arctic sea spiders, ghost octopuses, colossal squids over forty feet long, even modern-day piracy in the Caribbean. An ancient city 600 meters below the Guanahacabibes Peninsula, described by some as Atlantis, is based on actual scientific conjecture and purported sonar findings.

Drug cartels are building bigger and better narco-subs. In November 2020, Colombian forces seized the largest smuggling submarine to date, a hundred feet long with twin motors. Black market criminals have already sold Russian hardware to anyone willing to pay. Operation Odessa really did uncover criminals who came very close to selling a Russian submarine —with a captain and crew— to the Cali cartel. Countless articles include a photo of a mobster posing on a Russian naval base to prove he could do it. A Russian prosecutor who worked a case involving the theft of weapon-grade uranium stated, "Potatoes were guarded better." (*Chicago Tribune*, September 8, 2004.)

Acknowledgments

Special thanks to those who entertained my bizarre questions without reporting me to authorities: Nuclear submariner John Jones (ret.) US Navy STS1 (Sonar Technician Submarine); Matthias Eichenlaub, NATO Press Officer; Paul Ross, former lieutenant, US Navy; Robert Newstreet, former Boatswain Mate, US Coast Guard; Scott Ambrose, US Navy Reserves.

Check out John Jones' November 6, 2020 *Quora* article eloquently titled, "What stops me from hijacking a submarine that isn't on a mission if I had the crew and the know-how of the sub (theoretically of course)?"

Richard Wickliffe, May 15, 2022
Somewhere over the English Channel

About the Author

Richard Wickliffe's thriller *Storm Crashers* was awarded Best Popular Fiction at the Florida Book Awards. His screenplay for the tech-thriller was also optioned by Twentieth Century Fox.

Wickliffe has managed teams of investigators for twenty years with cases ranging from crime rings, to cyber fraud, human trafficking and Russian mafia. He's been published in journals in the investigative field and enjoys speaking about unique crimes, including the FBI's InfraGard Counterterrorism conferences and seminars in Las Vegas committed to accuracy in crime writing. He's the recipient of the FBI's Exceptional Service in the Public Interest Award.

Richard resides in South Florida with his family.

Other Titles from
Fireship Press / Cortero

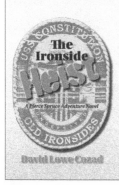

The Ironside Heist
by David Lowe Cozad

*America's oldest battleship afloat is in danger—
it's up to Pierce Spruce to save it.*

Time is of the essence as billionaire book collector Pierce Spruce and FBI Special Agent Robert Graham attempt to prevent America's oldest battleship still afloat from being hijacked by a rogue group of thieves.

Will they be able to maintain possession of the USS *Constitution*? Or has Old Ironsides set sail for the final time?

"David Lowe Cozad's *The Ironside Heist* is an enjoyable adventure book. Similar to the National Treasure movies—it weaves in fun historical references while keeping you engaged with the plot and characters."
—*Kennedy Dynasty Podcast*

Flight to Freedom
by Anthony Palmiotti

Being a prisoner of war isn't an option…

As Japanese forces corral almost eleven thousand prisoners after the fall of Corregidor Island in the Philippines, the remaining crew of the USS *Tanager* band together to escape to freedom. Pursued by a relentless Japanese officer, the escapees commandeer an old schooner. Through uncharted islands and stormy seas, they must outsail and outsmart Japanese forces sent to capture or kill them.

Inspired by a true story of early World War II heroism, *Flight to Freedom* is the story of a diverse group of people who just won't give up.